THE HATE EXTRACTOR

SEF HUGHES

First published in Great Britain in 2025
by Undercurrent Press

1st edition
ISBN 978 1 9998600 2 8

For Joe 90

PART I

ATLAS

Atlas Brown is a connoisseur of bad days. While others hoard their personal calamities without a thought, packing their mental shelves with whatever comes their way, he prefers to take his time. He holds his experiences up to the light, studies their attributes, assesses their uniqueness, and measures their value before either adding them to his collection, where they are categorised and filed for future reference, or tossing them aside.

Today's bad day is an excellent example. In it, he recognises a recurrent theme: that human beings are idiots. However, while it's an insight that often angers him, what makes this particular bad day worthy of his attention is its heady mix of anguish and remorse. And this morning, as he sits cross-legged on the carpeted floor of his metal box doing his best to ignore that infernal wind outside, the weight of knowing that he should've done more to counter this imbecility presses down on him. Because at no point in all his planning, in his years of research and development, or in his project's final execution, flawed as it may have been, did he factor in the stupidity of his species. They had needed priming. Educating somehow. It's obvious now, painfully so, because here they all are, in circumstances infinitely worse than before, when only a moment ago he'd handed them an opportunity to make everything so much better.

What's that? A chance to build a utopian future? Brilliant, give it here. We were saying only yesterday how great it would be to smash a big chunk of hope to smithereens.

Yes, as bad days go, this specimen is superb.

I hate—*you* hate—*he* hates—*she* hates—*they* hate.

I hate—I hate—I hate—I hate.

You hate—you hate—you hate—you hate.

He hates—he hates—he hates—he hates.

Only seconds have passed since he was sitting upright and taut, primed to get to his feet and on with a task that required his immediate attention. He was a man with a well-defined purpose cruising through his veins. And now he's on the floor, arms spread wide.

The base of his skull rests in a nest of discarded clothing. His eyes are closed and he is chanting.

She hates—she hates—she hates—she hates.

The transition from one frame of mind to the other is something he ponders only briefly. He was in one particular state and is now in a different one. Whatever caused the change, whatever intellectual journey he went on, that information is lost to him. In fact, the only remaining link between the two states is the wind. But that wind makes a sound, or a chorus of sounds, that Atlas prefers to ignore. Because that is no ordinary wind. This rare and fitful airstream hits the shipping containers just so, its unique trajectory transforming the aluminium stairs, railings, platforms, and window frames into the instruments of a surrealist symphony. Depending on its strength, it can resonate like fifty deep-chested fishermen emptying their lungs over the tops of various-sized glass jugs. At other times, it screams like the same men are being fed into a meat grinder. But even at its most ugly, it possesses a certain enchantment. In the days when the compound thrummed with people and all the containers were still in use, the technicians would lift their heads and watch as if they could see the gusts hurl themselves against the wall of living quarters, workshops, and offices.

If Atlas was so inclined, he could recall the time he looked out of his window and saw a man down there on the compound grounds. In a hard hat and overalls, fists clenched at his chest, he gazed into the heavens as he accompanied the wind with a credible rendition of *Nessun dorma*. It seemed to Atlas that the tempestuous orchestra was playing for the singer alone. This solitary figure, rooted between the looming gasholder and the half-built hangar, his powerful tenor carving a space between the airflow and the metal tubes and trusses to create a few minutes of beauty during an otherwise unpleasant time. Inspired by the performance, Atlas later tried his own collaborations. He imagined himself as a contemporary composer, a Glass or a Reich, someone capable of bending those deep piped whirs and purrs, widening the brayed flutes and fifes, curling the long, bellowed hoots and howls and sculpting them into an anthem for the ages.

But he does not care to revisit those times.

Too many memories blow in that wind.

In recent months it has modulated to a minor key.

And he is learning to ignore it.

They hate—they hate—they hate—they hate.

If he does hear the wind's music as he lies on the floor, it is little more than an acoustic cushion to his chants, a backing track he may or may not notice when it retreats. What is more interesting to him right now is an internal voice that's insisting he go outside.

Go out and get some exercise and fresh air and clear your head.

He agrees. He should.

But, also, he'd rather stay where he is.

He should get himself outside, down the stairs, away from

the compound, past the demolished factories, through the suburbs and into the city.

And he should do none of that.

The compulsion is strong in both directions.

I hate—*you* hate—*he* hates—*she* hates—*they* hate.

Pros and cons. There is life out there, that's a pro. He will see people going about their business, doing what humans do to get by in a world like this. It's good for him to experience that, the everyday, the mundane, the ordinary. Or as ordinary as it gets these days. It keeps his own existence in check. Helps him hold his purpose at the forefront of his mind. He is, after all, doing all of this for them.

There's life, Atlas, but not as we know it. And there he goes, laughing at his own joke and interrupting the chant. It feels good to crack his face. It happens so rarely these days.

Cons. Where shall he begin? How about the mental and physical effort it takes to go out? The possibility of attracting unwanted attention. And then the risk of injury. It's not as if there's a squad of first aiders to save him anymore. Disease, attacks from wild animals, losing his way. The ever-present threat of arrest followed by indefinite imprisonment. Need he go on? Who will look after the gasholder if something happens to him? He is better off staying right here, and that's before he even touches on the biggest downside of all: there is life out there. Yes, the plus is also a minus. The general population was barely tolerable before the world changed, but now, well, now. Now he dislikes it on a higher plane. A meticulously refined dislike. If it made sense to, he'd use the word 'hate'. And not the vanilla 'hate' that used to be thrown around with such abandon; the *I hate* getting up in the mornings, *you hate* wet summers, *he hates* women who wear trousers, *she hates* forgetting the punchlines of jokes. Atlas is thinking about real hate. The vicious, visceral stuff that once boiled his insides.

Like everyone else, he can't hate anymore. But without it he feels blocked. There is something inside of him that won't shift. A song in his head. Phlegm in his throat. A clot in a vein.

His organs itch.

He ought to be given special dispensation. A series of brief fantasies dart past his mind's eye: Atlas Brown sniffing hard at a hate nasal spray, smoking a hate stick, chewing hate gum, carefully applying a hate patch to his arm. Sweet, hateful relief.

He knows hate. Knew it. Knew it so well that he once hoped to capitalise on his expertise by devising *The Hate List Method*. HLM for short. The idea is of no use to anyone anymore. Still, it might have made him a pretty penny back in the day if he'd developed it into a fully fledged self-help manifesto. A tool for coping with modern life, written by a man who needed all the tools he could lay his hands on. A simple, practical meditation on hate because it's better to despise all things than just one.

HLM was about grouping. After an initial paper-based rant about everything the participant detested, from specific individuals all the way through to smells and inanimate objects, they were required to analyse each listed item and categorise it. Items naturally fell into the Source Hate or Sub Hate categories. For instance, back when he created the method, Atlas's list included his position as a Senior Researcher at the Facility. As per the instructions, he identified this as a Source Hate, grouped several Sub Hates under it, and ranked them from most to least loathsome. (Despite the name, it was not necessary for the participant to hate individual Sub Hates. Repugnance or even disinclination was enough. The important thing was that, when compiled, they contributed sufficient bile to their Source Hate.) So, under 'This tedious job', he itemised

the general lack of respect for my talents

writing up research

the morons I work with

this shithole of an office

and so on.

Similarly, during the analysis stage, the participant was

encouraged to look for opportunities to group seemingly independent Sub Hates with others in order to reveal new Source Hates, as yet unlisted. For example, an item on Atlas's initial list was the thinning skin on the back of his hands. On closer inspection, he saw it was associated with other items, including occasional impotence, permanent pain under one of his shoulder blades, deteriorating eyesight, the weird thing happening to one of his toenails, skin tags, and a receding hairline. This allowed him to see that these Sub Hates could be grouped under 'Turning 50'. He was then able to expand this new Source Hate to encompass popular music, social media, pubs, parties and more.

If he'd stuck with it, HLM could have provided people everywhere with the ability to think critically about whatever they felt hostile towards and focus their energies more efficiently. He had almost completed it. The only outstanding task was to develop a technique to deal with what he called the Super-Resistant Sub Hates, those which proved more immune to grouping than others. Again, using his own experience as an example:

skinny fingers
cheap pens
museums
cars
computers
shaving
smiling
being awake
going to sleep
gum chewers
politicians
shoelaces
air conditioning
asparagus piss
his ex-wife (because every good hate list should have one)

that hideous place on the Costa Brava where they spent their honeymoon and several of her over-celebrated birthdays

all birthdays, air travel, sunshine, beaches, foreign currencies, foreigners, other languages

abroad

flies, gardening, cats, tattoos, surprises, cyclists, nostalgia, maps, his hairy back,

and, of course, no list would be complete without himself

Dr Atlas Brown

Ex-husband to Bute Blue, the poet-novelist-artist

Brother to K, the musician-producer

Father to nobody

Doctor Hate.

Stay in, stay in, stay in. Go out, go out, go out.

Go out. Because if he does he may just turn this day around.

Because there are good days.

There are times when he can be quite the optimist. Times when he looks out of his window, takes in the sight of the gas-holder and allows his chest to swell with pride. And sometimes, when he's feeling this way, he'll whisper in a voice that doesn't sound like his

—all the hate of the world, right here in England.

Trapped and contained—

nice work, Atlas.

And on rare days like these, he knows there is never a straight line, that it scribbles its way forwards and sidewards, up and down, and sometimes even backwards, but always, eventually, arrives at its destination. Atlas the optimist is confident this line will loop back around to the Great Peace, those magical first months of oneness and togetherness, when it seemed as if a big, bright future for all would appear at any moment.

Or maybe the line will arrive somewhere even better.

. . .

This situation, this universal, paranoid inertia or whatever it is, is no more than an excursion.

Stars contract before they explode their atoms over the universe. That's all this is, society as it is right now. A temporary shrinkage. A tightening. The flexing of the human muscle before it uncoils and expands its mighty compassion upon the Earth, reaching out its giant arms and wrapping them around every man, woman, and child in an embrace of love.

No, too much.

Not love.

But something similar.

It wasn't his idea to call it the Great Peace. They did that. They, as in the experts in such matters. As a name, The Great Peace was passable back then, he supposes. It conveyed certain qualities of the moment. But he could have helped them think of a better one. If they'd asked. *The Silence. The Stillness. The Calm. The Tranquillity.*

At first, there were stories every hour. Armed conflicts grinding to a halt. Players in border disputes, terrorism, revolutions, and civil wars coming together around negotiation tables. Governments changing, some collapsing. The arms industry stalling. Hate crime, homicide, domestic violence, gang violence, sexual assaults, child abuse plummeting.

Atlas's greatest source of entertainment was the media's attempts to explain what was happening. An evolution surge, changes in solar activity, this god or that god had descended to Earth. Proof of a thirteenth zodiac in action. Extraterrestrial intervention. The specialists gathered on tv talk shows and panels. They analysed data and published journals. Some claimed it was a logical destination towards which the species had been moving for centuries. Others hailed the beginning of the True Enlightenment, a shift to pure consciousness.

On good days there's a lightness in his steps and thoughts. And there is nothing to regret.

All of it—it was all—predictable—and natural, he tells his reflection in the dusty mirror, his sentences dragging their feet, stumbling and tripping over his thoughts and intentions.

We're coded—programmed—to look for threats—aren't we?

We are, replies Reflected Atlas.

So—if the usual sources of—threat—evaporate overnight— we—we're bound to find—new ones—maybe we even find them in the—the disappearance of the original.

Correct as usual, Reflected Atlas says while giving Atlas one of his approving, reassuring looks, the kind that warms the latter's heart.

Atlas has theories.

He plays with one of them the way a child tortures a trapped spider, snapping off legs to see what happens. He has plucked every limb from this theory's sockets, and still it runs.

It goes like this: state-on-state violence brought nations closer for protection from those they regarded as threats. Strength in numbers. People looked outside their territories for others like them; they reached out to those who shared similar values and systems, who operated within recognisable moral codes. They formed alliances and created institutions. They promised to watch out for one another, to share intelligence and weapon technology. In some instances, they relaxed borders and visa restrictions, traded together, and forged bonds stronger than mere military coalitions allowed. And sometimes, as relationships deepened, they laid themselves bare to their partners. Human rights records, employment laws, race relations, nuclear weapons, carbon footprints, their strengths and deficiencies out on the table for all to see. They agreed to align more closely, to make their societies reflect each other's and raise the whole. Occasionally it worked. But even when it didn't, the ambition was there. They were doing more than hiding in a corner, waiting for hostiles to attack. Together they were striving for something better.

Striving, striving, striving until suddenly they found they no longer needed their neighbours. The Great Peace dissolved the adhesive. Physical threats were replaced by the metaphysical as populations remembered that those people, the ones over the border, the ones with the strange dress sense and weird music, were other. Their languages, skin colours, religious practices, their tendency to stand too close, their stand-offishness, the way they made their cheese, the way they didn't eat cheese, how they bothered you at market stalls, how they didn't like to barter, how lenient they were, how punitive. The differences that once made each other interesting, sophisticated or charming were magnified under a suspicious lens. People no longer trusted their international allies. They stepped back into their houses, pulled down the shutters, and brooded.

On good days, Atlas sometimes stands in front of his mirror and dictates a memoir he hopes will counterbalance his failure to predict this unintended dismantling of society. He clears his throat, fixes his gaze on a reflected corner of the room, and holds his hands together as if in prayer.

When he's ready, he begins with something like, as I watched the collapse of the United Kingdom—as a nation-state—starting with the—the unilateral breakaways of Scotland and Wales, then Cornwall and Yorkshire—and—of course—abroad—the independence declarations of Brittany and—and Catalonia—Texas and California—and the breakdown of the African Union—I realised these new entities were—what's the word—fluid—is

that it? It'll do for now. What I mean is that these entities—
would soon be dissolved by the—the emergence of multiple
smaller autonomies.

And I was—I was right. City-states and town-states began to
—to pop up everywhere—declaring themselves independent
from—from wherever they'd emerged. But—this wasn't the end
of matters—these—these places continued to split—like cells.
They're splitting now—still—as I speak—territories are
shrinking—and they'll carry on until borders become—meaningless—because—surely—there must be a minimum required
square footage—area of land—for a boundary to have any value.
For it—to—make sense. And—at some point soon—I hope—the
lines on maps will—dissolve—and we will revert to type and
start again—the return of the tribe—nomadic perhaps—able to
wander where we—we please. We'll begin over—and do it—
better. This time we'll do it better.

———

Worlds are shrinking, and Atlas's is the smallest of all.

———

He pulls on his shorts, the cleanest t-shirt he can find, and a
baseball cap left behind by a compound technician. When he
steps out of the metal box and onto the aluminium platform he
notices he's forgotten his shoes. Irritated, he goes back inside,
finds his brogues, sits on the bed, and puts one on. Then, realising if he is to walk any distance in them he will need socks, he
swears, removes the shoe and throws it through the open door.
He waits to hear it bounce on the tarmac twenty feet below.

His floor is cluttered with clothing, bed sheets, books, and
empty food containers. Somewhere under the mess is a pair of
running shoes. He bends and lifts a handful of papers, sighs, and
then drops them.

He wants his bloody running shoes and he wants them bloody now.

Shit, shit—shit.

Perhaps try under the bed, says Reflected Atlas. Just a suggesti...

Atlas interrupts the mirror with a gritted fuck you, falls to his knees, presses his ear to the floor, and spots the familiar white soles in the darkness.

———

Forty-three minutes later. Atlas feels calmer. He is sitting on a bench on the busiest street in town he can find, which isn't so busy at all. People around him move slowly, meandering between the few stores that remain in business.

He swallows. If he had water, he'd take a sip. Instead, he wets his tongue on the damp Castleport air.

A small group of middle-aged women has congregated a few metres behind him. He closes his eyes to concentrate better on what they're saying but their quiet voices usher him towards a familiar daydream, to a large auditorium. He is offstage, in the wings, listening to the imaginary audience's muttered impatience. They are waiting for him to deliver a talk entitled *Dr Brown and the Hate Extractor: The Moment of Revelation*. He has delivered it to many fictitious gatherings, and the time has come to shake it up a little. When he performed it last, he saw people in the front row yawning. Imagine! Atlas Brown, the man responsible for saving this miserable planet from the horrors of hate, pours his heart out on stage and they yawn at him.

He will not allow a repeat.

Someone in the imagined auditorium clears their throat. The tone suggests a heavyset man. There it is again, like a petulant outboard motor. And then another and another, each from a different part of the hall, a chain reaction of irritation. Atlas shrugs it off. They can wait. He has to get his thinking straight before going out there because these people have shown they aren't interested in the truth. They don't want a meandering autobiography. They crave excitement. A thriller. He needs a new way in. But really, the whole thing would benefit from an overhaul.

He searches for a way the story might have happened differently. Not better. Different and better are not the same. Nobody is suggesting he could have done a better job. And he takes a moment to remind himself that he made the best possible decisions under the circumstances at the time. He did all he could and has nothing to regret.

Let's be clear, things could not have gone better.

But they could have gone differently. And by things, Atlas means circumstances out of his control. The external factors. That's where he'll find the story this audience needs. The chance meetings, the accidents, happy or otherwise, the events that influenced his direction of travel. The problem, though, is their quantity. Thousands, millions, trillions of them coming at him from every angle, and most so minuscule that he couldn't have possibly noticed their influence. The tunes overheard en route to work, the weather, the unsolicited comments from strangers, the first news headline of the day, the second, the third, the scent of a handwash, the intensity of traffic, the ache of his muscles, the tightness of his underwear, the billboard posters, the street names, so many possible factors, bombarding him like cosmic rays, pushing his mind this way, pulling it that, each one with the potential to change everything.

It's just too much.

He needs a more straightforward solution.

Perhaps he doesn't have to identify a swathe of external factors to alter the story. Maybe all he has to do is imagine what would've happened if just one of them had brought about his idea for the machine in a more dramatic fashion. If the truth is too long and laborious, the fictitious version should happen quickly and theatrically. All he has to do is show these people, these figments of his imagination, the flash of inspiration. A big aha! moment when everything revealed itself to him. Something that will have them gasping in astonishment.

An image of his desk at the Facility appears. It's as good a place as any.

It was an ordinary wooden contraption. Dated, cluttered, and far too small for a man of his stature.

Stature.

For a man who deserved more stature than he was given.

An ordinary desk, possibly older than him, pushed against a windowless wall split lengthways by two tones of brown paint. Dark gloss at the bottom, lighter emulsion at the top, a neck-height horizon, beneath which loitered a school of excreta-quaffing researchers and their dung-guzzling assistants. And there, too, was Atlas, with his mug of expired pens, frayed blotter, an old paper bag of empty chocolate wrappers, and his stone-age laptop, closed. In front of him, slightly to the right, stacked against the shimmering ordure, is a pile of ragged notes and crumpled drawings. Scribbled on, torn from pads, tossed onto a heap. A heap that could have contained his breakthrough.

That's it, he thinks. Why the hell not?

The desk was where he collected his ideas. Those bursts of speculation, ill-formed and childish notions that occurred to him while he zoned in and out of the internal hum of boredom. Like a fatally inquisitive moth, an intriguing thought would flutter at his ears or nostrils, and in a well-practised manoeuvre, he'd stab it, impaling it with his pen against a scrap of paper which he would hurl onto the heap and instantly forget. So there it is. Why not tell them the Hate Extractor was born right there? That, instead of being coaxed out of its hiding place over so many months, it simply landed on that old wooden desk with a thump? Give the people the eureka moment they want.

He studies the fiction for a second and then concludes, yes, it's pretty much perfect. Because if it had transpired that way, his life, the whole narrative, all of it would have been different. All those years of frustration, all the stupid decisions he made, none of it would have happened. And that is all the persuasion he needs.

He walks on stage.

Applause.

He saunters to the microphone, keeping it casual, keeping it casual. He nods and smiles until the imaginary audience silences itself, then waits a few more seconds.

Atlas can't tell them what was on the paper because he is making this up as he goes along and hasn't yet figured out the details. The thinness of war zone atmospheres couldn't have simply occurred to him. It had to come through research. So even daydreaming about what hung in the air, never mind conceiving of a machine that would purge the world of it, was impossible. He opts for vagueness. He takes a breath and describes the idea galloping at him like a deer escaping a forest fire. He trapped it, wrote it down, and added it to his pile of defective concepts. And there it stayed, discarded alongside all the others he was unlikely to look at again. Until, months afterwards, the note fell off the desk as he rummaged around for a working pen or an extension lead or he doesn't know what.

From the corner of his eye, he saw a piece of paper seesawing towards the age-stained brown carpet tiles. He tells them he felt compelled to catch it and save it from the vacuum cleaners that would sweep through the Facility later that night. He says it was as if someone or something commanded him, looking wistfully into the lighting rigs. And as the audience seems amenable to such things, he proclaims that the moment he turned the paper over and read what he'd scribbled on it so many weeks before, the world changed. And judging from the volume of the applause as he raises his arms in triumph, they couldn't care less what the note said. Behold, he yells, the Hate Extractor! A machine. A mechanical wonder.

Made of nothing more than metal and bolts, but imbued with the power to rid us of our most destructive characteristic. And

Atlas finds he has come over all evangelical, shouting and slapping his chest like he's single-handedly driving the devil out of town, heavy breath and sweat behind every preaching word. A mechanism, he roars. A contraption to abolish warfare. Torture. Murder. That could purge the wickedness from the human experience. Suck. It. Out! Draw it down from the atmosphere like a giant vacuum cleaner. Cleanse our planet. Purify our souls. Expunge the serpent. Obliterate our demons. Crush the, crush the—

He is grinning when he opens his eyes. Like a drunk on a bench. But nobody is looking his way. No one looks at anybody anymore. It's always gazes, faces, heads down. As if making eye contact is going to get them into trouble. Robbed, arrested, or spoken to.

Benches aren't called benches anymore, either. Atlas believes the preferred term is street furniture. This one is more of a concrete sofa than a bench, long enough for ten adults to sit comfortably distributed along its hard, polished surface. Atlas is at one end, a woman at the other. She is older, eighty-ish, he estimates. He doesn't know how long she's been there. The bench was empty when he arrived. Otherwise he'd have sat elsewhere. He suspects he makes old people fidgety, so avoiding them is the polite thing to do. But she appears quite happy sitting there. Perhaps her vision isn't too good. Or she's deranged.

In front of her is a trolley, the kind that grandmothers pulled behind them when he was small. Old men with flat caps and wooden walking sticks, the women with tartan trolleys. Men don't wear hats anymore, and their sticks are aluminium, adjustable and ugly. The clunk they make as they hit the ground verges on the offensive. It's reassuring to see a trolley in the wild. It says something about the owner, about good traditional values and ethics, like readiness and circumspection. If Atlas owned such a thing, he would fill it with supplies from his metal box, a bottle of water, a sandwich, a change of clothing, a novel, and he wonders how he might acquire one. He could take the woman's. There are no wardens around and she doesn't look as if she'd be able to stop him. He would remove her belongings first, obviously. He isn't a monster.

She turns to face him and he ponders the possibility that he's been speaking his thoughts aloud.

He holds out a hand to her and says, water—please.

She looks away.

His life has included fleeting moments of plenty when whatever he desired was given to him without fuss. He would reach out and there it would be. Project Lung was like that. The beginning of it, at least. The problem with the new fictitious start to his story is that there is no room for Project Lung. It is a shame to jettison the Hate Extractor's actual predecessor. It was an official Facility programme that vibrated with potential in its early days. He could almost feel the electric buzz caress his skin. It had been such a long time since he'd made an impact, since he'd made some noise, and Lung felt like it might be the one to make people look his way and see something they'd missed. Why have we not recognised this guy's genius before? Give that man the status he deserves. Give him a promotion, a better office, a suitable desk. Give him everything he needs to do this again and again. Paint his damn walls if that'll help. All Atlas wanted was to inspire a little awe in those around him. Perhaps even impress his brother K. Maybe, but this was a taller order, make Bute proud of him. And for a few seconds during Project Lung, it seemed he was about to achieve it.

The early days were always the best. It was a known phenomenon. Facility people called it the E-Effect. Euphoria, energy, high expectations, excitement. All the Es compressed into a few weeks at the start of any promising project. His team fizzed with ideas, thrilled by possibilities. They chattered and joked while filling whiteboards with rushed, indecipherable numbers and incomprehensible lines, decorated the walls with post-it clusters, and speculated while eating lunch together, downing tequila in spontaneous after-work drinks, and messaging in late-night *what-if* WhatsApps. The fever had them. His lab brimmed with promise and life was good. And when Atlas wanted water, an ice-cold bottle was delivered to his waiting hand without hesitation.

His mind was wide open back then, at the top of the research summit, dazzled by the golden world below, giddy on the thin atmosphere. And yes, he knew it couldn't last, that it wouldn't be long until he and his team started zigzagging down from the heights, gaining momentum as they went, until, quite soon, the play became work. Initial results would disappoint. Idea after idea would hit a wall. Equipment would fail, bickering would lead to arguments, the blob of blame would grow and engulf them one by one, and the project would start to grind them down. But if you know there's a low on its way, you'd be a fool not to milk the high for all its worth.

Comedowns from highs like that were always hard but he was used to them. He knew that any worthwhile work was gruelling, that there were no quick answers. No aha! moments that exploded into being. It didn't matter how much tech you threw at a problem or how many big brains you had at your disposal, undertakings such as Project Lung invariably became repetitive and dull. That's why he skipped this part for the new edit, he remembers. It's just too slow for the always-on, everything-now generation.

Atlas takes in the old woman next to him and looks away again before she notices. She'd get it, he thinks. People like her are from a time when the slog still had value. They'd be happy to hear him talk about the tedious work of saving the world. She would listen without yawning.

He shoves his backside forward in the seat, extends his legs, and crosses them at the ankles. He links his fingers over his belly and stares into the sky.

If she was, say, at the front of a queue in a bookstore with a copy of his hypothetical memoir gripped in her tiny, wrinkled knuckles, he could tell her everything.

I hope you don't mind me asking, Dr Brown, but what inspired you to invent the Hate Extractor?

I don't mind one bit.

He'd give her the details. Nobody wants the ins and outs anymore, but, again, she's from a generation that appreciates the particulars. He'd tell her about the Project Lung tests he conducted with single-board computers. This clever, palm-sized technology was already infiltrating everyday life by turning objects into processors with web access. Cars connected to insurance companies, central heating boilers connected to mobile phones, refrigerators connected to food retailers, running shoes connected to running watches. They called it the Internet of Things. It had battlefield applications too. Helmets that let mission control know if their wearers were alive or dead. Armoured personnel carrier wheels that transmitted status reports to maintenance engineers. Gun triggers that informed medics of the mental state of individual soldiers during battle. But despite the plethora of frontline uses, Atlas was sure he'd find a gap in the war market.

He was interested in air quality monitors. Back then, hobbyists and would-be inventors rigged up their homes with these little green boards crammed with microprocessors, input and output ports, RAMs, and Wi-Fi and Bluetooth connectors. They made robots and game consoles. Home security systems. And they wired up sensors to measure the atmospheres of their houses, garages, sheds and greenhouses, sometimes connecting them to machines like dehumidifiers or extraction fans that could automatically alter an atmosphere's composition. Atlas wanted to develop a monitor that could be deployed in combat zones to observe, well, he didn't know what exactly. Perhaps he'd glean intelligence about chemical weapons or recent military activity. Lung was a discovery project. He would use it to examine the air of the most dangerous places on earth and see what he could pick up. And at this point in the story, he might drop in a subtle boast about how Special Forces installed his monitors in and around various conflict zones, as close as possible to the coordinates his team had identified, because that's the kind of clout this woman expects of him. Dr Atlas Brown, the future saviour of humankind, clicked his fingers. Suddenly, fatigue-clad men and women were risking their lives to mount inconspicuous solar-powered boxes on bullet-riddled embassy buildings, barracks, telegraph poles, village halls and schools across the world. Units distributed, mounted and connected to the cloud, and they were good to go. A complex web of tiny plastic spies inhaling the air, pinging data granules into the wide-area network and, via a satellite or two, back to Atlas's team in the Facility.

The old woman will nod encouragingly as he explains how they'd predicted great things ahead. How, while they waited for the data, they developed possible applications. Gun-mounted cordite sensors, early warning troop-activity systems, a web of war-crime detectors, all ready to present when they shared their inevitable discovery, whatever that might be. All they needed was a small win. Something to point them in a general direction. As the information started to come in, they searched for this something. They looked for anomalies, connections, patterns, anything unusual enough to raise an eyebrow. But the initial results were disappointing. Standard quality air, nothing suspicious or out of the ordinary. In six months, they didn't pull a single insight out of the numbers.

And then it turned to shit. She'd like that, this woman. A cheeky swear word from a famous scientist. But he'll balance it with a stern face as he tells her the Facility pulled the plug without so much as a warning. A phone call from a blunt administrator. Project Lung is officially terminated. Ask your team to report to the Orphanage in the morning for reassignment.

He would return the autographed book to the woman and explain that all he'd needed was more time, just another few months. Another year. But he was a middle-aged senior researcher who'd never made a name for himself, who commanded no authority and wielded no influence. He was expendable and how he felt about the decision was irrelevant.

So it wasn't just scientific curiosity that drove him to hack into the monitor network from his home lab and continue a de-authorised project. It was also indignation. Anger, he'd say, that's what inspired me.

And she would thank him for his answer and for signing the book, and then she might say something about how he'd shown them. How he'd had the last laugh.

Atlas leans his head to the side to look at the woman again but she and her trolley are gone.

In her place sits a row of male scientists. Severe brows, short beards, mouths that haven't laughed since childhood, all fastened tightly into white ties and tails. He should've made more of an effort. Atlas pushes his running shoes into the blue carpet of the new stage and listens to the translated speeches of the Nobel Prize speakers that snore into his head via an earpiece. In a moment he will walk across the platform to collect his honour from the King of Sweden. Then, at some point, he'll have to deliver an acceptance speech and a lecture on his work. This is uncomfortable. The problem is not that he hasn't dressed for the occasion. It's that he'll be required to thank the people without whom none of this would have been possible, etcetera, etcetera. And he isn't ready to say *her* name yet, not in public.

There is something that might be panic swirling in his shoulders and upper back. This is unusual for a daydream. It's also unnecessary as he doesn't even have to be here. If he wants, and he does, he can burn the venue to the ground and walk through the ashes, kicking the dry skulls of these grimacing fools into the air, then take himself off to a beach, somewhere warm, lean into a lounger, Aperol Spritz in hand, sunglasses, Piz Buin and cigar smoke, dozens of young scantily clad academics who, aware of his hatred of beaches, appear grateful for his presence. It isn't easy to imagine yourself on a hot beach when you're inhaling the Castleport damp, but he won't let a thing like that stop him, and now he's sipping a cocktail under a tropical sun. Much better, he thinks. This is how they should do all science prizes.

This is a great honour, he tells the speedos and bikinis. And I couldn't have done it alone. So I want to thank everyone who made me feel like a worthless piece of shit over the years.

It's a good start. He has their attention.

So, thank you to my brother, K. His contribution was entirely unintentional, I'm sure, but invaluable nonetheless. There is nothing quite like a younger sibling's meteoric success to highlight one's inadequacies.

They're clapping now. A female academic perches on the side of his lounger and touches his oily leg. He pulls away.

And thank you to that horrendous woman I used to call my wife. She has a special place in my heart where I've converted the left ventricle into a little fleshy throne room. The constant throbbing should keep her suitably uncomfortable until the day I die.

And, finally, my mother and father for their utter disinterest. Parental indifference can do spectacular things for a child's psyche.

Any questions?

Hands spring into the air.

No, I would not like to mention anyone else at this point. Thank you.

I don't believe in favourite colours. It's just light.

Six foot three and a half.

Advice? From me? That's very flattering. Well, let me see. A few titbits do come to mind. For instance, always follow your impulses. I'm not talking about those big dreams because that's where disappointment waits for you. It's the smaller stuff you should pay attention to, those gentle nudges and prods that lead you down paths you wouldn't otherwise have followed. Listen to the niggles, those unidentifiable lumps rumbling around in the recesses, making noises where there should be quiet, and allow them to guide you.

They're taking notes, which is good.

Okay, my last instruction for you is never marry. Or, rather, do, but not to a person. Marry your career. Because if you don't, if you just play at it and never fully commit, your work will take the plunge with somebody else. So, turn your back on ideas of romance and soul mates and, he apostrophises the air with four fingers, "finding the one". All of it is nonsense made up to keep you in check. It's religion. It might suit people who'd otherwise have no meaning in their lives, but not for you. Husbands and wives are fatal for the likes of you. They'll say they love you but in reality they want to destroy everything you stand for, whether or not they realise it. You're here to learn and invent and create and make the world a better place. Get hitched and you can forget all of that. Give your all to the science. Love it unconditionally. Pledge yourself to it.

This is a well-rehearsed performance. During and after his divorce, Atlas preached the dangers of attachment to anybody willing to listen, admonishing colleagues who failed to heed his warning. And even as he evangelises now, he continues to cement his position, shouting his protests from the narrow gun slit in his sturdy concrete pillbox. If only he'd been warned about the pitfalls when he was young. If only someone had taken the time to talk to him, ridicule him, or lock him in a room, anything that would have prevented him from ruining his career.

They've stopped taking notes. Now they're staring at him. Blank faces. And he wonders if he went too far, spoke too passionately on the subject. Does he sound bitter?

Do I sound bitter?

A little, one of them replies.

Right. Well, he shrugs, learn from my experience. I've been through the wringer so you don't have to. I…

and he hesitates again.

Did Bute actually compromise his work? Can he say that? And he shuffles through the memories like a croupier. Noteworthy incidents blurring past his mind's eye. There's nothing obvious. She simply wasn't very interested. She never asked how work was going or what he was researching, despite him breaking the official secrets act by making her the only person in his life other than K who knew what he did for a living. Even when he worked late or on weekends, she didn't inquire. Not once. What would a simple question have cost her? He wouldn't have expected her to care about the answer. It would've just been a nice thing to do.

Did she ever show any interest in him? She must have done. When they were courting, surely she asked him something about himself. She certainly knew enough to humiliate him in company. But only because he told her. Unprompted and unsolicited. So perhaps she didn't need to ask. Did he really speak about himself so extensively that there was nothing left to know? More likely, she was too preoccupied. All that writing, sculpting, painting, filming, private views, poetry readings, parties, and so on and so on. But he doesn't enjoy finding excuses for her. He was her husband, for crying out loud. Was a slither of curiosity too much to have expected?

The sound of muttering catches his attention. The academics are talking among themselves. Several in-depth discussions are happening simultaneously, and nobody is looking his way. He clears his throat but they don't seem to notice. So he tries again with a very audible ahem. One of the speedos turns, presses a finger to his lips and returns to his conversation. This is precisely what his marriage was like. He was a nuisance. A dull man making noise in the corner. The relationship advice he just handed out is probably what Bute would give if asked. Never marry. Especially a scientist.

But no, he can't say she tried to prise him from his work or attempted to get him to spend more time with her, and she certainly did not want children. So, it wasn't her insecurities that intruded on his work. It was her aloofness. Bute didn't care whether he lived or died but, if pressed, would likely have opted for the latter. And that is why his advice to these beach bums still stands. She distracted him by being unavailable.

After the divorce, Atlas subverted the Hate List Method to dilute his feelings towards Bute. The plan was to open the hate net so wide he would lose her in a new category. 'People' was his first attempt, but he didn't have the energy for all of them. He narrowed it down to roughly half the world's population: women. Again, too many. He tried instead with the women who had been a credible source of interest to him during his fifty years. He'd hoped to hate them all for a) the vast amount of his attention they took without asking and b) the way they glided out of his life so effortlessly. If there had been, say, ten or eleven of them, he might have been able to hide Bute under the bodies. But there were only five, and that was pushing it.

His penultimate attempt was to gather all the people who'd played an active role in bringing Bute and him together, consciously or not:

i) The couples who invited them to dinner parties in those first few months, who lied about how well-suited they were,

ii) the colleagues who stepped up the challenge of supporting his relationship by asking him about her, offering advice on how to take things to the 'next level', and teasing him whenever he was late or distracted,

iii) his mother, who, after finding out he was dating, phoned him every three days for updates, desperate for a clutch of grandchildren to ignore,

iv) the passersby, the diners, the waiters, the park walkers and their dogs, the taxi drivers, the flight attendants, and everyone else who saw Bute and him together and never once stopped them to explain it could never work,

v) makers of alcoholic drinks. No, not all makers, only vodka makers. Just a single brand: Finlandia, if he remembers correctly. And everyone who works for the supermarket chain he bought that particular bottle from because, without it, he and Bute would never have entertained a certain conversation that led to a certain conclusion. There was no proposal. It was a mutual decision reached during a discussion about evolution. It was the seventh date, according to the dinner party story they told while it was still amusing. A picnic in Bute's back garden. They established that both of them were horrified by the thought of creating offspring for entirely different reasons—she wasn't remotely maternalistic, and how could she possibly work with tiny apes running riot over her life—he believed it utterly selfish to bring children into a world as doomed as this one. Homo sapiens are finished, they agreed. All the best people refuse to procreate. Surely, this was the end of the line? There was wine and then the offending spirit, and at some point the notion of a permanent union unfolded in front of them, in which neither of them would ever pressure the other into producing heirs. It seemed perfect. Marriage was an excellent idea. Then, an awkward embrace, mouths pressed together like two pieces from opposite ends of the jigsaw.

vi) And then there was K. Atlas always found it easy to hate parts of his brother but not all of him. He hated his effortless success and style. His permanent happiness. He hated how nothing was ever a problem, no favour too great, no time too late to pick up the phone. Specifically, he hated K for putting Bute and him on a collision course, repeatedly inviting them to the same parties and dinners, and doing everything he could to bring them together. The clumsiness of his matchmaking and his corralling of mutual friends to assist his quest became the things in common the pair had lacked when they first met. But this was K all over. Big heart, small brain, irritating all around him by trying so hard to make them happy. However, Atlas can just about admit to himself that K believed he was doing the right thing. He adored Bute but thought her life could be improved with the addition of someone who could calm her fiery ways. He reasoned she would work more consistently and earn more money with a little stability. She needed a safe, levelheaded man. Someone she could come home to. Who would cook for her and listen. And there was his brother. For all Atlas's assurances and protests, K worried his sibling was becoming old before his time. Too serious. Bordering on the dull. He hadn't always been that way. K remembered his brother as a dormant volcano. A tall, lumbering, intelligent teenager, funny, kind and attentive, who would surprise all with rare, violent outbursts and random acts of emotional vandalism. But the lava flow had cooled and solidified, and now Atlas only worked. There was nothing else in his life. If only he had someone who could reignite him. It was clear to K that Bute and Atlas would be the perfect match. Neither was right for the other at that moment but given time they would mould one another into the partners they required. All he had to do was guide them together. The man was a fool but Atlas couldn't bring himself to hate him.

Finally, Atlas brought together all the elements he could remember of Bute's professional life and threw them into the therapeutic pyre. Like him, she defined herself by her work, so it seemed reasonable that if he destroyed it and the world it existed in, he'd free himself from her. So he assembled her poetry and all poetry, all literature in all forms, publishers, agents, and writers of every kind; her art and all art, everything you can make art with, the ink, paint and paintbrushes, easels and canvases, clay and marble and chisels; cameras, film, and tripods; her sycophantic lovers and followers, and every remotely creative person in existence; her shows and openings and all galleries, museums, and bookshops, and so the list continued. Then he stood back and gazed upon the heap of combustibles, snapped open a Zippo and tossed in the flame.

It was glorious. An inferno of hate that burned quickly and furiously. Books and wooden frames raging, tubes of paints bubbling, poets screaming, editors shrieking, the windows of quaint local bookshops bursting, free verse begging for mercy, skin melting, egos exploding.

It was strange to have a solitary moving image in his mind's eye for so many days. The blaze was so fierce it warmed his body through, his face flushed against the raw heat. Then, after a while, the bonfire began to disintegrate. He had nothing left to hurl into it, but all was well. The fire had done its job, he thought. Let it rest.

More days passed as he watched the flames shrink and calm, and the early fury succumbed to a glowing, smouldering soup with thick spirals of white-grey smoke that masked the embers of his contempt. But when the view cleared, she was still there, smiling at him from the cinders, unharmed and beautiful. She'd absorbed every single thing he'd tried to burn and was now more powerful than ever.

His backside is numb. City planners did not design street furniture for extended daydreaming. Nobody wants the penny-pinchers loitering too long in a place like this. Either go shopping or go home. But the stores are empty and money makes little sense anymore. Atlas rises to his feet, shakes his legs, and starts walking.

The country's recent experience with food banks is proving useful. They have a new name, something less loaded, less shameful, now that everyone has to use them: Provision Stations. Ration cards might also be in operation, but he doesn't know because he gets his food from Angela. To eat via official channels he'd need a recognised Castleport address and supporting ID, both of which he lacks.

Angela says the shortage is a supply chain issue. The movement of goods in, out, and through all these new territories, each with its own improvised checks and rules, is bureaucratic hell. If profits were involved, the extra time and hassle at checkpoints would be a price worth paying. But now that money is all but valueless, the motivation is merely humanitarian. With an entire population to feed, impatient truck drivers skip the more troublesome borders. It makes no difference to them who gets fed and who doesn't. In some places, inexperienced border guards make the problem worse. But Castleport has the wardens. She thinks they're more organised than most and partial to a spot of food bribery, which eases the flow. Supplies get through. Alexander sees to it.

Castleport's unofficial, unelected, and uniformed leader, Joseph Alexander, controls the wardens. Every day, more posters bearing his image appear on boarded-up windows. It's always the same portrait. A sturdy-looking middle-aged man. Thick neck and shoulders, neatly combed black hair, an enigmatic half-smile, and a vaguely regimental black jacket, shirt and tie, peaked cap under his arm. The headline above his head says

HOLD YOUR NERVE

It's quite a message, Atlas thinks. Is it an implied promise that things will improve or an admission that this is it, that you'd better get used to it? It's difficult to tell. Residents, relax. It will all settle down soon enough. Food, fuel, internet and all that stuff, it'll be back before you know it. So don't be angry or despondent. Hold on, keep the faith. Or is it, Residents, this is how it is now. With a little resilience and a little acceptance, it'll feel normal in no time. Hang on in there and you'll see.

There's always the possibility that he is speaking directly to Atlas. The all-seeing Alexander knows what he's done and what he's going through. Your work is important, Dr Brown, and we appreciate everything you have accomplished. Don't give up on us now.

Atlas looks at the faces around him as he drags his long legs in the general direction of the compound.

Life has malfunctioned. There is a glitch. The lubricant has dried. You can see it in the expressions of the ex-shoppers who gather by lampposts, the teenagers congregating under bus shelters, the solo pushchair pushers trudging along pathways. The elderly couples, their feet frozen at the windows of closed shops. A blankness is what they all have in common. Everything they thought they could rely on has been ripped away. The money in their pockets. The food in their cupboards. The shrink-wrapped products on retail shelves. The phone networks. One, two, three foreign holidays a year. The limitless supply of medicines. The safety nets. The right to ignore the world and the freedom to swan through their days without ever having to think about survival. That's what is missing from their faces. The nonchalance, the indifference that makes existence tolerable. And their eyes are bereft of sweet ignorance. Yet, while they seem more alert, more watchful than before, there is no terror. No anger. No rioting or looting. People have shrugged their shoulders and accepted their fate. Queuing for necessities, intermittent power, temporarily shut schools, barricaded banks, defunct ATMs, they act as if life has always been this way. And Atlas wonders how they'd behave if they knew it was down to him? All of this? Would they be so placid then? He casts aside the urge to run from a make-believe mob because, with no hate to fuel their rage, he doubts they would care enough to give chase. They'd be more likely to feel sorry for him. But some might want to talk. They may be interested in understanding what happened and why things have changed. Perhaps one of them will turn out to be an ex-journalist who'll track him down to the compound and knock on the door of his metal box.

Would you mind answering some questions, Dr Brown? It is Dr Brown, isn't it? I understand all of this is down to you?

Come in, come in. Pull up a chair, young man. Would you

like some tea? I've only got dandelion. Of course, it would be better with a dollop of honey too, but, well, the shortages.

He mustn't give the impression that he is some kind of amateur who accidentally discovered the Particle at home. In imaginary interviews like this, he makes sure the journalists understand that the project began in a high-tech underground laboratory alongside some of the country's greatest scientific minds, that institutional impatience and stupidity forced him to work in secret, and that that was why he had no choice but to make his breakthrough in a shed in his back garden. The whole thing seems far less shoddy that way.

Tell me more about the shed, says the reporter.

It wasn't just any old shed. Write that down. Definitely not a garden shed. It might've looked like one from the outside but it was pretty sophisticated, actually. A surprise gift from my wife. A way to keep me out from under her feet, I suspect. *The Garden Lab*, she called it. Impressively equipped for someone so clueless about such things. So not as eccentric as you might think. Not that I needed much of the equipment, a computer and a VPN to hack into the Project Lung monitors was enough at first.

The reporter scribbles into a small notepad and moves across the room. He sits on the bed, removes his trilby, and tosses it onto the duvet. Atlas notices the card wedged between the hat's ribbon and felt. In thick capitals, it reads PRESS. This is disappointing. It's like something from a comic strip. He thinks he should show him out and reimagine a more serious journalist. Someone famous from the BBC would be good. Perhaps they could do one of those in-depth tv interviews, an hour-long special in a darkened studio. A slow zoom in on his face as he makes his confession. Millions of viewers telling each other to hush as Dr Atlas Brown reveals all. But the cartoon reporter is already asking him to talk about the culture of the Facility. What was it about the place that drove you into exile? His pencil is primed.

Ah, interesting question. You'd better make yourself comfortable. This is a long story.

As a junior researcher, Atlas was happy to drink up the propaganda that poured from the Internal Communications Department.

No idea is too wild or unlikely.

Implausibility opens doors to the future.

Innovation begins by imagining the impossible.

Nobody escaped the headline platitudes that cascaded down the hierarchy via speeches and posters, educational videos, and intranet bulletins. The messages washed past the veterans, refreshed the withering dreams of the middle tiers, and flooded the minds of the juniors and Foundlings. And the recruiters dragged the clichés out into the world to ensnare the directionless bright young brains the Facility required for its survival.

They certainly worked on Atlas. He remembers his recruiter, a man who rattled through his customised script like a bucket of stones tumbling down a drainpipe.

A savage such as you needs somewhere he can, he can, you know, liberate that big brain of his and, er, make something of himself. Become, what's it, famous.

As they sat with pints of bitter in an ancient pub, the older man, Greville was his name, painted a picture for the twenty-three-year-old Atlas of a research utopia where science met creative freedom while skilfully avoiding the deadly nature of its business.

Atlas was smitten.

Mr Greville was a gentleman of sorts. Crumpled tartan suit and brown Crombie, tan tasselled brogues and a tired beige fedora. Rough around the edges and, from the sound of his voice, a little worse for wear on the inside too. They first met on the street, where he barred Atlas's path a few steps from the door that led to his bedsit.

Yes, you. You look like a boy who could do with some direction.

You look—like a—wanker.

Excellent, he croaked through a deafening smoker's laugh. I think we're going to get along. Come with me, Atlas, you lanky streak of piss. I'll buy you a, I'll buy you a drink. Yes, come on.

Two months later, Atlas accompanied thirteen other Foundlings on a tour of an underground labyrinth Greville called the Facility. It was a dense network of dimly lit corridors lined with doors that opened into tired but functioning laboratories and workshops. People in white coats over suits ignored the youngsters peering into their workplaces with eyes as wide as their gawking mouths. Very hush-hush, he told them. Those papers you've signed mean it's straight to prison if you utter a bloody word.

During induction, Greville explained the unique quality of this opportunity. The once-in-a-lifetime kind. That they should express themselves. Show the people here what you're made of. There are no boundaries, he rasped, only possibilities. And for a while in the Playpen, that felt true. Atlas and his fellow Foundlings had free rein. The facilitators said they should relax and enjoy themselves, make anything they liked. Familiarise yourself with the equipment, they said. Organise yourselves into teams, initiate projects, whatever. This is your space. Use it as you see fit.

There was a charge in the air. These guileless strangers came together, shared ideas, lent their limited expertise to others, and thrashed out concepts and theories. And while there was the occasional and inevitable falling out, a general harmony emerged among the Foundlings. Atlas experienced solidarity for the first time. Being treated as an equal compelled him to offer the same back to his new colleagues. It was as if he'd been plucked from what was shaping up to be an unremarkable life and dropped into the only place that could give him purpose. Sometimes Atlas still draws down on this glow of gratitude despite its brevity.

Then they graduated. During a reception event, they met various department heads who recruited them into existing projects and assigned them junior roles. Atlas can't remember how long it took but soon enough the true meaning behind Greville's motivational speech revealed itself. What the man had really meant was after they'd reached a certain level within the organisation, after they had kissed enough arse, after they'd given up all hope of ever expressing themselves through their work, after the idea of limitless potential had lost any meaning, only then, and not before, might they get a mess-this-up-and-you're-finished opportunity to run a small project of their own.

Atlas did what was expected. He worked hard, indulged in gentle politics, and befriended those he needed to. Eventually he made headway. From junior research assistant to senior researcher in eleven years. It wasn't bad going. He was the first of his cohort to do so. But then, somehow, his progress stalled. Almost three decades later, with only four moderately successful projects and a long list of failures to his name, he didn't have the clout to insist Project Lung should continue. He was supposed to swallow his humiliation and move on.

So, you broke the rules? asks the reporter.

Well, says Atlas, taking work home was a no-no. Get caught and you were looking at a prison sentence. But I knew the data was hiding something from me. I just needed a little time. So, I thought, sod it. My career was already in the bucket. Things would never change if I let the Facility walk all over me again. I had nothing to lose. And anyway, the world needs mavericks, wouldn't you agree?

The reporter half-nods like he hasn't committed to agreeing with this unusual man in his metal box.

You wanted to prove your employers wrong.

At first, yes, sort of. But after a while, that didn't matter anymore. It became part of me. I dreamt about it. Spent every waking hour thinking about it. And every spare hour working on it. I was obsessed.

Obsession. From the Latin *obsessionem*, meaning siege. A blocking up. A blockade. It was a siege on himself. With no home life to speak of, he threw every spare second and ounce of energy into the project. He neglected the Facility work he should've been attending to. If anyone from human resources had cared enough during those months to count his unopened emails, unheard voicemails, skipped meetings and missed deadlines, they would've concluded that he'd expired. Rumoured sightings were of his ghost, a forgotten scientist roaming the subterranean corridors.

While Atlas wonders if the reporter might turn this story into an extensive piece for one of the Sunday papers or, perhaps, become his biographer, he's also contemplating the anguish of the genius. It seems a bit hackneyed. He's unsure if that's how he'd like to be portrayed. But before giving this thought a proper outing, he notices the young hack has put on a pair of small round spectacles that make him look surprisingly similar to an early Carl Jung. Atlas lies back on the couch and finds he has an overwhelming urge to please the psychoanalyst. So he pauses and allows the psychoanalyst to explain that this obsession with his work was an attempt to fill several holes in his personal life.

Are you talking about my faltering marriage?

Ah, your marriage was faltering? Jung asks in an unconvincing Swiss accent.

Or maybe he's referring to the holes left by Atlas's parents when they died within three weeks of each other. His father from a brain haemorrhage. Then his mother, mugged while on her first excursion out of the house since becoming a widow.

Attacked by a teenage boy the size of a gorilla. He didn't kill her. Her heart did the dirty work. She collapsed at knifepoint, and the boy ran away. Later, he admitted everything to his girlfriend, who turned him in. Later still, he asked to meet Atlas. It was termed 'restorative justice'. A chance to rehabilitate, a step towards forgiveness, and possibly a sentence reduction. Atlas was the nearest thing the young man had to a living victim. Perhaps if he had been close to his mother, if he'd felt like a victim, he might have seen the merit.

Atlas suggests to the psychoanalyst that the death of his parents left a single hole between them. Small but not insignificant, more of a ventricular septal defect than a chest wound. But Jung parries with the idea that their demise removed a perceived barrier between Atlas and his own end, revealing a canyon-sized hole. And that he is standing at its edge, with K behind him, waiting his turn.

Yes, well, perhaps, Atlas says. A hole's a hole, though, don't you think? And before the psychoanalyst can argue, Atlas is on his feet, saying, thank you, that's enough for today. We have the hole analogy now, which is all I needed you for.

————

He sees he's reached the road that leads directly to the deserted industrial estate and the compound. Potholes at his feet, holes in his life, a big hole in the sky where the hate used to be. And the greatest hole of them all? The one he discovered in the data. Because that's what he eventually found. Holes! In his garden lab, surrounded by hundreds of printouts, columns of digits, tables, and graphs pinned to the walls, spread over the long worktop. Entire nights stood staring at them. Sometimes he would drink. The biting liquid loosened his brain and lightened his focus so he could follow the numbers as they danced from one printout to the next, and he'd swipe them from the worktop and replace them with others to let new movements take shape.

But he was lying on his side, on the sofa bed, contemplating a spell of sobriety when it happened, a soft eye on the thousands of numbers and shapes strewn across the floor and under his desk. It crept out like a cockroach from the gap under the skirting board, pausing, tentatively surveying the floorboards before taking a few more steps. Satisfied there was no danger, this tiny question scurried past his mind: what if he was looking at this the wrong way? He'd been studying the composition of the air, trying to find clues that would show something happening in the atmosphere. What he hadn't noticed, what was staring him in the face, was what was not there.

He levered himself up, put his bare feet onto the carpet of printouts, and picked up a sheet of paper. Yes, there it was, or there it wasn't. He grabbed another and another. They showed the same thing. The closer a monitor was to a conflict zone, the thinner the atmosphere. There was simply less of it. Nitrogen levels, oxygen levels, argon, carbon dioxide, methane, neon, hydrogen, all lower than they should be. Combined, it was a loss of just under three percentage points.

Ah, but what about altitude, you idiot?

He rose, his heart already sinking, and woke his laptop.

Jilib, 135 metres above sea level.

Sirte, 28 metres.

Tijuana, 20 metres.

Except for a few zones, like Marib, and almost everywhere in Afghanistan, nothing in the elevations could affect air density enough to explain the thinning.

How can the significance of this moment be conveyed to an audience? Simply saying it out loud never provokes a satisfactory response. It needs drama and enthusiasm, neither of which comes naturally to him. He has to practice speed, intonation, expressions, hand gestures, and whatever people use to communicate a dramatic turn of events. This was a turning point. The recognition that there was something else in the make-up of the skies the monitors hadn't detected, that there was an unknown substance or force in the air pushing all the other gases out, that realisation changed everything.

Suddenly.

All of a sudden.

In the blink of an eye.

Out of the blue.

Just like that.

But there he was, on the cusp of a breakthrough. Now he had something to look for. The hunt was on.

In the film version, he imagines they'll cut to a beautiful, shining laboratory lined with unidentifiable equipment and sleek computers. Atlas and his assistants in crisp white coats caught in a frenzy of testing and building, making the machine, saving the world. In reality, he stood at a cusp, and standing at cusps doesn't make great cinema. But that's how it was, Atlas plodding on alone, trying to answer a single question—what was in the hole? He took the mystery to bed every night where he entertained himself by turning it upside down, inside out, just to see what happened. Some nights, he'd rush downstairs and out to the garden lab to write something down or try something out. In the daylight hours, he'd take detours from his Facility duties to follow other sparks of ideas that occasionally inched him forward, just enough to reward his perseverance.

Working, working, working until, at last, he found it.

ARRINA

The conversation that became an argument, which grew into a slanging match and ended with her being ordered to leave the bloody house, was originally about pie, peas, and mashed potatoes.

The skirmishes were becoming rituals. Evening meals were the only time Arrina saw her father, and she preferred to avoid them. But she was running out of excuses. She could only pretend she was sick or eating out with friends (what friends? and with whose money?) so many times. With no job, she couldn't claim to be working late or attending a last-minute meeting. And so, as skipping dinner without plausible reason upset her mother, most days she joined her parents at the kitchen table at six o'clock.

Tonight's clash centred around Arrina's lack of gainful employment. If she had a paid position of some kind, her father would not have mentioned the cost of the meal after complimenting his wife on her cooking. He wouldn't have averaged out that cost across the week, factoring in the ever-increasing price of natural gas. Nor would he have divided that sum by three and informed Arrina how many metres of newsprint he'd had to watch pass through the printing press so she could stuff meat and pastry into her mouth.

Just think how proud you'd feel, her father signed, if you could contribute to the household expenses, give your mother some housekeeping, and repay some of the money you borrowed for your studies. His tone had been innocuous enough, the careful composure of a father keen to portray himself as someone who wanted only to guide his daughter toward a productive life.

If I had a job I wouldn't be here.

Her statement had come from under her breath, too quiet for her mother to hear, a simple record of fact that was not intended to provoke. If she had a job, someone like him or a new workmate or a chatty checkout assistant would suggest she got a place of her own. And Arrina would likely comply. It wouldn't be a thing she did or did not want to do, simply something that would happen, just as all the things that occurred in her life happened. However, while the words did nothing but declare a probability, her father watched them form on her lips with the disbelief of a man witnessing his name being engraved onto the side of a bullet.

His hackles were up. Arrina mirrored him involuntarily. Sensing an acute change in the room's atmosphere, her mother lowered her head until the tips of her fringe toyed with the mashed potato on her plate. And now that the foundations of the regular father-daughter spar were laid, he announced he'd given up hope of her ever leaving, and the pair proceeded to build one of their best.

You're out of touch,
you're spoiled,
you're stupid,
you're lazy,
and so on and so on until the two were standing,
him leaning in, look at me when I'm talking to you,
her poker-straight, I'd rather die,

him, lipreading, fists pressing down on either side of his half-eaten meal, then hands up, attacking the air with his silent shouts,

her, hands on hips, why are you such a wanker?

him, get out of my bloody house, you ungrateful little bitch,

the wife-mother seated below, between them, watching her tears make holes in the gravy.

Still shouting, she'd slammed the front door behind her, hoping the vibrations would not be wasted on her deaf father. She marched down the garden path to the driveway and the family car.

No coat, no bag, no car keys.

Orange street lights caught the drizzle she felt on her bare arms and face. She braced herself against the cold, kicked the weeds between the paving stones, and let the stiff wind point her in the direction of the park. She crossed the footbridge and stopped at the park gates. They were chained and padlocked. There had to be a way in because she could see youths gathered around the swings.

Youths. When did she start using that word? How old did she think she was, exactly? That's what living with your parents in your twenties does. Their ancient ways age you.

There were three other entrances. The nearest, back past the bridge and a hundred yards or so along the river. Perhaps she would find a hole in the fencing on her way. Arrina was about to begin her circumnavigation when she saw a figure on the bridge, standing in the middle, at the top of the arc.

Probably watching the water, she thought. Probably thinking of jumping. Probably a rapist or a murderer. Probably herself from the future, come to warn her about some terrible mistake she was about to make.

She took a few steps towards the footbridge. The figure moved.

When she stopped, it did too.

She calculated. If she turned around and walked away, she would look scared and vulnerable. Cut to a close-up of crime scene tape wrapped around trees, a blurry, upset dog-walker in the background being questioned by police, and her mother's tearful appeal for information on the local news. If she kept going in this direction, she and the dark figure would reach the end of the bridge at the same time. She'd be ready.

She was shaking, but of course she was, the air was freezing. Nothing ever happened here. This was a safe place.

Closer to the bridge, the figure looked female. Small too.

Her calculation was wrong, though. The woman was off the bridge before Arrina reached it. She wore a trench coat, a red beanie and a pair of yellow Adidas with green stripes. She was about forty. Maybe forty-five? And she was waving.

arrina-heal-i-understand-you-might-be-looking-for-a-job

Arrina Heal moved through life like an atom. She exercised no control. An infinite number of minuscule collisions had contributed to her arrival on the planet, and now her trajectory was at the mercy of endless influences as she tumbled along the path of least resistance. Energies pushed, pulled, halted, and accelerated her in directions she couldn't predict and never resisted. For Arrina, there was no alternative to the route the absent-minded universe created for her. To search for her own destiny was a wasted effort. Why strive to make a change in her life that would happen or not, regardless of her own actions? The choice between a futile fight or a carefree glide from birth to death had been easy, if it had indeed been her choice at all. The only consideration she gave to her voyage was to wonder occasionally where she would end up and what she might learn on her way.

The meeting with the woman on the bridge was nothing more than another collision. Now, three days later, they were sitting opposite each other in a cafe. The woman's name didn't suit her strained face, and the daylight revealed she was older than Arrina had assumed. Daisy's surname floated away before Arrina could catch it. Her colleague was a man. Blair. Younger but more serious. And while Daisy's words had a life all of their own, streaming out of her mouth like a party popper, Blair spoke little, which removed the need to make eye contact with him, and Arrina was all for not making eye contact.

Her father's advice, with whom relations had thawed now she had an actual job interview, was to remember to smile and be engaged. And while she appreciated his guidance, for who else cared enough to offer her any, he was still a fool. A narrow-minded, old-fashioned, chauvinistic, racist, impatient, tight-fisted, homophobic fool.

Make sure you look them in the eye, love.

It made her sick when he called her that. But not as sick as looking into people's eyes made her. *In* the eye. That's what it felt like, like she was inside them, in cold milky slime.

Blair's eyes were smaller than most, little balls of congealed yoghurt lined with short, sparse hairs. Daisy's were like stranded jellyfish begging passersby to put them out of their misery. But neither possessed anything as repulsive as her father's eyes, pinkish with a yellowy, translucent skin beneath which tiny purple worms feasted on putrid gelatin, held in place by dark double-layered lashes and flaking lids. She dreamed about his eyeballs sometimes, scooping them out with a soup spoon as he slept, exploding them under her heel, and hammering the worms with the back of the utensil as they tried to escape up her legs. She might have been ommetaphobic but she didn't believe so. Arrina wasn't scared of eyes, she was disgusted by them.

Look them in the eye, you never do that enough. It makes people think you're not interested or you don't like them. They never get to see the real you.

That is the real me, she thought.

Daisy and Blair on one side of the cafe table, milk-based coffees, cappuccinos or similar in front of them. Arrina sat opposite, her fingerless gloves curled around a cup of green tea. Daisy beamed at her.

we-read-your-research-paper-we-liked-it-very-much-didnt-we-blair-it-was-very-interesting

Arrina couldn't tell if a response was required from her. She searched the table for the words. She had long since ditched her stock of non-academic summaries of why she was interested in transonic aeroelasticity, what her research revealed, its implications on subsonic objects, and examples of practical implementation, as she never reached the end of her spiel before whoever she was talking to changed the subject.

She nodded at a bowl of wrapped sugar. Then, remembering the advice, she lifted her head and saw the woman staring directly at her. Arrina dropped her gaze back to her tea.

Blair removed an envelope from his jacket pocket and pushed it towards her.

Sign this, please.

Inside was a single sheet of paper headed *Official Secrets Act Declaration*. She did as he asked.

During the following thirty-three minutes, Arrina said only four words: yes, thank you, bye. For the rest of the time she listened to Daisy tell her about where she and Blair worked. They called it the Facility. It was a 'super-wonderful' place to start your career, full of hundreds of people just like Arrina who had the makings of great scientists but often lacked the, well, they didn't mean to be rude, but the confidence and personal skills they needed to break into their chosen fields.

Blair had pushed out his chair, his legs crossed away from the meeting. Daisy compensated by moving so far into the table that it looked as if its laminated edge might crack a rib.

If Arrina agreed to join, and it would be super-wonderful if she did, she would spend ten months doing a foundation in the Playpen, where she'd get safety training, attend placements at various live projects, and have time to absorb the institution's culture. She would also receive competitive remuneration, thirty days paid leave, health insurance, gym membership, and an accommodation allowance.

essentially-its-a-young-scientists-playground-you-can-do-whatever-you-like-and-get-to-know-yourself-better-as-a-researcher-explore-your-strengths-and-interests

Blair sighed through his nose.

We do important serious work.

of-course-we-do-blair-but-its-also-a-lot-of-fun-for-budding-young-scientists-like-our-friend-here-so-anyway-what-do-you-think-arrina

Arrina nodded.

does-that-mean-youll-join-us

She nodded again.

super-wonderful-im-so-excited

Daisy demonstrated this by grabbing Arrina's arm and splashing her new recruit's gloves with cold green tea.

———

Sam's calculation was indisputable; Arrina had belonged to him for precisely two months. The way he saw it, it was like buying a car. It was yours the moment you decided you wanted it. Imagining it on your driveway, the wheel in your hands, the pedals against your feet, the sound of the engine, that kind of emotional investment was as good as a deposit. The financial transaction and paperwork amounted to mere details. So while he and Arrina had been going out for just three weeks, she'd been his for eight.

Arrina didn't know about the first five. Her memory of their initial meeting was blurrier than his. She remembered walking by a public house she never learned the name of, even though she had seen it a thousand times going back and forth from home. Her habit was to pass by as fast as she could without breaking into a run to shorten the number of seconds she'd be subjected to drunken overtures and verbal abuse. She found it was better not to cross the road. By staying on the same side as the pub, her appearance before its patrons was sudden and surprising, giving them less time to think of something to shout, and she was out of sight sooner.

On the day in question, Sam stood at the pub entrance, sucking on a vape the size of a fist. As Arrina marched, a giant cloud appeared in front of her. She walked straight into it and inhaled a lungful of the sweet banana-flavoured fog. Slowing to empty her lungs, she coughed, wretched, and grabbed for her inhaler. She recalled seeing someone there, possibly a few people, but her primary memory was of feeling sickened by the thought of a stranger's expelled gases inside her. She spat and stormed away.

In Sam's mind, Arrina had enjoyed the smell of his vape. She'd smiled at him and then laughed at his joke about it being a foggy evening. This, he maintained, was when they established a connection, and he hadn't stopped thinking about her since. This bond strengthened outside the supermarket a week later. Sam was sitting in his van when Arrina exited through the automatic doors. Even from a distance he recognised her. She wasn't what he would call a looker. He usually went for prettier girls, not that he'd had much success. High-maintenance bitches, most of them. This one, though, she looked as if she'd be grateful for the attention. Plus, she was slim and blonde, and he liked that. The sides of her head were shaved and her clothes weren't exactly what he expected his women to wear, but these were minor details he could straighten out in time.

He gripped the van's door handle. This was his chance but he didn't know what to say. He watched as she struggled with a heavy plastic bag that looked ready to burst. It did. The contents rolled along the pavement. Sam wasn't a spiritual man but believed some things were just meant to be, and this was one of them. He swung the door open and jumped down onto the tarmac. When he reached her, she was stuffing canned food and tangerines into her pockets. He retrieved a tin of baked beans from under the wheel of a parked car and handed it to her. She snatched it from his hand without looking or speaking. Then, as she walked away with her coat and arms laden with goods, he called after her for her name. She shouted it as she stormed off. Afterwards, he remembered hearing her reply in the middle of his body rather than his ears. As if she had spoken directly to his heart.

He recovered himself just in time to say, I'm Sam, do you want a lift? before she disappeared around a corner.

She remembered the beans but not the person. She had no recollection of the exchange of names but it didn't surprise her that she'd given him hers. Arrina was also oblivious to Sam's sense of ownership. She was unaware he'd twice followed her to the Job Centre and home again. Or that he had sat next to her father at the local social club to get the measure of the man and had a brief conversation with her mother about the weather while they waited at the pelican crossing on the high street. Or that he'd watched her house from his van every evening for a week before the supermarket encounter.

When he eventually asked her out in the cleaning product aisle of the same store, she agreed, despite being betrothed to a man she had been seeing for over a year at university. This other man also considered himself her rightful owner, having proposed to her on the phone after she'd finished her doctorate and moved back to her parents' house.

It was during one of their daily telephone conversations the other man learned he had a rival. Incensed, he asked for his name and number and declared he was getting the next train. That evening, Arrina opened her front door to find Sam, smiling, burst lip, t-shirt ripped at the collar. He told her he'd had a call from the other man. They'd met in the park, argued and fought like teenage boys exchanging blows in a prearranged engagement. Sam thought it was funny. All that was missing was a crowd of yelling kids offering combat advice. But Sam didn't need the help. He said the other man was soft as shite. Hats off to him though, he landed a couple of decent punches. When his opponent stopped fighting back, when he was on the ground, weeping, Sam made him promise he'd never contact Arrina again.

The victory felt similar to the sensation he used to experience when he did well at the arcades, beating the high score on the retro games. He knew from that time that one big win often led to another. You enter the zone. You have momentum. And Sam had momentum that day. So he made a decision. He would marry Arrina. That would be his prize. He'd pop the question after she'd had little time to get over that other guy as he didn't want to risk a refusal. But he would do it soon. Two or three weeks seemed about right.

Sam arrived at Arrina's parents' house, his heart jumping, the engagement ring in his jacket pocket. She was already outside, standing at the front door, two suitcases at her feet.

Where are you going?

She sighed the word 'away' like it was the name of a faraway city.

What? You're going on holiday?

Arrina shook her head.

You're moving?

She nodded.

Where to?

Who the hell did this woman think she was? Didn't she realise what they had between them? He fumbled for the words to explain that she belonged to him now. She couldn't just up and leave, and certainly not without him.

You don't know what you're doing. I was about to ask you to be my wife. That's why I'm here.

Arrina said she wasn't allowed to tell him where she was going. Her voice did that thing he'd noticed before, as if it massaged the inside of his head, and within a second he was happy to just be there with her. Sam kneeled on the doorstep, extracted the ring from its box and held it up to her.

Will you marry me?

Arrina looked past him.

He followed her gaze. A black cab turned into the street.

Well, obviously, you're not going.

She grabbed a suitcase and reached for the other, which was now under Sam's arm. He pulled it closer and she missed the handle. Without looking at him, she carried the single case to the taxi, opened the boot and lifted it in. Sam got to his feet and brought the remaining luggage to her. He put it in with the other case and held the door as Arrina climbed into the rear seat. From inside, she peered past his shoulder and to the house. Her mother was at her bedroom window. Arrina waved but there was no sign of acknowledgement. Then Sam was in her face. She shrugged when he asked her how long she'd be gone and closed the door when he asked if she was ever coming back.

ALFONSO

Sound oozes in. The liquid warbling of budgerigars skips across the deepest, deepest whale song in a harmony that swaddles him tight. And all he wants is to stay right here in this mellow warmth. There is no reason, no reason in the entire world, for him to come out. It is too precious, too perfect to lose. And maybe it is this, the thought of holding on to it, that triggers the idea of its potential loss. So now Alfonso begins to slide, and, although he tries, he can't secure himself in this place because he has nothing to hold on with, no body, no limbs to reach out with, no means with which to grip the sides, and the comfort continues to fall away. And through the emerging gaps, the deep melody morphs into wails and cries, the chirrups into the chatter of a two-way radio.

A middle-aged woman was pleading her case when Alfonso noticed the disturbance. He nodded and smiled as she explained her predicament, rushing her words. She was irked, though she was trying her best not to provoke him. It wasn't uncommon for members of the local population to be upset when they came across Alfonso in the street. The uniform was to blame. It signalled a threat. Regardless of his attempt to neutralise its effect by choosing oversized jackets, trousers and peaked hats, all of which he believed gave him a harmless, clownish appearance, all they ever saw was a Castleport traffic warden. Alfonso mirrored her stance as well as he could because he knew this made it seem like he was listening, and people relax when they think they're being heard. It's a shame, he thought, to make her explain herself like this. He would have liked to have interrupted her some time ago, assured her there was nothing to worry about, and sent her on her way, but that was too risky.

Before reaching Ursula Street, it had been a good morning. Mil had received an unconditional offer from a university she was keen to attend, and it was the end of Jen's first week as the new assistant manager of her department at Leonard & Mann, a promotion she'd worked hard to get. Tonight they would celebrate with champagne and his special nut roast. After breakfast with them, Alfonso had practised his sun salutations, read a little while drinking his nettle tea, and taken a few moments to appreciate the front garden. His dahlias had looked splendid in the early light. It had been a delightful start to the day and he was in no mood to sully it by issuing this woman a fine.

On his way here it had been all sunshine and birdsong, the paving passing below him, the uneven joins pressing through his rubber soles. Small white clouds, a happy morning sky. He whistled fragments of made-up tunes until his phone beeped. Then he put on his peaked cap, turned the corner, and began his shift.

Alfonso always started at Ursula Street. He believed ticking off the most unpleasant part of the day straightaway was good for the soul. Something about how the words first and worst rhymed suggested the cosmos preferred it this way, and he was all for keeping the cosmos on his side. It was a parking disc zone, a technology-light income generator for the city council. To Alfonso's disapproval, these zones were springing up throughout the municipality. They were traps. To those familiar with them, a zone like this represented free parking, a rare thing in Castleport. They put people at ease. Made them careless. They absent-mindedly rotated the cardboard clocks to the wrong time, placed them upside down on their dashboard by the windscreen, or forgot them altogether, all of which were punishable by a hefty fine. The zones encouraged others to break the rules, mischievously setting the clock thirty minutes into the future. If caught, which they frequently were, they returned to find their vehicles clamped. The mechanism was also designed to ensnare drivers less acquainted with the concept. Hassled commuters parallel parked in infeasibly tight spaces and vacated their cars in search of ticket machines that didn't exist. Instead, they found small, lamppost-mounted notices. These official signs explained that this was no ordinary place to leave a vehicle and, if they wished to park there legally, they should locate a nearby retailer who would furnish them with a disc free of charge. With no further information, the drivers wandered from store to store, irritating shopkeepers. Meanwhile the traffic wardens swooped, slapping yellow plastic envelopes on their windscreens. Sticky-backed bad news.

This woman belonged to the last grouping. Alfonso was looking for her before she appeared. She ran towards him from across the street, a small child in one arm and an oversized handbag in the other. He smiled and waited. He'd already stayed longer than he should have. The rules were clear: violations were to be penalised immediately. This would have been an excellent beginning of the shift for most traffic wardens. No disc, £70 fine, move on. But Alfonso wasn't cut out for modern wardening. Not in this city. Those in the employ of Castleport City Council Traffic Department were known for their ruthlessness, a quality that contributed to it holding the title of highest-earning traffic department in Europe for the third year in a row, making the city more money than all the other revenue-generating departments combined. As a result, Mr Alexander, the head of the department, was a powerful man, feared by everyone except the wardens, who, by and large, worshipped him.

Mr Alexander's talent was his ability to create a particular culture within the department, one that lent itself favourably to the unforgiving collection of money. Initiation rituals, morning drills, group exercises, collective affirmations, and many other techniques instilled in his troops a militaristic consciousness. A disciplined brotherhood. They were Mr Alexander's foot soldiers, a militia of parking ticket-dispensing sociopaths. In the nine years since his appointment, he had systematically transformed his department, jettisoning the 'rabble of overweight, hippy vagabonds' and replacing them with a sinewy, hateful, all-male SWAT team. Of the old guard, only one remained. And here he was, still standing in Ursula Street, listening to the trembling voice of an illegal, the label the wardens had been ordered to use. It was beyond Alfonso how he was supposed to turn off whatever processor in his head computed the suffering of others. He felt sorry for this woman and sorry for this city in which he'd lived his whole life. Money was killing everything. As the place became slicker and shinier by the day, it grew more brutal. And its residents, now more than ever, were thirsty for some kindness, understanding, or anything that might soften the edges of modern existence.

PART II

ATLAS

Down, down, down. A slow, smooth, spinning descent towards the northern hemisphere, then towards Europe, towards northern Europe, and towards north-western Europe; down, down, and down, veering in favour of the British Isles, closer and closer until France, and Belgium and the Netherlands on one side, Ireland on the other, thin and disappear from view; down into the middle of England as the Isle of Man, Wales, and the Scottish borders glide away; down, down, down to an urban area, a small city that holds the shape of a sleeping, dreaming dog, and deeper still, down to an ill-defined district where criss-crossed roads slice the residues of disappeared factories and warehouses, bordered by sweeping suburban streets and wood-land; down towards a black spot, a high-contrast oval cradling the circular eye of a mottled white gasholder, the wink of a narrow, oblong hangar, and the tight-lipped wall of shipping containers; down through the roof of a single container, inside of which possessions are strewn over the carpet like islands and peninsulas orbiting a continental bed; down to a duvet mountain of undetermined colour, a naked lower leg stretching out across a murky beach; down and into a crevice and deep under the soft rock to the blinking face of Atlas Brown; down through his scalp and skull and into a warm April morning where sunlight shafts lurch through the garden lab windows and make slow-motion fireflies from floating dust, and where Atlas is standing at his workbench looking down, one elbow bent at ninety-degrees, a clawed hand grasping at air; down now to the bench where a wide-neck, bottomless demijohn sits alongside a pipette, a petri dish, and a half-empty bottle of whiskey; and down once more, all the way to the floor, to an open blue canister that lies on its side, spewing human fear pheromone over the scientist's bare feet.

There will be no adventures for him today. No leaving his box, no getting out of bed, and no lifting his head from under the covers. Instead, Atlas will stay right here and agonise his way through the day he came so close to murdering his wife.

The spill, and then the blackout.

The next thing he knew, two out-of-focus police officers loomed over his hospital bed. One of them informed him he was under arrest. Later, as they sat across a table from him in an interview room, Atlas noted that the one who did most of the talking, the one on the left, was little more than a boy. A boy with an angry face and a deep voice that said,

Mrs Brown heard a commotion coming from the shed.

Atlas shook his head.

No—it's a garden laboratory. Her—surname is Blue. She didn't—take mine. And she prefers Ms.

She claims she heard shouting and what sounded like glass being smashed. At first she believed there was an intruder in the shed.

Lab.

But after she called for you in the house and you didn't answer, she concluded it was you in the, the laboratory, and that you required help. So she went out into the garden and ran towards the lab while calling your name, intending to assist you. She claims that before she reached the door, and I use her words here, my husband burst out like a madman, stripped to the waist and wielding a fire extinguisher in the air; there was blood on his face, and he was screaming. Mrs Brown, I mean Ms Blue, alleges that you threw the said fire extinguisher at her, hitting her on the forehead. And then you proceeded to attack her.

Utter—nonsense.

Please, Atlas. Let the officer finish.

The third voice, not as deep as the child-officer's, belonged to Liam John, a solicitor Atlas had not met until half an hour before his police interview. Supplied by the Facility. A small man dressed in golf clothing. But it was the size of the man's tanned head under its luxurious helmet of jet-black hair that Atlas remembers now. His body appeared incapable of supporting a cranium of such proportions. Yet, there it was, holding it, not toppling over.

Don't worry, Atlas, he said before the officer arrived. Standard police nonsense, by the looks of it. We'll have you out of here in no time. Just follow my lead.

The officers entered the room and sat down at the table. The other one, also male, was older but slighter. Evidence pointed to him being mute.

Your neighbours called the emergency services, said the uniformed youngster. When PC Campbell and I arrived at the scene, you and your wife were lying unconscious in the garden.

So—her word against mine.

Atlas, John said, if you'll allow me. Officer, my client has no memory of the incident. We're awaiting various test results but it's looking increasingly likely that he blacked out before the alleged attack. As you can see, my client has also sustained serious injuries, so it is entirely possible that a third party attacked both Dr Brown and his wife.

Atlas's forehead throbbed under its bandage. At the hospital, a nurse explained that they'd removed several shards of glass before stitching him up. The cut ran from above his hairline, down his forehead, and stopped below his left eyebrow. Yes, it would scar, she said, but he'd been lucky he hadn't lost the eye.

The officer stared at Atlas. It was tempting to blow the boy a kiss. Or wink and say his mother would be so proud. Or ask him how his work experience was going. Or slam his palms on the table and tell him to come back once he's started shaving.

Domestic abuse is a serious offence, Dr Brown.

That's quite enough, officer.

She also has an injury to her forehead, Dr Brown. Only hers wasn't because of an accident.

But Atlas's mind was elsewhere. Of course it had been him. And whatever happened now, whether he'd be charged, whether Liam John could wave his legal wand to make it all disappear, he would still have to face Bute. Being locked up in a prison cell somewhere far away seemed infinitely preferable.

————

Spots of dried toothpaste under a thick layer of dust give Atlas's reflection a grainy look, as if he's activated a soft-focus filter on the mirror called Overplayed Videotape. This, coupled with the light from the adjacent circular window that flatters his bone structure and masks his wrinkles, means that the Atlas behind the glass is infinitely better looking than the one in front.

This is where he does most of his talking these days, standing bolt upright, addressing himself. Or, rather, this is where *they* do most of *their* talking these days, addressing *one another*. Atlas and his reflection discuss many things, from what he should do or eat that day and where he should go, to darker matters, matters of the mind, his mind. For instance, is he still compos mentis, and is the faint hissing sound he hears when he walks by the gasholder real? The pair also enjoy reciting and editing past conversations, repeating sentences Atlas said or should have said, fine-tuning his answers and questions and matching them to the most suitable facial expressions.

Above and to the sides of his reflection are approximately thirty centimetres of blurred background. The lower section of the mirror takes in his shoulders, chest hair, and nipples. The rest of his nakedness is hidden from view. He used to bemoan the absence of a full-length mirror, one of many complaints he had about his compound accommodation, but he's happy about it now. Instead of being in decent shape for a man of his height and age, which was how he considered himself in the days when he ran and ate better, his torso has started to pouch. He is pouching. And of that he'd rather not be reminded. So the mirror, as it is, works well.

Atlas clears his throat.

I've seen it—countless times. A thing happens—sometimes when you're trying to—solve a puzzle—and it's going around and around in your skull for—ages—months or longer.

Reflected Atlas grins.

Tell me how to solve puzzles too, oh, great solver of all things.

I will—just for you.

He winks at the reflection and makes a mental note never to wink again.

He has explained his problem-solving process to his reflection many times. These are rehearsals. And some, therefore, are better than others. But Reflected Atlas is a forgiving audience who enjoys it when Atlas becomes distracted by unrelated memories and ideas and wanders down new mental avenues away from the intended subject matter. It keeps things fresh.

Atlas's analogy today is a vast circular room with tall, smooth concrete walls. Maybe no ceiling, just sky up above, the occasional cloud passing by. On the floor are paths, large individual stone slabs laid out in concentric rings.

You are on the—the outer ring, and the answer—the solution you're looking for—is all the way over there—in the middle. Out of reach. You can't see it from where you are but you—you know it's there. You can sense it. The—more complex the problem, the bigger the room—and the greater the number of rings. The gaps between them—they're too wide to step or jump over—they're filled with all kinds of exotic plants—some toxic—some have thorns and some sting—they come up to your waist, like—a mini jungle. And the rustling makes you think something might be in the foliage—following you. And you're walking around the outer ring for—forever—looking at all the other rings—the ones you've got to reach so you can get closer to the solution. Or perhaps you're looking at the height of the walls—or at the ball of sky above you—and you're walking and walking—but you're not closing in. You can see that—that somehow you've got to turn these rings into a spiral that will lead you to the nucleus— where the answer lies.

Eventually—you notice something—perhaps a slight clearing in the undergrowth—next to you. It's not possible to cross—but you start to focus on your immediate surroundings—looking down as you walk—until you come across another clearing— and another. Then you spot one with a stepping stone—you know you passed here earlier but you were looking in the wrong place—for the wrong thing. So you step onto the stone—and into the next ring—nearer the solution. Your—mind has altered—as if by discovering the clearing and then the stepping stone you've opened your brain somehow—opened it up to surprising answers that might take you to where you need to be. That's how it works—a clearing—then a stepping stone.

Atlas pauses. His reflection is nodding vigorously.

I see where this is heading. It was like this for you, a circular path, and then finding the clearing at that ridiculous dinner party you didn't want to go to.

Atlas smiles.

You always know—where I'm going with these—lectures.

Reflected Atlas is about to remind Atlas that he invariably finds a way to the dinner party moment during these rehearsals but the latter is already there, remembering how important it was to Bute that he joined her that night. And he's assuming, as he always does, that she wanted him there to pour cold water over the flame of an unwanted admirer. And that he probably failed. It was a blathering, droning evening full of people and topics he had no interest in. Nobody tried to engage him, which was standard at these things. And when, eventually and inevitably, a discussion turned to a subject on which he did have an opinion, he had been silent for so long that he had lost the ability to speak. Or the privilege. He'd made his indifference clear and was being rightly ignored. So he pushed his chair back from the table far enough to be considered rude by anybody paying sufficient attention, drank red wine, and let his awareness drift between the conversations around him and the work he would have rather been attending to.

The occasional phrase or sentence carved its way through the white noise towards him. *Peter is such a darling, It was a hideous show, I prefer early mornings, personally, She has no talent, He did what?, There's going to be a renaissance, I am sure of it, The pigeon-chested fool makes me laugh so much, No, I love France, it's that, well, the people, Are you telling me you've never heard of Franco K Glover?, I'm ready for a complete change, That's not art, though, is it?, What's the phobia called when you're terrified of life?* And so this continued for what seemed like days until someone at the far end of the table said, *Honestly, it's like working with Ming the Merciless*, and with that, Atlas sank into a cold childhood memory. A forgotten nightmare, in his pyjamas, queueing outside the Cameo cinema, not to see Flash Gordon but to be challenged to a deadly game by a paranoid prince. Then into a leafy cave, and his legs are failing as he begs Timothy Dalton not to force him to push his hand into an ancient tree stump, inside which a scorpion monster readies itself to bite his fingers with its poisonous fangs. Then the helplessness as the famous actor plunges Atlas's puny arm into the murky hole. There is no relief from the fear when he opens his eyes to a pitch-black bedroom. The chest contractions, the screaming, the calling for his parents, his father's banging on the wall separating their bedrooms and his shouts of shut the hell up. He is too scared to reach out to his bedside lamp in case the scorpion monster is under the shade. He lies there, quivering, tears wetting the pillow, unaware that the terror will pass.

This dream memory, those seconds before certain death, relived amid a drunken dinner party haze of slipping faces and hot voices, clung to his throat for the rest of the meal, for the journey home, and for the hours back in his workshop.

It's interesting—isn't it? That nightmare had disappeared—there was no trace of it throughout my adult life—and suddenly there it was. Like my subconscious had been digging around—for something—to help solve my problem. There was nothing, nothing, nothing and then—bam—it was hanging from my neck like an albatross. No—that's wrong—it wasn't a punishment. It was a prize. Hanging from my neck—like a medal—a gift that would help me save everything. A golden external factor. Have I got that—is that right? It helped me—solve the problem.

I get where you're coming from. But can it be an external factor if it came from you? Should you be saying it was an internal factor?

But Flash Gordon didn't come from me—did it? Please—don't muddy the waters. This is already confusing enough.

For Atlas, the memory of the dream, it appearing to him when it did, was a revelation. And coincidences like that, if that's what it was, rarely occur in scientific research. So this one ought to be celebrated every time it crosses his mind. With a finger, Atlas draws a smile over his reflected mouth and then, after a second, adds a raised eyebrow.

Now—back to the spiral path. This is a prime example—you know—of what I'm talking about. That recollection—it cut a clearing through the undergrowth—but the stepping stone into the next circle—that was all my own work. I made the connection—as I played with the memory of how that fear had followed me—from my dream into my bedroom—and then from the dinner party to my workshop. But really—it must have stalked me for years. Shadowed me—lurking in the shade—biding its time—watching and listening for the perfect moment to—reintroduce itself. But now I had it and—afterwards—when the fear dissipated—I could think about it objectively.

Reflected Atlas smiles and raises an eyebrow so his features match Atlas's marks in the dust.

Oh, do tell. What were your objective thoughts?

A noise outside draws Atlas away from the mirror. The heat from the sun often causes the gasholder to groan, but he looks through the window anyway. There is nobody there of course. He lets his gaze float above the trees and fields on the horizon, way beyond the derelict Castleport factories, and remembers idling on the sofa in the garden lab, summoning up the energy to start another night shift. Slightly intoxicated from the red wine but not really feeling it, tired and a little sullen, as if the following morning's dooms were already upon him. With half an eye on the papers around him, he was thinking about fear. Why people felt it. The common denominators. Real-life fear versus dream-life fear. The difference between isolated, individual fear and that of groups. Did being with others lessen its effect? Or did fear reverberate and intensify as it bounced from person to person, the horror in their eyes justifying your distress? And was it possible to grade fear into levels of potency? Or was fear simply fear? No gradients or grey areas, just black-and-white fight or flight. And as he toyed with these questions, his thoughts merged with the work that covered the walls and floor around him. It was a simple idea. There could be no doubt that war zones played host to vast amounts of fear. While each conflict varied in geography and terrain, weaponry and chemicals used, vehicle types, death counts, and motivations, the one thing they all had was frightened people. Soldiers and civilians alike, all fearing for their lives and those of the people they love. He didn't need to research it: fear had to be present in hostile environments in greater concentrations than anywhere else. It was obvious.

It wasn't a solution. Fear couldn't change the chemical composition of the air. But it gave him an angle to consider.

What if, under the right conditions, human fear was a catalyst for a reaction of some kind? He might be onto something if he could somehow manufacture it, a chemical version of fear, and analyse the atmosphere in its immediate vicinity. And then he realised he wouldn't have to produce it all. That had already been done.

Angela visits him once a week and stays until the early evening. Occasionally she misses a visit but it's rare. For the first few months she tumbled in as if propelled by a wind of optimism, brimming with good news and ideas for the future. Another seven days had passed without him appearing in the press; she'd found a few cans of his favourite soup; she was closer to securing his new identity; she had located somewhere more suitable for him to live, a place not too far from the compound. Many of her plans were prefaced with the words' when things get back to normal.'

When things get back to normal, she might've said, we'll set you up in business, a small shop perhaps.

She uses the phrase less these days, which, to Atlas, means she's adjusting. And while good cheer still marks her arrivals, these occasions are more subdued now that 'normal' has become an abstract idea.

Lately she has been complaining about the smell of his accommodation. Last time, he forgot to air the metal box before she arrived and she refused to enter, insisting they talk outside. He suggested a stroll around the compound but she doesn't like to get too close to the gasholder, so they sat on the aluminium steps. Afterwards, she left a plastic bag of various detergents he hasn't brought in yet.

Cleaning though. Yes, he knows it'll be good for his head and general hygiene. She's told him all that, and yes, yes, he agrees. But she seems blind to the abundant evidence that proves he is not the disgusting pig she believes him to be: he showers once a week, washes his clothes every month or so in the machine in the laundry unit on the ground level, and keeps the cooking area of the kitchen box spotless. It's only in here, in his own quarters, that he has a problem. The bedding is the primary issue. The scent he's reluctant to remove must be gone by now, but sometimes he thinks he can still pick it up. When he pulls the cover over him, he catches, maybe, just the faintest trace. Fossilised skin cells, decomposing hairs, perfume molecules, they can't simply disappear. They've got to be here under the quilt somewhere, pressing against him, holding him imperceptibly gently, whispering reassuring words. And those same molecules could be anywhere inside his accommodation. Mingled with the dust that lies deep in the carpet, on his shelves, the books, on the windows, on and around the papers on his desk, between the keys of his computer keyboard. To clean the place, any of it, would be to abandon Arrina. He isn't ready for that.

Atlas craves and dreads Angela's visits in equal measure. He longs for the human contact, her conversation, those understanding nods when he complains about whatever new gripe he has, and, of course, the food and occasional bottle of something alcoholic. But he dreads being reminded of the dangerous burden he is to her. And one day she'll be caught crossing the border like a smuggler laden with illicit goods. She has a family. Four daughters and a son, aged between five and sixteen, a husband who is a big jazz fan and an aspiring sci-fi writer, and two working spaniels called Norman and Janice. What would happen to them if she didn't return home? Plus, he doesn't believe her when she says the provisions are not from her family's table. He'd be lost without her supplies but he can not bear to think of her own people going short for his sake. He can't be the only person unable to use the provision stations. There have to be other ways to find nourishment in this city.

He would miss her if she stopped coming. While he's sure she still thinks of him as an assignment, a hangover from the old job, she is steadily becoming his friend. Sometimes she brings flowers or a novel for him to read. He makes tea, and they play chess on the board she gave him after discovering they both enjoy it. They move pawns, chat about their lives, and perform little routines that inch them closer together, like when she asks how he is, and he says he's never been better, then laughs at her sceptical expression. It's a small thing, and it's always the same, but that is the point.

He'd miss her questions. He used to reveal as little as possible until he realised she already knew quite a bit about him from the brief she received when she agreed to take on the role. But there are a lot of gaps in her knowledge. And now he knows there's nothing he needs to hide anymore he has taken it upon himself to plug them.

What he's noticing is that these gaps belong not only to her. When life moves quickly it's easy to log the big things, peg certain moments as the story's key junctures, and leave everything else in the blur. But walking back through it all with her he sees external factors he'd forgotten about. Like the draft research paper he remembered while making Angela a gift of a secret he'd previously sworn to take to the grave. He wanted to give her something to thank her for all she'd done for him so far and to apologise for the trouble he'd caused her. Before extraction, she saw it as part of her job to find out what was in the agent that Atlas used to attract the Particle to the machine. She would ask repeatedly and attempt to trick, threaten, bribe or blackmail him into telling her. She wouldn't show it, but he knew she was infuriated by her failure. Even if it hadn't been his only leverage, the last person Atlas would have shared a secret with was Angela. But that was then, when life was different, when they were all under pressure and he didn't know who she really was. So sharing this information she had once sought so eagerly seemed the perfect reward. He dropped the revelation into conversation one evening as they played chess. When the excitement he had expected to see from Angela did not materialise, he immediately regretted his timing. Without taking her eyes off the board, she raised an eyebrow and asked, human fear pheromone? Is that it? Atlas detected a whiff of disappointment in her tone. She remained quiet until after she'd taken his second bishop and forced him to use his remaining rook to block a threat from her queen.

How did you get hold of the pheromone?

I—stole it. The Facility had a—stash.

Angela raised her eyes and looked at him.

Stole it?

At last she was interested and was soon asking Atlas how he'd known about the Facility's stockpile of fear.

I just knew—it—it must've been common knowledge.

And then it happened. The image of the draft research paper on the seat of a canteen chair appeared as clear as the chessboard in front of him. It must have been a good couple of years before he'd devised the Hate Extractor. Atlas had sat down with a tray of food in one of the Facility canteens, spotted the paper, and pocketed it. An action without thought. He likes to believe it was out of character, that he was distracted, and under normal circumstances he would've handed the report to the appropriate department unread.

It was a poorly written thirty-two-page paper with penned corrections in the margins. It described an attempt to genetically modify and weaponise a parasitic disease called toxoplasmosis. The infection was known to spread from rats to cats and then to humans, but the symptoms were mild for most people. The Facility was interested in its journey between rodent and feline. They knew the parasite attacked the rat's amygdala, the part of the brain central to fear and the fight-or-flight response, to render the animal incapable of fear. The next time the infected rat saw a cat, it walked right up to it, got itself eaten, and the parasite jumped ship. The researchers were looking to adapt toxoplasmosis to infect the human brain in the same way, devouring opponents' fear and rendering them easy targets. But it was messy and expensive, and the ethics department was becoming jittery. Also, the computer modelling suggested a possible uplift in attacks from emboldened enemy combatants. So the project was flipped. They would synthesise human fear pheromone, the hormone produced in the amygdala, the same chemical the previous work had tried to suppress. The new thinking was pheromone bombs. Dropped behind enemy lines, they could turn adversaries into harmless fleshy piles of terror.

The research was interesting but useless to him. Atlas shredded it and returned to whatever he'd been doing before lunch. Years later, in the hours after the Flash Gordon dinner party, when he was pondering fear and remembered that a manufactured pheromone already existed, the source of the knowledge, the paper, remained buried. But when Angela asked how he'd come to know about the pheromone and forced him to tug on the chain of memories, he snagged the confidential report and pulled it out of the sand. And yet another gap was revealed and filled.

Angela had returned her attention to the game.

What if you hadn't stolen the paper?

He shook his head.

I—don't know.

But 'stolen' is a strong word.

Whatever people may think of him, Atlas is adamant he's only ever broken one law. Admittedly, treason is a big deal but something about it being victimless blunts the edge. He was never a man to care about crimes against corporations. And the state, or the state before extraction, was nothing more than another uncaring conglomerate. So if it was stealing in a technical sense, if he is technically a thief, he exonerates himself.

Also, strictly speaking, theft within the Facility was not possible. Employees were encouraged to consider the place not as an organisation where hundreds of scientists worked on individual projects but as a single massive brain with the skills, knowledge, and acumen to solve any problem. No team or researcher had exclusive rights to anything they created. It was an open-source model in which every idea, invention, or development was up for grabs for as long as the approach improved the overall profitability of the institution. It was a giant free-for-all where any researcher could take your work and do whatever they wanted with it, from correcting its flaws to adding it to their own projects. Economics was at its heart. The greater the number of minds the Facility had circling around the most promising ideas, the better the chances of it reaching its financial targets. At least, that's how it worked on paper. Unfortunately, the only thing that mattered to the Facility workforce was *egonomics*. Status as currency. An individual's value to the Facility was directly determined by the value of their contribution to successful projects. What would have been the point of going to all the effort of breaking new scientific ground only for others to pick up your work, make it better, and take the credit? You'd be forgotten in an instant. No recognition, no plaudits, no glowing reputation. On the other hand, by protecting their ideas, researchers could grow their value within the system. So the reality of this policy of openness and collaboration meant teams went to extraordinary lengths to hide their discoveries.

The open source policy should have died slowly in a corner of a forgotten laboratory. And perhaps it would have if it wasn't for the fact that while Facility scientists believed their own discoveries were worth hiding, they liked the idea of everybody else's work being freely available to them. Hence the birth of an illicit trade in the secrets of others: an invisible, thriving cottage industry profiting from the perfect combination of capitalism, idealism, and egotism. Anyone could buy anything for the right price. The practice was both publicly frowned upon and privately condoned by the higher-ups. If it resulted in the Facility operating in the fashion they'd initially decreed, and if it created healthy market competition and the continual development of profitable state-of-the-art murder machines, well, what was there to complain about?

As Atlas understood it, a network of researchers operated the market with operatives in every department. It seemed straightforward. You let it be known what you wanted, and the market came to you. When Atlas decided he needed the pheromone, that's what he did. He approached a group of middle-ranking researchers gathered by the vending machines in the central vestibule, placed his hand on the shoulder of one of them and announced that he was buying. He lingered long enough for their confused faces to turn and see him, then returned to his desk and waited.

That afternoon, a man in his thirties appeared. He pulled up a chair and sat down.

How you doing?

I'm—okay.

The man's head tilted slightly to the right.

Are you sure?

Well—I could be better.

Thought so. And is there anything I can get for you that might improve your situation?

A—decent quantity of—human fear pheromone—that would help.

The man nodded, got to his feet and left.

Three days later, a woman pushed her head into his office.

Dr Brown, may I ask you a question?

Yes—of course—come in.

Atlas gestured to the chair.

Thanks, but I won't keep you long. I just wanted to get your perspective on something. Is that alright?

He nodded.

Would you say that naturally produced fear pheromone is better than synthetic? Or vice versa?

Interesting question. I assume—natural is better. No matter how good synthetic is, it's bound to be—lacking—in some way.

But I'm not sure it's—possible to produce natural fear pheromone—certainly not in—quantity.

No, you wouldn't have thought so. But there's talk of a production line right here in the Facility. Don't quote me on this, but they're saying a team has genetically engineered over a hundred chimps with a human amygdala and sweat glands. They're in these specially designed cages that allow the researcher to scare them half to death to produce an acute stress response. Apparently they have to intensify the fright stimuli faster than expected as the animals keep growing accustomed to however it is they're being terrified in there. They'll probably have to destroy them and start again with a fresh batch soon. But anyway, they collect the perspiration and isolate the pheromone. Or that's the rumour.

Right—well—going back to your question—if I were to work with the pheromone—theoretically, of course—I would opt for natural—providing the quality is—high.

My understanding is the quality is excellent. According to the rumours, they tested it on human volunteers and the results are impressive. Supposedly.

Better than the—other—synthetic version?

Yes. And more expensive. A process like that would be pretty intensive.

Of course. Out of interest—how much—in theory—what kind of cost are we—would someone be looking at?

It's a matter of economy of scale. The more that's required, the cheaper it is per unit. But if they halt production while they wait for a new batch of chimps, it could become prohibitively expensive. If you see what I mean.

Atlas sucked in his thin lower lip and bit down. He wasn't sure how much hormone he'd need. Or whether it would even work. He had envisioned dripping a micro-litre or two into his first test and then taking it from there. How much sweat could a chimp excrete in one scare session? Not a lot, he thought. And surely the hormone contained within that would be minuscule.

Again—if I needed such a chemical—I'd want to secure as much as possible—as soon as possible.

Thank you for your advice.

Atlas doesn't like to think about how many chimps were traumatised to produce the thirty litres of hormone that were delivered to his lab two months later. The unsigned note accompanying the blue aluminium canisters said more would be available soon if required.

He smuggled the canisters out of the Facility one at a time and hid all but one under a blanket behind the sofa bed in the garden lab. The remaining canister he placed on his workbench where it stayed untouched for several days.

———

The Control

He required a controlled environment and a reliable and precise way of measuring the air composition. He ordered a five-litre flask with a wide neck and a rubber-sealed lid. To its inside wall he taped an air monitor, which he linked to a laptop via the house wi-fi. Next, he closed the flask, refreshed the interface on the computer screen and made a note of the data.

Experiment 1

He removed the lid and placed the flask upside-down on the workbench. To the lid's underside, he secured a petri dish small enough to fit within its circumference. He adjusted his manual pipette to a single micro-litre, opened the canister and extracted the pheromone. Then, quickly, he resealed the canister and ejected the chemical into the dish. Finally, he positioned the inverted flask over the dish and pressed it into the lid's rubber seal. He set a timer for fifteen minutes.

At the end of the allotted time, he refreshed his screen. The air composition remained stable.

Experiment 2

He drilled a hole in the flask's side with a diamond bit and fashioned a stopper from putty. Then he reran the test with the same quantity of pheromone, opening the hole for fifteen minutes before blocking it up again with the putty.

No change.

Experiment 3

Atlas removed the stopper once more, set the timer for one hour, curled up on the sofa bed, and napped until he heard the electronic alarm bleeping. It took a moment to remember what he was doing in the lab. He rose, walked to the bench and reattached the putty stopper. His laptop had gone to sleep. He waggled his mouse and entered his password. Straightaway he could see there was no shift in the air composition. He was about to turn away when he remembered he had to refresh the screen. At first, it appeared as if nothing had changed in the data. Then a detail caught his eye. The oxygen level was at 20.9301%. But in the original figure, a pattern in the number had registered with him. He went to his notes. There it was, 20.9393%. It had dropped. Excited, he double-checked the rest of the figures. All of them were down. In total it barely amounted to half a percentage point but that didn't matter. There was something in the flask that shouldn't be, and he had it trapped. All he needed now was to calculate how much pheromone and time were required to reach the conflict zone levels of three percent. And then, of course, find out exactly what he had captured.

He did not tell Angela about his drinking. Or how the experiments grew more elaborate and reckless. Or how he used himself as a test subject. Or about the accident. She got the abridged version. The sober one in which he wrote up the findings, presented them to the Facility, secured funding, and, relieved from his other duties, dived into his discovery.

Bute didn't press charges. Nor did she confront him. Instead, she went away for a while, leaving instructions for him to vacate her life. Which he obeyed. He spent six months in rented accommodation while buying a house on the other side of the city. A hired contractor updated the property to his specifications, including a replica of the garden lab Bute had made for him but with the addition of a panic room at the rear. The false wall with a door that resembled a shelving unit wouldn't cost much more. It was the contractor's suggestion to put it in. He claimed they were becoming popular. Gives people that extra peace of mind, he said. To Atlas, it sounded like a good idea he'd never need.

In the meantime, he returned to work and did his best to scrape his reputation off the floor. His return was influenced by Liam John. He had let Atlas know that the Facility had been in two minds about whether to send in legal help when he was arrested. The new Facility Director, General Moss, swung the argument in Atlas's favour. John suggested Moss wanted to make a good impression on the staff and thought abandoning one of their own was poor optics. Instead, he believed it better to bring Atlas back into the fold and give him a second chance.

The human resource manager was sympathetic when Atlas explained he'd been unwell and was going through a divorce, but therapy was helping. He assured the man he would be back to his old self in no time. The manager told him there was no rush. He was a valued member of staff and everyone would do their best to help him recover.

For a little while Atlas considered doing what he claimed to be doing and actually hiring a therapist. The accident troubled him. His behaviour hadn't aligned with his perception of himself, personally or professionally. He was good at what he did. He could do the science and knew how to conduct solid research. Patience was something he had mastered years ago. His knowledge of the correct safety protocols was beyond reproach. So his actions in the garden lab perplexed him. It was as if he'd been caught in a fever he couldn't or wouldn't shake. Drinking while working was idiotic. He thought it was to blame for his questionable decisions, such as not wearing breathing apparatus while dealing with a potentially harmful airborne substance, like intentionally exposing himself to a substance he didn't understand. But it wasn't whisky that was undermining his scientific integrity. It was the substance itself. The Particle. He understands that now. It was there with him the whole time. When he first detected the change in the air composition inside the flask, not only was the Particle behind the glass, but it was also in the garden lab with him. He didn't measure that. And more of it arrived every time he repeated the experiments, every time he opened the canister, every time he dripped larger quantities of pheromone into the petri dish. His tiredness or drinking or marital problems weren't causing him to lose patience and rush things. Even at such low levels, the Particle's presence made him angry and careless. That's why he forgot to seal the canister and why, in his haste, he dropped it, spilling the contents onto the floor.

He has only a few seconds of memory of that moment.

The crushing panic as he tried to soak the chemical up with his shirt, wringing it back into the neck of the canister.

The oh shit, oh shit, oh shit.

The rising rage, punching the floor, the screaming from every pore.

The distorted vision.

The translucent, quick cells that slid over the surface of his eye, but then somehow in the air, crisscrossing like minute meteors, more and more, thickening until he could see nothing, kneeling in the heart of a colourless hurricane, maybe, maybe the sound of Bute calling his name cutting through the white noise.

And waking in hospital. Handcuffed to a gurney.

Atlas waited three months before he applied for funding for the new project. Too soon, he thought. He hadn't made amends yet. They'd reject him outright or drop his proposal into the slush pile alongside the starry-eyed submissions from young mid-level researchers trying their luck. But, somehow, perhaps thanks to a nudge from Moss, approval came quickly. And Dr Atlas Brown was back.

ARRINA

Arrina is unwell and hasn't gone to school. Her father has left for work and her mother is in the kitchen washing the dishes from breakfast.

She sits on her parents' bedroom floor trying on her father's shoes. The smell of the leather and the way their worn soles slip against her bare feet make her feel as if she's stepping into the grownup world. She believes all adults slide around inside their footwear. She likes to stand in front of the full-length mirror that separates her father's side of the fitted wardrobe from her mother's. Sometimes she tries to sign like him to her reflection, scolding the little girl for being lazy, but the sight of angry Arrina is too funny and laughter always breaks through before she can finish a sentence.

The magazine is under a pile of blankets she knocks over while reaching for an old pair of training shoes. She isn't very good at reading yet but there are lots of pictures for her to look at. They are of women, photographs, some in underwear and some with no clothes on at all. Most of them, even the ones wearing underwear, have their private parts on show. The photograph she is looking at when her mother enters the room is of a pretty woman with her legs in the air and her finger in her bottom. Her mother shouts Arrina's name at the same time as she slaps her on the side of the head, knocking her to the floor. Then she grabs the magazine, throws it somewhere Arrina can't see, pulls the girl to her feet by her ear and drags her out of the bedroom.

Arrina doesn't understand much of what her mother is shouting as she hauls her downstairs and pushes her into the hallway cupboard. Something about her being dirty.

She sits in the dark with the vacuum cleaner and brooms for the rest of the day. At one point, her mother snarls through the door for her to stop crying.

And eventually she runs out of tears.

Later, her mother asks in her soft voice if she is alright in there.

Later still, she is let out of the cupboard and sent to her room with a sandwich. This is before her father gets home. Usually Arrina would greet him at the front door, so when she hears his motorbike outside and the key in the lock she cries out for him even though she knows he can't hear her. He doesn't come to her and she daren't leave her bedroom. Arrina pushes her ear to the door when she hears her mother shout in the language they told her she doesn't need to know. It sounds like she is crying but it might be laughter.

She is playing with her dolls when she notices her father's footsteps on the stairs and then in the hallway. They stop at her door. A moment passes before he comes in, walks over to where she is sitting on her bed, and slaps her across the same side of her head her mother hit earlier. Arrina is holding her face and watching his stocking feet leave the room.

———

It took weeks for most of the new Foundlings to acclimatise to life underground. However, in an environment where a keen intellect was a prerequisite and social anxiety of various descriptions appeared to be a universal norm, Arrina felt right at home.

She'd fancied the Facility as a sci-fi nirvana with white plastic-clad walls and moving floors, housed within a series of metallic towers of various sizes scattered throughout a luscious woodland, each building connected to the rest through a network of glass tubes through which the brightest minds in British scientific research sped along in open-roofed electromagnetic shuttle cars, all lit with state-of-the-art lighting designed to promote optimum brain activity and furnished in the very latest in ergonomic thinking.

But it was none of these things.

Tired, subterranean laboratories, dusty two-tone Venetian blinds over internal windows, glossy mustard and cracked brown plasterboard, stacks of moulded plastic chairs awaiting repair, neglected rolling chalkboards, flickering, migraine-inducing fluorescent tubes, all linked by miles and miles of carpet tiles. It was a celebration of the most unimaginative dreams of the last century's future. Where polystyrene ceiling panels came to die. But something about the place suited her. As soon as the elevator doors opened, she knew this was where she was meant to be.

The night before her induction, Arrina slept soundly in a hotel room on the outskirts of a city she'd never heard of. She woke early, showered and dressed, and then ventured downstairs to the restaurant. Sat by herself as she waited for breakfast, she stole glances at the other tables, all of which were taken by single occupants of a similar age to her, all stealing glances.

She was the last to arrive in the lobby. The others had carefully spread themselves around the circumference of the large vestibule, heads down, eyes on phones or the polished floor tiles, shifting from foot to foot, waiting. There was no obvious place for Arrina to stand. She walked towards the group by the glass wall between the reception desk and entrance doors. As she approached, a nonverbal negotiation occurred between her and the circle. First, the people directly in front of her parted. Then the movement diffused like a ripple along the two halves of the circle as each individual agreed to sacrifice a few inches to accommodate her.

Arrina placed her bag on the ground, leaned against the glass, and turned her attention to the reception. A large man was sweating through his hotel uniform. He spoke to two middle-aged women on the opposite side of the desk, one of whom was asking if they'd accidentally booked a room in a hostel. The other female glanced around at the young people lining the lobby. Her expression was hard to read. It was either disgust or she was pleading to be saved from some terrible fate. Looking over his spectacles, the receptionist assured the guests they were indeed in a hotel, not a hostel, and that this er, he gestured with his hand as if scattering seeds, this party had checked out and was waiting for transport to its next destination. There is no need to worry, he said.

We must look pretty scary.

The voice came from Arrina's right. A short male. Short orange hair. Short orange beard. Short orange eyelashes. He was grinning at her when she turned in his direction. Breakfast remnants in his short teeth.

She nodded as she looked away.

Funny. Nobody'll admit it. Where they're going. It's bloody obvious. We're all off to the same place.

She nodded again, letting her head fall lower with every downward movement.

I tried. In the dining room. This morning. Three times. I said, are you a friend of Daisy's? Nobody answered. One ran away from me. Really. Scuttled like a beetle. Him. Over there. The chubby fella. By the stairs. Baggy suit jacket. Like I'd pulled a knife on him.

In her peripheral vision she could see the man's bitten fingernail pointing to the other side of the lobby.

I'm not asking you. Don't worry. Wouldn't want you legging

it. Causing a scene. His laugh exploded and the circle's foot-shuffling intensified.

My name is Arthur. Nice to meet you. He paused to allow her to reply. When she didn't, he laughed again. That's fine. I get it. You haven't scarpered. I appreciate that. Probably just excited. About being here. Not here. There. That place. The big secret. You know what I mean. Me too. It's good to have a job. Any job, to be honest. Money's decent too. But it's more than that. Isn't it? It's a chance. To make a difference, like. Do something important. Know what I'm saying? I'm excited as well.

It would be inaccurate to describe Arrina's feelings about the day ahead as excitement. The events that had led her to this hotel lobby were merely the latest in a lifelong series of bumps that had nudged her trajectory. She was no more excited by this bump than any other. They were all the same. Her being here wasn't an honour or a privilege. It was just another thing that had happened to her.

So, what's your name?

Arrina muttered a response and crossed to the far side of the lobby where she silently forced the man with the oversized suit jacket and a woman trying to hide behind a rucksack to part, causing another ripple in the human perimeter.

At precisely 9am, Daisy burst through the hotel doors and into the lobby. She stopped after a few steps, looked around her with an unlikely grin, and spread her arms wide.

here-you-are-my-wonderful-foundlings-look-at-you-isnt-this-just-delightful

Her smile seemed so extreme that Arrina imagined her ears touching at the back of her head.

well-what-are-you-waiting-for-come-on-gather-your-bags-and-follow-me-we-have-a-super-busy-day-ahead

Arrina sat near the front of the bus. It was a modern coach with antennae wing mirrors and a huge windscreen that gave her the impression they were gliding rather than driving through the nowhere-scape of hotel chains and roundabouts. Flying in a giant dragonfly, she thought.

Daisy stood in the gangway with a microphone to her mouth. Without taking a breath, she explained the order of things to come.

we-arrive-at-a-Facility-entrance-soon-where-youll-be-enrolled-and-security-checked-which-is-nothing-to-worry-about-unless-of-course-there-are-any-secret-terrorists-onboard

Her laugh shrilled through the speakers.

that-was-a-joke-only-a-joke-I-say-it-to-everyone-then-we-will-have-a-nice-icebreaking-session-not-that-there-would-be-any-real-need-for-that-now-as-you-probably-all-got-to-know-each-other-last-night-oh-no-oh-no-not-like-that

More ear-piercing laughter.

and-after-that-well-have-a-quick-tour-of-some-of-the-complex-and-hopefully-meet-some-of-last-years-intake-and-you-never-know-with-a-bit-of-luck-one-or-two-senior-researchers-too

The overcast outskirts of the city dribbed and drabbed into view. This new environment was familiar enough to Arrina. The branded pubs and bars, the fifties' semis, the topless young men walking broad, muscular dogs, the betting chains, teenagers with pushchairs, the fast-food franchises, and the omnipresent charity shops of a struggling suburban enclave, much like the one she'd left only the day before. The bus slowed briefly for a group of boys in school uniforms crossing the road as leisurely as they dared, laughing at their power to halt the giant motorised insect. Then it turned right and proceeded down a narrower street lined with pebble-dashed terrace houses and overflowing wheelie bins.

Arrina didn't see where the wall began. Its colour merged effortlessly with the dwellings that preceded it and of those opposite. A procession of concrete monoliths with bulbous heads, packed tight shoulder-to-shoulder, crowned with a single gleaming coil of razor wire. A prison, she thought. The bus turned left into a gap in the rampart and braked at a solid metal gate. Only when Daisy fell silent and stared at the entrance like everyone else did Arrina realise that the woman had been talking the whole way. A deep buzzing sound made all the passengers jump. Then a metallic clunk and the gates jerked and clanked apart.

The bus floated through a barren parking lot, the driver ignoring the markings on the tarmac as he piloted in the direction of the dark, low-level building ahead. The sign above the doors, in large, dirty, red letters, spelt out PRESTO. A supermarket, not a prison. Curled, faded posters boasted cut-price orange juice, freshly baked bread, and a new low-calorie lasagna, and behind them, through the unwashed windows, empty cash register desks and aisles of shadows. They travelled toward the entrance, took a sudden left at the storefront, a right along the side and again at the rear, and glided through another set of gates.

The feedbacking microphone screeched its return to life.

okay-then-my-dears-here-we-are-if-everyone-would-just-follow-me-please-follow-me

They gathered around Daisy before a lorry-sized opening in the supermarket's wall. Behind her, two hard-faced men in military fatigues emerged from the darkness. She introduced them as Corporals Harvey and Rosenberg. Harvey did his best to look harmless as he approached with a garland of lanyards while the Rosenberg addressed them.

Welcome to the Facility, he gruffed. This is the North Castleport entrance, and today will likely be the only time you'll be here. After your enrolment and security check, you will be assigned an access point closer to your department. Please put your lanyards around your neck and follow me. And don't touch anything.

The group followed the soldiers through the building and into an industrial elevator. Corporal Harvey closed the shutters behind them and Corporal Rosenberg pressed a button on the control panel next to him. And they descended into the Facility.

I meant what I said. At the hotel, I mean.

The man called Arthur had already tripped over the feet of two Foundlings while trying to catch up with Arrina. They were twenty minutes into their tour of the Facility. Enrolment and the security checks had passed without incident. To the new recruits' relief, the icebreaking session was delayed because of a lack of free rooms.

The group quick-marched along the narrow corridor behind Daisy. Arrina did her best to concentrate on the recruiter's machine gun spiel.

the-facility-is-enormous-the-story-is-nobodys-seen-the-entire-complex-due-to-its-sheer-size-but-I-think-that-seems-a-little-farfetched-oh-that-door-takes-you-to-the-showers-I-mean-I-get-that-most-of-us-are-allocated-entrances-and-workspaces-and-dont-have-any-need-to-wander-down-every-corridor-but-there-are-maintenance-people-and-security-personnel-and-that-kind-of-thing-who-must-have-seen-it-all-anyway-thats-what-they-say-its-quite-nice-I-suppose-it-gives-the-place-a-certain-something-mystique

According to Daisy:

1. instead of thinking of the Facility complex as a building, it was more helpful to picture it as a root system with a network of nodules, including research areas, meeting rooms, and storage spaces connected to one another with passageways of various designs, some of which were considerably longer, and older, than others;

2. while most of the complex could be traced back to the sixties, there were other underground facilities (with a small f) constructed around the time of the Second World War and some of these were incorporated into the Facility (with a big F) later;

3. she was aware of thirteen entrances and had more or less

memorised the location of them all, but there were undoubtedly many more she didn't know of;

4. as well as being assigned entrances, Foundlings would be allocated emergency exits near their workplaces, which were smaller than the main entrances and designed to be one-way, that is, heavily disguised on the above-ground side and often emerging in surprising places and, once, because of a fire in a lab, Daisy and her colleagues had found themselves in a stockroom of a small shoe store in a mid-sized shopping mall, causing utter confusion for the shop employees and customers when fifty or more Facility staff, many of them wearing lab coats, poured out of the room and through the shop;

5. their designated exits and entrances would change as they moved from project to project, but she was sure they wouldn't find that too taxing.

Arthur's appearance at her side distracted Arrina from Daisy's explanation of the rules governing the unisex toilets. He was a step in front of her now, looking back as often as he could without colliding into Daisy and the Foundling beside her.

I've got a feeling. An idea, I suppose. For here, I mean. We need to forge alliances. Befriend the right people. Shared mindsets. Strength in numbers. Are you with me?

Arrina wasn't sure what she was nodding in agreement to, or that she understood or was willing to join his alliance or whatever it was he was talking about. But Arthur looked pleased.

That's great. We'll talk again.

And he slowed so that the person behind him crashed into his back, causing the Foundling behind them to do the same, and the next, and so on.

A large room with desks arranged in a way that reminded the occupants of the exam halls of their youth. Daisy asked the Foundlings to sit a little closer to one another.

just-because-we-have-all-this-space-it-doesnt-mean-you-

have-to-use-every-inch-of-it-I-mean-its-kind-of-cute-that-youre-
all-so-shy-but-this-session-is-about-getting-to-know-each-other

Arrina sat in the front row next to Arthur. When told to stand
and introduce themselves one by one, he jumped up.

Arthur Bloc. Pleased to be here.

Daisy looked at Arrina. She stood, gave her name, and said
she was also pleased to be there.

With the script established, the remaining Foundlings introduced themselves. They were all pleased to be there. By the
time they'd finished, Daisy's grin threatened to split her head
in two.

well-done-everyone-now-we-are-going-to-play-a-game

The temporary accommodation was basic but comfortable. More
importantly for Arrina, each Foundling had their own room. But
the Playpen upstairs interested her more. While far from contemporary, it was the most modern environment she'd entered since
her arrival. It comprised twelve well-equipped workshops in
which the Foundlings were expected to devise projects, work
together, explore their strengths and weaknesses, and do their
best to forget about the close-circuit television cameras in every
corner.

Each workshop fed into a central hall that contained a self-
service coffee bar, breakout areas, a pool table, a couple of
pinball machines, and the longest and deepest sofa Arrina had
ever seen. On one wall, a large poster of black type on white
paper read

PLAYPEN RULES:

The rest of the poster appeared to be blank, which provoked
much laughter among the Foundlings until, upon closer inspection, one of them found a faint pencil scrawl beneath the title
that said

don't fuck up

Arthur Bloc promptly enlisted Arrina into his group. Other than him, there were already three members: Clare Norris, Bernado Bosch, and Ahmed Banu whom Arrina had noticed due to his impressively animated Adam's apple. They had no firm proposal about what to concentrate their efforts on yet, only Arthur's desire for the five of them to work together so well that by the end of Naturalisation they'd be recruited into the same project by a senior researcher who recognised their joint potential. The plan included decrees such as arriving early every day, leaving last, and not talking to the others, who, according to Arthur, were oxygen thieves. As far as Arrina could tell, his intention appeared to be nothing more than to foster an air of superiority.

I don't *not* like them. They just don't have it. What we have. We have to stick together. Together we have influence. We're better than them. We need to make it obvious.

Arthur's exclusionist tactic survived for less than a month. Every day, the common room buzzed with discussions about the various projects, and there was no way to stop people wandering into the workshop he'd tried claiming for his cause. Other teams frequently asked Arrina for her opinion, and she did not ignore the requests. In her one-to-ones, Daisy made it clear to all five that she expected to see more involvement with the Foundling community.

Arthur was furious until Ahmed suggested they all make a pledge to the cause, something the group could adhere to even if they had to split up.

That evening, they gathered in Ahmed's room. Arthur handed them each a piece of paper.

That's the oath. Take turns to read it out. Right hand in the air. Then stick to it.

Arrina scanned the first few words, 'I pledge my allegiance to Bloc's...' before the door crashed open. Two armed security guards were in the middle of the room. Daisy materialised between them.

ill-take-those-if-you-dont-mind-thank-you-you-wont-be-needing-a-silly-thing-like-this-because-as-you-know-this-is-not-that-kind-of-place-and-I'm-not-really-sure-why-any-of-you-would-think-otherwise-all-of-us-are-equal-here-and-nobody-gets-special-treatment-arthur-will-you-come-with-me-please

The group never saw that version of Arthur Bloc again. The new iteration of the man that appeared in the common room the next day was quite different. Diminished. Smaller, quieter, and compliant, sticking to Arrina's side. When Clare Norris asked if he felt okay, Arthur looked at his feet and moved his head in circular motions so slight that Arrina couldn't tell if the gesture was intentional.

Ever since Arrina Heal became aware of her voice as a sound that belonged exclusively to her, whenever she spoke she experienced a shock akin to hearing a recording of oneself for the very first time. To her ears, it sounded like a robin screeching at the more piercing end of its vocal range, far too high-pitched for a woman of her age. Like a child in a vice. An alien. A helium sprite.

A preoccupation with the quality of her voice affected her syntax, or at least the thought process that proceeded her word choice. Some utterances sounded tolerable as they squeaked through her larynx. Others clawed at her ears. In her teens, she'd tried grading the sounds she was capable of making. Those that she found less severe, with their slightly deeper, more open qualities, she ranked highest. Then she categorised her entire vocabulary by syllable parts to identify words that only used the best-ranking sounds or used them predominantly. Her aim was to develop a personal lexicon she could memorise and use with relative peace of mind. She spent weeks charting the phonetic possibilities in tables, lining up her preferred options, and cross-referencing these to form acceptable phrases. But it was futile. The constructions she could tolerate rarely formed sufficient meaning alone.

So, silence became her modus operandi. Monosyllabic half-whispers if absolutely necessary. As a very last resort, the shortest possible sentences formed from the results of her afore-mentioned research. She stitched the latter together by rehearsing the words in her head first and, if required, swapping them out for more suitable options. Unfortunately, the process often resulted in her forgetting the sequence in which the words should fall or the meaning she intended to convey.

But something had happened since arriving at the Playpen. As if exploiting the change of circumstances, her voice seemed to have independently liberated itself. And here she was, in her penultimate one-to-one, her insides as tight as a sprung bear trap, listening to Daisy explain her theory on why the other Foundlings clearly enjoyed Arrina's company so much.

how-you-speak-is-so-calming-i-noticed-it-when-we-first-met-but-now-I-can-see-it-having-an-effect-on-the-others-possibly-calming-is-the-wrong-word-its-weirdly-mesmerising-but-weird-in-a-good-way-of-course

Arthur and Ahmed confirmed it later.

It's your voice, Ahmed said. It's quiet but it works. People pay attention, they do what you say.

Arthur said, it's fucked up, but then everything here is fucked up.

The air was stiff before the first guests arrived. The Foundlings appeared to have forgotten their newly discovered conviviality. Daisy and Blair were too busy rearranging the plastic wine glasses and checking the PA system to speak.

Gawky, nervous, older versions of themselves stuttered into the room and took their seats. Arrina tried to estimate their seniority by composure. She searched for clues in their gaits and postures, their facial expressions and voices. But there were no signals. Every person who walked through the doors seemed as troubled by the forthcoming event as the one before. They flinched as all eyes turned to them, lowered their heads as if hoping to duck out of sight, sat motionless and invisible, and spoke as little as possible. Arrina wondered if she could ever endure this much discomfort in exchange for damp pastry and cheap wine.

Eventually, they had a full house. Daisy and Blair strolled up and down the seating area nodding and smiling at guests, with the occasional gesture being reluctantly returned. Intermittent whispered greetings, coughs, and the clearing of throats grated the silence. The door opened again. In walked a woman wearing a tight navy blue suit, black hair tied back, stern spectacles, and very red lipstick, possibly in her thirties. For a moment she was easily the most confident person in the room. Every head pointed in her direction. Then, from behind her, a man appeared. Spherical was Arrina's first impression. A medicine ball wrapped in tweed. Blair materialised by the man's side.

Good afternoon, General. Welcome.

The man flicked freckled fingers through the grey tufts on the sides of his head.

Ah, my apologies. Sarah got us lost.

The woman threw him an incredulous, open-mouthed expression.

No, you're not late. We've just settled in.

Right-oh. Where do you want me?

Daisy climbed onto the small stage at the front of the room and welded some words with impressive speed. Then she asked everyone to put their hands together for General Moss. The man rolled to the podium to a timid round of applause, which he wafted away.

Thank you, err, thank you all for coming today. Because it's a special day. I certainly think so. I know these events in the past have been relatively quick and modest affairs. But that's one of the little things I'd like to change here now I'm at the helm. These graduations only happen once a year and they should be celebrated. These young people deserve a warm welcome into the fold, don't you agree?

He paused. It took a while for his audience to realise he sought a consensus. Finally, Blair clapped and a smattering of researchers followed his lead.

Moss went on. His vague hopes for the future. The privilege of working with such clever people. Some of the other changes he was looking forward to making. He congratulated the new graduates, said he hoped they would be very happy at the Facility, thanked the audience, and stepped backwards to make way for Daisy's return to the podium.

The names of the graduating Foundlings were called out. One by one, they were washed to the front and back again amid the ebb and flow of bored applause, accepting their certificates from Daisy and shaking hands with Moss along the way.

Arrina Heal.

The slapping sound of the cold claps thickened as she stood up. So many eyes to ignore. She swallowed and took her first step towards the front, caught her foot on the leg of her chair, and fell on her face.

Silence.

Hot cheek against the carpet tile.

Someone's shoe near her head.

Someone speaking her name.

Are you alright?

She stood up again and looked around. All those eyes. She checked she was clear of the chair and ran out of the room.

its-okay-i-think-its-probably-happened-before-yes-im-pretty-sure

Those gathered around Daisy at the drinks table were unclear whether she was talking about Arrina's tumble and swift exit or that none of her young wards had been invited to join a project.

After the ceremony, Daisy and Blair had worked one half of the room while the Foundlings congealed in the other, hugging plastic glasses and studying each other's shoes. Periodically, one of them would be summoned.

daniel-oh-daniel-yes-you-daniel-would-you-come-over-here-to-meet-dr-johnston-please

A hesitant graduate would peel away.

The rest of the group watched their companions standing before nodding senior researchers as Daisy explained how well they did in a particular part of the training or described a personality trait she'd miraculously uncovered during the last few months. Then the flush-faced Foundling would return to the safety of the cluster, which parted just enough to absorb them.

Arrina, who'd slipped back into the room as Moss and his Sarah left it, wasn't called.

As the wine and food depleted, the guests drifted away until only Daisy and her Foundlings remained.

there-is-nothing-nothing-to-worry-about-team-nothing-to-worry-about-tomorrow-Im-sure-tomorrow-is-a-new-day-so-lets-cheer-up-and-help-clear-away-this-mess

Arrina held open a black bin liner while others dropped in paper plates and leftovers. Nobody spoke.

They'd heard about the Orphanage in passing from Daisy and in detail from Blair. He described the department as a Facility unit populated by unattached junior researchers. Similar to Playpen, with a recreation room, equipment for 'Orphans' to use to showcase their talents, and a budget for additional items should they be needed. He told them about entire departments being created around successful mini-projects, and of young researchers who, having discovered this new technology or that chemical, found themselves being catapulted up through the organisation. Now they would have to join its ranks, the

Foundlings lapped these stories up, grateful for anything with the power to counter the less optimistic tales of people who'd been in the Orphanage for so many years they no longer held out any hope of being recruited onto a project ever again.

After they'd finished tidying up, Daisy gathered her protégés together. Her jellyfish eyes wetter than usual. She cleared her throat and told the Foundlings that this was the last time she and Blair would work with them. If any project offers materialised in the next few days, they would be contacted directly. But, also, they should be realistic. Judging by the lacklustre uptake thus far, they might have to wait a while, that these things sometimes took longer than necessary because the decision-makers often forgot that they too had started out as Foundlings. Then her face hardened.

some-of-you-will-become-project-leaders-or-senior-researchers-yourselves-eventually-when-you-do-please-consider-recruiting-foundlings-come-to-the-graduations-meet-the-newcomers-and-help-people-like-me-nurture-new-talent

The tears followed. Bubbles of emotion erupting from half-eaten yoghurt pots. Blair turned away and left the room, sighing so subtly that only Arrina noticed.

Daisy tried to squeeze her goodbyes out between the sobs.

its-been-

-super-fun-

-working-with-

-you-all-

-youve-been-

-a-lovely-group-

-really-its-been-

The Foundlings stared at her. An arm, maybe two, half-reached towards her and fell away, unsure what to do next. The noise at the far side of the venue was a welcome distraction from the wet mess in front of them. It came from the entrance. A banging, like someone was barging it with their shoulder. If the crying was still in progress, the clattering and shouting from

outside swallowed it up. Arthur Bloc crossed the room and opened the door. In tumbled a middle-aged man in an old corduroy jacket.

Stupid door—bloody idiot door. Someone ought to get the bloody thing—get it bloody fixed.

Daisy pushed through the Foundlings, drying her face on her sleeve.

dr-brown-welcome

It took the man some time to determine who was speaking to him. He removed his glasses, wiped them on his untucked shirt, put them back on, and then found her.

Ah—you—is this graduation?

it-was

Seriously? Bloody hell—well—who's left?

youre-looking-at-them

How many?

twenty-two

Excellent. I'll take half—you, you, you—no, not you—you and you—and that group there. Come with me.

Not one of the chosen Foundlings saw Daisy's wide warning eyes and subtly shaking head.

———

The man who towered over them was thin but in good proportion. Nothing overly sickly about him, not even his eyes, the size of which were much reduced by the circular spectacles he struggled to keep on his nose. His entire head was amateurishly shaved, stubble that came and went in weekly cycles. Fingernails neat and short. No body odour to speak of. The raised scar that climbed from his right eyebrow up to his hairline added a criminal air. So did the way he avoided looking at anyone directly. Arrina caught the occasional glance in her direction but on the whole he focused on the empty space at his eleven o'clock, or at the paper or item to which he happened to be referring. This suited everyone.

Dr Brown called it a lab but to Arrina the room looked more like a workshop. The three rows of wooden workbenches with red and blue laminate tops lined the middle, and desks from every era edged two of the four walls. It reminded her of woodwork class, of Mr James and his habit of slapping the boys across the backs of their heads and leaning over the girls, his hands on theirs as he demonstrated the correct motion required to operate the plane. The so-called laboratory also acted as a storage area. Steeples of stackable tables and chairs dominated the third wall, and each morning, the young team deposited their coats and bags over the moulded plastic and grey powder-coated tubes.

At the other end was Dr Brown's office. A peeling mahogany veneer door with a head-height porthole covered from the inside with a sheet of newspaper, and a large dusty window obscured by beige Venetian blinds. This is where he spent most of his time those first few weeks, emerging every so often with a slip of paper held high.

I need someone to—fetch this, and one of them would take the slip and disappear.

The recruits felt good about their new positions. Although nobody knew anything about the project they'd been recruited onto, the atmosphere fizzed with an expectation that something important would happen soon. They spent most of this time collecting equipment from other Facility units, bringing it back to the lab, and filling the surfaces with their troves.

Take—the trolley, Dr Brown would say, it'll be heavy.

For weeks, they gathered and hoarded, walking in pairs for miles, searching for poorly signposted departments, pushing requisition slips through sliding windows, and taking receipt of whatever they'd been sent out to retrieve.

The lab became busier and more cluttered. But, other than that, nothing actually happened.

. . .

Confidence is a delicate child. A thing too easily undermined. And chatter from other junior researchers in the canteen did its best to do just that.

Dr Brown is mad.

He's on the verge of being thrown out of the Facility.

Every project he touches fails.

Your careers are over before they start if you don't transfer soon.

They tried to ignore condescending questions about their work and caught pitying glances and smiles spiked with subtle sneers.

Knowing neither the nature of the project nor whether Dr Brown was in complete control of his faculties, some new recruits struggle to stop the hearsay and accusations chipping away at their initial euphoria. They ate at the canteen less and less, preferring to take their lunches in the lab where they wondered aloud if they would have been better off taking their chances at the Orphanage. Arrina was in the minority. She'd made her mind up. Although she couldn't identify what, there seemed to be something about the man that would surface in time. She remained certain of that. And sure enough, on a day that started like every other, that something emerged. Dr Brown walked out of his office and asked them to gather around. He stood before them, glancing between the back wall and the paper he held.

So—we seem—we have everything we need—except one or two pieces on order. Anyway—that means—we can start the actual work tomorrow.

He paused, sighed through his nose, and turned to look at the air to his left.

Any—questions?

Arthur raised his hand. Dr Brown didn't notice. One of the others, a man called Frank, cleared his throat.

What are we going to be working on?

Dr Brown scanned his audience to locate the source of the question.

Seriously?

Yes, sir.

Atlas located Frank and deepened his brow.

How long have you been—working for me now? And don't call me—sir. If you have to call me anything—Dr Brown.

Sorry, Dr Brown. A little over four weeks.

And—you don't know—what we're working on?

Dr Brown raised his eyes to the ceiling and sighed again.

Well, actually, no, not really.

May I suggest you ask one of your—colleagues? And for future reference—always do that. I don't—don't have time to be dealing with stupidity—laziness.

With respect, Dr Brown, none of us know.

All the recruits stopped breathing at the same moment. Dr Brown's gaze skimmed over their faces as if they were hot coals. His glasses slipped down his nose.

Is—this—correct?

It took an age before their nodding became visible to the human eye. But, once underway, a rising number of quiet yeses and yeahs augmented the movement. Assertiveness rose and the affirmations grew louder.

Dr Brown shook his head.

Unfuckingbelievable—why the hell didn't you—you say something?

———

Graduation from the Playpen also meant relocating from their underground accommodation into a Facility-owned apartment block for junior staff members. Despite the cramped conditions and the poor noise insulation from outside and neighbouring studios, this provided more space and privacy than Arrina had ever enjoyed. Unlike her room at her parent's house or student digs, nobody could barge in through the door, nobody could root through her things while she was out, and nobody could give her a hard time about being untidy or walking around in the nude. This freedom felt unfamiliar and exhilarating.

However, one thing did not sit well. Downstairs, at the communal entrance, mailboxes groaned with the bulge of uncollected letters and leaflets. On her first day in her new home, Arrina emptied hers of the fast-food discount coupons and To The Occupier junk mail. And from somewhere within this mundane domestic chore came an emotional twinge she didn't recognise. Suddenly, more than anything in the world, she wanted to open that little metal door and find a small, stamped envelope inside, addressed to her in her mother's handwriting.

Arrina carried the strange sensation to work with her the following day. How nice it would be to hear from her, she thought, to find out what she had been up to, if she'd been anywhere, done anything. She knew of the strains that often defined mother-daughter relationships. She'd listened to flatmates at university complain of theirs. Mothers who interfered too much, judged too much, argued too much, preached too much. It seemed that there was always too much of something when it came to matriarchs. But she'd never related to the stories. Throughout Arrina's childhood, Donna had been there in just the right amounts. Admittedly, her idea of discipline was unorthodox, so maybe she punished her daughter too harshly, but Arrina had felt loved. And in a one-child family dominated by a father's unpredictable anger, that was an achievement.

However, when Arrina left for university, her mother fell silent. The phone went unanswered. And when Arrina came back for the first half-term holiday, it was as if only the physical form of this woman she'd once depended on remained. She no longer spoke or left the house and spent most of her time sitting at the kitchen table, staring at a hung etching of an unidentified bridge. Meanwhile, even though he refused to engage with Arrina on the subject, her father was doing something she thought impossible: he was looking after his wife. He cleaned their home, ironed their clothes, cooked their meals, made tea, did the grocery shopping. And he performed these tasks as if he'd always done them, as if it had been him, not his spouse, who had looked after the three of them from day one. And this is how things stayed for the seven years Arrina was away.

After completing her post-graduate studies, Arrina moved back in with her parents. It took a few weeks, but gradually, Donna Heal recovered from whatever she'd been suffering. The first sign was when Arrina returned to her bedroom after break-fast to find her picking underwear up from the floor. Saying nothing, she left with an armful of laundry. Arrina found the clothes cleaned, pressed, and folded on her bed the following day. Within two months, her mother was nearly her old self again, attending to her duties just as she used to. The only thing that failed to make a comeback was her voice. And so, apart from the arguments between Arrina and her father during the evening meal, the house remained silent, and her mother, now no longer a source of concern, faded quietly into the background of Arrina's adult life.

That might have been why it didn't occur to Arrina to tell her she had a job and was leaving again. Or why she failed to say goodbye. On the morning she was due to depart, she simply packed her bags and left. It hadn't seemed unusual when her mother looked down at her from the bedroom window and did not wave back at Arrina in the taxi. And in all this time she'd been at the Facility, she didn't once think of her.

While the pang was a surprise, Arrina knew to obey, just as she had always known to comply when the universe pulled her in an unexpected direction. On her next day off, she ventured out and bought the necessary stationery, unfolded the small wall-mounted table in her studio, and began to write. In her first letter, she described the new accommodation and recited the Facility-approved lies about her job. In the second, written the following night, she wrote she was eating well, had some friends, and was planning to visit soon. She composed the third, much longer letter a week later. In it, she recalled the time her mother watched her play for the school hockey team as it suffered its worst defeat in the institution's history and how the pair laughed so hard about it on the way home that Arrina had wet herself. And of the weekend they'd travelled to London together to watch Cats, when her mother stopped a celebrity tv chef on the street thinking he was an old friend from Poland. And another time, when she eventually relented and allowed Arrina to decorate her plaster casted forearm with flowers and jungle animals in bright felt-tip because it was due to be removed the subsequent day, only to realise later that the date she'd jotted the appointment into on the calendar was ten days too early. Then she dared ask her to write back.

ALFONSO

The hospital corridor is lined with gurneys on both sides. Bodies writhe on them in slow-motion spasms. Nurse and police uniforms step carefully over others on the floor.

Alfonso is shirtless, hands bandaged, a large bloodied dressing taped to his abdomen. A charge of pain builds in his groin, ordering him, instructing him to lower his torso back down onto the trolley where it is warmer and the sounds and lights are duller, less piercing. And now there is only the sound of his wife expelling cold air as they stand on Linsett Bridge. Below, two men on separate barges pass an oversized bouquet back and forth. Every time the flowers move, brightly coloured petals fall onto the water's surface, adding to the undulating garland surrounding both boats. He watches until the entire canal fills with petals and the boats are submerged beneath them. The men, petals up to their knees, remove their clothes and dive in. He is keen to join them but Jen stops him. Don't be silly, she says. Her fingers dance high above the canal and she tells him about a woman at work who wants to sell her an expensive watch. Before he opens his mouth to offer advice, a voice that isn't his whispers a warning between his ears.

Stay. Down. Careful.

He wants to turn and find its source but the bridge has begun to shake and the men in the canal have not yet come up for air. Alfonso looks for them, anxious to see their heads emerge from the petals. He shouts but the breathless voice drowns his words.

Taking us. One by one.

The undertones push his head into the water below the bridge, petals against his face and in his ears and mouth.

Can you hear me? Arrested.

He gulps for breath, eyes open, and is in the corridor again. There is a man opposite him, a metre away, prostrate like he is. His lips moving.

They're taking us away, one by one, and arresting us.

Alfonso manages a nod before his eyelids fall again.

Geese honks distracted him from the excuses of the woman on Ursula Street, and he failed to notice the suspicion in her eyes when she thanked him for not issuing a ticket. Only when he looked up in search of the squawking arrowhead in the sky did he realise it wasn't migrating geese he could hear but car horns. Their number had confused him. To hear so many simultaneously was unusual. He turned toward the racket and, as he did so, felt the air thicken and his neck muscles tense.

Alfonso's usual route took him from the top of Joshua Street, right past Jen's office block, along Albert's Lane (taking in Lindberg Road and all the Finches except Finch Square), up Ethan Lloyd and then circled back via Queen's Gate and Jet Lane before arriving at the city's centre. The noise seemed to come from east of Finch. Rather than keep to his beat, which would have taken him away from the irritant, when he reached the lower half of Finley Avenue where it crossed the City Chambers, he headed straight for the disturbance.

Alfonso's calm sense of public duty to seek out and resolve the nuisance was rudely punctured by a loud voice. Noisy bastards!, it shouted. He searched the faces of those around him for the culprit only to see that the pedestrians he was striding past were all looking at him. Had the outburst come from his own mouth? He realised his teeth were gritted and fists were clenched. Yes, it must have done. He stopped, mumbled an apology to everybody in earshot, and looked at his feet. Negativity like this just would not do. It had to be dealt with immediately. He relaxed his hands, closed his eyes, and took himself to his good place. In an instant he was in a lush green meadow bordered by blossoming trees. A gentle sun warmed his bones. On the ground, bumblebees bounced from one wildflower to the next, and speckles of pollen and tiny flying insects trailed light shimmers as they danced in the air. And here, in this field of his own making, he allowed his negativity to take shape. It often materialised right before him, but sometimes, as in now, it hovered above like a swarm of locusts preparing to swoop and devour him. All he had to do was look at the shadowy mass, confront it, and it would gradually disperse. Alfonso lifted his head to face his visualisation. It was bigger than usual, casting a shadow over the surrounding grassland. Instead of diminishing, it appeared to expand, vibrating as it grew. Down, down it reached until it surrounded him, filling his ears and snapping at his brain. It was useless. Eyes open again, he continued his march along the increasingly crowded pavement. He would try again later once he'd taken care of that intolerable din.

As he marched, Alfonso saw his annoyance reflected in the faces around him. Without exception, they were peevish and hot. Sideward glances and muttered exasperations and insults were being flung carelessly in all directions, bouncing off other frustrated brows and clenched jaws, magnifying in intensity with each contact before finding their way back into the centre of the traffic warden's throbbing head. How can so many idiots exist in one place? he growled to himself. A melting pot of every conceivable kind of moron. As the car horns increased in volume, he fantasised about punching random pedestrians, clenching his fists again as he imagined soft, greasy faces collapsing under knuckle. He caught himself. He tried to calm his racing thoughts by thinking about the gift he'd buy Mil when his shift was over, the meal they'd have later, the smiles of the two most precious people in the world, the gentle conversation, the congratulations. But it was impossible to hold the soothing images in his head while surrounded by bottom feeders.

PART III

ATLAS

Atlas knows this is a bad day, which is a good thing.

The bad days he knows about are better than those that hide behind him, stepping into his footprints, ducking when he turns, not revealing themselves until it's too late. The former, those inexperienced bad days, lose patience while waiting for him to wake. They get careless. They lounge around the metal box like it belongs to them and don't spot him open his eyes.

Then he's on the front foot.

I—see—you.

And he sees this one.

Against his better judgement, he has walked from the compound into the city. And he is thinking it's a ridiculous town with a ridiculous name. He knows this doesn't matter but can't resist condescending the place. There is something comforting in wallowing in the shitness of this place. And comfort is a resource he does not get enough of. So here it is. Castleport, exposed for its pointlessness. Its absurdity.

He begins with some facts. There is neither a castle nor a port in Castleport. Good start. It is a history-light, landlocked city with nought to offer. Is it even a city? He has scoured its quarters for anything, any little thing that might redeem it. But it is vacuous. Maybe once it had something about itself. Once upon a time. Before his time. The statues on Finch Square suggest that's a possibility. But as far as Atlas is concerned, the place is a blob of nothingness. The gravitas of a city is measured by its cultural offerings. This place offers nada. He's no theatre-goer but he knows there are no playhouses. He is unaware of a single music venue or public art gallery or library. No artistic movement of any note was ever born here. All it had were service industry jobs and retail therapy. Money in, money out. Shop to live, live to shop. But now the consumer ecosystem is gasping for breath; nothing remains but ghosts. Shadows of people who used to participate in the game wandering the streets and queuing for food. Scavenging and begging.

Things are escalating quickly. He should have stayed in the compound. Should have listened to himself. There'd been no need to venture out. He could have checked over the gasholder but that's on the list for tomorrow. He could have cleaned but, yeah. He could have attended to one of the million maintenance jobs that beg for his attention but it's difficult to know where to start if you're not in the right frame of mind. And he isn't. He could've spent the day staring at the ceiling and let the silence quieten his head. Instead, he's on another bench. This specimen is covered in plastic grass. It is situated on a street he doesn't recognise, yet it feels the same as everywhere else in this, this what-even-is-this-place-now. Someone has given it borders so it must be a country. The Republic of Castleport. Populated by the hopeless and the hapless. Those who lacked the gumption to leave or the courage not to come. He belongs to the latter. He lived here, lives here, because it was and is required of him. The Facility spoke and he doffed his cap.

These timid people who haunt the streets and line up for handouts, it's like they've always done it. As if nothing has happened. It is as if today is the same as all the days that preceded it. They're made of putty. A plasticine population moulding itself into whatever shape is forced upon it. Where is the fight? Where's the resistance? Create some noise. Protest or something. You're supposed to resist when others make your life worse. Stand up for your rights. Take to the streets. Men and women used to bring the biggest cities in the world to a standstill over the price of fuel, to stop corporations poisoning the planet, to end wars, to denounce politicians.

He can see himself watching these pliant people. It's a scene that flickers in front of his vision, himself through the lenses of the close-circuit television cameras. One at a time. There are plenty around, lots of options. Cut to the central lamppost POV. Cut to the gym rooftop POV. Cut to the bus stop POV. He feels watched by cameras that probably aren't functioning, feels watched by himself.

A new poster of Captain Joseph Alexander in his cap is smiling across the street. He is shining his teeth at the ghouls with their old carrier bags straining under the weight of free carbohydrates. HOLD YOUR NERVE, says the headline under his iron chin. Hold your nerve until all this feels completely normal. And if it isn't working for you right now, you aren't holding your nerve enough. Hold it more. Hold it higher. Hold it tighter. If it isn't working, you have nobody to blame but...

Ah, and there it is. There's the reason Atlas should have stayed in bed. He can barely form the thought but its presence is already lurking. All the signs were there. He saw it. He bloody saw it. And his internal alarm blared as he reached for the door handle. And his reflection, in its infinite wisdom, pleaded, Atlas, why don't you stay here today?

Like an idiot, Atlas had just laughed.

This—my friend—is what they call personal growth. You're looking at a man who—understands himself.

And yet, and yet, he went out.

You understand nothing, Atlas Brown, not until it's too late, his dusty reflection should have said.

And the pit of his stomach pulls at him.

Know your bad days.

Know you're bad days.

If this isn't working for you, Captain Joseph Alexander declares, you have nobody to blame but the buffoon, the klutz, the moron, the imbecile, the numbskull, the idiot, the plank, the fool, the fuckwit par excellence, Dr Atlas Brown.

Dr Atlas Brown, the architect of all of this.

The faces of these ghosts. Drained. Blank. Would they turn towards him if they knew? Would they find their anger if they realised the fault was right here in their streets, within pitchfork-stabbing distance?

Rule #1: Do not leave.

He ought to write a list of rules and pin it on this side of the door.

Rule #2: Stay in your box.

He has no memory of getting back. But here he is.

Rule #3: Under no circumstances go outside.

He sits on his sofa and removes his shoes.

It's peaceful at the compound, in his metal box. Nobody disturbs him.

Eyes of storms have a reputation for quietness.

Peaceful while the world rages around him.

But there is no rage. Only passive aggression. Closed borders. New borders. Shut a border, erect another. Smaller and smaller. Cross this line and you will regret it. You'll be sorry. But what are they going to do? They.

Captain Alexander and his crew.

Tiny tyrants.

Diminutive dictators.

Every time he goes into town, marching in formation, loitering on corners, more and more of them.

Single-brain-celled creatures multiplying like E. coli.

This is our territory now, you do what we want now, the squeaky voice of the new elite.

Reflected Atlas clears his throat.

Time to get the mallet out, Atlas?

I—didn't say anything.

You don't have to.

I'm fine.

Atlas does what he can to not think. Not thinking in general, that's what he likes to do best. He senses the thoughts heading his way and he deals with them. Most days. He's not bad at it. For instance, the gasholder is the largest object in view from this window and is right there in front of him whenever he opens the door to go outside. And what it contains and the cost of luring it there lurk behind him whenever he climbs back up the stairs. It looms over every moment. And yet, he doesn't see it. Doesn't think about it.

Not often.

Not as much as he used to.

He can step away from thoughts, most of them. But for those that refuse to give up, that follow him around like sunset midges, he turns to berserker meditation. He devised this refinement some time ago when the Hate Extractor project appeared doomed and he attempted to meditate his way out of his misery. No matter how he tried, he couldn't buy into the idea of allowing those unwanted thoughts to float on by like fluffy cumulus while he focused on the present. His thoughts, the persistent ones, were, and still are, of a different class. Heavyweight thoughts, dogged and ominous. This improved version of meditation matches the power of his thoughts with sheer brute force. Whack-a-mole for intrusive anxieties. Whack-a-troll perhaps. The moment a thought he doesn't like the look of rears its ugly head, he clobbers it with a mental rubber mallet. He hits it so hard it takes days to recover and try again. Out for the count, and the count is five days on average. Which isn't bad.

Any thoughts except those of Arrina

they're more

complicated

sticky

but there's no need to go near that right now.

Other than those, it's a foolproof system. Atlas doesn't even have to see the thoughts before he knows clobbering time has arrived. He can smell them. A metallic lavendery odour. Cloying and sickly. When he catches a whiff, he whips out his mallet and gets ready. The method deserves a book. Smashidations. Hitnosis. By the author who brought you The Hate List.

But no need for exorcism today. The calm of the metal box has soothed him. His mind is like a windless desert. Everything he doesn't want around is buried under the sand. He looks at the mirror from where he sits on the floor, his back against the bed.

Well done, Atlas, Reflected Atlas says.

He can't see his reflection from this angle but he knows it's there. Always is.

Well done. You've taken what started as a bad day and turned it around.

There's an intense sensation in Atlas's jaw that's threatening to make him smile. Relief maybe. Or optimism even. Best not to analyse it. But everything is going to be okay, and he laughs. He likes the sound of that so he does it again. His reflection joins in. Atlas stands up. He laughs out loud at the window, laughing at the gasholder out there in all its misery. Almost barking now, he roars at it from the pit of his belly.

Look at you—you used to think you were it—that you had it all—not so scary today though—are you? Pah! Prowling around your cage like a—like a

The cackles hack at his lungs and a coughing fit ensues.

When he recovers he exchanges a knowing glance with Reflected Atlas. He sits down again and tries to slow his breathing. The howling frenzy of a moment ago has given way to quiet, tender hope.

This is nice, he thinks. It's all I need.

Slide I: a photograph of the Hornet Combat Drone VI in flight.

Blank faces.

Atlas cleared his throat and focused on his notes.

This is—a—an autonomous, self-charging, low-flying, pilot-less—aircraft. Blah, blah, capable of synchronised swarm mode for—highly visible intimidation patrols in—unlimited—groups. It can stay airborne for up to—seven days—which seems unlikely to me. Includes JK11 fifth-generation missile avoidance system—blah, blah, blah.

Slide II: a demonstration video showing thirty Hornets in the sky, moving gracefully, parting like a school of fish dodging a shark attack as a missile approaches and passes by.

Slide III: a photograph of the B-Type Gas Mine.

This is supposedly modelled on—on conventional landmines—releases just enough chemical to—neutralise combatants within a—ten-metre radius. It says here it uses a fully—untraceable chemical agent in the—final stages of research—so the product will—circumnavigate limitations imposed by the Geneva Protocol and international humanitarian law. Also—it's expected to sidestep the Ottawa Treaty—by—not being a land-mine—not in the traditional sense.

Slide IV: a cross-sectioned three-dimensional render of the B-Type Gas Mine.

The B-Type—not on the market yet—pre-orders suggest it'll—do well.

Slide V: a 'dramatisation' of the B-Type in action. The title appears over an empty field.

THE NEW COMBATANT NEUTRALISATION DEVICE FROM BLACKPIN

The words fade as a squad of fifteen soldiers appears on-screen. They hastily cross the open ground towards the far left, rifles in hand, as if in an active situation. An RP voiceover explains the product's benefits as part of a comprehensive frontline defence strategy. It reassures the audience that the mines are designed for concentrated anaesthetic gas, only capable of rendering subjects unconscious for a limited time. Then, without warning, a section of the group collapses. There is no explosion or sound. The other combatants ready themselves for combat, on their knees and bellies, looking through the sights of their weapons as if searching for a perpetrator.

Believe what you will. Oh—and Blackpin—that's our trading arm—in case you don't know already. Search it—it's a big player.

Slide VI: An image of QiNT. The robot resembles a mini AT-AT captured as it clambers over the metal-effect lettering of its name. The composition is reminiscent of a movie poster.

This is 'Sniffer'—nickname—obviously—actually called QiNT—autonomous, all-terrain battle robot. Equipped with eyeNose1—a new sensor capable of detecting the full odour spectrum—can be programmed to track down individual scents —and individuals' scents.

Slide VII: A demonstration video of QiNT galloping over rough terrain. It could be Afghanistan somewhere. The shot cuts to a dirty-looking rag being secured into a compartment on the robot's front left leg. Back on the plain, the robot tears towards some rocks in the distance, its clawed metal feet thundering the ground, the terrifying clangour amplified as if to suggest that this alone would be enough to scare an insurgent into submission. On the other side of the boulders, there's a man with a head covering and an Ak47 slung around his shoulders. He crouches, peering over the top as the machine approaches him. The last few seconds show the robot's view of the action. The rocks get closer until the man can be seen between two boulders. Finally, QiNT stops and the man stands, surrendering his arms in the air.

There's a lot about this—but—in a nutshell—QiNT reaches running speeds of up to sixty-three miles per hour—armed with a light machine gun and—where is it—there—a motion-detecting 30mm auto-cannon. The recent update—Death March —catchy name—contains a suicide mode designed for extreme scenarios. Couldn't find any footage of it blowing itself up—more's the pity.

Slide VIII: A black screen with small white lettering. It reads Liquid Earth.

This is new—very in fact—not sure I'm supposed to know about it yet—but I do—so. Another landmine. Landmines are—popular here. I can't really explain what it—does—and I assume this is a working title—better just to watch.

Slide IX: An aerial shot of a muddy field. Dramatic music is playing but nothing is happening on screen. Then a tank judders into view from the right. A parenthesised caption ticker-tapes over the image. REMOTE CONTROLLED VEHICLE. The tank moves slowly toward the middle of the screen where a superimposed red circle has appeared, and the soundtrack shifts in key. The sound then cuts out when the camouflage metal encroaches on the circle. A small inset display appears at the bottom left of the screen, with a close-up side-on perspective of the tank. For a moment, the vehicle is moving in silence. Then it halts. In the aerial view, the earth around the machine appears to undulate. On the smaller display, its tracks have sunk into the soil. The undulations quicken, and soon they resemble ripples. On both screens, the tank sinks into the field as if dropped into a pool of syrup. Its long cannon is the last thing to disappear below the mud. The footage rolls for a few seconds more. Three or four bubbles appear on the surface of the ground and then the strange fluctuations cease. Other than the track marks, there is no sign the tank was ever there. The original black screen and white lettering return.

So—that's it. I don't know what—some kind of messing with the molecular structure of the—immediate terrain. I wonder how far down the tank—sank—if the landmine sinks with it—do they both keep—plunging—until the battery runs out? I'll find out in good time—I suppose.

Atlas had put it off for too long already. He didn't want to do it. Didn't see why he should.

He'd paced the perimeter of his living room reading slide notes out loud, one hand in his pocket, the other waving index cards in the air. Then with cards down, arms crossed. Then arms by his sides. Hands on his hips. Then freestyling. But as he walked to the front of the lab to address the young team, he reached for the security of his notes and put a hand in his pocket, then, as the videos played, arms behind his back. This was relaxed. Maybe even relatable and trustworthy. Open and vulnerable. He needed them to trust him.

Not so long ago, recruitment officers explained the precise nature of the Facility's business to new staff members. They'd had to do it at their initial meetings. But they had whined about how it made their jobs more difficult than necessary. Young people were becoming increasingly idealistic, they had said. The idea of joining an organisation that wanted to use their brains to develop defence systems and weapons of mass destruction was, more often than not, a turnoff. The recruiters demanded to be relieved of the burden.

Atlas remembers hearing about it. It was early in his career, still mid-level. He'd joked about it to his colleagues. His impersonations of a recruitment officer's whinging, breathy pleas to be taken seriously went down well. Most researchers thought the new crop of recruiters was a joke. Unlike Greville. He hadn't minced his words.

We make bloody weapons, his chest revving like an old outboard motor. We put the art in artillery. And if that isn't your thing, you can fuck off.

But this generation was spineless. No gumption about them. Grow a pair and work harder. That's what Atlas would have said if it had been up to him.

The recruitment officers were ignored until enlistment levels dropped. The higher-ups became concerned about the possibility of the Facility being unable to replace its ageing workforce. So they updated the policy. Recruitment officers would no longer have to inform potential recruits what was expected of them.

Instead, all intakes were to be gradually exposed to the Facility's business during training. A few dropped hints here and there. They were clever people and it wouldn't take long for the rumours to start, but nothing would be confirmed until they were assigned to their first projects. It would then be up to the project leaders to fill in the blanks. The theory was that the Foundlings would be so invested in their new jobs and improved financial situations by then that very few would leave. And it worked. The intake figures broke all records. And the increase in numbers through the door more than made up for those who left when they learned the truth.

The policy was in place by the time Atlas became a Senior Researcher. Whenever a recruit joined his team, he tasked one of the older researchers to do the big reveal. Atlas was good at identifying people with sufficient empathy to do a decent job. It was better that way. He had too much to do and the last thing he needed was to be reminded of what they made there. Concentrate on the science not the battlefield, someone had told him in the early days. Let others deal with the reality.

This time was different. Atlas was the only person on the team who'd been at the Facility longer than five minutes. He would have to explain to these youngsters what kind of organisation they'd chosen to work for, and he dreaded every second of it.

He began by asking how many of them knew the Facility's motto.

No response.

It used to be mounted on the wall—great big sign—in the main foyer—first and last thing you saw each day—aluminium letters around a foot tall—The Pursuit of Peace.

Atlas opened his laptop, asked for the lights to be dimmed, and turned on the projector. Then he gave the team a quick update on the Facility's most recent offerings: the Hornet Combat Drone VI, the F-Type Gas Mine, the QiNT, and Liquid Earth.

As he narrated the slides, he found he couldn't stand still. His feet pulled him back and forth, side to side, the projector's light kept catching him in the eye, the shadow of his cropped head intruding on the illuminated square on the wall behind him. Images of killing machines tattooed across his face.

This is—what puts food on tables. Roofs over heads—and so on—so forth. Can someone bring the lights back up?

He lifted one leg and half-perched on a table. Be relatable, he reminded himself. Help them relax. You need them. He could see their faces now. Christ, how he wished he couldn't. Why not just be happy you have a job? Millennials or gen-whatevers. Generation-Waste-of-Spacers, thinking they're owed something before they've even started. The idea of leaving the world to this cohort was enough to keep anyone over fifty up all night. God help us all.

He recovered quickly.

Do—any of you have—a question?

Most eyes were still on him, although a few pairs were staring at the floor. That was fine. He expected some fallout. Statistically, it was bound to happen. The rest of them would manage. He'd probably over-recruited anyway.

No? It's worth pointing out—we don't just do defence—you might have heard of Zoil—a synthetic soil designed to enable agriculture in arid climates—excellent invention—solves a lot of problems—improving thousands—maybe millions of lives. But —most importantly—it—turns a profit. Not as much as defence, though—that's where the real money is. Incredible the amount a state will pay—for the capability—to annihilate more people than its enemies can.

Too soon, he thought. Shit. Far too soon. And not even very funny. It just slipped out. He knew humour would be how those who didn't walk away would deal with working here, how they would soon bury the knowledge of what they did for a living under sarcasm and irony. But he shouldn't have said that. It wasn't even a joke. Just a flippant fact.

Anyway—I'm supposed to make sure you—you know what you've got yourselves into—before—before we proceed with the project. You—probably had a good idea already. But—if you didn't—well—what can I say? Welcome—to the Facility.

Some shaking heads. Gaping mouths. A few looked at one another with expressions Atlas assumed were shock. Possibly horror. He noticed an urge to tell them the emotions they were experiencing were not his fault. He was nothing more than the messenger. They really ought to have figured it out for themselves before now. Oh look, we've signed the official secrets act. Oh look, we're in a covert underground laboratory complex. And, if their recruiter had been doing her job correctly, oh look, some evidence of some of the deadliest innovations on the planet.

So why the stunned expressions? You've been in dream-like denial, he wanted to say. I'm just snapping you out of it. Get over yourselves.

He watched one of the group, a tall female, stand up and walk towards the door. She rummaged through the coats piled up by the exit until she found hers, and then she was gone. The remaining faces returned their gazes to Atlas. He had to move things on, to stop the truth from becoming septic.

He shrugged.

So—back to the motto—the sign I mentioned earlier—it disappeared one day. It was months before I noticed—someone had to point it out to me. The Pursuit of Peace—it vanished overnight—nobody bothered to look for it.

A murmur came from somewhere in front of him, but he couldn't hear the words.

Then a voice, male, too bloody right, it said.

Yeah—I agree. After the words disappeared—I started thinking about peace—about what it means—what it actually is. I think—at the fundamental level it's freedom from disturbance —not being bothered by other people—by anything. The best way for us—a human—to achieve this—to defend ourselves—is isolation—to take off to a remote location—to be alone—because nothing disturbs us more than other humans. A state's greatest threat is from other states. But a country—can't up sticks and relocate to rural Scotland—wherever. So—it has to find a different way to—to deter interference—stop other countries from becoming pests. So we have defence mechanisms—technology—right?—instead. And here—we—the Facility—make some of the world's most advanced technologies to satisfy that need. Therefore—in a messed up way—that doesn't sound so messed up the more you consider it—peace is what we do. We—you—are in the peace industry. Congratulations.

Their faces told him they weren't buying it.

What was he even doing? He should be at his desk. Trying out ideas, testing theories, designing new procedures, working out budgets. He had no business attempting to normalise murder machines to these people. He wasn't designed for this kind of thing.

—no—forget it—I'm not doing this—

He was close to shouting.

This—here—is the real world. You need to—channel—shape—whatever—how you think about things if you want to get by. It's the same everywhere.

Cards back in his pocket, arms crossed.

I mean—do you think advertising strategists—do you think they worry about turning the world into a giant landfill site? No —they're wondering about—about how to get the latest thing— whatever-it-is—into customers' hands. Making lives easier and all of that. Solving problems. Motorsport engineers—are they constantly fretting about their contribution to climate change? No—of course not. They're too busy smashing records in—in— fuel efficiency and aerodynamics. Even—the guy dishing out burgers at the McDonald's drive-through—does he spend a—a nanosecond contemplating how he's clogging up your arteries with animal fat? No. All that's going on in his head is—is I'm paying my way through—life—college—impressing my boss now the assistant manager role—or some other job—is vacant. What I'm saying is—there are—there are different ways to perceive all of this. Take pornography—the driving force behind the internet—for years—expanded what the web is capable of— ecommerce, streaming, virtual reality, live web-camming—no other industry has developed groundbreaking online technologies as quickly as porn—it blazed a path for everyone else but nobody talks about it—because—well—it's porn. Horrible, nasty, amoral porn. That's us too. The work we do here pushes science forward. That—that is what you need to focus on. We discover new materials—compounds. We bend physics—redefine possibilities. Here—in this weird rabbit warren—we're indirectly responsible for lots of amazing things—like solar power— because we had to figure out how to get electricity to—military units in the field. Baby formula! Mobile phone technology! GPS! People out there—they'd still be fumbling around with dog-eared A-Zs if it wasn't for us—or the likes of us. Flat-screen televisions—wireless remote controls—microwave ovens—you take all this stuff for granted—never giving a thought about their true origins. Well—you're sitting in it. This place—this is where modern life is born. We make life better—each new discovery is another lurch forward. But nobody wants to talk about it— because it's defence. Horrible, nasty, amoral defence. So—I suggest you crush any—qualms—or scruples—you feel stirring in your underdeveloped loins—and do what I do. Concentrate on the—the romance—on the idea that—somehow—the work you do here—one day will become a force for good.

He realised he'd been talking at his shoes. He looked up.

And if you can't—just leave—go—right now.

And now for—the good news.

Did he say that?

And now, ladies and gentlemen, boys and girls, the moment you've been waiting for… the good news! Are you ready? Hold on to your hats because this is it: the project we'll be working on is not a weapon. I repeat: it is not a weapon. You will at some point work on a defence project. But not today. Not here. Not with me. This is an exploratory project.

The air fills with sighs of relief, then cheers, whoops, and with those hats they'd been holding on to. The junior researchers hug, high-five, and slap each other's backs. Then applause for Atlas, rapidly clapping hands outstretched towards him, grateful eyes and the occasional tear of happiness.

Well.

The message was similar but the content was less profuse, and the reaction less dramatic. It was his usual hesitant delivery to an unresponsive house. But the mood lightened. He's sure of that. The change was minuscule but they were still in shock. He couldn't expect too much from them.

The difference—is—defence projects take new technologies— and find—innovative ways of turning them into—into weapons —and such like. Exploratory projects—they're about discovery— the real work—the creation of new technologies.

New technologies that others will weaponise?

It was the orange-bearded man at the rear. Atlas recognised him as the person who'd asked what they were working on, now with a look on his face that Atlas couldn't read. But this was interaction, and that had to be a good thing.

Yes—possibly—but that's not—what we focus on. The romance. Remember? We're—moving science forwards. Just— just forget about the rest of it—or—imagine a future—where the work you do today changes the world—for the better.

It won't, though, will it? It'll be a weapon.

It—might.

Atlas stepped forward, palms turning upwards invol- untarily.

But it may end up as a—a sustainable energy source. Or—a new kind of glue. Or some sort of—medical procedure that cures —I don't know—something terrible. Yes, the odds suggest defence—but who knows—who can predict the future. Can someone dim the lights again—please?

Slide XII: A photograph of the sky above Atlas's house, complete with a satisfying blue light-to-cloud ratio.

Whereas he'd considered himself distanced from the earlier slides, now it was personal. Here was a man who'd rejected the Facility, in spirit at least, and it had given him a second chance. He wanted to feel gratitude. He knew he ought to. But at that moment he felt humiliated. The Facility contained some of the greatest minds in modern science, people who could help him bring his idea to life with ease. It was too easy to imagine different circumstances. An experienced team. An A-grade lab. A generous budget. Everything he needed to make this happen. Was he supposed to be thankful for a decrepit workshop in the arse-end of the complex and a handful of children? Twelve Foundlings, for crying out loud. Eleven. Not an ounce of experience between them. And he, Dr Atlas Brown, had to persuade them that this was a worthwhile project. Why the hell should he care if a puddle of novices took him and his work seriously?

Slide XI: A photograph of a mid-blink Dr Atlas Brown. In front of him is a workbench. His arms are folded. Behind him are two metal-framed shelving units holding a variety of indiscernible objects. The apparatus on the bench is labelled with overlaid text (black with drop shadow) and arrows (red). There are two glass vessels. The one on the left-hand side is labelled 'Extraction Chamber'. The opening at the top of this vessel is unblocked. The vessel to the right is blocked and labelled 'Storage Chamber'. Inside each vessel, at the base, is a petri dish labelled 'Agent Holding Device'. In a hole in the right side of the Extraction Chamber, located approximately two-thirds of the way down, is a rubber stopper (white) labelled 'Bored Bung'. Taped to the stopper is one end of a short section of garden hose (yellow) labelled 'Extraction Pipeline'. A hairdryer inlet (black) labelled 'Suction Mechanism' is taped to the other end of the hose. The handle of the hairdryer sits inside a large ceramic mug (green) on top of a pile of books. There are three books. Only one spine (orange) is visible. The lettering (yellow) says Mid-Century Modern: Interiors, Furniture, Design Detail; Bradley Dunn. *The hairdryer's power lead (black) runs out of the drilled base of the mug and along the workbench to the right and out of frame. An additional length of hose (yellow, unlabelled) is taped to the hairdryer's nozzle. The other end of this hose section is taped to a rubber stopper (white), also labelled 'Bored Bung', which plugs a hole in the left-hand side of the Storage Chamber. The top opening of this vessel is sealed with a wide (unlabelled) lid or stopper, which is completely covered with tape. A device labelled* One-way Air Valve *is visible above and below the lid. A further overlaid label is positioned in the space over Dr Brown's right shoulder, parallel to his ear. It says,* Particle.

Atlas's hand cast a shadow as he outlined the basic principle and explained how the contraption worked. He mentioned improvements he'd made from the previous versions. He hinted at the toll the research had taken on him personally and professionally while trying not to sound desperate. He alluded to his exposure to the Particle, a moment that could have cost him his life or, worse, his freedom.

Then he stared out at his audience.

It was like talking to a field of cows.

They don't get it. They don't understand what's right in front of them. Atlas glanced over his shoulder at the contraption on the screen. It resembled an elaborate homemade stomach pump. And there he stood behind it. Like a tourist at the pyramids or the Taj Mahal. What had he been thinking? He looked like a joke. The whole thing, all of it, was a joke. Now all he wanted to do was turn off the presentation and tell them to forget it.

He wasn't in control. His mouth was forming shapes but the sounds coming out didn't sound like his. He was watching himself from above, from the side, from the back of the room, making a fool of himself.

It's—obviously—still early days, the man by the projector said. His voice was quiet. Apologetic.

Don't be put off by the—the thinking is more advanced than the—the important thing is, it works. Now I need some—help—take it to the—

Back in his sweating body. Droplets tracing shapes down his neck and under his shirt. A day before, he'd pictured them clambering to their feet, pushing to be the first to shake his hand, to tell him how excited they were to be on this journey with him. A moment etched into their histories, to be dusted off and shared with their children, grandchildren.

If only he could have given them more, something epic to fill the silence. A sucker punch to knock out their doubt and concerns.

They were not excited.

Their souls weren't stirred.

Their imaginations were not on fire.

What a fool he was to think it might have gone any other way. Such a clown. Such a, such a

He pushed his fists together, bowed his head, and resolved to give it one more try.

Perhaps I haven't been clear—enough—for you. I have discovered a particle—the Particle—it's an incredible and—terrible thing—like a parasite—airborne—that feeds on our fear —pours petrol on our panic and terror—burns our empathy—our humanity—to a crisp—makes us capable of the very worst we're capable of—reduces us to monsters—murderers and torturers and butchers—turns minor disputes into bloodbaths—it makes war possible.

Atlas turned and stabbed a finger at the slide.

I know where it is—this Particle—how it behaves—what it does and what it wants—and I know how to—how to—suck it out of the atmosphere—and trap it. I—we—can stop it. This could be the last—could put an end to—defence—the need for it—

Then he slumped. He had nothing left. The weight of the day was pressing down on him. He needed to sit. Needed to drink something strong. To forget all this ever happened.

There was murmuring.

There was no telling how long it had been going on before he noticed. Heads tilted towards one another. Hands covering words. Glances in his direction. A raised hand. Hair scraped back against her skull. Sunken eyes.

It is her.

He grips the rubber mallet but it's too heavy to lift.

Yes? Atlas said.

Her voice in his head before she speaks. Wrapping itself around his brain, massaging his temporal lobe.

When do we start?

ARTHUR

Arthur Bloc wanted more.

He had more than his mother, having already survived longer. If the stories were accurate, he had more than his father too. His own faculties to begin with. And he was on course to have more than his maternal grandparents. But Nev and Silvia were easy pickings. At twenty-five, Arthur earned more than his grandfather had when he retired. His sister Claire was still ahead but she wouldn't be for long. She'd had a head start. Married young to a man who'd done the honourable thing. A guy called Guy, three years older than Arthur and twice his size. Heaved breeze blocks for a living, talked about working offshore one day. Saving up for qualifications he could never remember the names of. They had a Nissan on tick and a council house around the corner from Nev and Silvia. Surrounded by childhood friends and their babies. Doing okay, maintaining it, heads above water, healthy kid. Happy for now, careful not to mess up.

Arthur wanted more than that.

More was a question of evolution and safety. The idea he'd automatically have more than his ancestors was flawed, he knew that, had never believed in it. There was no natural law. Or maybe once, for a short time in the last century, it had held true.

But you couldn't rely on something like that anymore. Now you needed hard work, cunning, and fear. Lots of fear.

More than anything, Arthur feared other people's apathy. He'd watched it take root in his friends when he was a teen, witnessed them settling for the meagre pickings the immediate environment could offer. When they spoke of joining the army, getting apprenticeships at local factories, going robbing with their brothers, or running drugs with the small-time crooks, he withdrew, extracted himself. He buckled down, avoided the socials, stayed in, didn't return texts. And he accepted the grief that followed, the inevitable punishment for thinking he was better.

Despite Nev's warnings that he was wasting his time, that he ought to stay put, Arthur got himself a university place. He was the only kid on the estate to go. As far as he knew, he was the only one who wanted to. Silvia said he was being selfish, told him to think about them, to think about his family.

Claire was delighted and furious. When he showed her the offer letter, she punched him in the chest and smiled. I never want to see you around here again. Understand?

And he was out. A northern college, as far away as he could get, studying for a degree in engineering, working in bars and call centres, ignoring the nightlife, attending everything, reading everything, cramming everything, all powered by his sister's postcards from home.

Dear Arthur, Kenny from school got eleven years for armed robbery.

Dear Arthur, Nev's been diagnosed with lung cancer.

Dear Arthur, The library burned down. Arson.

Dear Arthur, Guy lost his job.

Dear Arthur, Silvia had a stroke at the bingo.

Four frantic years of slog later, Arthur Bloc received a first-class degree and an award for academic excellence. It should have been enough but there was a snag. The dearth of engineers that had inspired him to pursue it as a career had become a glut. Job offers were scant and meagre and he realised he needed more than a first to continue in this direction. So he stayed put, secured a bursary for a Master's, and gave another two years of his life to studies and menial part-time work.

Claire promised to come to the graduation but pulled out the day before. Babysitter problems, she said. On the morning of the ceremony, he decided he wouldn't go. Instead, he would treat himself for the first time he could remember. A meal and a couple of drinks. He deserved it.

The Italian restaurant was a small, family-run establishment he had passed hundreds of times en route to lectures. He chose the spiciest, meatiest pizza on the menu and a half-carafe of house red. When he'd polished off the wine before the food, he ordered a beer and mistook the waitress's glances for something they weren't. He finished, paid the bill, and walked to a bar for some serious drinking. He had a thirst on. It wasn't too far. A traditional-looking place, lively enough.

After a beer, he regretted not telling the waitress where he was going and then regretted his generous tip.

After another, he made a comment about the barman's weight.

After another, he insulted a woman twice his age when she turned down his advances.

The barman asked him to leave. He refused and demanded another. A doorman appeared by his side. Arthur swung a loose fist in the bouncer's direction and found himself facedown on the pavement. He wiped the blood from his nose with his sleeve.

There was no security outside the next bar. He downed the first pint in one. The second slipped through his fingers and emptied onto his lap. The staff were indifferent. He slurred a request for something stronger. A small glass of clear liquid appeared in front of him. It wasn't enough.

More, he said.

He could no longer hold his focus on his hands. A woman in his narrowed field of vision told him they were closing.

There's a club at the end of the street that opens late, she said.

Arthur woke up on wet concrete between two commercial bins. His tongue like a shovel, eyelids like sandpaper, his face tight. He heaved himself up, leaned against the blue metal, and contemplated the avalanche of regurgitated sauce and chewed meat that was drying on the front of his shirt. Then, in a moment of panic, his phone was nowhere to be found, not in his jacket or his trouser pockets, not on the ground or anywhere, but, ah, there it was, under one of the bins a couple of feet away, with a cracked screen but working.

6.45 am.

He activated the front-facing camera. A dry, bloodied nose pointing in the wrong direction, one eye purpled and his lips swollen. A memory punched at his throbbing head. His hand pulling at someone, a woman, hauling her out of a cab as she tried to climb inside. The woman at his feet and a man screaming at him. Up in his face. Arthur belched it away.

The blue bins lined a narrow road. A fire door, a dead end, and the smell of rot to the right but signs of life to the left. He limped, paused to rest, hands on knees to ease his lurching stomach. On the street, a row of shops, a few parked cars, three or four people walking purposefully in the same direction.

The engine of the car nearest to him started up. The passenger side door opened. A woman got out.

arthur-bloc-i-understand-you-might-be-looking-for-a-job

ARRINA

The test chamber looked like a giant cartoon fish. The small access port at its mouth contained the mini-extractor and the Particle dispenser. At the tail, a ramp led to the vacuum-sealed entrance and its circular submarine-style handle. Arrina imagined the people inside had been gobbled up after falling from a boat.

The two volunteers sat opposite one another at the table. They performed various activities, as directed by Arrina's voice from the speaker in the chamber's ceiling. The first part of the experiment was based on a programme developed by the psychologist Dr Augustus Enderwick several years previously. Its purpose was to help train government field operatives to resist social cues that could prompt them to drop their guards and subconsciously 'humanise' enemy agents to the point of trusting them. Enderwick condensed into three hours a series of interactions between individuals that would, under normal circumstances, have taken many meetings over many days. The tasks included puzzles that required the subjects to work together, taking turns to ask and answer a list of pre-prepared personal questions as honestly as possible, and prolonged silences during which they stared into each other's eyes.

However, in a twist to the psychologist's technique, the participants inside the fish were not asked to fight the feelings they experienced. Instead, they were encouraged to relax and give in to them.

During this first stage of the experiment, nicknamed the 'bonding session', brain activity, heart rate, hormone levels and other stress indicators, including nonverbal communication, were observed and assessed until the team agreed the subjects had established a good rapport. For the second part, the tasks were switched to board games, with simple rewards and penalties to heighten emotional responses. The subjects competed under standard atmospheric conditions in which natural levels of Particle were present, then again after a 'mini extraction' that removed all traces of Particle, and finally, in a heightened Particle environment. Hypothetically, the subjects would demonstrate 'normal' aggression during phase one, zero aggression in phase two, and 'abnormally high' aggression in phase three.

The first subjects were female junior researchers. Lina and Belinda. Both twenty-six years old, of similar build and ethnic background. When Arrina interviewed them, they appeared enthusiastic about being the project's maiden guinea pigs. The idea of recruiting strangers from the Orphanage had sickened Arrina, but the reality proved more agreeable than predicted. It seemed Dr Brown had a reputation in the lowest echelons of the Facility. She only had to mention his name and the volunteers came flocking. A brief psychological assessment concluded that Lina and Belinda were of sound mind. Or as sound as could be found at the institution.

Stage one of the experiment went well. All signs showed the pair bonded successfully. Both subjects claimed to enjoy backgammon, so it was chosen as the game for the adversarial phase. They were given ten coins each. At the end of every game, the loser was to award the winner a coin, and the games would continue until either of them ran out of cash. The overall winner would keep the winnings. Lina joked about being able to retire when the trial was over.

Arrina watched through the fish-eye window as the pair played in normal atmospheric conditions. Ahmed stood behind her at the monitors, calling out changes to the stress indicators as they happened. Both subjects displayed some expected signs of anxiety. They were in an unusual situation, playing a board game against a stranger in a giant metal fish as other strangers observed their every heartbeat. Then there was the game itself. The five-thousand-year-old Mesopotamian distraction designed to mock a player's intelligence, to trick them into believing their luck is a hard-earned skill and their misfortune a deep-rooted flaw. It was no surprise that tensions were high.

One hour and thirteen minutes later, Belinda was out of coins. Via the speaker, Arrina asked the pair to relax while the team prepared for the next phase. Dr Brown stiffened. Arrina watched him. Until that moment, he'd been milling around, observing the proceedings and offering advice here and there. But now he had the look of a man listening to bad news.

Clear the—access port—please.

He approached the port, took a deep breath, and activated the extraction.

Now they all watched him. Intentionally or not, Dr Brown had provoked some discontent in the team by insisting he was the only person allowed near the agent, the substance used to attract the Particle. Only he knew what it contained, and only he had a key to the safe where it was stored. Earlier that day, to much annoyance, he'd ordered everyone out of the lab so he could set up the mini-extractor.

The situation had been causing hushed arguments for weeks. While some supported the doctor, believing he needed time to trust them, others moaned that he was being paranoid and unprofessional. How could they commit to a project while the critical component, the core of everything they were doing, remained hidden from them? As it was, their roles were merely auxiliary. We may as well be manual workers, one of them said, I didn't sign up to be a labourer. But despite the discontent, intrigue captured every imagination gathered around the test chamber, and as anticipation built, the grievances ebbed.

After extraction, the researchers resumed their positions. Arrina directed the pair to redistribute the coins and return to their tournament. The team took a couple of minutes to notice what was happening. Stress levels were plummeting. As they moved the counters, the players asked questions about each other's lives. They saw the funny side of bad rolls, offered suggestions when their opponent struggled to find the right move, and laughed so hard at a joke nobody outside heard that Lina knocked the board and scattered the pieces across the floor. Their smiles spread through the lab like a yawn.

The games were slow. Coins passed between Lina and Belinda repeatedly until it seemed there would never be a winner, so Ahmed suggested calling an end to this stage.

Again, Arrina asked the subjects to relax and distribute the coins for the final phase. Dr Brown reappeared at the access port. This time he released a controlled sample of Particle into the chamber. The change was immediate. The stress levels jumped. Eye contact between the pair ceased as they poured their concentration onto the board to set up the counters.

Dr Brown joined Arrina at the glass.

They were playing defensively this time, protecting their pieces and taking no chances. But ill-feeling seemed directed at the dice rather than at each other. Whenever one subject rolled a double or captured an opponent's piece, the other swore or looked away from the game, eyes rolling, arms folded, fists clenched.

The first game went Lina's way. Arrina held her breath and waited for something to happen. Nothing. No visible reactions. But the monitors told a different story.

Belinda won the second game. Lina was left with only one

checker on the board. The winner puffed out her cheeks in relief, and the loser forced a short-lived smile.

The third game began as cautiously as the others. Five minutes in, Lina took one of Belinda's checkers and placed it at the side of the board. Belinda lifted her face and stared at her rival. Then she whispered something the researchers couldn't hear.

Fuck you, replied Lina.

Camera 3: Belinda is the first to strike. She punches a fistful of backgammon pieces into her opponent's mouth. The force pushes Lina off her chair and onto her back. Before Lina has the chance to recover, Belinda is on her feet. She launches a chair across the table. The end of an aluminium leg cuts into Lina's forehead.

Camera 2: As Lina scrambles to her feet, Belinda climbs onto the table and throws herself at her rival, smashing both of them against the chamber wall, momentarily out of the cameras' reach.

Camera 4: Outside the chamber, Dr Atlas Brown and Arrina Heal peer through the observation window. The latter raises a hand to her mouth. Ahmed Banu, Arthur Bloc, and others join them.

Camera 1: The subjects are on the floor. They mash each other's faces with fists, bite into exposed skin, head-butt, and batter with broken table legs. Blood speckles their clothes. Belinda covers her face with her arms. Lina stands up and roars as she stamps on Belinda's shoulder, the floor, and then the side of her head.

Camera 4: Only Dr Atlas Brown is left at the window. From this angle, it looks as if he isn't watching the subjects. His face is tilted up slightly, and his head is making small, erratic movements as if following something as it darts around the chamber.

Arrina Heal and Arthur Bloc are at the access port. It is unclear which, but one of them activates the extraction process.

Camera 3: Lina's knees pin Belinda to the floor. She hammers her opponent's face with the heels of her clenched hands while tears pour down her cheeks.

———

Arrina felt lightheaded when they reached the canteen. If Arthur hadn't asked her to wait until the place was quiet, she would have eaten already. There wasn't much left to choose from. She took a porridge pot and a tea from the counter and joined the other two at their usual table, the one furthest from the entrance.

Arthur's feet were on the Formica. He didn't move them when she placed down her tray.

We need more ambition, he was saying. The project, I mean. It does. Not us.

Ahmed smiled as he considered his smoked salmon bagel.

Okay then, Arthur, we'll leave you to scope that with Dr Brown.

That's what I'm suggesting. In a way. It's not enough, said Arthur. It's wishy-washy. Discovery projects suck. There's no meat. It's boring. Predictable.

You are joking, aren't you? The tests we've been running are not my idea of wishy-washy or boring. And that first one definitely wasn't predictable. It was as predictable as a...

Ahmed opened the bagel and peered at the filling as if he'd find a suitable simile written on the pink flesh.

Arthur took a hit from his vape and exhaled under the table.

Not the project. Not that. That's good. It's excellent. Which worsens the problem. In a way. This thing. The discovery process. It makes us look like idiots.

Ahmed wafted the vape smoke rising around him.

Egotism isn't attractive, Arthur.

I'm talking about potential. Ours. Being wasted.

Whatever. Can you just stop that? It stinks. Arrina and I do not enjoy passive smoking. Plus, someone will see you.

It isn't smoking.

You have no idea what it is or what it's doing to your lungs.

Arrina gets it. Don't you?

Her face hovered over her pot, the spoon moving quickly between porridge and mouth.

Ahmed sighed.

So suddenly you know better than Dr Brown?

In this instance. Yes. He doesn't see what he's got. The potential.

Come on then, genius.

It's very simple. Even you might understand. We know we can trap it. This thing. This Particle. Brown says it triggers hate. And it looks like he's right. So what now? Keep testing its effects. Then what? Someone else picks it up. Our work. Finds practical applications. Correct?

Ahmed nodded. Arrina's head remained in the same position as she slid the empty bowl aside and replaced it with the mug of tea. Her glasses steamed over.

Arthur spread his arms wide as if to demonstrate the obviousness of his argument.

And then they take the glory. Yes?

Ahmed shook his head slowly.

It's hardly glory, Arthur.

That is a matter of opinion. And this practical application. What do you reckon? A weapon?

That's not our concern. Dr Brown said we shouldn't speculate about the Particle's end uses. It could become anything.

Think about it. Where we are. What they do here. What we have on our hands.

Ahmed turned towards the food counter where the catering staff were cleaning the surfaces and prepping for the early evening rush.

Yes, well. Possibly.

Or probably? Anyway. What I'm saying is. We should take it further. We should be the ones. If this thing is what he says. If we have something incredible. What? Just give it away? Wouldn't it be better. For everyone if we. I mean us. Took it to its logical conclusion? The sane conclusion?

And what conclusion would that be?

Don't be an idiot. You know. Brown knows too. He's just. I've no idea. Following procedure. Maybe. Playing it safe. A career to think about. Whatever. But imagine. Think what it would do for us. And him. If we go renegade. Do something crazy like. I don't know. Save the world.

You're being idealistic.

No, Ahmed, I'm being a scientist. You should try it.

Arrina's tea was drained. Now she watched Arthur's feet twitch as he spoke, their movements punctuating his speech. Calm lurches to the left for words, downward twitches for periods.

Ahmed shrugged.

I refer you back to my original question. Are you going to tell Dr Brown that he's doing his job, the thing he has been doing for decades now, the wrong way?

Arthur swung his legs off the table, pulled his chair in and rested hands on his lap. He looked at Arrina.

Not me. Us. We'll tell him. But Arrina will say the words.

ALFONSO

The corridor walls have disappeared. Through a single, barely open eye, Alfonso sees two figures, blurred, swiping their phones, their backs turned on each other. He recognises the faces. Their coats make an island on the floor at Jen's feet, her bag roosted on top. Behind them, beige paint and white dado trunking. Mil casts a look in his direction and returns it to her phone. The electronic sounds of medical equipment pulse gently, stroking his head, lulling him, encouraging his eyelid to close so he can return to the back seat of the family's Morris Minor on their way home from the seaside. Sand on his sticky fingers, the taste of ice cream where teeth meet gums. His mother's wide straw hat, a pink ribbon, the scent of sun lotion, the corner of her smile, the glances at his father, the soft sentences he doesn't understand. A cotton flat cap sitting above his father's hairline, eyes in the rear-view mirror saying hello.

—Mr McMurrough? Hello? Mr McMurrough, can you hear me?

Breath licks his forehead. The aroma of old chicken soup and a perfume he vaguely remembers. Kaleidoscope faces. Jen's, Mil's, Mr Alexander's and one other. Four distinct likenesses rotate in an anticlockwise direction. Then all of them together, like a bento box, Mil's blinking left eye and ear in one compartment, the stranger's smiling mouth and chin in another, his wife's and Mr Alexander's features sharing the remainder, circling, taking his stomach with them.

—Alfonso, we need to talk to you, say the lips.

As he approached the north end of Normanton Street from Perceval Square, Alfonso could see traffic queued along Hope Road, waiting to turn into the thoroughfare. Lines of vehicles snagged up the tributaries. From where he stood, it looked as if every car in Castleport was at a standstill. The noise of the horns was furious and continuous. Drivers, half in, half out of their cars, gesticulating and shouting. Even the pedestrian shoppers struggled to move, heel-to-toe, inching forwards, spilling onto the road. The entire city seemed to be trying to reach the same destination. Alfonso extracted himself from the pavement and pushed on between the trapped cars.

Normanton Street used to be the main artery through the city's centre. Recently regenerated and re-engineered, its four lanes reduced to two to make space for a long strip of narrow park areas, intelligent bus stops, kiosks, and several pieces of public art that now ran down its middle. *Las Ramblas* of the North, as nicknamed by a reporter at The Tribune. Named 'Recreation Island' by an out-of-town brand consultancy, the new Normanton Street was lined on both sides by fashion outlets, department stores and every high-street chain imaginable. More retailers than a small city could possibly sustain, according to its critics. Gyms, glassy bars and glaring nightclubs. And the mega-casino, a super church for Castleport's most devout spenders. It was a street designed to consume the consumers, to hoover up the city's residents, push them down its wide, shiny intestine, and deposit them bewildered and poorer onto Prospect Row.

As soon as Alfonso rounded the corner, he saw the problem. Twenty-six tons of tanker halfway down Normanton Street, extending perpendicular over the island and across both lanes. By standing on a concrete couch in the central reservation, he could see someone had wedged a Range Rover in the gap between the back end of the truck and a building, so now the only way for people to pass was to climb over the SUV or squeeze through the few inches that remained between the front of the cabin and a shop window. A hundred, or possibly hundreds, of shoppers amassed by the truck, clambering onto bus stops and occupied cars, climbing the sculptures and kiosks. They were shouting, horns blaring, children crying, engines revving. Normanton Street had fallen into hell. Alfonso watched them screaming, punching and pulling each other, kicking over bins. These creatures were unknown to him.

A crowd had gathered by the open door of the tanker's cabin. Alfonso pushed through, causing one woman to lose her footing and fall into another. Incredulous faces gave way when they saw his uniform. Alfonso peered inside. It was empty. He called out to be sure, in case the driver was hiding in there.

He's gone, a man behind him said.

Fucking legged it, growled another.

When there was no reply from inside, Alfonso climbed in and sat at the wheel. Opposite him was a red sales poster in the window of an electronics shop, beyond which several flustered assistants in matching checked shirts mouthed and gestured obscenities at him. Without stopping to weigh up the possible consequences, Alfonso lifted his hand into view, formed his fingers into a loose fist, and moved it up and down. The store staff exploded with fury and attacked each other. Satisfied, Alfonso removed his hat and jacket and looked at the controls at his disposal. It appeared simple enough. The key was in the ignition and the automatic gear was just a bigger, slightly more complicated version of the one in his car.

Below him, the crowd was larger and noisier now, cracking the solid air with pneumatic cries.

The light from the open door suddenly dimmed and a red, twisted face yelled just inches from Alfonso's.

If you don't get this thing out of the way, I'm going to rip your goddamn head off. Now move it, you piece of…

Alfonso slammed the palm of his hand into the man's forehead, forcing him to fall back into the crowd, which parted so he could hit the ground before it trampled him.

The traffic warden leaned out to the door handle and pulled it hard, jamming another man's head against the frame, his eyes scrunched up, his teeth bared. Alfonso eased up and the man fell away. Then he slammed it shut, wishing he'd thrust his boot into the intruder's mouth before releasing him.

He turned the key and the engine roared. When the people around the truck didn't move Alfonso pressed the horn, but its sound was indistinguishable from the cacophony outside. He checked the wing mirror. A banging on the passenger-side window distracted him. The glass shattered and a nine-iron golf club flew into the cabin, hitting Alfonso on the arm. A furious face appeared in the jagged frame.

Move your bastard truck, you wanker, move it.

The woman's last screamed syllable hung in the air as Alfonso stamped on the accelerator. The vehicle lurched forward and powered through the shopfront.

It seemed to take forever to find the brake. Then, for a moment, all was calm. Ceiling tiles fell silently. Shelving units and cabinets full of gadgets and laptops swayed. Glass glittered on the carpet. But there was so much more to destroy. At the back of the store, televisions and speaker systems were asking to be smashed. Smartphones and tablets and gaming consoles begging to be crushed. The prospect of obliterating the shiny surfaces, of mangling all those clean lines and expensive screens was so delicious Alfonso began to salivate. There was nothing between his vehicle and the orgasm of total demolition. His foot hovered over the accelerator.

The noise from outside had resumed. In his wing mirror, he saw people running, fighting, falling. Then, nearer, he heard a thud. He looked in the other mirror. Another thud. A man was striking the side of the truck, his truck, with a plank of wood. Alfonso's body spasmed. His fists flew at the wheel and the dashboard. He screeched through a jaw clenched so tightly that his skull was in danger of fracturing. Who did these imbeciles think there were? He grabbed the golf club from the passenger seat and made to open the cab door. Then he paused. Shop staff were now rounding on the cabin. Five of them, one armed with a sound bar and another with a vacuum cleaner. They were jeering at him, daring him to join them. He dropped the club into the footwell, placed one hand on the steering wheel, shifted the gear into reverse with the other, and pressed down on the pedal. The force of acceleration and then the abrupt stop as the rear vehicle smashed into the Range Rover and whatever else was in its way shook Alfonso around the cabin like a child's rattle. As soon as he could gather himself, he picked up the club again and exited the vehicle.

The street resembled a medieval battleground. People were hitting each other with objects and fists, kicking and pushing. Bloodied bodies sprawled over the road and plastic lawns. Upturned cars and toppled bus stops. A young man ran at him, yelling something about being late for work, only to be met with a nine iron to the head. Another man, older this time, came at him from the side. Alfonso only saw a movement, a change of the light out in the corner of his eye, but it was enough. He brought his elbow up to shoulder height and thrust it backwards, smashing the man's ear, crashing him to the ground. He stepped forward, feeling taller, fuller. Solid. There was nowhere to go, and that was fine. In fact, it was perfect. He was ready to stand and fight. To teach these mouth breathers how to behave.

He was surrounded by all the scum this dirty planet had to offer. They were all here, stinking up his city, the place he'd served all his adult life. Humanity needed a good hiding and he relished the idea of delivering it. He was invincible. Alive in a way he'd never experienced before. His muscles, blood, brain swelled with adrenaline. Thermonuclear fists. Atomic bomb feet. He lifted the nine-iron into the air and got stuck in.

PART IV

ATLAS

Night walks are good. No need for a rule against them. If you can overcome the fear of being caught for breaking the curfew, a foray into the city under the cover of darkness is well worth the risk. By overcoming fear, Atlas means to riff on it, surf on it, to fuel the night with it.

Angela worries about a warden patrol picking him up. She wouldn't be able to help if that happened. He'd be on his own. She says they detain people without ID and it's impossible to know where they end up. But Atlas has never seen a so-called nighttime patrol and is convinced they are propaganda bullshit. Rumours like that are an excellent way to control the population. Not that the Castleport street zombies, with nothing on their minds but the next food parcel, need controlling. No provision stations are open at night, and there is no reason to go out. So what would be the point of policing the curfew? If there is a threat to him, it feels minor.

He does this once or twice a month. He takes simple precautions. Just in case. Soft-soled shoes, loose black clothing. He sticks to back streets and avoids brightly illuminated areas and wide open spaces, but that's part of the fun. He can make it from the compound to Joshua Street without coming up for air. A network of pathways edge him through and around residential neighbourhoods and deliver him into the alleyway that runs parallel to Lindberg Road. The old running routine helps him here as he light-foots it from where the alley opens onto the north end of Finch Street to the tree cover on the south side. He sets off quickly before his body realises what he's up to. There is a kind of joy in these moments that he can't explain. It's like nothing he has experienced since he was a child. Perhaps longer. It is a weightlessness. It is as if his legs are made of springs, and he bounces from one to another with ease. Adrenaline, he thinks, doing what it does best.

Atlas is out of breath by the time he reaches the trees. He rests and eyes his destination, only a hundred or so yards ahead. These jaunts used to be random affairs. He took whatever route suggested itself, explored passageways he was too self-conscious to enter during daylight hours, and wandered behind rows of shops and office blocks. He found it liberating and exhilarating whenever he got himself lost again. And then he rediscovered the monuments on Finch Square. Ten of them. All black metal. Eight four-foot tall angels, each in a different pose, on ornate slim stone plinths that form a semicircle in front of two larger statues. A metal plaque indicates the smaller of the two is of Nathaniel Castleport III. Member of Parliament, Industrialist, Philanthropist, Poet, Son of the City. He's around seven feet high on a grander plinth than that of the angels, which gives him an extra five. He stands with a fedora in his hand, held against his chest, as he gazes up towards the central statue of another Nathaniel Castleport. Taller again. Presumably Nathaniel Castleport I or II. The plaque contains no ordinal. This man sits on a chair of sculpted buildings. A warehouse at his back, factories under his arms, a row of houses supporting each thigh. If artists who create such effigies are paid to flatter their subjects, to make them appear a little younger, a little better looking, and, perhaps, a little slimmer, then this man must have been a beast in the flesh. His iron effigy is monstrous. The sculptor either despised him or could not escape the subject's grotesqueness or girth.

Nathaniel Castleport I or II is positioned as if he's the city's very own Abraham Lincoln, a top hat mounted on a tuber-shaped head with dead-frog eyes, below which the skin sags in sympathy with a furious bottom lip. He is dressed in a long coat cut from enough iron cloth to dress ten men. His giant left arm is bent at the elbow, and his fingers appear to rub an invisible beard below his chin. The other arm thrusts forward like an aimed cannon, the downturned hand gripping the bulbous handle of a cane, the shaft of which disappears into the rooftops below. The overall impression is of an enraged creature poised to bellow globules of loathing at anyone who dares question his greatness.

The statues shelter Atlas from prying eyes. He feels comfortable here and enjoys spending a little time taking in the atmosphere and imagining the impact the space once had on the mind of the citizenry. It's the only place he knows of in Castleport that holds any evidence of forethought beyond traffic management and shopping. In any other city, he would walk past this hideous creature and his protectors without a thought. But context is everything. He's quite taken by the frozen theatre of Finch Square and its audience of townhouse legal offices. When he has absorbed all the ambience he can handle, he removes his clothes, scales the top-hatted sculpture, and curls up on the man's lap like an infant.

All thoughts about her are banned. It's for the project's ongoing welfare. Because if he descends into that rabbit hole, then everything is doomed. That's the theory. So it's a good rule. But it is not one that Atlas would write down and attach to the door or anywhere else because that would only make him think about her.

Don't think about the Primo External Factor.

Don't think about the first time you saw her because you do not remember which time that was, and you'll only end up thinking about all the times you ever noticed her.

Don't think about the hours you lost studying her through the Venetian blinds you left open just enough to see out into the lab without her realising.

Don't think about her awkwardness.

Don't wonder why she was attractive to you when nothing physical about her did anything for you; her shape, movements, choice of clothes, all of it unexceptional. There were millions like her, human beings like any other, with faces and bodies that don't register on any known scale. And yet he couldn't stop staring. Atlas has pondered the possibility of a spectrum of ordinariness in which the heights of individuality exist on the sparsely populated outer perimeter, while the epitome of dull, the essence of humdrum, resides in the middle. While most of us run as fast as we can from the grey kernel of human existence, away from the ordinary as if it were the most hideous of all fates, what if only the purest of minds refuse to resist, content to slip closer and closer to the epicentre and into utter indistinguishability? What's to say we should struggle against the mundane? Perhaps choosing not to fight is the purpose of life. Possibly we're supposed to blend in, and by reaching the nucleus of normality an individual attains perfection. The paragon of human. Is absolute beauty only found in the unremarkable? By resisting its allure, people batter and injure themselves, torn and scarred and ugly. But if a person surrenders completely, they exist undamaged by conflict. They are unblemished. Pure

her skin

Don't think about her skin.

But he is too far inside the rabbit hole now. While he's been lying there, the writhing burrow, this snake of soil and roots and worms, has crept over him and under Nathaniel's iron thighs, then over him and under again and again, and holds him firm. There is not a thing he can do, barely a muscle he can move until he has purged himself of every memory, every possible thought of Arrina.

———

It has always happened, this confusion. He is confident of that. It isn't age-related. Certain matters become disordered sometimes, that's all. He mixes up emotions. Especially other people's. Take Angela. He understands she cares about him and wants him to be safe. It's pretty simple when he thinks of it that way. His well-being is no longer a mere task on a long to-do list. He is an actual person to her now, not a job. She knows things about him, has a good idea of what makes him tick, and has an inclination of what he has been through and why he's not feeling great. Maybe she assumes Atlas is vulnerable. She must do. Just look at him. And what Atlas likes to do is gather up all of this generosity and concern, her kindness and sense of responsibility, and smash and grind it all up in the empty mortar of his skull until it resembles something like middle-aged lust. Angela does all of this because she is desperate to sleep with me, this is his conclusion.

Life was better when he didn't know his brain worked this way and did not feel the need to scold himself every day for being a dick. But it's a healthy sign of growth, as Reflected Atlas enjoys reminding him. None of this is supposed to be easy. While self-loathing is a chore, it is also the first step towa

no, no, no, he is getting sidetracked.

What he is actually trying to work through here is that he now realises he was wrong about Arrina.

This is what happened: he was flattered by the passion all these young people in his laboratory exhibited. Impressed by the way they threw themselves into the work. They clearly believed they were contributing to something worthwhile. And then the pestle got into action. It was his project, from his head, and they were working so damn hard, so enthusiastically, because they wanted to impress him. But he wasn't finished yet. He kept on grinding and grinding until he'd pulverised that reverence into naked sexual attraction. They lusted after him and his creative intellect. And that one, the uneasy, boring-looking one called Arrina, she desired him the most.

There.

You stupid old man, he says out loud, his words punching holes in the night. He did not know who Arrina was beyond the day-to-day work-related interactions. She reported to him at 10am every weekday, had him sign requisition forms, and asked him to approve the revised timeline, eyes on paperwork, all very professional and proper. So why her?

Her voice. Like a gentle cloud. A light soprano that bypassed Atlas's ears and slipped straight into his head. Soft tones that said good morning, that shared production problems, that asked if he needed anything else before she left for the day, and that exhaled mundane words that swept his thoughts aside and held his attention the way a cool windowpane against his cheek might, even as it challenged his authority.

Some of us have been talking about the project.

That's what—you're paid to do.

It lacks ambition.

I'm sorry—what?

The three of them standing in his office, her in the middle. Atlas at his desk, looking up from the document he's been reading, peering over his glasses so that only their legs are in focus, his forehead like a ploughed field, his mouth failing to find words.

We're sure our work has the potential to improve lives.

It—might.

And we believe we should be the ones who bring it to fruition, not the weapon designers.

He remembers leaning back into his chair and taking her in. She stood poker straight, hands by her sides. Open lab coat, yellow floral sack underneath. She looked like she was serious. Or nervous. Whatever, it was an expression he didn't recognise. Not yet. The others who flanked her were barely visible to him, one of them nodding, one shifted on his feet as if preparing to run away.

We should take the initiative.

But before that, was he already finding excuses to go into the lab to hear her speak? Was he asking for her opinion on any matter he could think of? Did he know he was doing it and believe that it was fine, that he simply enjoyed the sound of her voice? Did he tell himself there was nothing problematic happening, that soon he'd grow bored and someone or something else would replace her? This is a reasonable enough assumption based on his history. Infatuations came and infatuations went. Or did it begin when she marched into his office and changed the course of everything? Had he misconstrued this major turning point in his story, the world's story, one that would have required unfathomable courage and passion for her to initiate it the way she did, had Atlas mistaken all of that for her desire for him?

Physical distress provides effective relief from his psychological pain. And while it is nigh on impossible to move while in the rabbit hole's grip, occasionally he finds just enough give in its hold to push an elbow or a knee or even his skull against the statue's hard body. Or, if he happens to be in a suitable position, he can sink his teeth into the flesh of a hand or forearm. This discomfort is sometimes sufficient to distract him from the memories that trap him there. And the more acute the hurt, the better his chance of escape.

Atlas enters the compound and climbs the stairs that lead to his metal box. He winces from the ache in his left ankle. He wishes he had chosen a different joint with which to free himself. A wrist, for instance.

He is tired. He wants coffee. Strong, milk, two sugars. Dandelion tea has to be the poorest substitute. Bootleg coffee might be possible, but Atlas has no idea how to retrieve scarce commodities from the shadow economy. He doubts Angela does either.

She'll come tomorrow with fresh supplies and conversation. He should tidy up. Use the cleaning products she left. He could clean the window. That seems as if it might deliver the maximum return for minimal effort. But at the very least, he should bring the various coloured plastic bottles inside. Even after all this time she retains enough professionalism to make it impossible for him to know if he ever hurts her feelings, but it's foolish to risk it.

The bucket containing the products is full of rainwater. He bends down, removes the containers, and lines them up by the wall. The weak sunshine will dry them off eventually. He empties the water onto the stairs and watches it cascade into the compound. As he does so, he notices a movement on the tarmac. An orange blur darts behind the brick shed. A cat, he assumes. Here to eat the rats. Why the rodents are here, he has no clue. What are they eating? Or a fox. That would be nice. He thinks he might have an affinity with foxes. Intelligent outsiders, reasonably stylish, handsome even, persecuted. Out here on the aluminium platform, the sun is warming his body and he regrets wetting the steps. He'd like to sit on them now and soak up the heat.

The mess, which comprises one long table, ten chairs, and some basic kitchen equipment, is the only other metal box he uses on a daily basis. On the ground floor, the outlook of its glass frontage gives him an alternative perspective of the compound. From his quarters he sees everything, the whole gasholder and over the top of the hangar. Beyond, like a swatch of 1945 Dresden, a wasteland of flattened factories crashes into the trunks of narrow woodland, its green canopy clashing pleasingly with the red and grey brick foreground. Behind the trees, Castleport dissolves into piano key fields, lonely hills, and haze. But from inside the mess, all Atlas can see is the hangar's black corrugated steel curving away like an upturned whale. And if it's dark out, his skinny self looks back, hunched over a tin of cold macaroni cheese, spoon hovering near his chin.

Atlas slides the door aside, enters the mess, and selects a chair. At first glance, they're all the same. But he thinks the one he sits in while he eats is shaping to his backside nicely, which makes that piece of furniture more precious than the others. He doesn't want to risk damaging it by taking it outside. So he chooses a different chair, wipes dust from the seat with his hand, and drags it out into the compound, the feet of its back legs scraping tracks through the gravel.

As he walks, he notices the gasholder's shadow. He has seen this before, how the shade it casts is darker than any other in the compound. He doesn't like to look directly at it for long, but from his snatched glances, the murk seems sharp and complete, without penumbra. This is impossible, he knows that. His mind is only playing tricks on him but still he places the chair well away from it. Then he sits, faces the sun, and closes his eyes.

The Particle in its prison to his left, the Extractor inside the hangar on his right. And in the middle, Atlas. The catalyst. Because it was him, not Arrina Heal, who changed everything. It's ridiculous to give her either the glory or the blame. All she did was make it easier to act. That day in his office, when she and her colleagues explained what they thought should happen, all she did was help him find the courage to say the words out loud. He'd already sketched the rough plans and knew how he would design the machine. Yes, he had been worried. Maybe a little scared. Of course he was. Even now, with all that has happened, the idea seems so idealistic that only a science-fiction-obsessed child could conjure it without embarrassment.

So he will grant her one accolade: she helped him set the idea free and give it life. That's no small honour. He'd perhaps needed permission to talk to people about it. Imagination is fettered until given a voice. Arrina gave him that. But that is all she did. No more.

Although it was state-funded, very few people in government knew of the Facility's existence. However, old secrets are the hardest to protect, and the Facility had been in operation since the end of the First World War. So there were rumours and legends. During times of conflict, potential or realised, Whitehall spoke in hushed tones of an underground labyrinth somewhere outside of London, perhaps in the north, where the nation's sharpest minds in lethal technology stalked dimly lit tunnels that opened out into gleaming, futuristic laboratories where they invented innovative ways to murder foreigners. The story helped civil servants and politicians sleep better at night, happy in the belief that the country's fate rested with safe and deadly hands.

Savvy government employees knew to leave rumours as rumours, legends as legends. Sticking your nose where it wasn't welcome meant greasing the career ladder with your nasal mucus, ensuring a rapid descent. And even when the occasional misguided or ambitious accountant discarded the unspoken advice and tried to learn more about the fabled grotto, they struggled. As well as being hidden beneath the ground at an unknown location, it lay buried under a mountain of pseudonyms, creative bookkeeping, and other general administrative subterfuge.

On paper, Atlas was employed by a subsidiary of the maintenance arm of the Ministry of Defence. His payslip stated he held the position of senior engineer. His contract and the official secrets act forbade him from disclosing the truth to anyone. (For the most part, he obeyed. But insecurity and alcohol played a role in him telling Bute and K about the Facility on more than one occasion.) Officially, a little over eight hundred employees worked for the FMO, the MoD's facilities management operation: building managers and security supervisors, buyers, stock controllers, etcetera, which made the Facility a poor career move for scientists suffering from status anxiety. If you wanted to boast about your new research job, you went elsewhere. The Facility was for those who cared only about the science. The nerds. Obsessives and fanatics. The neurodivergents prepared to exchange badges of honour for the chance to reach towards the future, grab it by its ankles and pull it closer. These people could be counted on. They buckled down and did the work, happy to pretend to their friends and family up on the surface that their scientific ambitions were a thing of the past and that their passions now lay in health and safety, repairs, catering and cleanliness.

While the Facility was adept at keeping itself secret, it was impossible to keep one within it. Internal gossip and rumours spread like a lab-made virus. Atlas gave no announcement to his team about expanding the scope of the project. Arguably, it didn't qualify as news. The tasks they'd already embarked on would remain the primary focus. Full Extraction, as he'd begun to call it, was a new side programme led by Arrina and supported by her two colleagues. Just an area of research that warranted some scrutiny. No big deal. Because big deals were at risk of being seen as changes in direction by the higher-ups. Autonomous rewriting of objectives was not a good look. However, thinking through possible applications while working on an exploration project showed initiative and a willingness to make an impact. And it was customary to present these to the Board alongside the main findings of the authorised work at funding reviews. Appendix fodder. Starters for ten. Jumping-off points for whoever took over when the exploratory activity concluded. Disappointingly for Atlas, downplaying the minor restructuring did not deflect attention. One week after extending the project, Bart Noble, the closest thing Atlas had to a friend at the Facility, stopped him on his way to lunch.

I hear you're going to put us all out of business.

Atlas studied the man's sneer.

I'm sure there'll always be a—a market—for expensive explosives.

Minutes later, as he queued in the canteen, a junior researcher ahead of Atlas asked him if there were any vacancies on the team. Atlas looked first at the man and then at the busy seating area. Heads turned away. He growled an incomplete insult and marched back to the lab to have a stern word about discretion.

—————

When Atlas stares at his face in the mirror for long enough, there comes a point when he no longer recognises himself. He knows his reflected self is a version of him but it hasn't looked like him for a while now. The most obvious difference is its smile.

Smiling makes him feel foolish. Smiles tell people a man is malleable, that he lacks the grit to see things through. Reflected Atlas smiles continually. Atlas knows this is an attempt to cheer him up, to motivate him, to keep him from standing too close to the edge of the abyss, but it's beginning to grate.

Atlas is confident that Nathanial Castleport's scowling countenance never once broke into a grin. There's power in that kind of control. Unsmiling men get on in life. Nobody takes them for pushovers. Serious men with serious plans do not smile. Not genuine smiles, anyway. Cruel smiles, they're okay. Dismissive smiles, too, the brief ones that only move your mouth while your eyes remain cold.

Arrina told him to smile more, to be friendlier to his staff. Let them know you're on their side, she said. And, of course, her words penetrated. It was back then when the chatter about the project's new-direction-that-wasn't-a-new-direction ramped up to an unstoppable momentum. The team was going through its first E-Days experience, which Atlas knew wouldn't last. He needed to channel their energy into the work. Arrina suggested he modify his behaviour and show people they were important to him. He tried. He coughed up platitudes as if they were fur balls whenever one of them wobbled, worked at speaking to them as equals, asked for their opinions, and discussed non-project subjects like their health, the weather, and anything else he could think of. It was too late for name badges so Arrina created a spreadsheet with names next to a brief description of their owners. He'd wander through the lab, throwing out a "Good work, Tina" here and a "How are you today, Mark?" there. And he would smile.

Her plan was a success, he concedes that much. Arrina's strategy made them happy, and they worked harder. Before long they were building each other up, congratulating one another, high-fiving and backslapping like they'd already won. The place was electric, and their zeal, he sees now, was a supercharged external factor.

Atlas moved more people to Full Extraction and the pace of work picked up. They based the machine on his rough prototype. He supervised the design and development of a suitable pump and closed conduit that could transport the Particle into the storage chamber. The concern was leakage. It was imperative that once the Particle entered the extraction area, it had nowhere to go other than into storage. The process had to be frictionless and airtight. While the team concentrated on the pumping elements, Atlas drew up some ideas for containment. His calculations showed there were approximately 43,000 cubic metres of Particle, an almost inconceivably small quantity when held up against the five and a half quadrillion tonnes of atmosphere around the earth. If the Particle was evenly dispersed, its presence wouldn't be an issue as it would be too weak at any one location to have an effect. But the updated Project Lung research proved the existence of Particle concentrations in specific geographies, or Fear Zones, as they'd taken to calling them. Atlas still didn't know the exact quantities required to turn these areas into autonomous slaughterhouses but he'd get to the finer details later. His initial sketches were of a graphene-lined steel tank capable of holding 50,000 m3, to be buried in a country with a low natural disaster threat. Uruguay and Poland were high on his list. Extraction would have to happen at the storage site as transporting the trapped Particle was out of the question.

Atlas's aching grin played no small part in persuading his team to accredit their new sense of belonging and wellbeing to him. Thanks to Arrina's intervention, he had their trust and deemed it safe to bring up the subject of insurance. It was a little thing, a niggle he had, that this was a project that might need an extra layer of protection. It was just in his head, a case of mild paranoia, he was pretty sure, but this irrational voice was loud enough for him to pay it some attention.

He leaned on the frame of his office door and beckoned them. It took a few minutes before he had them all assembled and silent before him.

You're well on your way—to altering the course of history—and your careers. So this work we're doing—it has to be safeguarded.

They looked pleased to be hearing this.

What I mean is—we have to be careful. Because sometimes projects can—go wrong. For all kinds of reasons. And we have to be prepared for that—to happen—to us.

The tall blond man, who the spreadsheet had identified as Cory, raised his hand.

What might happen?

Nothing—nothing—I'm sure of that. But it pays to be prudent—don't you think? To ensure we're one step ahead—just in case. But what I'm about to ask of you may seem—a little—illicit. And it is—a bit. But you're not to worry about it—it happens all the time—other teams are always doing it—it's normal. But also forbidden—very.

This insurance would protect their project, he said, and their futures. They would build a clone of the new machine. Every component would be made twice, and the copies smuggled out of the Facility and stored at a safe, undisclosed location. And they would do it all in secret. But this would not be like an ordinary Facility secret. This one had to be kept from anyone outside of the immediate team. If it leaked, they'd all be finished. And with the most natural smile he could muster, he explained if any of them were uncomfortable with the plan, he would understand, and they would attempt to complete the project without a safeguard and hope for the best.

She's almost gone now. Her face and her voice are being pulled out to sea by the retreating tide. Other memories are washing in, cleaning away the remaining traces of her. Here comes a description, Times New Roman, the words Male, Short, Broad, Redhead on a spreadsheet. Atlas recalls the list of features but not the name of the man they belonged to. He did know it for a while, he's pretty sure. He can feel the shape of it in his mouth. He remembers calling it out in surprise when this Male, Short, Broad, Redhead, this MSBR, impressed him with his fake invention. It's the initiative that Atlas recollects. Such enterprise from this fledgeling who'd said nothing for days while everyone else in the lab discussed ways to acquire the necessary materials to build the ghost. That's what it was called, the cloning of the machine. Ghosting was treason. There were stories of senior researchers hoarding weaponry parts, assembling them elsewhere, and attempting to sell them on for their own gain, being caught and never seen again. Atlas and his underlings had to gather all the elements they needed without raising suspicion. It was too dangerous to attempt via the black market. They had to be cleverer than that. Then this spreadsheet description of a person cleared his throat and announced he had an idea. He named it the Bliss Gun, a fictitious project that would explore the development of a device that could destroy the dopamine and serotonin transmitters of enemy combatants, resulting in mass depression on the battlefield. MSBR planned to submit it for approval, with himself as project leader. If it worked, the non-fictitious team could get hold of everything it required for the ghost's construction. If it failed, MSBR would take the flack.

The young scientist scratched a pen over the various forms, submitted the project for approval and waited for the rusty cogs of the Facility's bureaucratic engine to process the request. Atlas should have stopped it. A better man would've done. He was convinced that all the researcher would succeed in doing was getting himself arrested. But, a week later, permission arrived and the Bliss Gun was in business. More form-filling followed, and parts for the ghost machine were soon being stockpiled in one corner of the lab.

What the hell was his name? Atlas can picture him perfectly, that ugly mouth of his beaming through his badly cut orange beard. He can hear the man telling him he ought to buy a van to move the parts to wherever he planned to store them but that he should first drive it to the Facility each morning for a few weeks to negate any potential suspicion. And he did. He bought a Ford pickup with a jammed CD player. Its heft suited neither Atlas nor the quiet suburban street on which he lived. He was too flimsy for the vehicle. The driver's seat did its best to make him unwelcome, the steering wheel sneered at him, the pedals fought against his legs. Scientists choose small, innocuous cars, preferring their work to speak for them, not their earthly possessions. So, inevitably, the new monstrosity attracted attention in the car park at the Facility's main Castleport entrance.

Predictably, Noble was one of the first to mention it.

New wheels, Atlas. Did you get a pay rise?

Home renovations. A bit of—a project. Getting my hands dirty—all of that. Temporary solution, though—hate the thing.

For three months, he parked it in a camera blind spot identified by MSBR. By then, the wheeled goliath was a regular fixture and the guards at the entrance had stopped checking Atlas's identification as he came and went. But they waited a little longer and a little longer again before daring to move the first sections of the ghost machine.

Atlas congratulates himself for getting through an entire portion of his story without her, even though, in reality, she'd been present the whole time. This proves it can be done.

However, the next section is more problematic because she was the only other person to play a part in it. He had needed help to unload the pickup at the other end and carry the parts to his hiding place, but no, it didn't have to be her. There were stronger team members who were better built for that kind of labour. One or two of them actually offered to join him. Obviously, he should have accepted. But by then, even before he'd asked her to come instead, he was already playing around with this idiotic delusion, pretending that she and he were a couple. It was his way of diverting his attention away from a fear of being caught with the cloned equipment. A distraction technique of sorts. Or, at least, that is what he told himself. And if he allowed the fantasy to project a present in which she adored him, eagerly slept with him, listened intently to his ideas and opinions, supported his decisions, and, maybe, occasionally cooked for him, it was only a form of method acting. Just a harmless exercise to keep his nerves at bay. So, he couldn't take anybody else with him but her.

He should erase her. That's the best thing to do. He could have transported the ghost machine sections by himself. It would have been difficult but possible. Or the story could be that once every week Atlas and, let's call them Tim, he's pretty sure there was a Tim on the team. Okay, let's try that again. Once a week, Tim and he took the pickup to the south end of the narrow alley behind the row of houses where Atlas lived. They each collapsed their respective wing mirrors so the vehicle could be coaxed between the tall garden walls that undulated like wet cardboard. He stopped the truck, aligning the passenger door with the recess that held the peeling wooden entrance to his backyard. Tim exited and squeezed between the side of the pickup and the wall until he reached the tailgate. Atlas followed, taking care not to impale himself on the gearstick as he climbed from the driver's seat. Once they had emptied the truck, Atlas clambered back in, drove it out of the alley, and parked on the street. By the time he'd unlocked the front door, walked through the property, into the garden, and opened the old door to the alley, Tim had arranged the parts in order of size. After they'd carried everything into the garden, Atlas instructed Tim to wait in the house. Then he opened the panic room in his garden lab and brought the materials inside.

But here is where the substitution comes undone. Because Atlas did not linger in the panic room thinking about Tim waiting for him. Nor was it Tim's body he imagined pressed into his sofa, or Tim's hands touching the books on the shelves, or his eyes taking in the place, assessing Atlas. And it wasn't Tim who sometimes agreed to a glass of wine and a chat about work, was it? No, it wasn't. Atlas did not cook for this man or watch him eat while describing how the world might look after extraction. And Tim was not the person who waited until after six drop-offs before asking Atlas why he didn't want help storing the parts inside the garden lab. And when Atlas answered that it was complicated, that it was a mess in there, it was not Tim who pointed at Atlas's forehead and said in that voice, *that's where the real mess is*. And Tim didn't laugh like an explosion of butterflies, like an old sash window opening on a dusty bedroom. And whoever this Tim is, that was not who Atlas went to kiss without thinking, and the face that grew closer, the mouth that closed when the laughing stopped, and the soft lips that didn't pull away did not belong to a man called Tim.

They belonged to her.

ARRINA

Dr Brown had the body of an old man emerging through the skin of a younger one, hints of his future physicality appearing in the lines of his neck, in the scratches of white hair, in the slight sagging of his chest and belly. On the turn. Mid to late autumn, she thought.

Inside the Facility, he was in control, the adult in the room. But outside, he presented a different persona. Nervous, always on the verge of tripping over his feet and smashing his face, apparently incapable of making a decision or taking action. He would babble in the truck on the way to his house, stall the vehicle at traffic lights, and hurt himself as he tried to carry parts that really needed two people to move safely. But despite this chaos, she knew what he wanted. So she kissed him.

It was a hurried affair, as if he feared her changing her mind. Naked in less than a minute, falling onto his living room couch, him on top of her, then her on top of him. Ungainly, like a poorly fitting shirt.

While he slept, she toured his house. She touched the art, moved the markers in the books on his bedside table, squeezed half a bottle of shower gel down the sink, folded over the corners of a few magazine pages, pushed a fingernail through the leaf of a cheese plant, plunged licked fingers into a box of granola, turned up the temperature of his refrigerator, and put some random pieces of cutlery in the recycling bin.

When she returned to the living room, he was still sleeping. She dressed quietly and left.

It became a habit. Not entirely unpleasant but not altogether necessary. Dr Brown expected her to be the one who accompanied him and helped carry parts from the pickup. He expected her to put her arms around his shoulders when he held her by her waist, to kiss him back when he pushed his face into hers, to take off her clothes as he removed his.

In those conversations afterwards, Dr Brown (call me Atlas) asked about her life before, as if this, whatever *this* was, marked a new time. It seemed to her that in these question-and-answer sessions, which circled around past lovers, he was searching for something to hook on to or a place he could occupy.

Arrina thought of the interior of her head as sacred ground. Just because she accepted where the universe sent her did not mean she had to open up her inner life to whoever happened to knock. Nothing was written that said she could not protect herself. At university she watched people turn themselves inside out over and over until she could no longer recognise them in the black hole gravity of their love dramas. Their work suffered. One or two abandoned their studies altogether, unable to exist in the same institution or city as their counterparts. An undergraduate she'd known attempted suicide because a woman he'd slept with once refused to speak to him afterwards.

The trick, she reasoned, was to decline entry. No matter how badly they wanted in. They needed you to need them, to depend on them for your sanity, to give away all sense of a free and autonomous you in exchange for emotional addiction. Their willingness to box up their dignity and self-esteem and hand it to you was supposed to be enough reason for you to do the same. She found it easy to sidestep the offerings. Just as she could refuse to be scared by a horror movie by keeping in mind that nothing she saw was real, only actors and special effects and someone's ideas of what she should find frightening, she evaded falling for people by being mindful of the chemical reactions in the brain that caused individuals to make false associations between those they've slept with and their future happiness.

Dr Brown talked a good game. His disastrous marriage, how he would never live life that way again, that his work gave him all the love he needed. But he spoke about it too much. Like an ex-addict making noise to drown out a hunger that never relents. Whether or not she liked it, he'd already let her in. So that's where her insurgency began.

(*I can tell you about my sex life. I've never had a love life.*)

She surprised herself with how easily she invented the cast of men and women. One after the other, they sprang to being on her tongue. Names, hair colour, ages, likes, dislikes. She told him she never thought of them like that, as lovers. She hadn't loved them. Hadn't made love to them. And they didn't, as far as she ever noticed, love her. Two or three might have been briefly and unhealthily obsessed, but there was no love. No feelings of tenderness moved between any of them and her. They were fucks. She was a fuck. They fucked, and that was all.

He winced but pushed for details as if rubbing his palms in broken glass would toughen the skin. He laid next to her, the sides of their hips and legs pressed against each other, and she fabricated funny stories, weird requests, awkward situations, and unusual locations, and he laughed like a coughing dog in the right places. Her torture victim begged for more. Every act, the highs and lows, the ins and outs.

She invented an older man (*no, not as old as you*) who used to take her to expensive hotels (*his name was Frank if you have to know*) and treated her as if she were a queen. He had her try food she had never heard of, wines and champagnes that cost the earth, and presented her with beautiful jewellery and clothes. He'd pull out her chair for her, stand whenever she rose from the table, hold doors for her. No man had behaved towards her like this before. Then they'd return to the hotel room and everything would change. The flick of a switch. He would speak to her as if she were nothing, tell her she was shit on his shoe. In bed, he threw her around like a rag, her face pressed against walls, against carpet, arms up behind her back. Forced his way in. Stretched her mouth. He ordered room service and invited the staff at the door to join them. Sometimes they agreed, and he commanded her to open her legs for them, called her a whore, and masturbated. Then, in the morning, it was as if the previous night hadn't happened. Once again, she was the most precious creature ever to have walked the planet. They breakfasted together and his driver returned her to the student halls.

Dr Brown watched her as if she were a screen. No acknowledgement, not even a wince as she planted seed after seed, sentence by sentence, each genetically modified to proliferate, nourished by his insecurities, that would later push their gnarled branches into his imagination as he lay alone in bed. Arrina occasionally wondered why she was compelled to hurt him but always concluded that this battle was neither her doing nor her responsibility. The universe was acting through her, and who was she to question it. This, like everything she did, was inevitable.

THE MEETING

Two middle-aged white males approach one another, right hands outstretched. Both men are smiling in quite different ways. They've never met before.

The shorter of the pair, overweight, unruly grey plumes quivering from the sides of his head, and a tight three-piece tartan suit, has been alone in this wood-panelled room for an hour planning the discussion he is about to have. Now that he has settled on a strategy, he's feeling confident. It's essential that this meeting goes well because, as with all encounters during the initial months of a new appointment, a good result will set the tone for his leadership. He is determined to be perceived as fair but firm. Luckily, the person he is meeting is already indebted to him, so he should be malleable enough. However, because the man is known to suffer from mental illness, and as he is unused to dealing with people like that, a certain undercurrent of unpredictability is pulling at the foundations of his certainty.

The other middle-aged white male, cropped charcoal hair, tall and thin, in a black suit, circular spectacles perched precariously low on his nose, and a fresh scar on his forehead, has just entered the room. Before going through the door, he was nervously optimistic. However, something is amiss. There should be a full committee, primed to interview him, but Moss is the only other person here. The charcoal-haired man tries his best not to look alarmed. As far as he's concerned, this session is supposed to be about funding. This is all wrong. It must have to do with him overstepping his project's framework. Ideally, he wouldn't have alluded to the transgression in his report at all, but the rumours about what they'd been up to had become so prolific he felt he had no choice but to include the information. He had written about it as if it had always been a part of the primary focus of the research. But now, seeing that the meeting is not what he expected, his legs weaken as he shakes his superior's hand.

Atlas, Atlas, come in, come in. So good to finally meet you. How the devil are you? Thank you for coming. Take a seat. Coffee? Tea?

No—thank you, General—I'm fine.

Something stronger?

Thank you—no—too early for me.

Please, sit. Are you sure? You had breakfast?

Yes, sir. I had a—had a bite on the way here.

Splendid. Then, let's get to business.

Will anybody else be—joining us?

No, just you and me today. Excellent. Well, then. Difficult to know where to start, if I'm to be honest. So, I'll jump straight in if that's alright with you.

By all means.

Right then, here we are. So, Atlas, as you might be aware, part of my job is to assess projects for secondary funding. I've been looking through my predecessor's files, and it seems that most applications have been relatively straightforward, making it easy to decide which should get the money and which shouldn't. Needless to say, the majority don't.

Yes, sir. I've been in—the latter camp—a few times.

From what I can tell, everyone here has. The important thing is not to take things like that personally. Very few get through and that won't change under my custodianship. It's not that I wouldn't like to approve them all. Well, not all of them. From what I've read, some of them are a little, how should I say, well, they're a tad fanciful. That's not a comment on your work, of course. But, unfortunately, there's a budget to adhere to and we must make decisions based on potential returns. To be honest with you, this is very much like running a business.

Yes, sir.

An obscene amount of work goes into these projects before they reach my desk. I appreciate that. But money is money and all of that. We only have so much, and I have to ensure we spend it wisely. Are you sure I can't interest you in a coffee?

No sir—I mean—yes, I'm sure.

You won't mind if I do? Early start today. Sarah, bring me coffee, please. No, he doesn't want one. Thank you. Actually, I'll have one of my special coffees. Anyway, Atlas, this is beginning to sound all very negative, which isn't my intention. Thing is, once in a while, a project comes along that really stands out. Like this one you're working on, the, the hate, what are you calling it again?

The Hate Extractor, sir.

Ah, yes. Hate Extractor. Fascinating. A good name, which always helps. You know, to grab one's attention. How long has it been in development?

Six years—on and off. Took a while to gather the—evidence. I wanted to make sure—I could present a sound case. Plus, I would've reached this stage sooner, but a few other—things— required my attention—I've been doing a lot of the work in my own time.

Bloody marvellous. That's what I like to hear! A true profes- sional. Old school dedication. I admire your diligence, Atlas. A project like this could quickly have been filed under 'fanciful' if it wasn't for all the work you've put in. If everyone took the same care, our job here would be a hell of a lot easier. Or harder, if you get what I mean. You should see some of the proposals that come through here. Some of them are dazzlingly amateurish. Anyway, enough about them. A new era and all of that. So, back to the here and now. You know, Atlas, it's all about teamwork, don't you think?

Yes, sir.

Glad you agree. The thing is, the projects that are approved for secondary funding rarely get through without a tweak or two. Actually, can't remember reading about a single one that has. They always need just a bit of, how should I say, channelling. Yes, a slight shift in direction. Only to make them economically viable, you understand. Yours has already changed course, am I right? You started out on a discovery project and then expanded your remit?

We—we became interested in possible—applications.

A good call, Atlas. I mean, entirely against the rules, which you know. A big gamble that paid off. So, what do you intend to do with the funding?

The silver-winged man has been looking forward to this moment. This 'slight shift in direction' is grossly irresponsible and would be penalised under normal circumstances. Indeed, his predecessor would have come down hard on a misdemeanour like that. The scientist not only knows this, he's been nervously waiting for some kind of reprimand. Watching him subtly squirming in his chair while bracing himself for the hammer blow was entertaining but not quite as satisfying as the relief that's dancing like drunken horses over his face right now. And in a few seconds, the scientist will relax and lower his defences, and he'll be exactly where he needs him to be.

The man with the cropped charcoal hair is doing everything he can to control his reaction. It's as if a mild electric current is rushing from his feet to his head. He wants to stand up, raise his arms, perhaps even jump up and down because he feels this energy in every part of his body. This must be it. He is finally getting through to them. After all this time, they hear him. They understand him. They recognise him for what he is and they actually like it. Thirty years and here he is. But right now he has to gather himself. Whatever it takes, he has to remain professional.

Ah—I thought—well, we've—er—we've—taken the prototyping as far—far enough. So—we'll build the final version. When completed, the machine will be sufficiently robust to—to pull the Particle out of the atmosphere—and pump it into the storage vessel—that still needs designing—I have some ideas I'd like to explore. And after that—we need to work out how to destroy the trapped Particle. But that's for later.

Very good. And this Particle, remind me, how did you discover it?

Through Project Lung—before your time—didn't amount to much—air monitoring tests in conflict zones. After we'd abandoned it, I went back to—found a gap in the data—something the monitors weren't picking up—it couldn't just be empty space —and—eventually—I worked out what it was—the Particle.

Ah, the curious mind. Splendid. Others would've given up and moved on to the next thing. But there you were, squirrelling away, acting on a hunch I dare say. Like a, what's it, like a scientific detective! Looking for the missing victim, as it were. A credit to the Facility.

Thank you, sir.

I'm serious, Atlas. Tell me about this gas you found. I understand its potential, but not the thing itself.

A particle—that's what it is—not a gas. It's quite simple. Let me—if you don't mind—I'll start by asking you a question. Do you know—what hate is?

I beg your pardon?

Please—humour me.

Oh. Well, hate is, well, hate is just hate. A strong and rather negative emotion. The polar opposite of love, I suppose. There's bound to be a more scientific way to explain it. I am more of a soldier-politician than a psychologist. To someone like me, it's the thing that starts wars. Fuels the madmen. That kind of thing.

And—where does hate come from?

Is this really necessary, Atlas? Very well. As I said a moment ago, it's an emotion. It comes from the mind.

Which is what everybody says. But what if—instead—it was more like—an infection? In French there's the phrase—*j'ai la haine*—I have hate. *Avoir la haine*, to have hate—something we possess rather than—than—something we do. Something we contract—like a disease. Thinking in those terms—hate has nothing to do with love—not opposites. It kind of makes sense that they should be but—but they're not connected. If they were opposites we couldn't experience them simultaneously. But the thing you said—that it—fuels madmen—I agree with that. But what if it was like a microbe—always in the air—always present but in—in higher concentrations in some places than others? And—what if we only found higher—higher concentrations of it near people experiencing—intense fear?

Which is what you've discovered to be the case.

Our tests show that when subjects in—stressful environments —are—exposed to above-average concentrations of Particle they —become—hostile and violent. We also tested Particle-free environments—exposed subjects to increasing degrees of antagonising behaviour—emotional irritants.

And?

Nothing—one hundred percent described states of euphoria —happiness.

There's a rather woolly section in your paper. Something about this explaining various atrocities? It seems a little farfetched, no?

That—that's the direction of the evidence—acts of barbarity —restricted to war zones—almost always. Or—we believe— where large numbers of people are—afraid.

It seems that the fear of unrest—or violence—attracts the Particle which—as I said—promotes hostility and violence, which—in turn—creates more fear, which attracts more Particle, which attracts—well—you get the picture—the best example of a —a vicious circle—I've come across. But so far—we have only found high concentrations of Particle in conflict-intense geographies—which is where we've been measuring it.

You've looked elsewhere, I take it?

Not enough—we'd like to do more tests—but so far—we've only found a trace present in peaceful territories—up to now.

And so, thanks to your slightly unorthodox change in direction, rather than simply identifying and defining the Particle, you want to remove it from the atmosphere? And then I suppose all these people fighting in wars and whatnot are just going to drop their weapons, give each other a hug, and go home?

Well, yes—

And this agent, there's a mention of it but no details.

Yes—that's a mistake—there should be a page in the report that—please forgive me—I will rectify immediately—it's a pretty basic compound—sorry—I'll get the information to you later today.

A woman enters the room without knocking. The men fall silent. She is carrying a tray with a white mug, steam billowing like a tiny locomotive, and a small plate of biscuits. As they wait for her to serve, the silver-winged man reflects on the change in the room's atmosphere since the conversation began. He fancies himself an expert on such matters. He likes to observe the flow of communication between individuals and how mood, tone, and syntax alter as discussions move through the various stages of negotiations. He is particularly interested in his own behaviour in these circumstances. So much about this man irritates him. His speech, the way he seems incapable of allowing a single sentence to escape his mouth before doubting his own words, is infuriating. And his questions about hate, well, they were bordering on impertinent. It's no surprise that he feels increasingly hostile towards him. Not that the scientist will have noticed. He appears oblivious to anything other than his own story. The problem is, it would be helpful to introduce a little trucu-lence about now to unsettle the man, but it has to be on his own terms. He cannot be seen to be getting riled. Certainly not in an important meeting like this. The silver-winged man takes a slow breath and reassures himself that everything will be okay. He can relax. It doesn't really matter how this conversation goes, as it won't make a blind bit of difference to the outcome. There is only one end to this.

Meanwhile, the man with the cropped charcoal hair perceives different changes. The most obvious is the thick smell of the coffee and whiskey oozing from the cup that's just been placed on the desk. The other is his own revitalised optimism. The upset he experienced previously has evaporated, and so has his earlier flurry of relief. He is on an even keel now and is confident the Facility has seen the potential of his project. He is keen to continue with his explanations as soon as the woman has left the room. As she turns to go, he notes that the other man does not attempt to disguise his gaze, which follows her rear until she closes the door.

So you were telling me you've developed a machine that can end all war. That's basically what you're saying, isn't it?

It sounds very—grand when you—put it like that. But—yes.

Thank you for answering my questions, Atlas. I needed to ensure we understood your paper as you intended.

It's my—pleasure.

Do you know how much the UK government spends on defence annually?

Not—precisely. Quite a few billion—probably?

A little over sixty billion pounds. Small fry compared to the Americans. They're in the region of six hundred billion. China spends around one hundred and thirty billion. Then there're the Saudis and the Russians, who spend about eighty billion each.

That is—a lot of money.

Indeed. Globally, the amount is approaching two trillion. That's dollars, but it's still rather large.

Imagine—if we didn't need to—you know—spend all that money on weapons.

Exactly. We've been pondering that very subject since your research came to light.

The impact we could make—on poverty—and disease—or climate change—if the money could be used for good.

Absolutely agree.

And we would have world peace—in—in our lifetime.

We would. If your research is accurate, that's precisely what we'd have. No more war and no reason to spend so much on defence. World peace, as you say. And therein lies the problem.

The—problem?

Yes, the problem. You see, Atlas, war, or at the very least the threat of it, it's what you might describe as a bit of a going concern.

I don't—

How can I put it? The money we've been talking about, thousands of billions of dollars, it's a vast amount. You can't just take that out of the global economy.

I'm not sure I—

Look at it this way. Say the MOD stopped funding research. What would happen?

I'd—be—out of a job—I suppose.

You would. And so would thousands of other people. Not just scientists and researchers and such likes but an entire ecosystem of professionals and businesses, you know, manufacturers, dealers, and the like, all of it would suddenly be redundant.

—I'm—not—

These organisations would simply fail. Overnight, countless people, from CEOs to factory floor workers, would be out of work with no means to pay their bills and mortgages.

Maybe, though—a price worth paying—for the benefits.

I know several experts who would be happy to debate that with you. You see, we're not just talking about this country, are we? What we'd be doing by creating total peace is making millions of people around the world unemployed. Pension funds would disappear in a puff of smoke. Economies would collapse. Is it starting to sink in, Atlas?

So—

Atlas, if your machine can indeed achieve everything you hope it might, it will cause an international catastrophe.

But—

What I am saying is that we have to be economically realistic.

Realistic?

Total peace is a threat to global stability.

I don't—with all due—respect—you're missing the bigger picture. We're talking about—ending—ending all conflicts around—the power to stop people from massacring each—

On the contrary, I fully understand. And the world cannot afford, literally cannot afford, for that to happen. And I certainly can't sanction funding something that would lead to a world-wide financial meltdown. Think of the misery that would cause. People everywhere starving. Riots in the streets. Total mayhem, Atlas.

That's completely—

Atlas, enough. I can't give your project the green light as it stands right now. I understand this isn't what you want to hear, but there are lots of influential people who have a lot invested in, in, well, in defence.

Invested in war—that's what you were about to say—isn't it?

These things are bigger than you and me.

So—that's it—is it? We have a chance to—to end all that suffering and—and you're shelving it for—for profit?

· · ·

And there it is, another change. The silver-winged man sips at the cup and enjoys four or five seconds of the new dynamic. If he'd been so inclined, he could have used empathy as he changed the scientist's project. But where's the fun in that? And soon, when he puts his coffee down, he will shift the trajectory again. If the researcher is disappointed now, wait until he gets a taste of this.

The man with the cropped charcoal hair stares into the corner of the room at the ancient hatstand and the coat that's been hanging there since his first review some fifteen years ago when his funding application was declined by a different director and a full committee. But the garment doesn't register. He is only aware of his organs turning in on themselves. He has to bring this conversation back on course. This meeting has to conclude with the project being funded. The best way to do this is through dialogue. He understands this. But what he wants to do right now is stand up and shout at the stupid, greedy little man sipping on his hot morning whisky.

There's no need to be so dramatic, Atlas.

Dramatic? I can't believe—we have the opportunity—we can change the world! And all you want—

And we still can, Atlas. But in a slightly different way.

Different how?

Your project will get funding, but not in its present form.

But you just said—you mean—we can carry on?

Yes.

Oh—but—I see—I—thought—I must have misunderstood—sorry, I—

No need. I like your passion.

Right.

Your proposal is to create a machine that will rid the entire world of war or, to put it more precisely, eradicate our desire to fight one another, yes?

Yes.

The Facility thinks this is an excellent idea. But we have to do it in a way that protects our economic interests.

I see—so—

It's all about strategy, but you don't have to worry about the details. We'll deal with all the hows and whens, but right now we need you to, well, reimagine implementation. And that will have an impact on your research.

How should I—reimagine it how?

Before I tell you that, I want you to know that, in my opinion, you are the best person to lead this project.

I'm sorry—what?

Well, some people here say you're a little too, how should I say, that you are too idealistic. They think of you as one of those fanciful scientists we discussed earlier.

I don't—follow.

Alright then, bluntly, I had to fight to keep you on this project. Atlas, there are people, some of whom are far more influential than me, who want to hand it to someone they can trust to deliver the desired outcome. Dr Noble's name has been mentioned. You know him, I think. But I've given my professional guarantee you are indeed the best man for the job. In other words, I have put my career on the line for you, Atlas, and I don't expect you to disappoint me.

I know him—thank you—I won't.

I'm sure you won't.

So—the project—you said something about—reimagining?

Right, well, yes, the implementation has to change. Rather than removing the Particle from the atmosphere wholesale, you'll explore how to extract it on a more bespoke basis. We've concluded that the only way we can avoid economic disaster is if, at the end of the extraction process, we leave the world with a single political entity that has the experience and deftness to assert the appropriate control on the international markets.

Some sort of—global government?

In a manner of speaking. It's contentious, but the idea has a lot to be said for it. Some of our best thinkers claim it is our last chance to move forward as a species. And when you think about it, that makes perfect sense. I mean, we've already proven we can't solve global problems in our current situation. Like the climate crisis. There is no point in addressing that at a national level. It has to be tackled internationally. Otherwise, we're done for. Then there's cyber security, money laundering, economic migration, huge issues that don't recognise borders. Borders only hinder solutions. So, yes, a world government. In a roundabout way.

In—what sense?

Well, it's a complex and emotional thing, really. Ideally, you'd have all the nations happy to hand over their jurisdiction to a higher level of authority that operates federally. But there's no chance that countries like the United States or China will cede power. Not only them. Sovereignty, national identity and all of that twaddle. It all gets in the way. Nobody's going to just give it up. So, 'roundabout' in a sort of Her Majesty's Government controlling everything sense.

I think—I think I'm missing something.

You're not.

I—I really don't think—I'm—.

Come on, Atlas. Keep up. You are to develop a way to weaken certain nation-states so we can take control of them one by one. You will work out a method of extracting the Particle from specific geographies to render local armed forces ineffectual while not impeding the activities of our troops.

You want me to—weaponise the Hate Extractor?

Don't be so negative, Atlas. We are eradicating war. But we're doing it in such a way that we preserve the structures that make us all safe and secure.

Controlled by Westminster?

To some extent. Some private interests too, of course.

I—don't know what to—say.

Thank you, perhaps? Agree to this slight change in direction and everything will be just tickety-boo.

That's not—I mean—shouldn't—wouldn't it be better if—maybe the United Nations or someone does it?

It most certainly would not. The UN would make a dog's dinner out of it. Look, our preliminary plan sees us occupying the major powers over a fourteen-month period once your work is completed. Within another year, we should have pretty much everywhere under control. Everywhere that counts, anyway. People will hardly notice what's happening. You still get your peace, and we get a new world order that works in our favour. It's a win-win. All you have to do is ensure your machine is up to it.

No—I'm sorry, General—I don't think—I want to be a part of this.

And I'm sorry too, Atlas, because, well, you have no choice. Unless you'd like me to call in Noble? I can do that. It's not a problem.

No—I don't want that.

Good. You just need a little while to mull it over. Take a few days off. I understand that this will be a shock to the system, but you'll see sense in this approach in time.

General, I—

You have one year to isolate the extraction to specific regions and protect our troops from the effects. We have secured an external site where you'll conduct the research, which we'd like you to have a hand in setting up, and we've started recruiting a more experienced team to work with you. If you need extra resources, just ask. Sarah has a file containing the details, including the geographies we'll be looking at in the first instance. Thank you, Atlas. Close the door on your way out, there's a good man.

PART V

ATLAS

Angela is three days late. It is a pity because he's cleaned the box, in a manner of speaking. If she'd arrived on time, she would've been disappointed. That morning, when Atlas woke and remembered he still hadn't lifted a bony finger and that she could turn up at any moment, he felt a familiar twinge of failure. When she didn't show up, he seized this second chance by the throat. The result is a compromise of sorts. But as long as you don't look at the bed, the mess of his desk, the mirror, or anywhere beyond the sofa really, it's looking pretty good. Even if he says so himself.

Three days is a long time. She has been late before but never like this. There was that once, just after the new border between the compound and wherever it is she lives appeared out of nowhere. Forty-eight hours later, she turned up with supplies and a smile, boasting about how easy it was to find a road that wasn't barricaded. Atlas suspects they've now cordoned off that route and she's still looking for an alternative way through.

Or she's been detained.

Or she's ill.

Or, no, he doesn't need to go there.

It could be anything but Atlas knows he has to be sensible because the chances are that this is nothing serious. She'll turn up in the next ten minutes and they'll laugh about him being on the verge of panic.

Even if she doesn't come until a week on Thursday, that's no big deal. He has enough food to keep him going until then because she always brings too much and he never eats a lot. He has a small wall of canned soups and so on in the mess. If he paces himself, it'll last longer. Twice as long, maybe. He'll be fine. Everything is alright for the moment. For many moments spanning over several weeks. He's also got the medicines she's brought over time. Illness has been kind to him. Lack of human contact has its benefits. So, right now, he just needs to meditate to focus his mind on the present.

Atlas in the mirror nods in agreement.

It's been a while since he last tried meditation. But now is probably a good time.

It is a question of where. Meditating on the edge of the bed will make him want to lie down and sleep. The seat of his desk chair is covered in notes he would rather not disturb. He assesses the room. The sofa presents the same problem as the bed. He could sit on the newly cleaned floor or on the Eames. But they're not quite right either. Perhaps the box itself is the issue. The answer might be a different environment, and he's about to go to one of the other metal boxes when Bute's head appears. It's translucent and impossible, decapitated, floating somewhere in under his upper eyelids.

But her voice is very convincing.

Hello Atlas, I thought you'd be at work.

It's a surprise but he knows why she's here. The last time he saw her was the first time he tried to meditate, three weeks after his meeting with Moss. They were divorced by then, and he lived alone, striking distance from town, far enough away from work to claim travel allowance. Like now, he didn't know where to sit. He was in his house, that little haven he appreciates these days more than he ever did back then, and was about to perch on the wooden stool in his bedroom to test its suitability when the doorbell rang.

From outside, there was little of note about the dwelling. A mid-sized Victorian terraced townhouse on an unremarkable street. To Bute, it would have aligned perfectly with Atlas's general appearance and demeanour: skinny, tall, conservatively dishevelled. When she arrived at his front door, a poorly fitting thing in peeling blue and rust, she would've assembled her assumptions of what would come next, complete with sights and smells. The small tantrum of a garden to her left would not have allayed her concerns.

He did not invite her in.

He hadn't seen her in two years. With the door only half open and his body wrapped in a white kimono blocking her view into the hallway, he listened to her description of the items in the cardboard box at her feet.

Hair tied back especially, the scar dripping down from her hairline, keeping the official grounds for divorce at the forefront of the visit.

I thought you'd be at work.

Then why are you here? was the response Atlas refrained from giving.

This is the last of it. I was going to leave it on the doorstep.

If you find anything else—just—burn it.

Redecorating. Moving on. Thought it was about time. You know?

Don't come here again—please.

Then Atlas took the items and closed the door mid-reply.

He congratulated himself and dropped the box on the hall floor. Back upstairs, he considered the stool again. Then he put the meditation cd into the player and laid on his bed. If he fell asleep, so what. It was better than being conscious.

The inside of Atlas's home was at odds with its outer appearance. Mid-century furnishings, off-white walls, tastefully hung abstract paintings, reclaimed floorboards. A tour would reveal several healthy monsteras and other large plants, shelves lined with colour-coordinated books, occasional piles of interior design magazines, modern fittings, etcetera. Clean lines paired with pops of pigment courtesy of designer lamps, rugs and ceramics. If a visitor were to keep a keen eye out, they might also notice the small cream-coloured boxes a little above head height. Each room had one, sometimes two. Each box contained a single-board computer connected to numerous sensors. Before moving in, he'd had the house wired to within an inch of its life. Wires were fed under floors and through cavities to connect the sensors to a central hub that linked to an app on his tablet with which he monitored the light, temperature and air quality of every corner of his house. So much wiring existed in Atlas's terrace that if the original materials used to construct it were removed—bricks and mortar, window and door frames, plaster-board, sills and joists—the cables would retain the shape of the building, like an illustration of the blood vessel network of a strange-looking animal. Less than a year later, he changed the system to wireless and demoted the cabling to insulation.

Bute had arrived on his doorstep on the day he was due back at work. It was the third delayed start. Atlas hadn't been into the Facility since his supposed funding meeting. Initially, he had thought about returning early to show willing. If he were a political player, that would have been good form. Then he phoned to postpone his return by a week, citing ill health. Six days later he telephoned to do the same once more. Now, lying on his bed, staring at the ceiling, he wished he'd called again yesterday. He still couldn't face it.

Other than the vintage eight-arm chrome pendant light and

the areca palm edging into the lower left of his field of vision, there was nothing else of note to look at from this position, but he was aware of the bedroom and its contents around him. The walnut and brass wardrobe with doors open wide, the matching walnut and brass bedside tables sporting small teal ceramic lamps and various unread books, magazines and papers, the hand-tufted wool rug in ecru and charcoal in need of a vacuum, the pointy yellow Sternzeit chair partially hidden by multiple items of clothing destined for the laundry basket that he kept in the hallway. Radio news leaked in from his neighbour's kitchen. A blackbird repeated itself in a nearby garden. A car squeezed past the parked vehicles lining the narrow road at the front of the house.

He hadn't lied to the Facility. He was ill. It was depressing that he'd needed a GP to inform him of his depression. That shouldn't have been necessary. All the signs were dangling from the roof of his skull.

I.D.I.O.T.

Intranet of Depressing Irrational Ominous Thoughts.

And now another human being knew his weakness.

A mild case, the doctor pointed out. It happens to the best of us, don't be too hard on yourself. We can fix this. Have there been any changes to your lifestyle recently? Any traumatic events? A death in the family or a change at work?

He didn't like the direction of the consultation. Why look for external factors when there was so much evidence inside of him? Why deny himself the satisfaction of taking the blame?

Atlas has never been a quick thinker. While at university, a tutor likened his thoughts to a school of whales, unhurried but substantial, occasionally breaking the surface in a thalassic extravaganza, spouting mild genius over the ocean.

He liked that then. Less so now.

Slow might not be stupid, but slow was to blame. He should have spotted the dark cetaceans earlier than he did. Perhaps they'd been hiding in there somewhere, among their innocuous cousins, skulking towards his cerebrum ever since his meeting with Moss. But he had been too slow to notice, and two days later he realised he'd been lying in bed for what seemed like a week and had no intention of getting out of it again. It was as if the monsters of melancholia had appeared out of nowhere, and now their fat heads were pushing against the inside of his cranium, blocking out the light, bringing with them the full realisation that his work had been turned against him. From behind his eyes they whispered a song to him.

You're a fool, they sang,
You've been an idiot,
Only a moron would think it could've been different,
You may as well die.

He'd wanted pills from the doctor. Tiny depth charges to drop into his puddle of a mind that would blow the blubber to slimy pieces.

You don't want drugs, she said.

I do.

Trust me, you don't. Not yet. It's not that bad yet. You've got a way to sink before you need medication.

Sinking.

She gave him exercises. The address of a mental health website. Told him to take up running again. To lay off the alcohol. And presented him with a meditation cd.

Atlas wanted to feel anger as he hauled himself back to his house, but he was too defeated to conjure anything more than a mild malaise. If his own doctor wouldn't help him, she must have understood he deserved this. Everyone on the planet must've sensed it by then. They'd been failed by a man who couldn't argue the merits of a machine with the potential to alter the course of history and direct it towards a future that might favour them for a change. Instead, he was going to turn it into a weapon. And even if they hadn't known the nature or cause of the defeat, they would have felt its ramifications deep in their guts and in their bones. A species-wide despair was underway. He could smell the disappointment. And the pity he saw in his doctor's eyes wasn't for him. It was for her other patients and her family, for all the people she knew, and for those she had yet to meet. Her eyes said I'm not helping you because you're not helping us. You are doomed because we are. Your life is over because you're wasting your chance to save ours. Your career is finished because the world is fucked.

It took a while before the breathing became easier and the hard edges of chrome light and palm leaves slipped out of focus. As his lungs inflated and deflated, Atlas could feel the rising and falling of his chest, the movement of air in his nostrils, and the pressure from the bed pushing against his buttocks, back, and legs. The rhythmical motion transformed into a gateway through which he began to reach fractional moments on a quiet plain somewhere. No troubles, no strife, just him in the universe. But these slices of nothingness were thin.

The voice on the cd encouraged him to waft away any thoughts of Moss and the project and Bute and Arrina and his GP and all the troubling sounds and images that floated by. You are not your thoughts, it said, your thoughts are not you. Think of them as clouds in your mental sky; simply note them and return to the breath. A light touch, a flick of the wrist is all you need to move them aside.

Meditation. It sometimes seemed like he was taking a feather to a knife fight. Atlas's thoughts weren't clouds. Often they were giant leeches with enormous tusks and claws that dragged themselves over his body and head, slashed their way into his eyes and mouth, and sucked away his ability to function. By flicking his wrist he only produced more of them. So he ad-libbed with an oversized rubber-ended mallet with which he battled them behind closed eyelids. He swung at them for days, smashing them to the floor, mashing and pulverising until, in time, the bloodsuckers weakened and Atlas grew a little stronger.

The thoughts changed, but still they didn't resemble clouds. They became waves. Gnashing waves with jaws and teeth, a storm that thrashed towards him, twisting and frothing, reaching for him, one after another, hellbent on pulling him seawards, rolling him over, dragging him under and chewing him up. They threw themselves at his legs, often falling short, receding with the shsheeewwrrrcchchch, shsheeewwrrrcchchch of saltwater churning sand, only to make way for the next attack. But as ferocious as they seemed, he did not have to fight these thoughts. He could, if he remembered in time, step backwards.

Step away.

And there, shsheeewwrrrcchchch, the wind howls at his ears, pushes him closer to the water while the arms of a clock rise to the heavens, and he is following the instructions uttered by the woman at a desk to go into the room ahead of him. He is surprised by what he finds. Atlas, Atlas, come in, come in. Moss alone behind the long table. He'd expected more people. There were always more people, sitting in a line, watching him enter, and he would nod at the faces he recognised from last time and stumble like a bad clown towards the chair in the middle of the floor. The likes of Dr Simon, the Chief Scientist, Lieutenant-General Bryson, and three or four department heads questioning, listening, and taking notes. A panel of peers and purse-stringers, experts willing to hear his plea. A row of polite inter-rogators. You are invited for "a chat". But don't be fooled; this is no chat. It's a summary execution. A firing squad. A live snuff show. That's how it is supposed to work. You've submitted the research, and you know why you are there. Results reviewed, the impact-investment potentials calculated, advice listened to, and decisions made. Some tough questions, a reminder that your future is, once again, in their hands, a brief explanation of concerns, and then a pre-determined verdict.

Your project dies here.

Nice try, though.

We're sorry.

Better luck next time.

But the whispers had been positive, and while waiting to be called in, he had been sitting outside, sweating his way through a terrible case of optimism. His attempts to self-medicate by silently reciting all the reasons for his previous rejections, from the too expensive and too ambitious to the too niche and too ridiculous, failed to ease his symptoms. But he wasn't cured of hope until he walked into the room and saw only Moss.

Atlas, Atlas, come in, come in. So good to finally meet you. How the devil are you? Thank you for coming.

He looked around, half expecting to find the others lurking in the corner, hiding in the curtains, spying on him, studying his gait, looking for the telltale signs of incompetence.

Please take a seat. Coffee? Tea?

No, thank you—I'm fine.

Something stronger?

Hard surfaces amplified his voice, his head shaking ever so slightly, his neck tensing to stop it.

Please sit so we can get down to the business of destroying your dreams.

Step away.

And also here, shsheeewwrrrcchchch a retreating wave engulfed by its descendent and three imaginary soldiers from the Sudan People's Liberation Movement-in-Opposition emerge from the froth, bent over, hands on knees, catching their breaths, with their eyes on their man, the man they've been chasing through the streets of Bentiu, now cornered where the external walls of two adjoining yards meet at a right angle. It's insane to exert yourself in this heat, to gallop like the gazelle. But there is a glut of madness in this place today, and nobody cares if these men use up more than their fair share. The youngest of the three, little more than a boy, straightens up and shouts at the man. You think you're going to escape us? You think you can trick us? We know who you are, we can smell your Dinka piss from a mile away, stings my nostrils, makes me want to chop you down. And the soldier slashes his machete in the air like he's cutting at his words. The man has nowhere to go. He can barely breathe but his eyeballs have never been more alive, flicking from the space between his captors to their weapons to the walls at either side of him. He is crying and begging them to please don't kill me, please don't kill me, I have children, I have a wife. There is a ledge in the wall behind him and to his left, but one of the soldiers is too close. Could he race at them, rush them, find a gap maybe? The older men are slower. He could run between them but they are all walking towards him now, laughing and shouting, waving their blades and the gaps are shrinking. He turns to the wall and jumps as high as he can, fingernails cracking as he scrapes back to the ground. There is something in the terror on the man's face and his bulbous eyes as he gets to his feet, in his babbling, his juddering body and the way it sways side to side, in how his legs give way as they approach him, his vulnerability, weakness, and helplessness that fills the soldiers with a familiar energy they have no word for. Like a fire. A lust. A power surges from their groins up their backs into their heads and arms, like a thirst of the bones that must be quenched. The youngest always strikes first. The machete cuts through the fingers of a hand that tries to block the blow, and the blade digs deep into the middle trapezius. The man's head lists into the wound, his beige shirt darkens. In a final effort, the man attempts to launch himself at his attackers' legs but only falls at their feet as another blade lands.

Step away.

And again, shsheeewwrrrcchchch as the sand fizzes with saltwater and his guts fizz with jealousy as Arrina in bed talks of old lovers, skimming from one to another with amusement, sexual flaws and specialities, the sex toys they bought her, complaints from the neighbours, being caught with a boy in the hills near her parents' house, what was his name again? the moments and reasons they left, or she left, the strangers, the social media stalkers, the lucky escapes, and he chuckles to cover up the comparisons he makes between these young men and this ageing divorcee.

You're the oldest man I've ever slept with.

Does she think hearts harden with age; that he only pretends to listen; that he is not in love with her; that her stories do not force his innards to tighten and tighten until there is no room left in his body for rationality; that he is not imagining what it will be to exist as nothing more than another of her anecdotes told to a future man, the one about the boring old guy, old skin, old ways?

Step away.

A penultimate shsheeewwrrrcchchch that seethes up the side of an old stone pier and onto the boots of a winter-uniformed guard holding the barrel of his rifle against an islander's fore-head who lies on her back as other men, un-uninformed, tie her four howling children to her limbs, one to each, and the islander pleads as the guard presses the barrel harder onto her skull, clattering her head against the damp stone slabs, screaming abominations like a kennel, and it is all he can do to stop himself from pulling the trigger. And now they've secured the children, the men lift her by hands and feet and stagger to the water's edge, as near to it as they can, and swing her from side to side, counting down from three.

Step away.

Meditation over, it occurred to him to fetch the cardboard box Bute had brought. It might be interesting, mildly so, to see what he'd left at the house they used to share. He slid off his bed, into the hallway, and down the stairs. But instead of continuing to the front door where he had abandoned the box earlier, he turned right to the kitchen and out into the back garden, where he lay down on the small lawn that separated the lab from the house.

He stared at the sky and closed his eyes when the sun appeared intermittently between bulbous clouds. It was warm enough for him to open his dressing gown and expose his naked body to the rolling vastness above. It felt good. Like the air was cleansing him, gently blowing away his failure. Maybe this was forgiveness.

I'm sorry, he said.

It was a whisper, as soft as the breeze that moved the hair on his chest, groin and legs, that seemed to say, yes, Atlas, this is indeed a good time and place for your apology, and the universe is ready to listen.

So he repeated it. A little louder, his voice cracking as the air collected his words and delivered them in an instant to every living being, from the blackbirds to the blue tits, the great apes to the great whites, causing them to pause and weigh up his request for pardon.

I'm—sorry, louder still, on the verge of shouting.

And finally, shsheeewwrrrcchchch like a shell against the ear, lapping at a floor-length tablecloth at a dinner party where he knows nobody but everybody knows him. There is no K, no music, no promoters or artists. This is something else. Brand new people with glassy skin and nylon hair, ten, eleven of them sucking on fine wine and exotic meats, conversations swirling under laughter and compliments to the chef, bravo, bravo. Atlas floats from one exchange to another, catching scraps. The housing market is a bubble fit to burst; these politicians are idiots to think this or do that; Shanghai is a fantastic city as long as you're not native; no, no, no, that's a common mistake but actually a parakeet will have your eyes out given half a chance; and score the crotch with the sharpest knife you can put your hands on.

The scene judders and halts, gripping the guests in suspended animation, mid-flow, eyebrows arched, drinks raised, mouths contorted. And then fast-rewind. They rise from their chairs and, not looking behind, speed-walk backwards out of the room through the terrace doors and into the early evening while throwing clipped, unnatural gestures. They reverse all the way to the far end of the swimming pool where they gather and arrange themselves facing away from the house and towards the view of the valley below. Atlas, backtracking in a cream suit and beige open-neck shirt, returns his drink to a waiter's tray and retreats from the company until he pauses at the moment of his arrival, at the top of the stone stairs by the side of the property. His foot hovers over the next step. His eye-line is locked on a bird frozen against the blue sky. There is nothing, nothing, and then the sound of chatter on the soft air signals the action has resumed and Atlas descends the steps. He approaches the others by the pool. The waiter offers him a glass of bubbling wine. The guests are enjoying the panorama, pointing lazily to clusters of white buildings dotting the steep green slopes that cradle them. Against the lush canopy, they look like broken teeth.

As Atlas nears, a tall woman in a purple dress and oversized sunglasses turns to face him.

Oh, here he is.

She spills the words as if pointing out yet another abandoned cottage on the valley opposite. But the others nod in agreement; yes, here he is.

A man in a green suit and slick-backed grey hair cranes his neck to see. Yes, it's him. Shall I do the honours?

The woman in purple pulls the man's shoulder back.

No, let me.

Then a small voice squeezes through from somewhere behind the group.

Actually, I was rather keen on doing it.

The guests part and a child, four or five years old, dressed in a toga, walks through the gap.

Dr Brown, it gives me great pleasure to inform you we all, that is, all of us, you know, humanity in all its manifestations, we all forgive you. I can't speak for other species, of course.

Before Atlas can thank the child, the others burst into laughter, put down their glasses, and applaud.

Inside, the dining room appears broader and deeper than the building in which it is housed. White linen nets billow like ghosts over the floor-to-ceiling windows that line the space on all sides. The chairs and the covered table are the only furniture in the room, positioned by the entrance. Waiting staff watch the guests like perched jackdaws. Atlas takes a seat at one end of the table. Toga Boy is to his left, and a younger, taller, slimmer version of General Moss is to the right. The latter is instructing the woman in purple, who sits across from him, on how to skin a rabbit.

There are a few ways you can do it, Moss Man is saying, but some of them are fiddly. I like the simplicity of the hanging method.

Toga Boy leans into Atlas.

You shouldn't be too hard on yourself.

Atlas nods as the boy continues.

The idea of ridding the world of hate is appealing, I sympathise with that. But it wouldn't be without its problems. For me, hate is an excellent thing to have around. A kind of motivator, a little help to get things done.

A motivator? Atlas either says out loud to himself.

Now Moss Man is telling the woman in the purple dress she just needs to make a couple of string loops for the animal's hind legs so it hangs upside down, ring the ankles, score the crotch, and gently inch the pelt down. It only gets tricky when you have to ease the arms out of their sleeves, he says. And around the head, of course, which takes a little bit of light manoeuvring.

Yes, a motivator, Toga Boy replies. Something that gives people a sense of purpose. We define ourselves by our hates. And those of us who understand it don't want to be rid of it. We've only just learned how to use hate as a tool that can really move us forward, and then you come along and say you're going to take it away. It's easy to forgive you because we're happy you failed.

Atlas, on the verge of laughter, shakes his head.

Hate isn't a tool. It is the nearest thing we have to evil. Everything, every aspect of life, would be much better if it didn't exist, if it had never existed.

Toga Boy sips his wine.

I can see why you'd say that. But you are only focusing on the side effects. All that unpleasantness is unfortunate, I admit. We'd all rather it wasn't the case. But everything useful has side effects. The combustion engine, medicine, the wine you're drinking. You are a scientist, you know this.

Atlas exhales.

I'll tell you what I do know. Side effects are only acceptable if they're outweighed by benefits. Significant positive benefits. The problem with your argument is that if hate has advantages, and that's a big if, they come nowhere near to outweighing the so-called side effects.

I need to provide a little context here to help explain where I'm coming from. Is that okay with you?

Atlas nods.

So back in the day, if a king needed an army to defend his realm from invaders, he'd simply ask the shire lords to raise a militia from the population of villagers and farmers. You'd get a knock on your door and before you could open it, you'd be charging across a field waving a rusty scythe at a bunch of scary-looking Vikings. You had no choice. There were severe penalties for those who refused. And because of that, in those days, fighters didn't believe in much more than getting home safely to their families and crops. Which doesn't make for a very effective killing machine.

The Moss man is saying that with one or two modifications, his rabbit-skinning method works on people too.

Atlas rubs his forefinger and thumb up and down the stem of his wineglass.

Killing machines?

But as he speaks, he realises his brain is working in a way he has never experienced before: it can concentrate on two conversations at once, not only dedicating an ear to each but also dividing itself so that it processes the information it's receiving from both speakers with equal deftness. While the boy is telling him that, ideally, what you want is a large body of people totally committed to the cause and prepared to throw themselves at the enemy, the woman in purple is asking Moss Man, in a decidedly flirtatious cadence, if he's ever skinned a man alive. Moss Man laughs suggestively as if to say yes, he has, but he won't be admitting it to her. Not yet. Not here.

Toga Boy, who doesn't appear to notice this second conversation, continues.

To be honest, I find it incredible that it took military leaders so long to realise that a soldier is much more effective when he fights for something bigger than himself. Genghis Khan might have ruled every inch of Eurasia if he'd spent some time stoking up hate in his soldiers instead of fear of what would happen to them if they didn't fight.

The woman in purple gasps as the Moss Man announces that

someone in the know once told him that if you get to the stage when you're ready to rip a man's skin off, either the man knows nothing or he's too far gone to tell you anyway. But he still has his uses. Theatre of Fear, he called it. A very powerful tongue loosener but it's not for the faint-hearted interrogator.

The woman chuckles.

Oh, I'm sure it isn't. Do go on.

Toga Boy clenches his tiny fists.

To hate something, you have to love something. It's yin and yang. You need to believe in an idea so strongly that people who don't believe in it become a perceived threat. Even their existence is a danger to you. To who you are. And so you start hating them. Obviously, that means you've got to attach so much weight to the idea that it defines you and everything you stand for. People adore buying into weird ideologies so it's not that difficult. All a leader needs to do is plant the idea into some fertile brain mulch, water it occasionally with a bit of propaganda, and then sit back and watch the hate bloom.

Moss Man is asking the woman to imagine shooting a prisoner dead in front of the person she's interrogating. He gets a fright, sure. But he's probably seen it all before. It's no big deal, really. Plus, if he'd rather die than give you the information you want, then a bullet to the head is quite an attractive end to proceedings. What you're saying to him is, if you don't talk, that'll happen to you. And he says to himself, thank god, bring it on. But if you skin a man alive in front of him, well, now that's a different story. Moss Man lowers his voice. A different story altogether. And the woman in purple laughs like a bath of slurry.

Atlas shrugs.

Religious wars, they've always been that way.

As he replies, he realises that not only can he focus on these different exchanges, but he is also able to think about the fact that he is doing so. His brain is actually working in three sections. Is his mind broken? Or has some genius streak that's been lying dormant suddenly awoken? Perhaps it was the child's act of forgiveness earlier, a gust of relief so powerful that it lifted an old iron manhole cover somewhere in the depths of his psyche and let his true potential escape.

People drone on about how religion is responsible for so much fighting and killing but it only accounts for something like seven or eight percent of all war throughout history. Did you know that? And if you take any of these wars and look for the real motive, it's never actually religion. It's a land grab, or economic, or political. Look at the Taiping Rebellion. You have a guy, Hong Xiuquan, who claims he's the brother of Jesus. He mixes up a dubious version of Christianity with a generous helping of other Chinese religions and folklore so that it's palatable, then establishes an illegal state called the Heavenly Kingdom. His followers love it. He tells them they're God's chosen ones and that their neighbours, the Manchus, are evil demons who want to annihilate them and everything they stand for. The solution? Exterminate the Manchus and steal their land. And there you have it, all the hate you need for the deadliest civil war ever. About thirty million people die. And, yes, the Heavenly Kingdom lost in the end, but they gave it a bloody good go. Incidentally, the hating worked both ways. After he died, his enemies dug up his body, beheaded it, cremated the remains, and then fired his ashes from a cannon! Hilarious. I suppose they wanted to make sure he was really dead. But if he'd succeeded, Hong would have been powerful beyond belief. It didn't work because of one thing: a perspective problem. As in completely losing perspective. He went too far. Too fanatical. Do that and you risk letting the real world that surrounds your invented reality dissolve until you no longer understand it. You're left flailing around in a sea of ignorance. Which, of course, eventually drowns you. That's what'll happen to Hitler. The signs are all there. It's a form of collective madness that's going to eat the Germans from the inside out. But that's by the by.

The Moss Man is half-whispering now. Just as you did with the rabbit, you hang the traitor up by his ankles. I say traitor, but he might be a spy or a politician, it doesn't matter. Anyway, you should have some adrenaline ready in case he passes out. You want to ensure he remains responsive throughout as it makes for a much better performance. A hose pipe connected to cold water works too, but it's not as reliable. Then you ring the skin around the ankles with the blade. In all likelihood, your interviewee will be squealing juicy information at you like a demented piglet by the time you're down to the other man's balls. Nobody wants to see a skinned scrotum. But, really, it would be a shame not to finish the job. And, you never know, you might manage to squeeze out another couple of tasty morsels from your man before you're done, if you'll pardon the expression.

He's losing her, Atlas observes. Her attention is being tugged by another story further down the table where a man is talking about going undercover to investigate conditions in a South African diamond mine.

Atlas leans towards Toga Boy.

Hitler is dead. He died decades ago.

Did he? Yes. Yes, you're right. Of course. Just imagine I was speaking in the past tense. What I'm saying still stands. Victor Hugo said that certain people can't love without hating. I'm paraphrasing. He was trying to make a point about specific personality types. There's more to it, though. All humans love to hate. It's obvious, isn't it? How can we even know what love is if we don't hate? And vice versa. You can't have one opposite without the other.

Toga Boy pauses.

Am I boring you?

Atlas shakes his head.

Not at all. However, everything you have just said is utter nonsense. This assumption that love and hate are polar opposites is wrong. People are always confusing love with good and hate with evil. Yes, good and evil are diametrically opposed by definition. But you can hate good things and love evil things. So love isn't an appendage of good, and hate doesn't necessarily have close ties with evil. Love and hate have nothing in common. Love is an emotional response. Hate, which I've proven, is an airborne virus. But no, you're not boring me.

Well, do say if I become tedious. I'd despise myself if I were sending you to sleep. Or more asleep than you already are.

Atlas laughs. Moss Man, who has stopped talking, is eyeing him. His eyebrows pull a confused crease down his forehead.

Are you laughing at me?

Now Toga Boy is chuckling.

He was laughing at me, actually.

No, I think you're wrong. I saw him.

Toga Boy leans forward and lowers his voice.

That's because of that issue of yours we talked about last time. Remember?

Now it's Moss Man's turn to laugh.

You little turd.

He rises to his feet, causing his chair to fall backwards and clatter on the tiled floor, and walks out to the veranda, still chortling.

The boy watches him go, then turns back to Atlas.

Okay, so they don't have to be opposites. It's all about balance, of putting your following at odds with the rest of the world without pushing them, or yourself, over the edge. What you do is tell me that how I live is special. Call it freedom or democracy or, you know, some other banal but catchy name, then hang a religious banner over it and point to an enemy out there who wants to take it all away. There doesn't have to be a logical reason for this. A simple 'they hate you because of what you have' should do the trick. Then show me how they deny their own people the very thing I now cherish more than breathing and make sure I understand it is my moral responsibility to free these strangers and protect my way of life. Do it right, and I'll be there cheering the soldiers boarding the trains and ships. Fuck it, give me a gun and I will happily shoot anyone who threatens the ideals you've manufactured for me. I won't need threats of losing my land, or promises of gold, or bagpipes and drums to get me into the mood, and I won't need death metal blasted into my ears. I'll be as invested as hell. And there you have it, the makings of total war. Human beings fighting for ideas rather than because they've been told to. I'm getting pumped just talking about it.

Metal striking glassware interrupts the conversation. A stout woman dressed in a butler's uniform is standing away from the table, her eyes fixed on Atlas. Again she hits the side of a large brandy glass with a spoon.

It's time to run, she announces.

As Atlas and the other guests get to their feet, the Moss Man returns through the veranda doors, followed by several staff members. Some of them are stretching and touching their toes.

The butler claps her hands.

Ready to burn off some of those calories and doubts?

The guests make their way out of the house, down the driveway and onto the gravel that leads towards the valley they gazed at earlier. And now they're running as if their clothes are on fire.

Atlas hasn't run in a group since he was at school. The sports master would force them outside into the winter rain and onto mud tracks that led down into the woods. Spurred on by the threat of no lunch if they failed to complete the course within the allotted time, the boys dragged their half-formed bodies through the sludge and cold misery, flecks of brown on their pained red faces. But this, now, hurtling down the slope in the dry heat, cheered on by crowds of walnut and fig trees, vibrant green leaves clapping in the gentle breeze, Atlas is filled with sunshine and bright blue sky. And while it's become clear to him that this entire episode is not a passing thought he forgot to step away from but a deep dream as he sleeps exposed to the elements in his garden, he believes he will run the slopes of the beautiful valley for the rest of his life. He laughs and skips as high as he can, trying to push his head into the slithers of cloud above. My doctor was right, he shouts to the other guests, all I needed to do was take up running again!

Toga Boy appears at Atlas's side.

I'll run with you if that's alright. I'd like to finish our conversation.

Good, because I'm beginning to think you might be a little mad and I want to give you the opportunity to prove me wrong.

It's not madness to believe we need hate.

All you've managed to say so far is that people fight better when they hate each other. So I'm not convinced.

I hadn't finished. We'd be nothing without hate. It defines all the great movements. And their leaders too. It keeps the pages of history turning. Churchill defined himself by his hatred of the Nazis. De Gaulle, too.

A flash of colour distracts Atlas. He turns to his right just in time to see the woman in purple tumble headfirst into the roadside foliage.

Toga Boy sees it as well.

People should be more careful when running at speed.

She was still wearing her sunglasses.

That can't have helped.

Have you noticed how easy talking is, even though we're sprinting? I don't think I could fall over if I tried.

It does seem remarkably effortless. But then, we are in your dream. Next time, you might find it more satisfying to throw that torture fanatic into the bushes.

Perhaps. So, you were saying?

Yes, Bonaparte said France's crowning immortality would be its hatred of traitors, tyrants and slaves. What else fired up people like Castro and Lenin to change society if it wasn't hatred of those opposed to them?

Okay, I'll buy some of that. But you're still talking about war. A lot of good people die horrible deaths because of this hate of yours.

It isn't just my hate. It's yours. You only invented that

infernal machine because you hate hate. Or you hate being a failure. One of the two. Possibly both. Only you can answer that. I imagine it is more of the latter, though. So you see, hate drives innovation. I mean, think about penicillin, pulled directly from the hatred of suffering and death caused by bacterial infections. Without hate, we'd still have child labour. Or as much of it as we used to. It's the hatred of poverty that fuels attempts to exterminate it. Fire came from the hate of cold, dark nights. The car from the hate of walking. I could go on.

I'm sure you could. You are grossly oversimplifying all those examples, you know that, don't you?

Atlas, this is a dream designed by your subconscious to make you feel better about your failure, and I'm just a strange young boy wrapped in a bedsheet who occasionally dumbs things down to help you. But it's working, isn't it? Are you getting this now? Your machine threatened to bring the species to a halt. Yes, you may have prevented a few million more gruesome deaths in the future, but really, is that too high a price to pay for progress? Billions and billions of people reap the benefits of it every day.

Atlas feels something on his neck. He lifts his hand to investigate and finds a worm. Instantly, he throws it away, disgusted to have had it against his skin. The worm lollops through the air, turning slowly, straightening and contorting until Moss Man's face gives it somewhere to land.

Atlas opened his eyes. Under him, the grass cooled his body through his dressing gown. Above, the garden air was warming up and the English clouds were dispersing. And among the latter somewhere was the Particle. Floating, ricocheting from atom to atom, lingering, waiting to be summoned. Waiting for its next moment. Its next opportunity to bore its way into the minds of frightened people. To poison them. To warp their behaviour. To turn them into devils. And Atlas had the power to stop it from ever happening again.

Bollocks to forgiveness, he thought.

Bollocks to the economy and progress.

Bollocks to the Facility and bollocks to the vested interests.

He, Dr Atlas Brown, could not let General Moss and his god complex decide the fate of humanity. The man had no right. The simultaneous discoveries of the Particle and how to imprison it were a sign from the universe or a deity or the collective human spirit or wherever, it didn't matter. He possessed the knowledge. That was all that mattered. And to not use it, to allow it to be weaponised, would be indefensible.

He needed to be clever, needed a plan. For that, he needed space and time. Yes, he would return to work. He had no choice. But it would not be today. Or the day after that. He would call them again, he'd take another couple of weeks, maybe rent a cottage somewhere. He would go to K's party. He would do whatever the hell he wanted. Space and time were his secret weapons, and they would reveal to him what he had to do. Meanwhile, he had the agent, including the sample from the lab safe. The Facility didn't even know what it was, which meant Moss's threat of sidelining him was empty. The only thing they could do without him was panic, and he had no problem with that.

———

Angela is six days late and I'm going to starve.

Step away.

Angela is six days late and Alexander's army is on its way.

Step away.

Angela is six days late and these fools, when they get here, these idiots, they'll damage the gasholder and release the Particle.

Step away.

Angela is six days late and if everything I've done isn't already a failure, it will be soon.

Step—

He opens his eyes. He must speak to Reflected Atlas because what if they do come for him?

There is a good chance they'll come eventually, agrees the reflection.

But they won't know what's here—in—the gasholder. Angela wouldn't—tell them that.

It seems unlikely. She's made of sturdy stuff, that woman. And even if she did, who'd believe her?

But—if they take me away I won't be here to—to look after it.

Reflected Atlas shakes his head.

Not if they take you away, no.

That's bad.

Worse than that.

But—she's only six days late. It could be anything—couldn't it? Her husband—he could be unwell.

Or there's a fuel shortage.

Or—she has a bad migraine.

Does she get them?

No idea—possibly—and they can last for days.

Reflected Atlas looks pensive. He is staring in Atlas's direction but something about his expression gives Atlas the feeling that his insides are being examined.

What?

Just a thought.

And?

Well, you raise an interesting problem.

Do I?

You're going to die.

Thanks for—that.

And when you do, there will be nobody to take care of the gasholder.

That—that—is an interesting problem.

We could say, well, never mind, you'll be dead, why give a shit what happens after that?

That's a possibility—who knows—all of this might be a stupid dream and—and maybe I'm still lying on my bed back in my old house—trying to calm the hell down.

That's not helpful.

You're right. This is—hideously—real.

Atlas raps his knuckles against the wall beside the mirror to prove his point.

Do we care what happens after you croak it?

Can we speak about my—departure with a little more sensitivity?

Okay, after you're gone, passed over, shuffled off, in whichever gentle and painless way that might happen, what then?

It's obvious—isn't it?

Really?

We—need a person.

Who?

We don't know yet—do we. We need—we need an heir.

Someone to inherit your little empire?

Well—an apprentice, I suppose—to train up.

You've found people to help you before.

Interesting—I'm detecting—a certain—distancing going on here. This is an us thing. It's not just about me—we're in this together.

What did I say?

You keep saying you—instead of we.

Okay, fair point. *We've* found people before.

Yes—*we* have. But that hasn't—always worked out—very well, has it?

Angela did. By the way, I'm not pressing the past tense on purpose.

She did—is. She is working out just fine.

And you found her through the American.

Atlas laughs. He hasn't said the American's name out loud for a long time and he's happy that Reflected Atlas is keeping up this tradition.

Yes—but he found us. She was—part of the package.

What I think I'm trying to say is that you, I mean we, need to get out there and find someone. Atlas, go fetch us an heir.

Atlas steps away from the mirror. He's had enough of this conversation. He started with one problem and suddenly he has another. This is uncomfortable. It's easy for his reflected self to tell him to go out and solve this issue or that complication but he doesn't understand what it's like. You can't walk up to someone and say, hey, want to dedicate your life to the continual containment of hate? And to make matters more annoying, the American with his intense, vigorous face is now prowling around his thoughts.

Angela came via the American, and the American came via that invitation, the one from K. Atlas remembers it in his kitchen, propped up against a fruit bowl full of utility bills, charity appeal letters, and blackened bananas, with its neon orange plastic and transparent lettering that he barely noticed until after his meeting with Moss. Then, once his world had become a bleaker place in which to exist, its gaudy design jumped out at him every time he entered the room.

When he lived with Bute, it rained invitations. She'd pretend Atlas was involved in the decision-making process by permitting him to join her as she weighed up the advantages of each offer: who would be there, career advancement opportunities, potential alcohol quality, distance from home. Most went straight into recycling, often with little consideration. The remainder would loiter on coffee tables, desks, and window sills, where they would be discussed in passing. Private views, the opening of such-and-such a show, some debut author's book launch, someone-or-other's thirtieth birthday party, the wedding of whats-it and who-ja. Would they be worth the hassle? What kind of return would she receive for the effort? Would the hours of labouring through countless dry conversations with people known and unknown bear fruit?

These deliberations were invaluable. Events that yielded sales, commissions, valuable new contacts, or anything else that progressed her career resulted in a Bute high. Sometimes they'd move on to other parties spawned from the primary function. Or maybe head to a nightclub where she would dance and he would drink. Especially fruitful evenings could even lead to a few minutes of semi-enjoyable sex. If, on the other hand, the event produced nothing of value, a dark sulk would descend. So any effort spent minimising Bute's potential ruinous moods was worthwhile. And, as he had some say in assessing each request's viability, Atlas also bore some responsibility for positive outcomes. Didn't we do good, she'd squeal afterwards, feeding his hunger for approval. Luckily for him, when things went badly, Bute's impenetrable despair had no room for anyone else's incompetence but her own. As long as he got her home quickly and kept out of her way for two or three days, he was off the hook.

For Atlas, the entire process from start to finish represented one of the few positive experiences his marriage ever offered him. So it was no surprise the habit stuck after the divorce. He mulled over every invitation that landed in his inbox or on his doormat with a level of rigour that would have made Bute proud. Of course, the quantity and quality plummeted. But five or six times a month, an invitation would arrive. He'd read it, calculate the likelihood of his ex-wife or someone she knew being there, research the artist or author, and leave it to linger by or in his fruit bowl. If it was still there by the time the date finally arrived, and if he was feeling sufficiently frivolous, he would go.

He enjoyed buying art and appreciated the occasional reading. And, despite himself, it was agreeable to surround himself with creative people. They made what they wanted. Expressed themselves freely. He found their blind determination to control their output uplifting. And the tinges of envy he experienced were quashed quickly enough by his sense of moral and intellectual superiority. They could bask in their freedom all they liked, but he, Dr Atlas Brown, was doing the real work.

However, the plastic invitation on the counter promised none of these benefits. K, his brother, was a musician or a producer or possibly both, who lived in Los Angeles. Most invitations he sent were to events in places like New York, Johannesburg, or the Balearics, making them easy to ignore, but this one was in London.

It'll be good for you, K claimed on the phone. Get out of the house. Break the cycle. Book a train ticket and come down. We'll have a blast, bro. Trust me.

Atlas could only sigh in response.

———

One hour, he promised himself.

The taxi pulled up outside a warehouse where a long line of people reached beyond the sleek glass doors. He walked to the front of the crowd, causing faces to twist.

There's an effing queue, mate.

Atlas avoided eye contact while wondering if they would have challenged him if Arrina had been on his arm, if he'd looked like someone, like a man who got VIP invitations, who went to these places, a guest-list native.

A shadow beat pulsed the evening chill, duff, duff, duff, duff, duff, duff, duff, duff. The rhinoceros at the door found Atlas's name on a clipboard and motioned him inside.

Within four metres of the door, the floor space disappeared. In its place a snake pit of glittering cheekbones and closed eyes and shining shoulders and raised arms, twisting and writhing. Louder now, clearer, dum, dum, dum, dum, dum, dum, dum, dum, dum. Atlas was disorientated in seconds. Red air, blue layers slicing through the haze. Bodies moved against him on all sides and the music shook his innards. Someone at his back jumped up and down, forcing him to move to the rhythm, doom-doom-doom, doom-doom-doom, doom-doom-doom. He tensed his legs to steady himself and messaged K.

sounds like an elephant
being strangled
by barbed wire
while it kicks a bass drum

He looked at the time on his phone. There was no way he could stay for a full hour. He cut it to forty-five minutes.

K appeared at his side. They tried to hug but the proximity of others made it impossible. His brother shouted in his ear. He hadn't seen the text. He'd spotted Atlas from up there, pointing with his head.

You stick out like a mourner at a pride parade.

Thirty minutes.

K pulled him through the crush until they reached the stairs at the side of the hall. Another enormous bouncer nodded at K and opened a rope barrier. It was calmer on the mezzanine. Most guests sat at tables. The one K led Atlas towards was more crowded than the others. People turned as they approached. K introduced Atlas as his older brother.

Brother—just brother—is fine.

There were a few cheers, and various bottles and glasses rose in Atlas's direction.

He's a scientist, but don't ask him what he does. It's a state secret, K pantomimed in a shouted whisper.

For—fuck's sake, K.

K's face clenched.

Facilities management, he shouted, he's big in facilities management. Then to Atlas, he said, sorry, everyone's pissed, they've already forgotten. Nothing to worry about, I promise.

Ten minutes.

Soon he was holding a glass of champagne and listening to a woman explain the point of the party over the thrum.

It's a launch. River Long's new album, *Afterthoughts*. K produced it. It's kind of a big deal.

By the second glass, he was experiencing a feeling not dissimilar to enjoyment. A man on his left asked what K was like as a child.

Typical little brother—pain in the arse.

The man snorted.

By the fourth glass he was nodding and holding out his spare hand towards the woman at the other side of the table pouring tequila shots.

Wikipedia says the K is short for Kobe. Atlas has also read that it stands for Kingsley, Kyser, Koda and Killian. His real name is Kenneth. Kenneth Brown.

Naming the firstborn son after the maternal grandfather was a five-generation family tradition. So it should have been Atlas's name. But his parents, believing themselves above ancestral archaisms, named him after a titan instead. The response was frosty. Atlas's mother's mother stopped communicating with her, and her father had her husband barred from his golf club. His mother's siblings expressed their disapproval in various ways, including forgetting her child's first four birthdays, a crime she never fully forgave. Even his father's parents got in on the act, accusing the young couple of being disrespectful and urging them to change their son's name. So when their second boy was born, rather than call him Prometheus as planned, they yielded and christened him Kenneth. It wasn't the perfect solution but it scabbed the wound.

Kenneth Brown. Aesthetically, it was way off the mark for a successful musician/producer/DJ. And while K worked so much better, it didn't stop Atlas from cringing whenever he heard his forty-five-year-old brother introduce himself. But then,

here was Atlas, a fifty-year-old white male dancing so enthusiastically in a heaving, sweating nightclub he was struggling to
breathe.

It was dark outside when K pulled him off the dance floor and
through the exit. Atlas remembers people were still queuing to
get into the club as he sat on the pavement with his shoes in the
gutter. Above him, the group from the mezzanine spoke of
where next. Some suggested their houses and apartments, other
bars, nightclubs. The pros for one venue were quickly countered
by its cons and the pros for another. Fast sentences and laughter
made him lightheaded. Atlas needed to go back to his hotel. He
felt tired. A little on edge.

An American accent stood out from the chatter.

We've had a great night but we have a busy day tomorrow.
We can drop a few people off on the way back.

A black limousine appeared.

K's hands under Atlas's armpits eased him onto his feet.

Time for your bed, I think.

The vehicle chiselled through the city. Music played behind
end-of-night conversations. Atlas gazed into the streets, turning
only to turn down invitations to go for more drinks. The car
made a few stops. Soon, only Atlas, the American accent, and a
French-sounding woman remained. He knew her face from the
table, one of three women with the tequila bottle, they'd allowed
him to lecture them on something he believed to be pressing at
the time. Whatever it was, it had already faded from his memory.
The couple chatted quietly, tersely. Her voice was soft, his like
radio static. She looked annoyed. He didn't make eye contact as
he spoke. Then he murmured something unintelligible and
turned to the nearest window. Atlas offered the woman an
apologetic frown when he caught her glancing his way.

I should—probably—get out here.

She looked outside.

Is this where you live?

My hotel is—it's close enough.

Nonsense, said the woman, we'll take you all the way.

It's okay—I can walk from here.

The man sighed at the window.

Look, we've come this fucking far. We're taking you back whether you like it or not.

Atlas has always woken up in the wrong place. Wherever he is, when he opens his eyes for the first time each day, he is unable to identify his environment. It's as if someone or something has lifted him from his bed while he slept and carried him to an unknown location. And although he's known the phenomenon since childhood, he continues to wake in a state of confusion. The reaction lasts until he reaches for his glasses and the blurred objects and colours framed by early eyelids sharpen and orientate him.

Cold poles, like chrome arms with lightbulb hands, against pavilion grey eggshell. His house. His own bedroom in his own home. All is well.

A giant veined paper orb like a moon suspended in dust-purple space. Purple space? The Oldham Avenue house, in Bute's room, in Bute's bed, her to his left.

The shards and curved glass of a chandelier dangling from an intricately painted, multi-coloured rose in the centre of a lurid green ceiling. Oldham Avenue, his room, in his bed, alone.

Dust-encrusted cobwebs fluttering around a bare bulb, a white flex against white cracked plaster. His student digs, Broughton Street, Edinburgh. Yes, of course.

Six large bulbs with orange filaments hanging from brown corded cables that loop down and up, slung through brass fixtures, forming abstract numbers or letters. This is. He knows where this is. It's coming to him. A hotel room. In. In London.

In London, wishing he'd stayed at home. All this way for a

hangover larger than the oversized pillow that holds his head as if it were an unexploded bomb.

Atlas looked at his watch. The train had gone north without him. The idea of looking up the next one was too much.

Just find your phone and tap the app, he told himself.

He rose from the bed, filled the small kettle, set it to boil. He fingered the selection of complimentary sachets and took a measure of himself as the air swelled with the smell of moist, molten plastic. Not so good, he concluded and thought of his meditation cd. You won't need it, he'd told himself before he left. It's a quick trip to London, in and out, SAS-style, back before you know it.

The Dooms is what he called it when he was younger. He used to find a particular pleasure in those periods of remorse. He'd sit back and observe the psychological process as if from a distance. It amused him. The human being, so eager to undermine its place in the world in exchange for a few hours of joyful intoxication, always sure it's getting a good deal until it wakes up to an arcade of agonising introspection. He believed this was the only opportunity people got to lift the veil on the false narratives they needed to function and to see life as it truly was, and they did it again and again because they craved the truth. And the truth, to Atlas, was funny. Funnier still was the thought of millions of others waking to the same gloom, unprepared and ill-equipped to handle the pointlessness of existence. Lately, however, the relatively new idea of him being responsible for the continued destruction of his species had rubbed the shine from the joke. As he stirred hot water into the granules, he wondered if he would drink if it worked the other way around, if hangovers arrived before the drunken joy.

The envelope slipped under the door to his room as he walked to the bathroom. Something about this cream rectangle's brisk, soundless movement over the dark blue carpet and how it would now lie there without a sound until he saw fit to pick it up gave him pause. The item spoke to him of time, patience, and good manners. It seemed discourteous to react to it so soon. It asked to be left to rest for a while, even if only a few seconds more. As he lifted it from the floor, he realised it also spoke of money. This was an expensive envelope, embossed above the seal with the letters MF.

Dear Dr Brown,

I behaved atrociously last night. Please allow me to apologize in person at lunch today. My car will be outside your hotel at 12.30pm. If you'd rather not, I'll understand. I'll instruct my driver to wait ten minutes.

Yours sincerely,

Milo.

He texted K.

Who is Milo
?

U got it. Good.
How's ur head this morning?

I did. Who is he
Head hurts

Nice guy wants to say sorry
said he was a dick last night.
U were off your tits

Surname? Need to search him

Farfalla.
Maybe fafarla something like that

investor type from NY
don't know him really
might be buying into the record company

By 12:35pm he was in the back of a black Bentley, disappointed in himself. The driver informed him they were heading to an Italian restaurant. Atlas didn't catch the name. It would take half an hour. Thirty minutes to decide how he should behave. By accepting the invitation, he'd already capitulated, which vexed him. Bute would have thrown it away whether or not she remembered the night before.

Last-minute invites stink, she'd say. I am not an afterthought.

But Atlas could still make the meeting difficult for this Farfalla person.

He'd be distant. He'd pretend he thought someone else had invited him. He'd turn to leave and see what happened. He'd make sure this man understood he was neither interested in him nor his apology.

But, seriously, who did he think he was? Sending a car to his hotel! Did he expect Atlas to be impressed?

Here he was again, being pushed into doing something he didn't want to by a man with more power than him. More power because Atlas had let him have it. Ah, to be able to scribble a few words on a piece of paper, throw it out into the world via whatever means, and know that the lickspittles will come running. Pitter-patter, the sound of mere mortals scurrying to bask in your monied magnificence.

No, he decided, I'm not doing this.

Atlas told the driver to stop. The doors clicked unlocked. He looked out to his left, then to the right. There was an entrance to a tube station just around the corner. He could just go. He had things to do. A train to catch. A bed to lie on. A void of self-pity to stare into. He opened the door and got out.

He stood watching pedestrians pass in both directions, the car door open behind him. The day was warm, sky blue. He noticed a couple of glances, people wondering what someone like him was doing next to a vehicle like that.

Give us a lift, mate, shouted a young woman, her companions covering their laughter with their hands.

Atlas felt foolish. He wanted to walk away. He scanned the other side of the street for encouragement.

Sod it, he said to himself. If I go there now, it's because I've chosen to. I am in control. This is up to me.

This way, sir.

Atlas followed the waiter through the half-full restaurant to a set of open double doors. On the other side, ten or so men stood by a small bar. Every face in the room had turned to him. Finally, his eyes settled on K, beaming. Atlas nodded, careful not to look relieved.

The American's voice erupted from the group of well-dressed bodies.

Everybody, this is him. This is the scientist I was so hideous to last night. Welcome, my friend. Thank you for coming.

Atlas's shoulders almost touched his ears in the man's embrace. He did not resist being manoeuvred into the crowd for too many handshakes, introductions, and backslaps to count.

You didn't tell me—you were going to be here?

K was sitting next to him.

You never asked.

And did I ask you to—to explain to him—what I do?

You didn't need to. You told his girlfriend all about your job as she poured you your fourth and fifth and possibly sixth tequila. You'd make a terrible spy.

Opposite, Farfalla was recalling the car ride from the night before.

I was a monster, wasn't I, Atlas? A total monster. May I call you Atlas?

Atlas spent the rest of the meal fielding questions about his work he couldn't answer. But the people around the table were enjoyable company, ready to laugh and make gentle fun of themselves and each other. His hangover and misgivings soon drowned under two, perhaps three, glasses of red wine. They also quizzed Farfalla about his background, if he liked London, and his opinion of the new president, all of which he answered in expressive detail.

After lunch, Atlas sank into a large leather armchair, a brandy in one hand, a smouldering cigar in the other. He couldn't remember the last time he'd smoked indoors.

Come, Farfalla had said, guiding him away from the others. I want to talk to you about sciencey things. I've invested in a renewables project in New Mexico. One by one, the other guests, including K, made their excuses and left.

Sciencey things?

I'd like your opinion.

And so they'd sat, and Farfalla talked. Atlas did his best to concentrate under the alcohol fug. A solar technology, something based on photosynthesis, a desert, and research by a famous Dutch scientist he'd never heard of. Farfalla scrolled through emails and read out paragraphs, showed photographs and drawings.

Atlas mustered a scholarly nod and uttered the required platitudes, yes, it sounded interesting, the kind of work the world needs right now, yes, you should be proud to be part of it. And Farfalla seemed pleased.

The conversation veered from technology and down the roads of the places they'd lived, where they were from. School, the American's children, Atlas's divorce, the emptiness of politics. Farfalla furnished each subject with anecdotes and rumours, and Atlas chuckled and grew to like the man he'd been determined to hate just three hours earlier. And he wondered if he was looking at the most honest face he'd ever seen. It was the way it moved. Each emotion Farfalla felt was right there, dancing on his face, morphing from joy to anger to love to disdain every few seconds. His cheeks flushed, eyes watered, lips curled, forehead furrowed, eyebrows scowled, teeth beamed. It was as if his features were incapable of staying still for a moment, an autonomous physiognomy that betrayed its wearer's every sentiment the instant he experienced them. It must be exhausting to be so expressive, Atlas thought. Surely, he would be better off burying at least some of them.

Waiting staff swept in and cleared the tables, brought more drinks, emptied ashtrays, and Atlas wondered when he'd last used an ashtray.

It's okay—for us to—to smoke in here?

You can do whatever the hell you like.

Atlas laughed.

I wish that were true.

You don't believe me? Name one thing you can't do.

I wouldn't know—where to start.

Farfalla's eyebrows dived deep into his face.

Come on. Just one.

Cook a decent lasagna.

Atlas watched the man's eyes roll and lips purse.

I'm being serious.

Fine. I can't—save the—save the world.

Bullshit. Of course you can.

Atlas laughed again, and Farfalla's grimace turned into a smile, then into what he supposed was a ponderous expression, then wide-eyed wonder, and back to the grimace.

Okay—how?

If it were me, I would just do it. Obviously, I need an idea, the thing that's actually going to save the world. After that, all I'd require is resources, which are there for the taking.

Yes, well—you've possibly got the money. But for someone like me—I don't have access to the resources. I might know how

—exactly how to save the world but—I can't—do a thing about it. People—such as me—have to persuade others to give them what they need.

Then do it.

Yes—of course—as easy as that.

He pondered Farfalla's mental stability as he watched his facial muscles tango. If a man with a face like that approached Atlas on the street, he'd give him the widest possible berth. Sane people protect themselves. They put up a barrier between their internal goings-on and the outside world. The kind of openness Farfalla exhibited would likely lead to injury or worse. At that moment, Farfalla looked upset with side helpings of anger and disappointment, and Atlas suddenly felt guilty.

I'm sorry. Too much to drink—I think. For sure, actually. I didn't mean to offend you. All I meant was—is—that it's not always easy to—get people with the money to—to do the right thing.

It sounds like you have some experience.

You could say—I've built a career on it.

More brandy arrived. Atlas looked at the glass in front of him and imagined the state his head would be in the next day. How utterly doomed. Farfalla stared into his drink as he swirled the liquid around the tumbler. His face had slowed down a gear. There was a slight smirk, a frown, and then a raised eyebrow. His large eyes met Atlas's.

I don't need to explain myself to you. I'm only going to tell you this to push a bit of positivity into the conversation. And maybe even a little hope.

That would be—nice.

I mentioned the project in New Mexico. That's my money doing some good, and if all goes well, I'll get a reasonable return. Sometimes all you need is a half-decent strategy to make people listen to you. Money wants money. If it does a bit of good in the process, then great. So here's a story. A man came to see me a few years ago. He worked with poor families in this little town somewhere near Mexico City. He told me that charities were killing his neighbourhood. His people were too reliant on handouts, that was his theory. He was passionate about it. He'd go on about teaching a man how to fish instead of giving him a can of tuna. So he was determined to create a company that could provide the community with microloans. Small advances so they could buy tools and earn money to wean themselves off the charity. He wanted to help them set up businesses and drag themselves out of poverty. But banks aren't interested in lending like that. Not enough profit, high risk. So I said I'd help. They pay a small amount of interest. I make peanuts back, but it is a profit. And it's actually working. He was telling me about a woman who trained to be a seamstress when she was younger but then got involved with some guy who liked his drugs too much. She started using and in no time she had an addiction and the guy disappeared leaving her with four kids. Long story short, she manages to get off the crack, borrows money from us, buys a sewing machine, and starts an alteration business. She paid off the loan within a year and hired two other people. Then she borrowed more money for extra machines. And he's got plenty more stories like it. Bores me senseless with them every month. We've made somewhere in the region of two hundred of these loans and only about three percent of them have gone bad. So we're making money, they're making money, and some good is getting done. And most importantly, I feel better about myself.

Farfalla's expression skipped and jumped. The deep brows of concern to a wide mouth of mirth to the narrow eyes of curiosity.

You see what I'm talking about?

It's a bit—depressing—to be honest.

Why?

Money. Profit. Wouldn't it be—better if people did good for—for the sake of doing good?

What? They do it all the time. That guy in Mexico, he isn't

making a bean out of this. He has a day job. He's a programmer, writes code for websites. I might hire him for a project soon. These poor families he works with, he does that in his own time for free. It's his passion, like I said, he needs to do it. But money though, yeah, it's heartless. Money doesn't care whether it's running an orphanage or running drugs. If it can reproduce, it'll get involved. If it can't, it won't. End of story. But honestly, there's always profit if you look hard enough. In fact, I'd say that if there is good to be done, there are dollars to be made.

As Farfalla talked about money, Atlas pictured it as an organism, a manufactured virus developed in an ancient laboratory, a pandemic infecting the lives of everyone, corroding decency, and causing the very issues Farfalla said it solved. It's like trying to cure alcoholism with a spoonful of vodka, he thought. Wipe out money and you eradicate all our problems. Why was this such a difficult concept for people to grasp? Money wanted to turn the Hate Extractor into a weapon. Perhaps blindness and stupidity were also symptoms of the infection. He downed the rest of his brandy and slammed the glass on the table between them harder than he intended.

I've heard—enough.

Farfalla's face was still for the first time that day.

I—have a project. It will do more good than—than you can imagine. And it won't make anybody any money—it can't—it'll —do the opposite. It'll ruin entire industries—destroy thousands of jobs and livelihoods around the world—pension funds will collapse, and—I don't know what else. It might even—might even wipe out money itself.

Bullshit, said Farfalla. He was smiling again.

Okay—can I ask you a question?

Sure.

Do you know—what hate is?

· · ·

Farfalla instructed the driver to take them to Castleport via Atlas's hotel.

That's a three-hour drive, sir. Possibly more.

Perfect.

He slumped into the backseat and leaned into Atlas.

I want to be a part of this, Atlas. This is destiny, I can feel it. You and I meeting like this, it's no coincidence. This is kismet in action, my friend. Fate has brought us together. You and me, Atlas, you and me.

Atlas breathed treasonous air. The weather had shifted. All around them, heavy storm clouds heaved and spewed raindrops the size of walnuts that bounced off paving stones and hammered the car's roof. The pessimism and guilt that had been keeping Atlas company for so long rapped on the windows, reminding him of his obligations.

Now is not the time to desert us, they said. We're not finished yet.

They knew they were losing him. They had no choice but to act. But Atlas was shielded from them. Farfalla's words, his face and eyes, his unbridled optimism surrounded the car in a protective bubble that buzzed with power, an impenetrable force field of positivity. We can do this, he was saying as he produced a decanter of whisky from a small compartment. There is nothing we can't do. You show me how and I'll show you how. We can do anything. We can save the world. You and me, Atlas.

Farfalla followed Atlas into the house and dropped onto a couch. Atlas went to the kitchen to pour more drinks. And there, at the counter, glasses in front of him, bottle in hand, he realised he'd made a mistake. He had never betrayed the Facility before. But now he'd broken the official secrets act, and in doing so, he'd become a traitor. This was serious and had to stop. I will tell him I made it all up, he thought. I'll apologise. Make a joke about it. Say it was revenge for yesterday. That would have to do. He poured the drinks and headed back to the living room. Farfalla was asleep on the sofa. Atlas put the drinks down, threw a blanket over the uninvited guest and climbed the stairs. Everything will be okay. He'll have forgotten by morning, or I'll insist he does. It'll be fine. He removed one of his shoes before collapsing onto the bed.

Atlas's phone pinged just after ten.

A text message from Arrina. No missed calls from the Facility. It was the first time in days they hadn't tried to get hold of him. It was, he suspected, good news.

How u doing?

He didn't have the energy to reply to her, to type like you don't want to know, like I spent yesterday eating the cement dust I produced while banging my head against a concrete wall, like someone has pushed tacks through my eyelids as I slept, like every organ in my body is queuing up, waiting to be shat into the bedsheets.

Water, he needed water. The effort required to sit up was enough to push the moon out of orbit. Yesterday's clothes stuck to his skin. He stripped, found his way to the bathroom, and headed downstairs. Two untouched glasses on the coffee table. Shapes in the fog began to form. The lunch, Farfalla, drinking. Cigars. He stepped over a blanket on the floor and scraped into the kitchen. The backdoor was ajar. Well done. You drunken idiot. You might have been robbed. Murdered in your sleep.

His fingers felt the water go cold. He filled a pint glass and took large, loud gulps. Icy tributaries ran from his neck to his chest, crisscrossed over his stomach and rushed to meet his groin and the tops of his legs.

Knees.

Ankles.

He filled the glass and repeated the process. Putting it down, he forced his head under the running water, rubbing it into his hair and over his face while he gasped at the sharpness. Then he turned off the tap and reached for a towel. That's when he looked out the window and saw that the door to the garden lab was wide open.

Ancient cerebral mechanisms clunked and rasped. He was always fastidious about locking the lab and hadn't opened it since his meeting with Moss. Part of him believed he'd never open it again. Rusty cogs groaned, heavy pistons creaked, a weak jet of steam spurted out from somewhere behind a cognition piston, and a ticker tape tapped and ticked and presented him with a message: there is someone in there.

He dropped the towel, pulled a drawer, grabbed the first dangerous-looking object and rushed through the backdoor.

Nice spoon.

Farfalla's smile frolicked about his face.

Atlas looked down at his hand and saw he was still naked.

Been checking out your hardware.

Farfalla laughed this time, the volume turning Atlas's stomach.

Sorry, I couldn't resist.

It's—a soup ladle—you shouldn't be—in here.

I have to say, a bit of an anti-climax after everything you said last night. I was expecting something like a Batman car.

Come on—out.

Atlas followed Farfalla back into the house, wrapped the discarded blanket around his waist, and turned on the kettle.

I shouldn't have—it's secret—an official secret. Everything I do is. This is very—really serious. If it ever gets out I told you—I don't—

Relax, Atlas. I'm not telling anyone about it. It's not like they would believe me anyway.

Farfalla reminded him about their pact, how they were in this together now, and how he would bankroll the project. But that he needed more detail. He had to understand how it worked.

Atlas wanted to free himself from the man's constant talking, to disappear so he could nurse himself. Painkillers and bed, maybe some food if he could hold it down. But they were in his lounge by this time, sitting opposite one another on the two sofas with no sign of impending release. The Largo was on the wall behind Farfalla, the white form haloing the top of his head, and Atlas drifted to the last person to come between him and the painting. Arrina. He was in the same position, on the same sofa, naked like now, wrapped in the same blanket, and she said, *I think we might kill art. I think. I think art is a byproduct of pain, and if we take that away, there'll be no reason to make it anymore.*

On her feet, her naked back towards him, her face up close to the artwork. It was the texture that had prompted him to buy it. From a distance, the image was pleasing and vague. There was movement but little in the way of structure. Whenever he took time to look, it seemed different. A snowscape or sea froth or bleached desert. Fluid, he supposed you might say. But when he stood right in front of it, its character became more apparent, more beautiful. In the busy gallery where he first saw it, he thought he could hear the painting as the chatter behind him melted into a winter wind, sand scratching the earth's surface, the simmer of saltwater, brush stroking the canvas, the artist's breath.

He should have replied that pain was the one thing they'd never be able to take away.

Atlas answered Farfalla's questions as vaguely as he could without sounding evasive, made more tea, explained and re-explained the theory and the results, and outlined his rough thoughts on costs and the issues still to be resolved. But when the American tried to draw him on the agent, Atlas had to make clear he wouldn't be elaborating on its ingredients for the time being. Farfalla shrugged and said he understood.

Atlas went upstairs to wash and dress. As he showered, he noticed a few green shoots of optimism rising in his gut and that, interestingly, he had no wish to trample them to dust. Once he was ready, he took Farfalla back into the garden lab where he unlocked the panic room and pointed out the machine's various components, his assembly drawings, and the storage tank. And at some point during all this he realised he had decided to trust this man.

ARRINA

They waited. Dr Brown's no-shows were not unusual but this was the longest yet. They'd assumed he would return to the lab straight after the funding meeting with the board. Then they expected to see him the following morning. Then after lunch. Or the next day. Or the next week.

Rumours filled the vacuum. The meeting hadn't gone well. They were all out of a job. He'd been transferred to another Facility unit. He'd been sacked.

They looked to Arrina for answers, so she called him. Then she borrowed Ahmed's car and drove out to his house. She tried the door before knocking. She whispered through the letterbox. Phoned again from the garden gate.

Later, he began replying to her text messages with one-word answers.

Resting.

Ill.

Fine.

Soon.

Dunno.

Maybe.

No.

Arrina handed out tasks, supervised, and pretended things were okay, and everyone seemed happy enough to believe her.

A man and a woman appeared on the Friday of the second week of Dr Brown's absence.

Hello, we are Terence Holt, said Terence Holt, pointing at his chin.

And Lucy Anchor, said Lucy Anchor, pointing at her chest. We're from ProCo.

Terence said, the Project Coordination Department.

And Lucy said, that's if you didn't already know.

Tall. Dressed in his-and-hers navy suits and skinny black loafers. Both with airy blonde hair in the process of escaping that morning's styling products.

And you're Dr Brown's famous team, continued Lucy. So many good things being said about you. It's so great to finally meet you all.

The pair worked the room, shook hands, took notes of names, asked about job roles, said what a fantastic start they'd all had to their careers, what an exciting future they all had at the Facility.

Lucy did most of the speaking. A chocolate voice, lots of teeth and bright eyes. Terence nodded and grinned and perused the worktops.

Lucy said, work will resume next week when Dr Brown is back.

And Terence nodded and said, he has been under considerable stress and needs rest. Our medical doctors have been in touch with him, and he's feeling much better.

Everything is fine.

He'll be back soon.

Who's in charge while Dr Brown is away?

Her colleagues' glances, nods, and nudges prompted Arrina to hold up her hand.

If we could have a word, said Terence through his nose.

They led her into Dr Brown's office.

Please sit.

They stood shoulder to shoulder, looking down at her. They spoke in tandem, sometimes to her, sometimes to each other, in a conspiratorial tone.

It's vital you keep the team happy.

Brown has a lot of work to do when he gets back.

You'll all have a lot of work to do when he returns.

This is an important project.

It has attracted a lot of new funding.

I'm not sure if she needs to know that.

Well, she knows now, and it might help her maintain morale until he returns.

We're counting on you.

The Facility is depending on you to show your full support.

Yes, I just said that.

I am reiterating so she understands the importance.

I'm sure she gets it.

We're not saying you'll be held personally responsible for any deterioration in group self-esteem.

No, we're not saying that at all.

We understand you can only do so much.

Yes, exactly.

But you are in the best position to keep their confidence up.

To make sure they don't drift off to other projects.

Or get poached by other teams.

This is an excellent opportunity for someone like you.

People are watching.

Don't let us down.

Is that understood?

The pair reappeared the day after Dr Brown had been due to return. Earlier, the team had arrived to find the lab ransacked. Papers and equipment cluttered the floor but there was no damage as far as Arrina could tell.

Two other women in matching suits and a couple of security officers accompanied Lucy and Terence. In a harsher voice than the one Arrina remembered from last time, Lucy instructed everyone to remain seated.

She said, we have a situation and need to speak to you all individually. Do not be alarmed. This is nothing more than procedure. And, please, don't touch anything.

What we said out there about not being alarmed, Terence said to Arrina as Lucy closed the office door behind them, that doesn't apply to you.

You should be very alarmed, agreed Lucy.

Papers and folders slipped beneath Arrina's feet. She sat and braced herself while she watched Lucy and Terence jostle for position on the other side of the desk. Everything about them seemed different now. Their skin looked rougher and dryer, their hair coarser and, most disturbing of all were their wet bloodshot eyes, like fertilised hens' eggs emptied onto saucers.

Right, so.

Where is Dr Brown?

When did you last see him?

We have photographs.

We know you were at his house?

You two are close?

We didn't ask you that.

You were sleeping together.

Well, what would you call it?

Did he force you to have sex with him?

Are you sure?

Lucy took Arrina's phone and demanded the passcode. She scrolled through her texts while Terence asked if she didn't think he was a bit old for her.

Did he tell you about his plans?

Don't be clever.

It doesn't suit you.

Please, don't lie to us.

It won't do you any good.

It'll do you harm, actually.

Your career.

That's what we're talking about.

You're lying.

You've already lied about the last time you saw him.

Don't play with us.

Where is he?

Where is the agent?

What's in it?

Who else are you sleeping with here?

You know it's against the rules?

You have no idea what you've got yourself into, do you?

Besides escorted trips to and from the toilet, nobody left the windowless lab for so many hours they lost track of time. Phones and watches were confiscated, laptops removed. Food arrived, boxes were cleared, more food arrived. People slept on the floor under workstations, others fought to stay awake. Terence and Lucy disappeared and reappeared. Other men and women dressed identically took their places while they were away. The questioning continued in shifts.

Sometimes the interrogations inside the office became heated, and muffled shouting and crying could be heard by those outside, who could do nothing but stare at the closed blinds while waiting their turn.

———

Livid. Fucking furious.

Arthur's hands slammed the air in front of him.

They accused me of being a thief. Hammered on about it for ages. Said I'd stolen something. And gave it to him.

Before releasing the team from the lab and suspending them from duties, Anchor and Holt had made clear they were forbidden to communicate with one another and would be watched to ensure their compliance. But the people assigned to do the watching seemed clownish in their ineffectiveness. The junior researchers tricked them with amateurish disguises and decoys and joked about the doomed state of the country's secret services. Regardless, they made sure to be careful when they met, rendezvousing in parks, by canals, cemeteries, never more than two at a time. Arthur had been keen to meet Arrina. So here they were, she and him, like spies in black and white cold-war Berlin, moving in and out of deep shadows. Between trees, behind statues.

Arrina had seen the newspapers. Dr Brown had become a wanted man. The list of misdemeanours was impressive and utterly improbable. But, guilty or not, the press had spoken. He'd fled abroad. Interpol hot on his heel. His bank accounts frozen, millions of pounds confiscated. Considered dangerous, potentially armed. The photograph, probably intended to generate a sinister air, was flattering. Heavy darkness around his cheekbones, chasmic eye sockets, exaggerated scar on his fore-head, slightly grainy, like an old headshot from police records. Looking straight at the camera, at her. In real life, he never really did that for long enough for the image to carve a place in her visual memory.

Arthur's words came at her like a train.

The agent. That'll be what they were talking about. He kept it in the safe. Didn't he? Never said what was in there. But we all suspected. That morning, after the break-in, it was open. Just slightly ajar. Did you see? I'd never seen it open before. Had you? I took a quick peek inside. Because, well. Wouldn't you? And it was empty.

His voice was shaky, his eyes pink under the orange lashes. Arrina focused on the gravel and drifted closer, bracing herself to comfort him. But Arthur kept widening the space between them.

I thought the Facility raided the place. Like everyone. That they took the agent because who else? Looking for clues or something. Especially after they went all Gestapo on us. But then they asked me if I'd taken it. Which got me thinking. Only Brown knew the combination. So maybe he took it. Made it look like a break-in. But it doesn't make sense. Why mess up your own lab?

Arthur pulled a hip flask from his inside jacket pocket, unscrewed the lid and offered it to Arrina.

Suppose it doesn't matter now. Nobody comes back from suspension. That's what they say. What a waste. We had a good thing going there. Then Brown goes and blows it. What an arse. The stuff in the newspapers is probably true.

They continued to walk, narrowing and widening the gap between them.

And then. Get this. When I refused to confess. They said they had photographs. Of Brown and me together. Compromising ones. I mean, come on. I've been nowhere near the man. As if. He's barely spoken to me. Said they'd make them public. It's ridiculous.

Arthur let his mouth fall open as he took in the sky. Arrina followed his eyeline. Under a smooth grey blanket, two birds hovered side by side, appearing to make no progress in any direction.

Unbelievable is what it is. I mean, what the actual fuck? Who would do that? Sleep with him. You'd have to be mad. Even if I were that way. He's disgusting. And old. And smells weird. The idea makes me sick.

Arrina didn't know what her face was doing when Arthur Bloc turned to her for a response but he saw something in her expression that tore down his dismay and replaced it with child-like delight.

Wait a minute. You?

She shook her head and made to speak.

Oh my god. Arrina Heal. You've got a dirty secret. I mean. Obviously he was interested. But bloody hell.

· · ·

It was another two weeks before Arrina saw Arthur again. It occurred in a stuffed elevator as it burrowed deep into the Facility. He was hidden from her at first, behind the shoulders of the other passengers. There hadn't been the time to find out who else had been instructed to return to work. A late phone call had told her to report at the Orphanage at 9am the following morning. She would alight at level twelve, the lowest she could descend aboard this lift, although she'd heard of a second elevator nearby that went further. What happened on most of the other floors was a mystery to Arrina. There was no signposting, no hospital-style markers on walls to point visitors to their desired departments. From this side of the sliding doors, each level looked identical.

The usual voicelessness permeated the elevator, eyes clung to the various corners, vents, and warning notices. As the contraption descended, the routine gnawing and grinding of its antiquated workings were accompanied by weak coughs and rasping nasal passages. They stopped at the first floor. This one she did know. The home of the Playpen and several administration departments, including human resources and payroll. After a delay, doors slid wide and exposed the occupants like sardines in a freshly opened can. They braced themselves for one of their number's polite requests to be let through and for the doors to be held as they pushed through the bodies and burst out into the empty corridor. But nobody spoke or moved. At level two, three people wrestled their way off, and three forced their way on. She suspected this floor served some kind of air defence research function because of the high-ranking Royal Air Force officers she had seen alighting here.

Similar tussles ensued at levels three and four. But soon, the elevator began to empty. At level six there were only four people left. Arrina dared to raise her eyes. The two women in front of her wore white lab coats with tied-up hair and spectacles. She leaned back just a little to look between their shoulders to check if she would recognise the other person. And there he was.

Arthur Bloc, watching the numbers on the control panel illuminate and dim one by one. By level nine they were alone. Arthur was still fixated on the blinking button. Arrina cleared her throat as loudly as she could.

There was no surprise in his face when he turned. A nod and a slight grin, as if they still met this way every day.

Good to see you. Going down?

He let out a single laugh.

She explained she'd been called in.

Glad to be back?

Before she could respond, the elevator stopped at level ten, where she knew the discovery laboratories were located, including the one Dr Brown had been using. Arthur nodded again and alighted.

See you around.

The doors closed and Arrina continued down to the Orphanage.

ALFONSO

—Oh, Alfonso. What a mess you've got yourself into.

Mr Alexander sips hospital tea and purses his lips. He continues, saying something about knife wounds, about Alfonso being tougher than he'd thought.

Alfonso watches him brush invisible crumbs from his jacket and place a hand on the peaked cap that rests on his crossed leg. He talks through his always-smile about the footage he's seen and the people Alfonso hurt.

—You were like an animal. It's quite a watch. It was as if everyone just lost their minds. Especially you, Alfonso. Brutal, and he shakes his head.

Mr Alexander rises from his seat, walks to the window by the bed, and parts the blinds.

When he speaks again, he says he can't be seen to condone behaviour of that kind. He mentions Mil and Jen, prison, disgrace on the council, wasted potential. As he puts his hat under his arm, the metal insignia of the traffic department catches the light.

His hand sweeps his hair as he moves to the foot of the bed. He talks about team morale, about sending the wrong kind of message, protecting reputations, this month's figures, and smashing targets.

—So I've dealt with it. I had a quiet word with the Chief Inspector. I reminded her about our department's substantial contribution to her budget and how awful it would be if that somehow changed.

Mr Alexander reaches down and pats Alfonso's leg.

—It's all going to be fine.

His always-smile is bigger now. As the man leans down, the sight of it reminds Alfonso of earlier hallucinations. A floating mouth combined with the features of others. But this one, the real mouth on a real face, grows nearer until Alfonso can feel its lips against his ear.

—It's decision time, Alfonso. Now that we've both seen what you're capable of, I want you to have a little think about how you might channel this newfound gusto of yours when you return to work. You know, when I was watching you beat the living shit out of those people, it occurred to me, if only Alfonso could apply a quarter of that enthusiasm to his job, he'd shoot up the ranks in the blink of an eye. Alternatively, you could leave.

Alexander moves away and straightens his back. He pauses to examine the grapes in the bowl on the bedside unit under the emergency pull cord. He frees a fruit from the cluster and holds it close to his face, rolling it between his thumb and forefinger.

—Just resign. Let me hire a younger, more able man. That's what I'd prefer, to be honest with you. But like I say, this is about appearances. Sacking you after what you've been through would be hard on the troops. I've got to consider their feelings, haven't I. So, anyway, decide.

He drops the grape back into the bowl.

—And do it quickly. We wouldn't want these annoying charges returning to bother us in the future, would we?

PART VI

ATLAS

This is a treasure Atlas retrieves from the archives on special occasions. It goes as follows. He once scoffed at Moss's ideas of a new empire, a global government run from Whitehall. But on bad days like these, he craves it. He imagines the beautiful order of systems and controls. He yearns to be inside the gargantuan automaton, a small cog meshing with his fellow men and women, shoulder to shoulder, turning because there is nothing else to do but turn, a minor piston out in the extremities of a mechatronic limb, mindlessly, contentedly pumping under pressure, one of a billion ball bearings easing the movement, rolling and rolling and never questioning his place in the apparatus. The purposefulness of being a part of something so much larger than himself, a component in the machine, the idea of it tastes so good. And it's made all the more delicious because of this alternative. This collapse of his making. This disintegrating, rusting tangle of broken parts that are cracking and crumbling by the day, thousands of micro-territories worldwide just like this one, with populations who can see no further than the end of the food queues. This monumental mechanical failure. This meltdown. Slow-motion demolition. An unabating splintering of structure and everything that ever kept him and all those around him safe. The fractures and fragments, the endless smashing and shattering of what he once would've blithely described as normal life. And in this wreckage, scattered about the world like unexploded submunitions of the latest cluster bomb technology, are places, mini-states, run by incompetents, sitting above decaying nuclear missile facilities or at the feet of neglected atomic reactors. Who's to say there hasn't already been an accident and a radioactive cloud isn't drifting across Europe poisoning every living thing in its wake? In other enclaves, self-anointed emperors go about their days unaware that they are the custodians of unmonitored laboratories stuffed to the brim with factory-made viruses. Who will prevent the next flesh-eating plague from escaping when the building inevitably falls apart? And there's this place, with its giant drum of the deadliest substance on the planet being tended to by a recluse who believes his reflection is an autonomous, sentient entity. If this is the alternative to Moss's horror show, then the man was right all along and Atlas is sorry he ever thought he knew better.

———

It's been two months since he last saw Angela, similar to the length of time he was in hiding. There is a parallel he recognises and it gives him some solace. Maybe she is lying low somewhere. He hopes that, if she is, she enjoys her experience as much as he did. Hiding suited him. Or rather, being hidden did. There was no desperation or fear or any of those other emotions commonly associated with it. Others were keeping him safe because he was worth something. And, of course, he found that flattering.

During this time, he began seeing his life as a story with a beginning, a middle, and an end. And if he is still living within a story, Angela must also be in her own, one that brushed against his for a while. It's not that she has disappeared altogether. She is somewhere, working through her plot line. Maybe she's being hidden by people who need to keep her safe, just as he was. It might even be that they're hiding her so she can return to him when whatever danger she is in has passed. These allies may understand the importance of his work and, by extension, hers. And if that's the case, perhaps she is being looked after well. It is important to him they take good care of her.

His hideout was comfortable. He liked the minimal decor, the concrete flooring and the intentionally unfinished walls. Well-designed bare-bones furniture. A bedroom for him, another for his revolving security detail, a simple, amply equipped kitchen, and a living room with large sliding glass doors that led onto a balcony. The view was of a sea. He didn't know which one and never found out. He will ask Angela when she comes back. She'll know. No reason to keep it from him now.

It was there he first met Angela, Farfalla's head of security. Their initial conversation, him furious that he'd been drugged, her apologetic but firm.

She said it had to be done. This is a zero-risk operation; we can't afford a leak.

He shouted at her. Who the hell was he going to tell? And she'd listed names.

There were holes in his arm, three he remembers. But the first dose must have come from the whisky Farfalla had handed him at the pub. That was the last thing he remembered. A toast to future success. They'd planned his disappearance only minutes before. It had been a face-to-face meeting in a pub in Manchester. Everything had to be in person. Nothing written. Nothing digital. And no patterns. Random venues in random locations. Hence, the free house in the north of that sprawling city. It took Atlas an age to find it, and when he did he was convinced the clapped-out murder hole had to be the wrong place. But Farfalla was there, sitting in a corner away from a creak of old men who looked too regular for their own good.

Over drinks, the American explained it would take a few weeks to secure a site for their work and set everything up. His people were researching locations suggested by Atlas, including Poland.

Atlas explained that the Facility would start looking for him the minute he didn't return to work.

Not so long ago—they wouldn't have noticed I wasn't there.

Farfalla nodded as if he knew this already.

The choice was simple. Either Atlas went back to work and feigned interest in progressing the project in line with the new directive, or he went into hiding. Farfalla said he had a place where Atlas could hole up and people who could handle everything. They'd keep him secure and fetch whatever he needed from his house and lab before his employers noticed anything. The pair agreed he should disappear as soon as possible.

Atlas excused himself. He stood at the urinal and stared at scrawled, indecipherable graffiti on the old beige-tiled wall. They were actually about to do this. Together, they were going to rid the planet of hate. Nothing else mattered to him now. It felt as if he'd been on this trajectory his entire life, and here he was, on the verge of making history and defining how the world would remember him. Doubts swung at him but they were easy to dodge. He had faith in his new friend and, at that moment, quite a lot in himself.

There were two whiskies on the table when he returned. The men chinked glasses, toasted the future, and drank.

His entire time in hiding was set against a classical soundtrack. Most of it was music he didn't recognise but felt he should.

There was no phone or internet access. But there were books so his afternoons and evenings disappeared into stories. Grey, Orwell, Kafka, Ballard, Nabokov, Atwood, García Márquez, McCarthy, Smith, O'Brien. The effect on him was unexpected. He had always enjoyed a little fiction here and there. A chapter or two of the latest big prize winner, just enough to take his mind off the day's troubles before turning off his bedside table lamp and instantly forgetting the story he'd just started. Therefore, reading this way was new. It was an intense experience that brought him to his own story, something he'd never contemplated before. At night, in bed, he sculpted the narrative of a man who saved the world. From his troubled youth to his troubled adulthood, the rises and falls, the minor triumphs and the spectacular failures, the loves and the clashes, all of it, every detail powering his story towards its conclusion. Someone will write this one day, he thought. Or he would. A memoir of a secret saviour.

In the mornings, he worked. His notes from the lab had been retrieved and his new team, Farfalla's people, security-cleared and serious-faced, arrived in batches to take briefings. Atlas handed over adjusted plans for the Extractor, specified equipment and safety processes, storage requirements, taking care to give them only the information they needed to know. When they pressed for more detail, the whys to his whats, they left frustrated. A career of protecting ideas at the Facility had taught him to keep things back to ensure that he, Dr Atlas Brown, remained at the heart of the project.

Even if you are expecting it, the moment you discover you are a fugitive wanted by international authorities can be jolting. Atlas estimated it would take months if it ever transpired at all. The reality came as a surprise. A threat to national security in the blink of an eye. He found his new status both terrifying and pleasing.

The report of his changed classification came from Angela on her fifth visit to the hideaway. He already despised her because of her type, this wishy-washy woman, devoid of character, taking up space with her extra pounds and loud voice of nothingness, adding zero value to the world. She claimed to be responsible for his security. It seemed unlikely that Farfalla would choose someone like this to protect him, with her absurd collection of primary colour trouser suits, poorly dyed hair, and that northeast accent with a sing-song cadence that wasn't remotely serious enough for the job in hand. And the way she laughed, it boiled his insides so violently he wanted to push his fist down her throat to rip out the cackles at the source.

His heart sank whenever he heard she was coming and sank further when she arrived, always bursting his hideaway bubble with those sickeningly sweet tones.

Hiya, pet. Looks like you've had a little break-in.

She handed him a tablet with the video primed to play. Farfalla's team recorded it an hour after they'd removed the final contents from Atlas's garden lab. Three dark vans howled down his street, screamed to a halt, and belched armed personnel out of their sides. Dressed in black, with helmets and goggles, torches on their rifles, they broke down his shabby front door and disappeared inside, leaving two of them to stand outside like sentries. It happened so quickly. Atlas imagined he'd been there, in bed. Or making his cup of valerian tea, relaxing in the bath one moment, a high-tech muzzle pointing at his chest the next.

The lights in neighbouring houses flickered on. Curtains twitched. Atlas watched Lawrence, the banker who lived across the street, march down his garden path, his flapping dressing gown revealing pink pyjamas under the orange streetlights. A sentry yelled at him and he turned on his heels.

Further shouting became audible at that point. It seemed to come from inside the house, and for a second Atlas thought they'd found someone in there. Intruders, perhaps. He had been burgled three times since he'd bought the place and it would've been joyous to watch these stormtroopers drag the little shits out onto the street, guns at their heads. But, disappointingly, they emerged empty-handed.

An Interpol Red Notice appeared online twenty-four hours before the newspaper stories. He was wanted for drug trafficking, people smuggling, and money laundering in one hundred and ninety-five countries. The tabloid press demanded his head on a platter for running a child sex slave ring. Both used the photograph from his Facility ID card. Shot eighteen years ago, it flattered present-day Atlas, its resemblance to his fifty-year-old face fleeting to say the least.

The stories ran for days.

Doctor Hate, they called him.

There's your new name, Angela said as she dropped the newspapers into his lap.

Someone from the Facility must have fed it to them. Sending a message. A joke that only Atlas would get.

Nothing he read made him laugh. One piece covered K more than it did Atlas. After speculating on how the latter used the former's fame to lure children into his 'disgusting enterprise', it took some of K's lyrics out of context, found secret messages buried in choruses, suggested he was part of Atlas's operation, perhaps funding it, introducing his older brother to his 'wealthy pervert friends'. Atlas asked Angela to get a letter to him. She smiled and shook her head.

Some articles included quotes from colleagues and neighbours. He'd always been reclusive and a bit weird. There was something creepy about him. One woman, whose name Atlas couldn't place, was horrified that she'd once introduced him to her children. Mr Lawrence Corn, 37, the man who'd launched a charm offensive the day Atlas moved into the house hoping to persuade him to become his Friday night drinking buddy, was quoted as saying you have to wonder about men of a certain age who live alone.

Against Angela's advice, he snipped the articles. He needed them to remember who had said what for the diary he would never keep, for the justice he would never get round to finding, for the revenge he would never take.

We can't call you Doctor Hate, said Angela, but do have a little think about who you'd like to be.

Perhaps she brought up his identity at a later meeting. She wasn't one to dump too much reality in a single serving. Even she showed more consideration than that. Whenever it happened, Angela explained that Atlas Brown would not be a name he could use once this was over. He should think of it as mere nomenclature and distance himself from it, psychologically speaking.

The old Dr Brown was now a digital phantom. 'Cyber puppet' was the term Angela used. One of her security team, who specialised in such matters, dangled the algorithmic marionette from virtual strings and danced his electronic fingerprints across eastern Asia. He enjoyed the idea of his apparition leaving a trail of fiction behind it as it slipped through borders, sent text messages and emails from a spectral phone, logged on at internet cafes and mysteriously disappeared seconds before the local police appeared.

But what this Angela woman didn't seem to understand, and he was reluctant to explain, was that he would need his name when it was all over. This became clearer as he chiselled away at his unwritten narrative. He was making history, and one day he would lay claim to his legacy. People would want to know him, to know who was responsible for the new world in which they lived.

It's possible that while in hiding, Atlas asked after Arrina. He likes to think so. He thought about her, he remembers that much. He missed her. Mourned the loss of her. He assumed the entire team would have been redeployed to other projects by then. Maybe some had been sent to the Orphanage. She would've moved on. Whether or not he'd vanished, a woman like her was never going to hang around a man like him for long. And certainly not for the man who, she probably believed by then, had lacked the courage to return to the lab to announce his failure to secure the funding or, worse, to confess that he had capitulated and agreed to weaponise his discovery.

Would he have told them? It might've been easier to replace

the whole team than explain himself, standing there, hitting the side of an empty coffee mug with a spoon, hello, can everyone gather around, thank you, now, you know we were going to save the world? Well, there's been a slight change of plan. We're making a weapon instead. Any questions? Those blank, wrinkle-free expressions staring back at him.

Nor was she going to hang around the man who kept sex slaves in a darkened warehouse, who traded in migrant misery, who ran a complex criminal network that flooded school playgrounds across the British Isles with narcotics.

Whether he was missing her or mourning her or regretting ever having looked at her, he was in the process of leaving her behind alongside everything else he'd abandoned. No matter the intensity of his craving, she was gone, and he would have to get used to that.

Historical Interlude

In the late 1700s, while the French Revolution raged, a very different kind of uprising was underway. Although few people realised it at the time, scientists in France and elsewhere were up to their necks in the Chemical Revolution. Historians claim this insurrection spanned over two centuries, beginning in the 16th. However, for this story, we are only interested in the activities of one man over a somewhat shorter period.

The individual in question was Antoine-Laurent de Lavoisier, a nobleman chemist from Paris. During his career, he identified and named hydrogen and oxygen, discovered the latter's role in combustion, created the metric system, and invented the law of conservation of mass. The well-heeled Parisian also proved to be a prolific social reformer and humanitarian. He spent much of his time and money improving the French capital for the commoners: urban street lighting, clean

drinking water, air quality, prison standards, and public educa-
tion. Furthermore, as securing funds for science was no easy
task in those days, he used his wealth to establish a state-of-
the-art laboratory as a sanctuary where ambitious young scientists could develop their experiments free from financial
worries.

Unfortunately, these endeavours were overshadowed by his
reputation—many Parisians believed Monsieur Lavoisier to be
an utter bastard. This was due to the great man being a driving
force behind one of the most violent and reviled tools in
the *ancien régime's* armoury: the *ferme générale*, a company
designed to collect tax from farmers. Worse still, he commis-
sioned a wall to be built around the city to streamline the collection of duty from the beleaguered poor.

This was not a good look for the altruistic scientist when
the *Reign of Terror* began. Lavoisier was convicted of tax fraud
and selling adulterated tobacco and sentenced to death by guil-
lotine. His appeal failed to persuade La République to spare the
life of this fine scientific mind, and in May 1794, Lavoisier lost
his head. (In an excellent example of 'science karma', Jean-
Baptiste Coffinhal, the judge who threw out the appeal, was
executed a few weeks later.)

Before his decapitation, Antoine-Laurent de Lavoisier built
the very first gasholder, or, as he called it, the *Gazomètre*, to aid
his work in pneumatic chemistry. Meanwhile, on the other side
of the English Channel, a Scottish inventor named William
Murdoch had just discovered how to distil flammable gas from
coal. Soon afterwards, Murdoch joined Boulton & Watt, an engineering and manufacturing firm based in Birmingham. While
there, he constructed a mechanism to heat coal and produce the
gas, which he used to illuminate his home and office. However,
he didn't have a way to store it. So, James Watt Junior, the son of
Murdoch's employer (and a man who also got into a spot of
bother in Paris during *La Révolution*, though not enough to lose
his head), helped Murdoch adapt Lavoisier's contraption. It

worked well, and the company produced a larger version at its first gas works.

With the help of his understudy, Samuel Clegg, Murdoch went on to construct a second gasholder at Salford Twist Mill in 1805 and a third at Sowerby Bridge. From 1850 onwards, after the first telescopic gasholder was built in Leeds, these giant metal barrels started popping up everywhere. Then, in 1890, William Gadd of Manchester firm Gadd & Mason made a monumental leap in the technology with the invention of the spiral-guided gasholder. By the start of the 20th century, one would be hard-pressed to find a British town without such a mechanical wonder.

End of interlude

The scene of a bustling gasworks fades to black as the camera cuts to post-industrial Britain, a couple of centuries after Lavoisier's posthumous exoneration.

Two figures pick their way over a crumbling brick and concrete desert towards a giant iron memorial to more optimistic times. Like a churchyard of fallen headstones, the remnant footprints of demolished factories and warehouses divide the ground between the men and the shrine. From this distance the structure resembles a beetle on its back, legs thrust up to heaven, the smooth dome of its underbelly vulnerable.

Farfalla stopped and spread his arms.

This is perfect, he announced. There's more than enough storage, and all this vacant land means we can do everything we need to right here.

Atlas checked his ego. Had he really expected another secret underground laboratory? Had he imagined a hollowed-out

volcanic island in the middle of the Pacific or a converted super-
tanker off the coast of India? He might have fantasised a little.
But this. This was a wasteland. Worse than that, it was a wasteland in Castleport.

Farfalla lurched forward several paces in front of the
scientist.

We have to be inconspicuous, and that's what this place is.
That road over there. You see it?

He pointed to his right, where all Atlas could make out was a
derelict bus stop shelter.

It leads to a decommissioned recycling plant. Nobody comes
here. We'll put up a few temporary buildings, build something
like a hangar where we can assemble the machine, and gate the
entire area off.

Have you—you've already bought it, haven't you?

I knew you'd love it.

The men stumbled nearer the gasholder.

This is the—I can't—this is the exact opposite of what we
need—it's not even—we can't—it won't work.

Farfalla's eyes and brows pirouetted as he looked up at the
metal framework.

We're going to make this happen.

Twenty iron columns linked by six horizontal iron circles,
and every space between them crisscrossed by thinner trans-
verse braces that fill the men's view with diamonds and triangles
that appear almost lace-like compared to the rest of the structure.
And there, in the centre, the empty container itself.

We're lucky, said Farfalla. They're being dismantled up and
down the country. We got this one just in time. Trust me. This is
going to be perfect.

———

Atlas's new home was inside a pair of the fifty-six shipping
containers that formed a barrier between the road and the gas-

holder. Seven containers long, four high, and two deep. His first sight of them from the back seat of the blacked-out SUV put him in mind of toy bricks stacked with little thought to aesthetics. Faded reds, oranges, greys, blues, various freight logos and states of repair, a faceless dam of rusting metal, a non-spectacle in the post-industrial landscape.

However, the other side of the container wall took a sulking Atlas off guard. He couldn't reconcile what he'd seen on his approach with the painted matt black metal, the fitted windows and doorways, and the silver web of aluminium walkways and steps that connected it all. The lower two floors were offices, workshops, a mess, and a toilet block. The remainder served as sleeping quarters. Atlas was in the top row, at one end, next door to Farfalla. It was a cuboid of luxury, its grandeur heightened by the incongruity of the surrounding landscape. A large, comfortable bed, a double-seated sofa opposite a mounted television, his Eames lounge chair, a couple of his rugs over the heated floorboards, a small drinks fridge, and various plants, including a monstrous monstera from home, all sat within smooth, insulated, plastered walls.

A sizeable circular window illuminated the accommodation during the day, and four low-hanging pendant lights did the work after dark. A mirror half a metre to the left of the window, the same shape but a little smaller, created an effect that pleased Atlas, as if the new quarters had two eyes, one looking out, the other in. And then there was the back wall. At its foot stood his bookcase, its shelves packed neat and tight, precisely how it had been in his home study. Above it hung three of his favourite paintings, including the Largo. These additions to his metal box were a surprise from Angela's team, commandeered during the final retrieval visit to Atlas's house. He might have shed a tear had he not been so worried about their removal somehow alerting the Facility to his whereabouts.

He took in the view only once on that first day in his new

accommodation. Forty metres away sat the gasholder, empty, dead looking. Like a collapsed circus tent. The ground around it and at the base of the container wall had been levelled, and a wide area of black asphalt sunsetted to the edges of the compound. At its perimeter was an eight-foot-high wire fence, and beyond that, industrial badlands, razed factories, and demolished warehouses that crumbled the land until it dissolved into a narrow wood in the distance.

The only other structure within the site was a red brick shed that stood alone behind the gasholder, only visible because the latter was empty. Maybe three meters wide and six long, with a flat roof that sloped at the far side, wedging itself into the ground. It was a sturdy-looking thing with a metal door. Atlas marked it as a potential future refuge when life on the compound became too much.

The site was acquired by a company called Castleport Aerobiology, which was owned by an offshore structure of some kind, which, in turn, was owned by something else, some type of fund or other, and Atlas's ability to comprehend liquidised and dripped, dripped, dripped out of his ears and nostrils as Farfalla clarified how the purchase couldn't be traced.

Atlas had only asked the question to be polite. He had no interest in the answer. Even if the American had explained his ability to buy the site and fund the project was down to him being some kind of high-achieving career criminal and the Hate Extractor was his chance to make amends with god, Atlas's response would undoubtedly have been the same: a nod at a world he didn't understand and an attempt to move the topic elsewhere. As long as Farfalla was paying for what he said he would, fulfilling his end of the bargain, that was good enough.

The conversation did move. First, to the distant wood and fields beyond it and how, if they covered the lower half of the view with their hands to block out the ex-industrial unpleasantness, it was like gazing upon an idyllic corner of the English countryside; then to the catering arrangements that had become complicated because of the wide range of dietary requirements among the technicians; and then to whisky-fuelled hypotheticals.

Would you have made it?

They both held glasses, Farfalla on the sofa, Atlas in the Eames. This was his third visit to Atlas's metal box, enough to make it a tradition. They'd drink, talk about the project, drink some more, and then leap into unchartered territory.

Would I—have made what?

The machine. The way the Facility wanted you to.

—no.

But?

But—I wouldn't have had a—a choice.

There's always a choice.

You're right—I made a different one—we did.

And how do you think things would've worked out if you'd gone in the other direction?

A total—catastrophe. Moss—his idea—that we'd stroll through the doors of the White House—the Kremlin—drop our people behind desks in the Élysée Palace and the Bundestag—unopposed. Perhaps the machine might've—with enough work—we might have adapted it—to do what he wanted—suck the life out of any resistance—before it even started. But for what? So we could—I don't know—plunder the planet all over again. Insanity.

Maybe a new world order isn't such a bad idea, though. One power in control of everything. In a way, it makes sense. Providing it's run by the right people.

And therein lies the problem.

Yeah.

And it isn't like we—the British—can boast a decent track record.

No.

The idea—makes me feel sick—can't even begin to imagine the—

I understand what you're saying. But the nasty crap you are thinking of, that was an empire trying to quash opposition. If there's no resistance, perhaps it wouldn't be so bad.

I'm no historian but—take away the massacres and torture and concentration camps and—all that stuff—there are examples —you know, exporting food from India and Ireland while people there were starving to death—stripping wealth and resources— forced labour—the whole thing only existed for profit—profit over life. That's our way. We are the capitalist shit on humanity's shoes.

Farfalla smiled all over his face.

We're saving the world twice. From itself and from the British.

If we—I hope so. Yes—we are.

His new desk was an upgrade of sorts. The large glass plate with heavy, grey Z-frame legs was in a shared office space in a ground-level box until he asked for it to be moved to his living quarters.

He had the two technicians who struggled with it up the narrow outside stairs pull his bed into the middle of the room and position the desk facing the far wall. Its ugliness soon disappeared beneath a paper whirlpool.

The printed to-do lists and critical paths were becoming his life. He experienced no pleasure in ticking items off as every completed task gave birth to another three. Progress was swift. He knew he should've been excited. This was everything he'd been working towards. But it suffocated him. The pressure clogged his lungs and squeezed his heart. And he found it impossible to tune out the sensation. Whenever he tried to meditate, the frenetic energy outside in the compound grounds crashed through his gentle cloudscape and pushed him into a panic. Each hammer strike took him closer to the moment he would have to assume command. And he wasn't ready.

He'd thought the hangar would take at least a month to construct. But they built it in four days. From his window, he watched in horror as cranes swung giant metal arcs in the air. Yellow hardhats beckoned them a little more to the right, a little more to the left until they were lowered into position, where workers with tools rushed in to secure them. Truck after truck rumbled the earth, a relentless march of deliveries, arriving, emptying, and departing. Cement mixers, turning and pouring, followed by a swarm of long-handled rake-like implements that pushed the grey mixture into every corner. Meanwhile, furniture and carpets arrived to furnish the empty sections of the container wall, and fitters and assemblers buzzed in and out of each metal box, transforming them into practical, inhabitable compartments. And the noise. The cacophony of construction. Clanging, hammering, screeching, booms and bangs, bleeping, this vehicle is reversings, zapping drills and whining screwdrivers, the crunching and scraping, and on and on.

And the shouting. Someone down there obviously suffered from a severe hearing impairment. Mike. Mike, Mike. Mike.

And the laughter! What did they find to laugh about? There was nothing funny going on down there or anywhere else.

But there were also days, slightly better days, when Atlas persuaded himself that the sound of progress was the sound of delay. For as long as it persisted, he remained safe from the impending circus performance in front of these highly professional technicians, these experts, as Farfalla insisted on calling them.

I'm bringing in the sharpest minds because this work needs, you need, brilliant people, he had said more than once, word for word, like he'd rehearsed it.

More of them arrived, these so-called brilliant people. Atlas watched them alight the minibuses and carry their holdalls to their temporary homes, all grins and arrogance. But where had Farfalla found them? How could Atlas trust them? They may have possessed the skills and experience his Facility team lacked, but they were not his people. In the days that followed their arrival, Atlas was sure he caught some of them looking at him, smirking as they turned away. He had no doubt that the snippets of quiet conversations he overheard were about him. And when he had no choice but to speak to them, something in their eyes revealed their disdain for him. He amused them. So he retreated to his box and hoped that the time when he would have to work more closely with these people would somehow never come. He visualised a terrible virus savaging them, a police raid and a mass arrest, a terrorist attack, an earthquake, a once-in-a-generation flood clearing the place of these experts and their equipment, and him in his metal box being swept out to sea where he would live out his days making fishing lines from computer cables.

Still, he couldn't avoid them altogether. Meals were served in the mess. It was constructed from four shipping containers, two by two, allowing a single long table to run down its middle. They ate in three shifts. Atlas always went in with the first. It was cleaner and calmer then. There was enough clutter and disorder around the compound without him having to contend with it at mealtimes. Occasionally, technicians would sit opposite and try to make conversation, but mostly they gravitated to the far end of the table. Perhaps the discomfort he experienced in their company was mutual. That's fair, he thought. He wouldn't want to eat with the boss, not one like him. It would have done nothing for his digestion. And, predictably, the early shift became quieter and quieter, as the technicians assumed correctly that Dr Brown would be there, scowling at his food.

However, his expression was more likely a wince than a scowl, a result of the effort required to control his thoughts about Arrina. He tried to restrict himself to subjects such as how useful she would've been at the compound. The woman understood him and the machine. She knew what was at stake, what they could achieve, and would have been able to inspire these people, these expert technicians, just as Farfalla wanted Atlas to. She would have had them imagining a future worthy of their hard work. One word and they'd have been hers for the taking. And with that, despite his efforts to concentrate on the practicalities of having her around, his mind would drift towards her voice and how her mouth moved, those small lips of hers, how her words circumnavigated his ears and found another way in. Then he'd be fighting with himself to keep her clothes on, to not see her sitting on top of him, bent over his sofa, not to feel her pressed up close, warming his body under a thin sheet. But the aches returned as they always did, one gripping his groin like a vice and the other standing on his chest like an elephant. And there they would remain until he cleared his mind of her.

But soon enough, the dreaded day arrived. The compound was ready and the handpicked team of specialists needed his leadership. Farfalla gathered them in the hangar before he informed Atlas they were waiting for him.

Don't overthink this. Walk in there and talk about your vision the way you described it to me. They're keen to hear from you, Atlas. You've got nothing to be nervous about.

Atlas looked at his desk for something to take with him that might help. He hadn't prepared. Hadn't wanted to, as if by not doing so he could delay this moment and maybe these people would just get on and do the job they were supposed to do. Because why did they have to be motivated anyway? They were being paid well enough. They didn't need the big-picture stuff Farfalla was so keen for them to have. The thinking had been done. They needed to implement his plans and do their damn jobs.

There had been an idea rumbling around in the background of Atlas's brain that he would befriend a technician, a man or woman who'd displayed natural leadership qualities as they prepared the compound. His intention had been to observe them all from his window or stroll among them as they worked. Atlas would spot this candidate straight away and invite them for a coffee, and after an informal interview he would ordain them project manager. From that moment on, he would communicate with the wider team through this new conduit while remaining at a distance, the mysterious genius, his thoughts occupied with grand theories too labyrinthine for mortal minds. But he hadn't observed them. No, he had stayed in his box instead, hoping that one day soon there would be a knock at his door or perhaps just a slip of paper pushed under it that said they had finished. The machine and gasholder were ready to go. He'd walk out there, turn on the extractor, and head home.

You're the man, Atlas.

Farfalla's dancing face did its best to be encouragingly sincere.

You can do this.

Atlas grabbed some papers and followed him out, swearing to himself.

Inside the hangar, they'd arranged the chairs in a circle. It looked like a group therapy session. There were two spaces left. Atlas and Farfalla sat down and the chatter ceased. Eyes flickered between the pair. Behind the people opposite him were the crate upon crate of machine parts, ready to be unpacked and assembled. Beyond that, the arched space moved away until it hit a semi-circular wall at the far end of the building.

Farfalla's beam was almost audible.

Everyone, this is the famous Dr Brown. Dr Brown, this is everyone.

Waves and nods and bright faces. Atlas panned the audience and attempted to return their enthusiasm. I can do this, he said to himself, trying to drown out the prickling anxiety. These people are here for me. They want to know me, to respect me. This is easy. Come on.

My name is Dr—Atlas Brown. At this very—moment I'm—I'm on the run somewhere in—South America.

Some laughter and more smiles.

Okay, this is okay, he thought. Stand up. Atlas stood, placed the papers on the seat of his chair, and pointed over their heads. Those boxes behind you—they contain what I hope will—with your help—become a history-changing machine. I initially wanted to make it at my—previous place of employment but there were some—disagreements—about its application. We were at crossed purposes.

His hands were shaking. He shoved them into his trousers and left the circle. Heads followed him as he walked towards the crates. Movement will distract them, this is fine, just keep moving.

If we do our job right—we'll wipe out hate and everything attributed to it—wars—violence—

Farfalla was leaning forward, nodding, fists clenched on his lap.

So that should be—fun.

Laughter again, more this time.

But we need to get it right—and we have to move quickly.

Atlas had circled back around to his chair. He picked up his papers and glanced at them. Don't do that. They'll think you're reading this, that you've been rehearsing. He folded them in half, then quarter, and pushed them into a pocket.

I wrote something for today—for this speech—but now I'm in front of you it seems—it seems irrelevant. I'm—sensing you're starting to see—see how important—the importance of your roles—that we have to—act quickly because—we believe my previous employer will try to replicate the machine—they—they can't—well—they can, but it's going to take them—they don't have—the—

And then it fell apart.

—they—you see—they haven't quite got—what I'm trying to

His words began to trick him. They hid from him, rushed

under his feet to trip him up, pretended they meant one thing only to reveal their true identities as they left his lips.

What I'm—what I'm—I'm trying to—is, it was no—no good —it—sympto—

Farfalla's face was a smiling horror. The other expressions in the hangar rippled like reflections on a disturbed pond as mouths attempted to form the shapes that would coax Atlas's sentences out into the open.

—symptomatic problems—it's complicated—if—Arrina were here—you'd understand—what I'm—

Farfalla stood.

What Dr Brown is saying is that his previous employers don't have everything they need to complete the project. But we do. Isn't that right, Atlas?

Atlas nodded, unable to offer anything else. He sat down. A clean, fire-sharp heat in the side of his head, just under the skull, cut down into his neck and shoulder and distracted him from the blurring at the periphery of his vision.

Then there was an unfamiliar voice. Its deep, floating syllables seemed to mutate, twisting and stretching so far it was as if they began nearby and concluded outside the hangar somewhere, their meaning pulled way out of his reach.

Much closer was Farfalla's voice.

Atlas, perhaps you'd like to answer that?

He came to in his bed.

Back then when it was new, the memory foam carried every inch of him just so. It was like being suspended in warm air. Beautifully designed, he thought. But now, not so much. He wakes most mornings with pain at the small of his back, stiff shoulders, and often a crick in his neck that forces him to turn his entire body to look left or right. He refuses to entertain the possibility it's his body's integrity, not that of the mattress, which is letting him down. But when he woke that evening, he marvelled at how the bed held him.

The artificial lights in the compound crept through his window to paint an elongated oval across the ceiling. He closed his eyes again without spending a moment to wonder how he'd got there and fell into a deep sleep.

Hello Atlas. Atlas, wake up.

It was good to hear her voice.

He was naked except for a baseball cap, sunglasses, and boxing gloves, floating belly-up in a small brick-lined pool of blood. Below him, discarded shards of metal and glass waited for him to sink. To his right, the gasholder's plexus of iron braces and columns split the light from the rising sun, cutting three-dimensional shapes into the thick air. Around the pool, cows, sheep, ponies, and other species Atlas didn't have names for grazed on wildflowers in a vivid green meadow. A halo formed in the clouds above him. Arrina's face drifted into the circle.

Atlas, it whispered.

The word glided towards him, negotiating the air like a feather, a soft twirl here, a slight glide to the left there. Down, down, down, this ethereal utterance graciously acknowledged gravity's pull until, there it was, taking a moment to hover in the warmth rising from his chest, and then, descending again, it landed with the subtlety of a live wire. Of white-hot coal. Of a shuriken. Shockwaves tremor through his ribs and limbs and Atlas is more awake than ever before.

Shit—where—what time is it? My glasses.

Atlas lifted himself onto his elbows.

Almost lunchtime.

I'm so hungry—wait—what? When did—how come you're—what's—going on?

I've been kidnapped. Bag over the head, bundled in the back of a van. Want some tea?

Atlas didn't laugh.

Waterboarded until I agreed to come.

If you could be—serious—please? What day is it?

Tuesday. And it was all a bit cloak and dagger.

She climbed under the duvet, her jeans touching his bare leg.

I found a note in my bag. From your friend, Angela.

She's not—my—friend.

She said you needed my help.

I—don't.

That's what she said. Not in the note, later. When we met. After we'd given my tail the slip.

You've been followed?

Not only me. The whole team. Ever since you ran away. They make it very obvious we're being watched. Mine always wears this red coat.

I didn't—run away. I disappeared—there's a difference.

They interrogated us when you didn't come back. And the newspaper stuff, it was all quite bizarre. Lots of paranoia flying about the Facility. There was a bit of a split between those of us who thought it was total crap and those who weren't so sure.

Who wasn't sure?

Then we were all suspended. Some still are. I've been assigned to a new thing, this weird torpedo that's boring me to death. Arthur hasn't, though. Remember him? He's back on your project. I see him sometimes in the canteen. He says it's a whole new set of people working on yours now, except for him. It has a different name, too, numbers and letters, not sure what it is. I don't know anybody else on the team. It's all very secretive.

Who's running it?

I have no idea, never asked.

Did they—after I left—say anything about me?

They had lots of questions about you. Then nothing. It's like you never existed. Like you vanished. But then, you had. I thought you might have done something stupid.

Such as?

Then, when I get home from work the day before yesterday, I find this envelope in my bag. They must have slipped it in while I was on the bus or something. Inside, there's a note that says HE needs you.

He—as in—me?

Maybe. It was capital letters, Aitch, Ee.

Right—so, what happened?

I'm getting there. In the morning, when I leave for work, there's this woman I don't recognise standing by the front door. She starts walking next to me, smiling and saying hello, and I go a bit faster but she keeps up. So, I'm glancing over my shoulder for the woman in the red coat but I can't see her, and this new woman tells me not to worry, the person I'm looking for has been held up. And we keep walking and she says her name is Angela, that she's your friend.

She isn't.

You said. So this non-friend of yours asks if I want to talk, and I say nothing but she tells me anyway, what you're doing, where you are, which is hilarious by the way, not North Korea like the media's saying. When she's done, she asks if I understand and gives me a choice. Either I go to work and forget everything she's told me, and she kind of warns me nicely about the repercussions if I ever tell anyone about you, or I join you.

And what did you say?

I told her no way and went to work. Are you an idiot?

But—did she let you know the—the consequences of coming here? Of—joining me?

Yes.

And then she continued to talk about her journey, about the gasholder, and about the people downstairs in their overalls while Atlas fought the urge to wrap his arms around her and push his face into her neck and thank her for coming, thank you, thank you, I've never needed anyone so much in my life.

————

There is something quite beautiful about pissing from a great height. There's a twenty-foot drop from the door of Atlas's metal box to the ground. In the mornings he likes to open that door, step to the edge of the walkway, and urinate into the new day. For an instant, the crescent connects him with the gravel below, a hot fluid arc hitting the ground with a satisfying splatter. And if he's lucky with the light, a rainbow will shimmer there for a moment or two. A full bladder on a bright, frosty morning creates the best effect. While his body is still warm from sleep, a magnificent bow of steam will hang in the air for seconds after the last trickle of piss has left him. The sight of it never fails to impress him. When the compound was populated, he only did this at night. And only then when he was too drunk to climb down to his usual spot by the windowless side of the converted shipping containers. He stopped using the shared facilities soon after he arrived. Too many people emptying their bodies in the same small space. The smell, the awkward greetings, he couldn't cope with it. But now the place is his own, aerial urination is a daily ritual.

As he relieves himself from the walkway, behind him and to his left is Arrina's old accommodation. Angela decided not to have her bunking with the other technicians, who shared metal boxes, four cots in each. Instead, she gave her Farfalla's. That suited Atlas. It was good to know she was close by. Arrina settled back into her role as his mouth and ears, which meant he no longer faced the prospect of dealing with the day-to-day management of the compound. With her handling the more minor issues, the sheer quantity of which had previously overwhelmed him, he could crawl into his comfort zone and the infinitely less stressful work of solving the big-picture problems, like how to leakproof the gasholder. And, of course, her proximity made her discreet visits to his quarters easier.

Her accommodation was marginally more comfortable than his, but they spent their nights together at his. The first evening after her arrival, she entered uninvited, removed her clothes and joined him in bed. Later, while he slept, she left. When she didn't come back the following night, it seemed only natural and polite that he should attempt to make a return visit. He tried her door but it was locked. There was no answer when he knocked. Through her window he saw her lying on a sofa, legs crossed, arms behind her head, looking up at the ceiling. He thought better of tapping the glass and returned to his box, angry at himself.

There was no pattern to her visits. It seemed she appeared when she felt like it. Sometimes three or four times a week. Other weeks, not at all. Attempting to arrange a more regular schedule was out of the question. Too desperate. All Atlas could do was wait and hope and take solace in the fact she didn't appear to be receiving any other visitors. Yes, he'd listen for movement on the metal stairs outside, for the sound of her door opening and closing, for voices, laughter, and intimacy. But lack of evidence did not mean it wasn't happening. Or wouldn't happen. Nor did it mean the technicians weren't looking at her, wanting her. It was, perhaps, only a matter of time before he heard a light tapping at her door.

He would fight the urge to look through Arrina's window whenever he walked past her box to reach the stairs. He had to remain aloof, just the right amount to keep her interested. She was attracted to Dr Atlas Brown, the inventor of the Hate Extractor, the great scientist destined to end all war, to save millions of lives, and to eliminate so much misery and pain in the world, a scientist preoccupied with big ideas and how to realise them. So that's who he had to be, not the other person, the small man who woke with a headful of self-doubt and a hollow knot in his stomach. So instead of peering inside to catch a glimpse of her, he would turn away and take in the view of the compound, the gleaming hangar and rusting gasholder, assess the men and women down there working for him, for him goddammit!, and do everything in his power to be the leader he was supposed to be.

Her old metal box is unoccupied now. Despite that, as he stands there in the morning chill, penis in hand, he senses its presence over his shoulder as acutely as he would if someone were standing there watching him. The container has become a shrine to a person and a time it pains him to remember. And later, when he passes it on his way to do whatever he decides to do today, Atlas will avert his eyes as he does every day.

The American once joked that he and Atlas would fall out if they ever ran out of topics they could disagree about.

Quarrels are our love language, he would say whenever he sensed the scientist's exasperation.

The arguments occurred in private, in Atlas's quarters. And the one he remembers now wasn't the first or the last. Nor was it the most drunken, although they'd consumed several cheap whiskies with green ginger wine. Having given up pressuring Atlas to mix more, Farfalla had resorted to pouring them himself, adding too much sweet wine and spoiling the drink. Which was how this particular dispute began.

Atlas couldn't tell him he despised being told what to do. That would've handed him too much ammunition. And he could not admit to resenting how Farfalla expected everything to stop when he turned up. He came roughly twice a month by this time, usually unannounced, arriving in the afternoon and leaving the following day after a night on Atlas's couch as he no longer had his own accommodation on site.

Every visit was the same, his ridiculous smirk waltzing over his face as he announced inspection time.

I'm checking up on my investment. Let's go.

They would start with the scaffolding inside the gasholder, then on to the extractor hangar. The technicians in their matching overalls and hardhats would nod and move out of the way as the two men marched around the compound. Atlas pointed out where they'd made progress and listed the key issues they had overcome since the last visit. And he'd watch Farfalla pretend to keep up with the detail.

Excellent. Good job. Well done, everyone.

He aimed his words at those on his payroll. They would thank him and return to work as their employer moved on to the next item. Then, when the pair had done the rounds, it was into the main office to look at schedules and discuss the new challenges, the missed deadlines, expected delays.

Wrangling over costs was part of the routine. Atlas had a continuous need for more equipment and materials.

You can't—predict the price—of something like this.

It always started lightly, with friendly eyes and open body language. Then one of them would step closer to the edge of the hole neither wanted to jump into.

Farfalla might shake his head and mumble a common complaint, shuffling nearer.

You've been outside the real world for too long, Atlas. Things are in danger of spiralling out of control.

And as the good humour evaporated, Atlas would step closer still.

I'm—not your accountant.

No, you're a money pit.

Sober, both men would see how close they'd come to the edge, the darkness at their feet, and instinct would tell them to retreat, to change the subject while making a mental note to return to it later.

But this visit had been different. After the tour, Atlas followed Farfalla to Angela's office.

She sat behind her desk, Farfalla perched on its edge, and Arrina was cross-legged on a chair. Atlas stood with his back against the window. The fifth presence, the subject awaiting discussion, lingered in the background, in an invisible corner, while the others eased their attention towards it.

The weather had little impact on their work but they talked about it anyway. What a pleasant start to spring. A bit of blue sky really changed the atmosphere of the place. Angela had seen some daffodils growing behind a crumbling brick wall just outside the compound on her way in that morning. Farfalla had travelled from Berlin, where snow had fallen for a week.

The early sunshine warmed Atlas's shoulders as he listened to the small talk. He knew something was coming. A cut to his funding, probably. Discussions about such matters had always started like this at the Facility. Why should it be any different here? It struck him as an odd idea that a blow like that could be softened by chitchat. Let's pretend everything is fine for a few moments, chat about last night's tv, check in on everyone's day so far, maybe wish someone a happy birthday, then we'll chuck a hand grenade onto the table. Is that okay with everyone?

Angela was smiling.

Isn't it lovely that Arrina is settling in?

Farfalla's face cartwheeled, and Atlas nodded.

Her experience of the project before it was liberated is proving to be really helpful. Anyway, she's been a dear and told me all about how things were at the Facility and what's changed since you absconded, Atlas. They seem to have no idea where you are or what you're doing. So that's good. The consensus appears to be that you are probably abroad. However, there are some concerns that you might be trying to sell your work to an enemy state. But as long as they think this is happening somewhere far from here, there's nothing to worry about for now.

Farfalla shrugged.

So what's the problem?

Yes, well, as you're aware, they're building their own version of the machine. We always assumed they'd do that eventually. From what Arrina's told us, we're probably in the lead thanks to our head-start. But, and it's a big but, she doesn't have information on the full extent of their progress. So, there's some guesswork going on here. Of course, we've never been overly worried because we thought they didn't have the agent.

Atlas cocked his head.

What—do you mean—why the past tense?

Nobody knows—anything about it—except me.

He looked at Arrina.

You were the—the closest to the project and you—you didn't—did you?

She shook her head.

Angela sat forward in her chair.

The trouble is that they might now. Or be on the verge of knowing. They have a research team working on it exclusively. With Arrina out, we won't be able to learn more about their progress. This isn't a dig, Atlas, but if I knew what the agent consisted of, I could find out how far they've got. But as you don't want to share that information, the prudent thing to do is to assume they're at least level pegging.

Farfalla's brow threatened to touch his chin.

Level what?

Level pegging. Even-stevens. Drawing.

The American nodded as his face settled down again.

You must admit, Atlas, it would make things much easier if you'd tell us what's in it.

Atlas pushed himself away from the window and walked closer to the desk.

It doesn't matter—the contents—the agent—it's irrelevant—their plan is—it's different from ours—they think they can develop localised extraction—which is impossible—and then use the Particle as a weapon. And—let's not forget they take an age to do anything—it's a slow, lumbering—mammoth of a place. We'll have all gone home by the time they get started.

As Farfalla lifted himself off the desk and moved to the vacated window, his features tumbled and reassembled repeatedly.

I agree with Angela. Think about it. One minute you have all the technology and knowledge you need to seize control of the whole world, and then, just like that, it's gone. Poof. The brain you depended on most disappears with everything he needs to go freelance, and he's the only person alive who knows what the agent is made up of. He can't build the machine by himself, so he might, and probably will, try to find somebody to help him make it the way he originally intended. And here's the thing, if the Facility can see the potential for the Extractor on a geo-political level, what is stopping some other state from seeing it too? Suddenly you've got Russia or China, or anyone else for that matter, marching their troops into other countries unopposed. So what are your options? Wait for your lumbering mammoth of an organisation to get its shit together? Or are you going to pool all your best talent and resources at warp speed? I mean, what choice do they have? They don't know where you've gone or what you're up to. So they have to believe the worst and act on it. What's the alternative? Treat it like some kind of lame land-mine project? It's unthinkable for people like that. I say we assume they're ready.

Atlas raised his palms.

It's—okay. We're moving quickly. Things are—happening as planned—more or less. There's a problem with the—the gash-older lining but—but it's being sorted—will be—just as soon as the—the new silicon arrives. We're ahead—it's fine.

Angela shook her head.

But what if we're not ahead?

Exactly. Atlas, we have to move faster. Bring extraction forward. Arrina will help you. Angela, too. She'll be here full-time. And if you need more people, we'll get more people. Or equipment or whatever else you need. But we have to move faster.

And so later, back in his box. After food, after drinks, and after three games of speed chess, all of which Farfalla won well, Atlas exploded a fine spray of the badly poured drink from his pursed lips, coating his cheese plant with a cloud of sticky vapour.

What on earth—is that?

If you don't like it, you mix them, like I asked in the first place, said Farfalla.

It's disgusting. It tastes like—like a child made it.

Why always so dramatic, Atlas? It is so tiring.

This—you see—this is what happens when you rush. When you don't understand what you're doing. This—is a prime example.

I'm serious.

It's like—it's like you've got a—deep-rooted need to—to ruin things.

The refrain had circled in Atlas's mind since the meeting. Since being told he wasn't working quickly enough. There was something deliciously satisfying in hurting Farfalla. It was the man's face. Atlas could see the effects of his insults in real time.

That's what—people like you do. You take beautiful things— and trash them.

Farfalla's features collapsed.

Don't do this.

I can do—whatever—the hell—I want. You said that to me. Remember? I won't—kowtow to you—or—your money. Others might—but not me.

Jesus, you're boring.

Atlas shuffled forward and leaned in.

It—it must be so tedious for you—your ungrateful little scientist puppet—getting above his station again. If only he knew his place.

Farfalla sighed and let his head fall back.

I won't be drawn into this.

You're—up to your neck in it already. Up to your neck in— filth. Everything you touch—it turns to shit. This so-called drink —this entire project.

Is that a fact? It's flattering that you've spent the time getting to know me and my bad habits so well.

I don't need—to know—I can smell it on you. You all smell the same—the stink of money.

Farfalla rose from his seat, his face swarming.

Now you listen to me, you piece of shit. Without my money what have you got? I'll tell you. Nothing. Sweet FA. I'm not listening to this. It is tedious. You're tedious. Your problem is you're ungrateful and pathetic. I've had enough.

He turned and walked towards the door.

Atlas leapt to his feet.

You—you've had enough? I'll show you enough—you—you

Atlas threw himself at Farfalla, unsure what he'd do when he reached him. Less than a second later, he was in a headlock, his face pressed against Farfalla's ribcage.

Let me—go!

His flailing arms hit a wall and the calf of one of Farfalla's legs.

Calm the fuck down, Atlas.

Farfalla released him and pushed him back into the middle of the room. Atlas crumpled on the floor, hitting his head against the leg of the Eames.

Another voice entered the box.

Is everything alright?

It's fine. The doctor had a little too much to drink, that's all.

Through his tears, Atlas could make out a man in the doorway and someone else behind him.

Atlas's vowels stretched over his frustration.

You've got—my entire life—in a headlock. The whole—fucking—the whole fucking thing. You can walk away—but I can't.

It's not supposed to be a prison, Atlas, but you're making it that way.

That night, Atlas's sleep fragmented into many dreams. In one, Angela and his brother sat side-by-side on a stage within the compound, cellos between their legs. They played with eyes shut, their heads vibrating to a duet that sounded like children begging for mercy.

In another, a hundred versions of his zombified mother and father chased him through a restaurant kitchen that went on for miles, where the chefs and servers assisted his escape by putting obstacles in his parents' way and suggesting hiding places that never remained hidden for long.

Then he was outside, spying on a man he knew was Farfalla, although he bore no resemblance. Atlas hid behind a wooden crate and watched him enter the hangar. From where he crouched, he could hear a noise like a rhythmical cough. The sunlight made it difficult to see into the building so he moved nearer. The din grew louder. Inside, hundreds of soldiers stood in formation, facing the Hate Extractor, pounding their feet onto the hard ground. The man who looked nothing like Farfalla walked around the machine. With each orbit, the closer he got to it, the faster the stomping tempo became, so by the time he was near enough to place his hand on the metal side of the Extractor, the beat had bled into a roar, like boulders being turned in a giant cement mixer. Suddenly, the man struck the Extractor with his fists. A thousand blue lights illuminated the structure and lit the faces of the watching troops. Then Atlas heard a thin scream. He lifted his head to trace the sound. A movement by the top of the contraption caught his eye. And a second one. A small shadowy shape shot down into the funnel, accompanied by another shriek, more shrill this time. Two more. Below, the man raised his arms as the shapes and cries increased in number. Disturbed by the intensity of the noise, Atlas retreated back into the compound grounds. But although the stamping was quieter out there, the screams were louder. A strong wind blew in every direction. He pushed back to the crate, hunkered down, and covered his ears. A dark tornado stretched from the hanger entrance up into the air, narrow at the base and widening like the funnel until it seemed to hold the entire sky in its grip. It moved from side to side, bulging and contracting and screaming, tiny fragments breaking away and rejoining the heaving central body. As Atlas stared, he realised that the mass comprised millions of blue-black objects or forms. This was no twister. It was a giant murmuration trying to twist itself free from the drag of the machine's suction. Countless squealing starlings were being vacuumed out of the sky.

ARRINA

Arrina understood that being buffeted through life by the whims of the universe did, from time to time, result in loneliness. And she soon discovered she missed the Facility. It was as if those last weeks there had never happened. Being held against her will, the interrogations, the fear, and the worry, they all evaporated beneath the hankering. There she had friends. It seemed reasonable to describe them as such. She could even stretch to the theory that it wasn't just the machine and all it promised that she had worked so hard for, it was also for Arthur, Ahmed, and the others. But here she had nobody to whom she could dedicate her energies.

Her relationship with Dr Brown remained cordial. She continued to sleep with him because, along with everything else, he expected it of her. It was part of the role she'd found herself in. And it was okay. The sex was still as dull and predictable as ever but she had known that would be the case. But the time she spent with him wasn't as easy as it used to be. The man had changed. On that first night at the compound, when she entered his quarters and woke him from his dreams, he seemed just as she remembered. But the daylight revealed something new. His eyes looked a little more sunken and his skin a little more grey, but this only added to his general shabbiness and did not disturb her. It was the essence of him that appeared to have altered, or as if the side of him she once liked had been replaced or crushed by the pressures he faced. The temper tantrums stood out as the most visible change. She had never seen them before, these long, excruciating rants, moments of fury that scared and disgusted her. Even when things had become pressured at the Facility, he'd never lost it like that. The less obvious changes included a minor loss of self-confidence, a slightly shorter attention span, a near-imperceptible stoop in his posture, and the faintest stale under-note in his odour. In isolation, each mutation was negligible, a nothing. But together, they represented a sinister transformation she needed to be wary of.

When he was away from the day-to-day demands of the job and when he wasn't obsessing about her past partners or potential new ones, elements of his old self resurfaced. She remained impressed by his ambition. This had been attractive at the Facility. So, striking out on his own in this way, how he'd sacrificed his freedom for the greater good, she could admire that. Still, this did not lead to closeness in their relationship. There was no friendship. He made no genuine attempt to understand Arrina, preferring to build his own version of her from assumptions and stereotypes. Even her basic likes and dislikes were of no interest to him. It didn't take a psychoanalyst to recognise her extreme discomfort in social situations. Yet he seemed to believe she brimmed with so much poise and assertiveness that there was no need to ask if she wanted to become his go-between, the person responsible for circulating his orders in the compound. Like the sex, he expected consent. Yes, she'd been his voice in the Facility but this was different. This young woman with next to zero leadership experience or personal skills appeared out of nowhere to order around these experts, most of whom were twice her age. Unsurprisingly, they resented her authority. Arrina could see them growing tired of Dr Brown's tortured genius persona. And she was nothing more than his marionette, relaying his often bizarre and unreasonable instructions. In their minds, she shared the blame. She wouldn't be finding allies among them.

While Arrina didn't object to being alone, she pined for the old days when she, Arthur, and Ahmed worked without a care in the world, when everything was about the project, the team, getting the best results, sharing the burden. It hadn't felt like a job. This, though, this was work. Hard, laborious work. Her father would have been proud.

The end was in sight, however. She knew it would take longer than Angela and Farfalla hoped for, even with the new urgency that so irritated Dr Brown, but the Extractor was almost ready and the modifications to the gasholder were progressing well. Soon enough, the universe would shift again and bounce her away from him and his machine.

Two bags and a cardboard box appeared in Arrina's quarters at the start of her second month at the compound. They contained her belongings from her apartment. Clothing, toiletries, her ancient laptop, four unread self-help books, a small maneki neko she'd owned since childhood, and a bundle of utility bills wrapped in an elastic band with a note that informed her they'd been paid. Seeing these possessions again took her by surprise. She hadn't asked for them or even given them much thought, believing them lost to the life she had left behind.

When she unpacked, she found a postcard from her mother at the bottom of one of the bags. Communication with the outside world was prohibited. Angela had confiscated her phone before she arrived and told her that emails and letters were forbidden. Then, this hadn't presented a problem. Arrina understood the need for secrecy, and she'd given up on hearing from home by then. She had suspected her father of intercepting and destroying her attempted correspondence. But the possibility that her mother was too angry with her to write back had also crossed her mind. She remembered the figure standing at the bedroom window all those months ago. She wondered if she had been looking at someone who couldn't believe she was being abandoned once again. But this postcard changed things. One side held an aerial photograph of Glen Coe. On the other, a brief note mentioned her father's illness. Nothing else. It was dated five weeks previously.

The conversation with Angela was awkward. Arrina showed her the message and asked for her phone so she could speak with her mother. Angela refused. If the Facility traced her location to Castleport, they would conclude that Dr Brown was also there. Then Arrina suggested using a public payphone instead. Again, no, due to the likelihood of her parents' line being monitored. They needed to be very careful.

The Facility is under our feet, dear. We'd be sneezing in the lion's den.

They eventually agreed that the only sensible course was to have Arrina's letter posted from abroad. Angela would provide a PO Box address and have someone check it regularly for a response. She admitted it would slow things down but it was the safest option available to them.

In dry weather, Arrina would take a sandwich to the far side of the old brick shed with the metal door. This was the furthest she could escape from her duties while remaining in the compound. She'd fashioned a small seat from loose bricks against the outside wall, and here she would sit, eating her lunch and letting her eyes zone out across the distant fields through the chainlink fencing. She rarely had time to think about anything other than the gasholder. Hermetically sealing a drum of that size without compromising the spiral-guided mechanism was more challenging than she'd expected. On four occasions now, having thought they'd mastered it, tests had proven them wrong. New leaks appeared, or the movement was undermined, and they were forced to repair, reseal, and start again. Patience was wearing thin and it was her job to keep the technicians focused and motivated. Hiding behind the shed, itself almost hidden behind the gasholder, granted her ten minutes to catch up with herself.

Angela had given Arrina no reason to distrust her. She had a warm and comforting demeanour, verging on maternal, the antithesis of the hard-faced security she'd known at the Facility. It seemed as if the woman had misunderstood the role of Head of Security and considered herself responsible for people's mental health, caring for and nurturing them, building up self-esteem and a feeling that all was well with the world. That may have been why Farfalla hired her for the project. She calmed things just by being around. Despite that, Arrina found it difficult not to suspect Angela of withholding her mother's reply. She waited a month before asking if she'd been sent a letter. (You'll be the first to know as soon as it does, lovely.) When another month went by, she enquired again. The answer was the same. But what if she'd written back? Of course, Angela would have read it before handing it over, which struck Arrina as reasonable. Security was security. But what if her mother had asked her to come home? Would Angela pretend nothing had turned up? It felt possible.

To leave the compound would cause problems. And although never stated outright, she was sure she would not be allowed to go. But how would they stop her? The security guards at the gate couldn't if they tried. There were two. Both elderly, certainly past retirement age. She'd been heading up to the entrance to see them for a while. They liked to chat about their lives. They made her tea and shared their biscuits. Ed, who worked the day shift, won her affection with packets of chocolate topped or chipped or dipped delicacies they would finish in one sitting. But the best stories belonged to Bernie. She would spend longer with him in the evenings when she didn't have to work late. He'd tell her about his time as a magician. For forty years he'd performed at the working men's clubs and cabarets, playing card tricks and pulling rabbits out of hats. (It was basic stuff, really, but I loved it.)

Bernie had appeared on television three times (when they used to air proper Saturday night variety shows; you don't get that kind of family telly these days). He'd met the Queen (lovely woman), got drunk with celebrities Arrina had never heard of (before your time, love), and travelled the world on cruise liners, entertaining the guests with table tricks and jokes.

He'd lost his wife in the early days and never remarried. By his own admission, Bernie was also beginning to lose his memory. He was happy to admit when he made things up to fill in the gaps (no point letting the truth get in the way of a good story now, is there?) She had asked him to show her something from his act, and he laughed and promised he would, one day soon.

Neither of the security guards inquired about her life. But nor had she offered anything up. She liked to believe that these men, or the Old Guard as they'd been nicknamed by the technicians, were there to impart the great moral lessons, to speak of their lives like parables. The trials and tribulations of a comparative youngster were unlikely to interest them.

Ed and Bernie never alluded to being under orders to prevent people from leaving. Perhaps all she'd have to do was crouch under the barrier and walk out. They might try to stop her but she doubted they'd succeed. Especially Ed. He was shorter than her and moved as if he wore concrete boots. He could raise the alarm, but what then? Other than those two, the only other person in security was Angela, and she probably wasn't physically capable of stopping her either. Would the other technicians run after her and drag her back inside? Maybe it would be left up to Dr Brown himself.

K

An interview published in a national Sunday. K has won an award for a score he created for a Korean film director. The journalist writes that the musician/producer laughs while explaining he was surfing on the back of the filmmaker's talent. Did he think he will be nominated for an Oscar? No, of course not. This is the first time he has collaborated in this way and there is still so much to learn. There are many far more gifted composers who deserve a nomination. His latest album, Decay, is sombre in tone compared to recent recordings. What inspired this new direction? The musician says there is nothing new in the recording's direction. There has always been an undercurrent of melancholy in his compositions, and he references his 2010 release, *The Chapel of Joy*, and the choral backing tracks he uses on *Inside*. However, he admits a sombre mood has risen to the surface of his work recently. He writes most of his music within an emotional bubble in which a single strong feeling can take precedence over others. He is unsure from where this 'internal atmosphere' emanates; it is just a reflection of whatever he happens to be going through during the composition period. Perhaps it was an echo of how it feels to be growing older (the writer notes that K will celebrate his fiftieth birthday in a month), but it could just as easily be influenced by the climate emergency or this political toxicity that nobody can escape from these days. It's relentless. Or that every time you read a newspaper or watch the news, they've invented yet another novel way for humanity to perish. Nevertheless, the artist believes there is also some optimism in his compositions. You don't have to be upbeat to be positive, he says. He wants to give his fans hope. His music is intended to act as a kind of salve, to soothe and console. Do the mystery around his brother's disappearance and the subsequent allegations play into his music? The journalist reminds readers of the charges that await Dr Brown when, or if, he resurfaces and notes K appears uncomfortable with the question. The musician says Atlas and he are very different people. Obviously, the episode has been upsetting on a personal level. He doesn't know the truth about his sibling, and the chances of him finding out the truth of the situation seem to diminish as time passes. He has no idea if he is even still alive. So, yes, that probably fed into the music. How could it not? But so did the baseless speculation the British press saw fit to publish about the musician's involvement in the crimes his brother is accused of committing. The claims made by these newspapers had a profound effect on his life.

Decay will be released on May 28th on Prometheus Records.

PART VII

ATLAS

He is hiding in a wheelie bin. They may be called something else now. Mobile refuge receptacles or trash trollies. But it's a bin and he's upside down inside of it, and if he doesn't rectify the situation soon he thinks he might lose consciousness and then what? Off to the incinerator. Buried under landfill.

If it wasn't the middle of the night, if the sun was pushing light through the blue plastic walls, he'd be able to see the shit his face is pushed up against. But he can discern the soft echo of his breath now that it's safe enough to breathe the putrid air again. It sounds like someone behind him exhaling into his ear. But the good news is the voices outside have retreated. He'll wait a few more minutes before attempting to extract himself from the predicament.

Nobody would think it to look at him right now but in recent weeks Atlas has discovered that food scavenging is an art. And where there's art there is dignity. It's a multilayered discipline that draws on an individual's powers of observation and deduction, stealth and speed, intuition, and a well-honed sense of smell. These are needy times and food waste is scarce. However, finding enough to eat is still possible with the correct approach.

The curfew is stricter these days. Uniformed wardens patrol the main roads on foot, so he sticks to the side streets and alleys. He knows these routes well enough now, and as they tend to cut through the residential areas, he has no need to risk the wider, better-lit thoroughfares. But that doesn't take all the danger out of the enterprise. People don't like strangers roaming in their backstreets and going through their bins. He isn't sure why it concerns them, but to prove it does, he has an arc of scabbing teeth marks on his left forearm courtesy of a German Shepherd let loose by an overprotective homeowner. Atlas has revised his approach and has been more considerate of late. He watches the quieter houses, those with a small number of comings and goings and only one or two illuminated rooms. His working theory is that fewer mouths mean more waste. Large families throw little away. It's also more advantageous to target homes where the bins are kept in the alleyways behind. He has found several locations where three to four dwellings match this profile. He visits them in strict rotation.

Atlas ventures out after dark. If the residents are going to dispose of their waste, they will have likely done so by then. It is better to strike when the scraps are fresh. When all seems still, he makes his move. The plastic bins are tall with hinged lids at chest height. Step one, lift the lid and inhale its air through his nose. The gases within these sealed containers create a complex miasma, and it takes a great deal of concentration to single out edibles among the rot. The longer the container has been closed, the more intricate the aroma. It's a task made infinitely easier if the bin has been emptied in the last day or two.

It is a feat of modern civilisation that, while the world disintegrates, the refuse in this tiny corner of England continues to be collected. This, alongside the wardens who march through the streets displaying all the military gusto they can muster, is a message from Alexander.

I'll protect you. Your homes are safe.

Whether this is a laudable public service or a worrying escalation of unelected power is of no concern to Atlas. He's here for food, and the collections make it a more tolerable exercise.

He might describe the various smells as layers between which his nostrils rummage until they identify a few recently discarded carrots, unfinished jars of baby food, or beans wedged in the bottom of an emptied can. Once he knows something of value is to be had, the next stage is excavation. Unless the bin is three-quarters full or more, he lays the receptacle on its side, taking care to arrange the hinges to his left or right so he can open the lid like a door. Atlas then crawls inside and retrieves the debris he wants.

This was the position he was in tonight when he heard the voices. At least two males. He froze. There were no discernible footsteps but the increasing volume of their conversation told him they were getting nearer.

First voice, it's true.

Second voice, laughing, no way.

First voice, honestly, they were out all night looking for them.

Atlas climbed deeper into the bin and pulled his legs clear of the opening. The curfew meant they were likely wardens. He'd never seen them away from the main roads before. It was a troubling development. Then the voices were very close.

Second voice, will you look at that? What a mess.

He could hear their feet scraping across the crumbling tarmac towards him.

First voice, badgers probably. I've seen them lift the lids and pull stuff out.

Atlas held his breath. The men were right next to him. He could see a pair of legs silhouetted at the opening. A foot moved and kicked the lid shut.

First voice, we caught one a few months back. Barry skinned and cooked it. Tasted like shit.

Second voice, more laughter, deep and menacing.

The bin rocked. Atlas reached for his shins and held them tight.

First voice, what are you doing?

Second voice, tidying up, aren't I? Keep the place spick and span.

A moment later, Atlas's entire weight was pressing down on his head and neck. The bin was upright.

First voice, he reckoned it tasted like pork, only sweeter. It bloody didn't.

And the men continued on their way.

———

Even with a glorious early morning sun outlining its curves, the machine was striking in all the wrong ways. Lying on its side on the back of the flatbed truck that hauled it out of the hangar and into the open air, the Hate Extractor looked vaguely egg-shaped, like an oversized cement mixer held together with dull steel and rivets the size of fists. Atlas stood next to Angela as they watched the transport come to a halt.

She chuckled.

It's a funny-looking thing when you see it on its own like this, don't you think?

Atlas sighed his frustration.

No offence meant, obviously, she said.

A team of technicians rushed forward to attach the pipeline to one end of the machine, connecting it to the gasholder. With this adornment, the effect was of a stranded sperm cell. Atlas hoped that later, in its upright position with the funnel fixed at the head, the machine's comical appearance would disappear into the shadow of its potential.

The entire workforce gathered outside to watch the thirty-minute test run. Today was a big day. If all went well, full extraction would follow soon, so an air of stiff excitement stood among them. Atlas cast his eye over the technicians and wondered if they were as disappointed as he was in the machine's appearance. This wasn't the first time he'd wished he had created a more spectacular-looking contraption, one more fitting to the job. Presentation mattered. He had always hated the design of NASA spacecraft. Design, pah. The last one he remembered seeing was nothing more than a shambolic pile of shoe boxes and old umbrellas wrapped in tinfoil and mounted on a rusty shopping trolley. Tidy your work up, for god's sake, he'd think. The whole of humanity is going to see this. Have some pride.

If Moss hadn't got in the way, he might have had a budget to collaborate with a product designer. Together they could have developed a large black box, minimal and sleek, with a single line of dim red lights running up the side that lit up one by one as the machine's internal fan blades powered towards optimum speed. Or a giant brushed aluminium tube with revolving ends that whirled and emitted a pleasing hum as it sucked the Particle out of the sky.

The issue at hand. That's what Atlas had to keep at the front of his mind. This wasn't a show. This wasn't a movie starring him, the maverick scientist about to alter the destiny of humankind because terrorists had kidnapped his daughter. Or because he wanted to blow up a giant meteor on a direct collision course with Earth. He had a job to do. He was a professional working in challenging circumstances who'd given up much more than he should have to see this through. They would never thank him for it. The world would never know. The change would seem normal. Wars and violence would stop and people would believe they'd simply evolved into better humans. They'd speculate about whether they had reached some sort of inevitable equilibrium. Was that not enough for him? Why did he deserve recognition for this work? He'd sacrificed everything for this project because he had a duty to do so as a member of the species.

Sacrifice. A tricky word. *Sacrificium* from *sacrificus*. *Sacra*: sacred things. *Facere*: perform. A show for the gods, staged in exchange for a return, to seek favour or avoid retribution. Look, I've killed my goat, now give me a good crop. Look, we slit the throats of the seven virgins, so please stop this famine. But sacrifice wasn't what it used to be. People sprinkled the term around the place, pretending to themselves and others that it represented their complete selflessness. Surrender without gain. They'd gloss over the expected payoff. But, secretly, they always wanted restitution. A mother turns to an unruly son and tells him he's ungrateful for everything she has sacrificed for him. She ritually slaughtered her career, her connections to her unencumbered, childless friends, and her carefree life to nurture him. And in return for her offerings to the deities of maternity or the patron saints of mothers she wants a particular pattern of behaviour. But he has gone and ruined the new paintwork with crayons, failed his exams, fallen in love with a man, become an artist, married someone from a lower class and a different race, hasn't make a fortune to support her in her old age, or made a fortune and won't support her, doesn't call, no longer visits her at the care home, and she feels cheated.

Sacrifice is a risk. This trade with the gods is stacked against you, even if you define the expected return. Your goat for a bountiful crop. Your best years for a large house and a nice car. Defined. And maybe, only maybe, delivered.

What had he sacrificed?

His own home. He couldn't go back. Could never sell it. He had walked away. More accurately, he'd fled.

His family. A brother. Does an ex-wife count? Probably not. Definitely not.

Friends. Not really.

His reputation. There hadn't been much of it in the first place. What there had been was now smeared like excrement across a pig's arse.

His identity. Yes, this was the biggest one. Who would want it now? Negative equity. Close the door, push the keys through the letterbox and walk away. But in the heat of the moment it had seemed worth it.

Worth it? It would be. Could be. He'd have to wait and see how it felt post-extraction. When it was done. When hell had been yanked from the sky and the world tumbled gleefully into some ill-defined utopian future like a giggling newborn landing in a bed of soft, warm feathers. Because that's what all of this had to be down to: how it made him feel. When it was all over, the secret to the success or failure of a history-changing, universe-altering, dimension-shifting event would be found in the chemical reactions triggered in this solitary cluster of cells called Atlas Brown. Would it make him feel good enough to believe the sacrifice had been worth it?

Yes. One hundred percent yes if he went down in history as the man who saved the species. As it was, with this prospect ruled out, the deal he negotiated with this sacrifice was ill-defined. An investment with no guaranteed return. But, honestly, he knew deep down how he'd feel when it was all over. And even if he sat at his desk and wrote it out a thousand million times that the only reward he needed was the knowledge he'd made planet Earth a better, safer place, even if he opened his door and sang it into the night, chanted it every morning and every evening, even if he tattooed it onto his chest in Latin, it would never be true. What he really wanted in return for his sacrifice was the whole world. And whatever happened now, he would feel cheated.

Atlas led a team around the Extractor for the final checks, whispering to himself, breathe, Atlas, breathe.

For the sake of the test he needed to concentrate.

He stood in front of the machine, as ready as he would ever

be. It wasn't the rehearsal Atlas had wanted. The hangar remained out of use after he'd decided a week ago to make alterations. The gap between the funnel and the retractable roof section was too large and presented a potential danger. His solution was to build a platform to raise the Extractor by two and a half metres. As yet, he hadn't worked out how to secure the pipeline that would have to run from the machine's new height down to the floor before heading outside to the gasholder.

He'd been told the alterations couldn't be done in time. Farfalla called to complain.

It's like you're sabotaging this.

But Atlas had insisted.

The temporary scaffolding inside the building left enough room for the machine's storage but not its setup and operation. He should've also postponed the test run. But the pressure to stick to the schedule was mounting. He could see technicians' eyes rolling as he inspected their work on the platform. He felt the heat of their seething as he informed Arrina of the extra alterations he wanted. Tempers grew shorter. Resentment scratched through the compound. Every hushed conversation sounded like insubordinate chatter. Arrina insisted his judgement was not being questioned. Her words massaged his anxiety and eased his mistrust of those around him, but the effect never lasted long.

He would stick to the timetable. The test would run on schedule and he would show them he was in charge. That he knew what he was doing. And if that meant moving the machine outside, so be it. Afterwards, they would take it back inside, analyse the results, and make any final adjustments before Extraction Day. And soon his struggle with these people would be over.

They checked the connections and fixtures, inspected the pipeline, and tested the power and the backup generator. Then they entered the gasholder itself. This was the most crucial component of the entire project. Extracting the particle was one thing but the whole endeavour was meaningless without somewhere secure to store it. For months they'd worked to hermetically seal the telescopic drum. They lined it with rubber and a resin that would maintain its integrity for a hundred years. Atlas had no idea how that number had been calculated and found it unconvincing.

Farfalla had shrugged.

It'll be enough. You'll have figured out something else long before then. Maybe we'll build your underground tank.

They'd conducted several tests in recent days. The container had been filled, emptied, and filled again. Measurements were taken, leaks detected and resealed, and extra linings were applied. Then the tests began again. A belt and braces approach that satisfied Atlas in the end. Nothing could escape. Theirs were the last human eyes to see the inside of this spectacular feat of engineering. Atlas's gaze followed the matt black tubular wall up into the darkness that swallowed the light from the rigging lamps below.

He nodded. Hate will feel right at home here.

Outside, he watched the giant drum being lowered until the edges of the gentle dome levelled with the earth. And he lost himself to a moment of reverie. This vast mechanism that he used to think of as a rusting monster hellbent on destroying his dreams had been repurposed into a wonder in only a few months. And now all his hopes rested on it. Voices on a nearby handheld radio yanked him away from his musings. Four vehicles approaching the gate, one of them said. For a second, Atlas couldn't move. Four vehicles? They weren't expecting anyone. He scurried towards his box, stopped, composed himself, and set off instead in the direction of the machine.

Where was Angela? She had assured him everything was watertight. The entrance of the compound was visible from where he stood. The security guard leaned into the window of the first SUV. Then he straightened up, returned to his cabin, and opened the gate. The convoy sped into the grounds, gleaming black gloss and blacked-out windows.

They'd found him. He wasn't prepared for this. He turned and clattered through the door of the nearest office. A technician sitting at one of the desks let out a small scream of surprise. Atlas assessed the room until he settled upon the tall shelving unit behind the technician.

Dr Brown. Is everything okay?

Yes—quick. If we're fast—we can pull the shelves away from the—hide behind them—hurry—they're here.

Before the technician rose from his chair, Atlas wedged his fingers between the unit and the wall. He heaved with all his strength. The top of the shelves lurched and the entire thing keeled forward. He watched as the files and books and then the metal structure crashed onto the desk the technician had just vacated.

They both stood motionless, staring at the destruction. Outside, vehicle doors banged shut. Muted voices spilt onto the tarmac. It was useless. Atlas had been so close to finishing. And now this. There was nothing else for it. He would have to go out and face them.

Nine men and two women, all suited, most in sunglasses, some talking on phones. Atlas exhaled a deep breath and marched towards them, sweat stinging his eyes.

—hello—what—what can I do for you?

A woman in shades and a sleek ponytail stepped nearer to him.

Dr Brown? We're shutting you down.

Atlas could feel the weight of the compound's stares. The woman took another two steps in his direction.

And I'm placing you under arrest.

She covered her mouth and coughed. Was she smiling behind her hand? Was she actually enjoying this? Atlas's stomach tightened and his head swam.

I'm sorry. This is just too cruel.

She turned back to her colleagues and her body convulsed.

Look at his face!

At first, Atlas thought she might be having a fit. It occurred to him that now would be the moment to make his escape. Which was when he realised she was laughing. He scanned the others. They were smiling. A man stepped out of the crowd, removed his sunglasses, and held out his arms.

We're here for your big day. I thought you'd be happy.

When it became apparent Atlas had not enjoyed the joke, Farfalla ushered him into the main office. He sat at a desk.

Atlas's entire body was shaking. He leaned against a busy whiteboard to steady himself.

And who—the hell are these—people?

Close friends and colleagues. Nothing to worry about. You'll get ink on your coat, Atlas.

Atlas glanced at his shoulder and moved away from the board.

You can't—it's not—it's not okay—to—you can't do things like that—I thought—I thought that was it—this is not a—it's not a fucking joke—what we're doing here—it isn't a joke—you can't —if you do anything like that—again—I'll—

Farfalla's face seemed to turn inside-out as his features dive-bombed each other.

Okay, okay. No more surprises. Jesus. I promise. I was just trying to make you laugh. But no more. Okay. I'm sorry. I didn't want to upset you.

Atlas nodded.

How is everything? All set for today?

We're ready to—go.

Well, what are we waiting for? Let's get the show on the road.

Is—that what you—is that what you think this is—a show?

Farfalla sighed and stood.

Come on, Atlas. Let's get started.

• • •

The machine was in position, its warm-up hum barely audible over the excited chatter. Atlas walked through the assembled staff and visitors, his legs still weak. He climbed onto the flatbed and placed his hands against the machine's lower panels.

Okay, okay, okay, he murmured. This is going to be okay.

He nodded to Arrina and the crowd fell silent. She gave a single nod back and touched the screen of her tablet. The small light on the side of the machine switched from amber to green. The first whoosh buried the Extractor's warm-up purr. A second arrived a moment later, then another. Whoosh, whoosh, whoosh. The lulls between each rush of sound shortened until there was nothing but a continual deep thrum. The two technicians monitoring the pipeline by the gasholder turned to him simultaneously and raised their thumbs. Atlas looked over at Arrina, who responded with a tight smile.

And that was it, extraction had started.

Atlas lifted his eyes to the sky.

So far—so good, he shouted to the gathering below him.

Through the light applause and Farfalla's whoops, he tried to imagine colourless nanoscopic particles rushing towards the Extractor's funnel, and, for a moment, he fancied he could see streaks of translucent motion marking the air. Then he felt a teardrop on his cheek. He wiped it away and choked down the emotion. Overwhelmed was not a good look. He climbed down from the truck and approached the gasholder. Its rhythmical grumble had become so familiar during these last few weeks that Atlas often caught the whistles or hums of technicians as they accompanied its clunking cadence. But today the sound had greater resonance. This was the noise of the drum expanding as it filled with hate. When once it had been purely mechanical, devoid of meaning, now its metallic utterances seemed sinister, a colossal robot growing more bleak and terrible with every passing second and no one was inclined to whistle along.

He turned again to the assembled crowd. Everyone stared at the gasholder as its enormous barrel inched upwards. Atlas wondered if they were realising the significance of his work for the first time. Were they able to comprehend what was happening in front of their own eyes? Did they grasp the monumental nature of this moment?

That's when he spotted Farfalla walking with one of the men who'd arrived in the convoy. The man appeared older than the others. Cropped grey hair, a short white beard, and a broad back that strained against the panels of his black suit jacket. Farfalla opened the door to the main office in the container wall and ushered the man inside.

The test run took thirty minutes but the Extractor would continue in clean-up mode for another four hours, which was how long Atlas believed it would take until they could be confident the pipeline was free of the Particle. The gasholder's barrel now stood at a little under one metre in height. A team in hazmat suits and masks circumnavigated it with handheld leak detectors. Cooling fans were whirring, and most of the compound technicians had congregated in small bands while three of their colleagues prepared the harness they would later use to lower the machine back onto its side.

Farfalla's other guests loitered by the main office's door. As Atlas manoeuvred through them, the woman who had played the joke on him earlier put her hand against his chest.

Just a moment. They're almost done.

I—I need to get something—out of there.

The two men were what he wanted out of there, away from the plans and anything else the stranger might see.

They won't be long.

As she spoke, Atlas noticed she was wearing a small earpiece. The attention of the others was on him now. Up close, with their eyes hidden behind sunglasses and their actual heights revealed, they seemed more menacing. One of them moved to block Atlas.

Now—hold on a minute—you can't do that.

He turned to address the woman. She was holding two fingers to her earpiece.

You—don't have the right.

He's coming out.

The suits pushed him out of the way as they arranged themselves into a human corridor leading from the door and into the compound grounds. The man with the white beard appeared first. He eased himself down the two steps and walked into the column. As he reached the centre, the entire company enveloped him and moved away as one, leaving Atlas standing alone.

Farfalla was in the doorway.

Ah, Atlas. Just the man. Come in, come in.

Farfalla signalled for Atlas to sit.

The American took position behind the chair opposite, drumming the headrest and biting his lower lip. An empty coffee cup stood on the desk between them.

I've got some great news.

The test—it went well.

Of course! My apologies. Certainly looked that way. That's excellent.

I need to make a few minor adjustments—but other than that, everything is ready to go—for full extraction.

Perfect. That makes me so happy.

What's your—news?

Right, well, it's very good news. You're going to love what I have to say.

Farfalla sat down and Atlas leaned forward.

I'm all ears.

Tell me, what is your greatest remaining worry about this project?

The storage—and disposal of the Particle—as you know.

Yes! And what if I told you I've solved that problem?

—what?

Farfalla stood up again.

I almost can't believe I pulled this off.

What—what on earth—what are you talking about?

That this man might've solved the problem that had troubled Atlas for so long was ridiculous. Whatever Farfalla had 'pulled off', Atlas was keen to kick it to death as soon as he answered.

I've sold it.

The American's face lit up like an ecstatic child while Atlas's scrunched into a fist.

You've—what?

I've sold it. The whole lot. And for a considerable amount of money.

Farfalla strode around the office, pulling fingers through his hair. You're going to be rich, my dear friend. Stinking rich.

You—bloody idiot. You—you fool! Utter—utter moron. That doesn't—you haven't solved a thing.

Farfalla stopped. He stared back at Atlas, his features melting.

At best, you've just—given the problem to someone else. At worst—I don't—I don't even want to think about it.

You're overreacting, Atlas. This is a great deal. You can forget about the Particle and enjoy some wealth for once.

You don't—understand. The Particle—it needs to be protected and—and destroyed. Not—sold—that doesn't solve a thing—who—who's bought it—and why—have you even asked yourself—no—we can't—I won't allow this.

Farfalla returned to the chair, eyes fixed on the desk, forehead creased, eyebrows attempting to cover his sockets, lips pursed, then pouting, then pulled straight again.

No, it's you who doesn't seem to understand, which is a little disappointing. Look, you're the brains here and I'm the money. You brought the idea and I brought the finance. I've paid for everything you need. Haven't I? Have I refused you anything? Do you have any idea how much this project of yours has cost so far? No, you don't. You've never asked. Never shown the slightest interest. And that's okay. You're sticking to what you know and I'm sticking to what I know. I am making a return on this investment whether you like it or not. I own every single thing here. I pay all the wages. I own the land and all the equipment. I own all of it.

You don't own the machine—or me.

No, that's right.

And—if I walk—you've got nothing.

Again, you're right. But, equally, what will you have?

The feeling was a familiar one. If Atlas was the man he ought to be, he would walk away. Abandon it all and leave the Particle in the sky. But both men understood he'd never do that. That he wasn't strong enough. Had this been Farfalla's plan all along? To corner him in his own dream? To let him get so close to its fruition and then change the terms. It was absurd. Was he about to trap all the hate in the world only for Farfalla to sell it? Surely doing nothing was better, safer for everyone? And who was this person? And what possible reason could they have for wanting to own it other than to use it as a weapon, the very thing Atlas had given up his old life to prevent from happening?

Atlas studied the printer in the corner of the room. With enough force, he could crush Farfalla's head with it and hide the body until extraction was over. Did he have the strength to do that? He'd have to be quick. What if Farfalla stopped him?

Please Atlas, you just need to frame this differently. You'll walk away having transformed the world into an infinitely better place. And you'll be a rich man.

And you even richer?

That's beside the point.

I'm struggling to see—what choice I've got.

You have plenty of choices. I can think of six. Seven, actually. You know what they are. Stop being so puerile. There are several forks in the road in front of you. I'm not forcing you down any of them. But the one you wanted to take, the one that leads to the future you've dreamed about where you're the hero and we all skip off into the sunset with our big happy faces, that one doesn't exist. It just isn't there. Never was. But in its place is the next best thing. It is a simple choice. The path of least resistance. If you follow it, you get to complete your project, change the world, and make a ton of money. But you can put your ethics or moral code or whatever it is in the way if that's what you want. It's up to you. You can walk away and let the Facility trap the Particle. You can burn the whole enterprise to the ground. You can do lots of things. But don't you dare suggest that I'm forcing you to do anything.

Atlas was unsure why he thought staring at Farfalla would change his mind, but that's what he did. He fancied he could see the back of his skull through his eye sockets, that he might be able to reach in there and smash his ignorance against the bone walls, push it into a corner and kick it until he saw sense, saw things the way Atlas did. Maybe this is all stupidity was, an invisible tumour blocking oxygen to the frontal lobe that rendered clear thinking and sensible reasoning impossible, and normal brain function would only be resumed after its destruction. But as he thrashed around inside Farfalla's head, it occurred to him that the man's idiocy could work in Atlas's favour. He had to stop himself from smiling at its simplicity. The sheer beauty of it. He would agree to the sale. Then, after extraction, he'd claim it was too unstable to move, that they needed time to settle it into its new environment. They would be in uncharted territory. It was something they couldn't have predicted. Then he would invent further complications and assure Farfalla he was working on solutions but that they'd take a while. Years perhaps. Meanwhile, secretly, he'd develop a way to neutralise or destroy the Particle. As a plan, it was possibly quite brilliant.

Atlas broke his gaze and nodded, trying his best to appear resigned to this new fate.

So—who is this—our great benefactor?

He's an Estonian entrepreneur. Oblonsky. Made his money in

mobile phones, I think. But he's into renewables and politics now. A nice man. He's got a good heart. I like him.

A—good heart?

Yeah. He has a warmth about him. I can't explain.

Okay—what is Oblonsky—and his big heart—what are they planning to do with the Particle?

It's going to be an insurance policy. A deterrent. He's worried about Russia's intentions in the region.

So—a weapon? Doesn't he realise Russia can't—won't be capable of anything—of hostilities after extraction?

I didn't see the use of pressing that point with so much money on the table. Look, in the unlikely event he ever releases the Particle, we still have the machine, don't we? We just suck it back in again.

Atlas burst into laughter.

Is that—seriously—is that your plan? To suck it back in?

It's always an option. If things go wrong. Which they won't. This is Estonia we're talking about. They had the Singing Revolution, didn't they? They're not exactly a violent bunch.

I am not happy about this—this decision—I want to make that clear.

It's very clear.

Atlas rose from his chair and opened the door. He scanned the compound. Those were Farfalla's people taking readings and measurements, cleaning down the machine, sweeping the ground, painting container offices, driving forklifts, comparing notes, and making charts. It was important to remember that. He could trust Arrina but nobody else.

And—I don't want Oblonsky and his—secret agents—whatever they are—hanging around here while we're working—is that also clear?

Abundantly.

Farfalla joined Atlas at the door.

One last thing. The customer wants a sample from the test batch. They're sending someone to collect it tomorrow.

Atlas strode into the compound with the confidence of a highland bull. Here was a man who made decisions and acted without question, altering the course of the future as he blustered forth. The devil take your consequences, to hell with your piddling doubts. This was Atlas Brown, Dr Atlas Brown, crumpling Milo Farfalla's grubby little plan in his fist, ready to be flicked away, dropped into the nearest wastepaper basket and forgotten. He was at the door of the hangar before he realised that with every step forward he'd left a thin slice of his newly found backbone on the ground behind him, and now, like a stick of chalk dragged against a brick wall, there only remained a stub, only a fingernail's worth, only the thinnest sliver of the grit and certitude he'd possessed in such bounty just a few seconds ago. He was no longer smiling, no longer holding himself tall. He barely had the energy to stand unaided. Of course he wasn't capable of foiling the American's deal. You pompous, pathetic man with your superiority complex, he scolded himself. Put yourself back in your box and let the grownups get on with the work. Which is what he did. He turned and marched back to his accommodation, buried his face into a pillow, and screamed into it until he could taste blood.

The Yemeni Crisis, seventy-eight thousand people killed.

The Afghanistan Conflict, almost two million people killed.

The Syrian Civil War, over half a million people killed.

The Somali Civil War, approaching half a million people killed.

The Mexican Drug War, thirty-nine thousand people killed in battles, one hundred-and-forty-eight thousand people killed in organised crime homicides.

The Kurdish-Turkish Conflict, forty-three thousand people killed.

The Boko Haram Insurgency, forty-seven thousand people killed.

The Indo-Pakistan Wars, between fifty and one-hundred-and-thirty thousand people killed.

The Israeli-Palestine Conflict, twenty-six thousand people killed.

The War in Darfur, three hundred thousand people killed.

The list continued in his head, the rhythm hypnotising him.

The Kivu Conflict.

The Libyan Crisis.

The Ituri Conflict.

South Sudan.

The Caucasus.

Cabo Delgado.

Katanga.

The Maghreb.

All of them

happening

right

now.

Images of corpses, piles of them, children wearing a terror they should never have to know, drones, rattling machine guns, suicide bombers with eyes closed, lips tight, bloodied machetes, gas attacks, mass executions. How many killed today? In the last hour. How many faced death as he lay in his bed? It was an exercise of balance, holding the weight of one outcome and comparing it with that of another, the heft of all that dead human flesh versus the threat of the Particle being used as a weapon. If he never found a way to neutralise it and it remained in the possession of a country that might never use it, that might never work out how to deploy it without destroying itself, then surely he'd made the right decision. The atrocities of now versus latent savagery. Secret mass graves versus a giant drum of hate. Child soldiers versus a deterrent against invasion.

On the edge of sleep, while being taunted by imaginary lorries queuing outside the compound, flanked by foreign soldiers in First World War gas masks, a revelation occurred to

Atlas, one that would soon be buried and forgotten under vivid dreams and a fitful slumber: with no hate present, would it not be impossible to release the Particle knowing the harm it would lead to?

He woke to the sounds of a piercing, repeating shrill outside. A circle of light on the ceiling. It took longer than usual to remember where he was.

He checked the time: 5:45 am.

Through the window, down in the compound grounds, he saw a man he didn't recognise climb out of the cab of a colourless, unmarked tanker. In front of him stood three technicians. By the time Atlas had pulled on his trousers, grabbed a shirt, and opened his door, other technicians dressed in hazmats were emerging from the various buildings. Arrina was walking down the steps of the container wall.

Atlas sat on the step to his metal box, the cold air creeping around his exposed neck and feet. He watched the tanker driver refuse a biohazard suit, letting it fall to the ground when a frustrated technician thrust it into his chest. Arrina spoke to the driver, then looked Atlas's way, too briefly in the early morning light for him to read her expression. He would not be telling her about the buyer. He would explain this interruption away, say it was for tests that couldn't be run at the compound, maybe some kind of legacy programme, one of Farfalla's ideas. He'd think of something if he had to, but evasion was his best bet. She enjoyed his vagueness, enjoyed the mystery. Also, she let things go. He liked that about her.

Atlas watched a small team connect the gasholder and the tanker with the pipeline. When the transfer was underway, he got to his feet, closed his door, and returned to bed.

The dimmed rhythm of activity outside helped him relax back into his mattress where he searched for an abandoned dream. He could remember the aroma from an old orange-coloured coffee bag mingling with his father's voice reciting a story of a horse and a lion, and something about a small girl that he couldn't quite grasp, red curly hair perhaps that reached the floor and tripped him over. But just as the familiar character of the dream started to come together, a change in tempo from the compound blocked his progress. Irritated, he opened his eyes. Gravel was being crushed under heavy boots, far too many of them. And unfamiliar voices too. He sighed and pushed himself up from the bed. In the new scene below, the tanker was gone. In its place was a minibus, around which stood twelve armed figures in pseudo-military uniforms and helmets. Within minutes, Atlas was among them, pushing one of them in the chest back towards the bus while spitting into his phone.

I said—I told you—you agreed—his people—they're not welcome here.

Arrina ushered him away from the new arrivals.

I'm sorry, replied Farfalla. Oblonsky informed me about it afterwards. He's protecting his investment, that's all. They won't get in your way.

They're carrying—guns. And one of our people—security guards—one of the old guys—was so freaked by it all—he quit— upped and left.

As he shouted, Arrina opened an office door and signalled for him to enter.

We'll replace the guard. And the weapons are only to protect you and the machine. There's nothing to worry about.

Protection—from what?

It's just how Oblonsky does things.

———

Atlas is hungry. Tortuously, desperately, devastatingly hungry. And the queue for food is seven million miles long. There is no way he's joining the end of it. They bleat at him as he limps down the line.

Sorry—I don't—I never do queues.

He uses the most authoritative voice he can swing.

Make way, please—I have an—appointment—I have an appointment.

At the front is a small lorry. Two men in the back are handing cardboard boxes to a man on the ground. Three wardens stand off to the side. This is who Atlas approaches. One of them is checking papers and directing people to collect their food parcels. Another chants one box only, over there, one box only.

Atlas chooses the oldest warden but before he speaks he realises it's the youngest, with a red peevish face, who's in command.

Hello—warden. Is that—what I call you? Or—do you prefer officer—or sir?

What is it?

I—am Dr Atlas Brown and—and I've come for my rations.

Join the queue.

Yes—but—you see—I'm starving and I—I have important work to—

Join the queue.

Atlas spots the older warden taking him in.

You!—you recognise me—don't you—please explain to this —to your colleague—it's me.

Empty laughter from the queue behind him. Fuck off to the back, mate, someone shouts. Others join in. Get in line like the rest of us. Who do you think you are?

Atlas turns to them.

It's—me.

He points to his face with both forefingers.

You know—Doctor Hate—from the newspapers.

But nobody is looking at him. Just like that, he has disappeared from their thoughts. The distribution has resumed as if nothing happened. Those in the line gawp at the truck, necks craning. Do they seriously think they can ignore him away? That they can simply turn their heads and he'll melt into the road? Don't they realise Dr Atlas Brown, saviour of the human race, the great liberator, the genius himself, is here in the actual flesh, in the actual starving flesh? Dr Brown, the most tenacious scientist of all time, isn't going anywhere until these people understand this is the real deal, that he is who he says he is, and they hand over some bloody food.

Gentlemen. Gentlemen—I think—there's been a—a misunderstanding—we seem to have got off on the wrong foot.

The wardens refuse to acknowledge him. He steps closer.

Excuse me—gentlemen—officers—please.

Nothing. Atlas turns his attention to the truck. The people who've had their IDs checked are taking their boxes, saying thank you, and stepping aside. It looks like a friendly enough transaction.

Excuse me—sir. If I could take my box—I'll be on my way.

The man sighs.

Go away.

Atlas points at his face again.

I—am—

Yeah, I heard.

The man hands a box to a young woman with a small child strapped to her back. Atlas is close enough to see inside. Onions, a bag of rice, cooking oil, eggs, various vegetables and wrapped items. His stomach lurches.

Look—I just—want something to eat—is that too much to ask?

The man in the truck turns away and reaches for another box. The woman has gone and now an elderly man extends his arms towards the lorry, waiting for his rations. Atlas can sense the wardens coming closer. He pushes in front of the old man, knocks his outstretched arms out of the way.

You owe me. All of you—all of you do—you—should be—you should be worshipping me—like a god—like a—I am Doctor Hate—

Either you go away or you'll be arrested.

It's a voice from behind him. A warden.

—please—

Atlas finds he has fallen to his knees and his hands are joined in prayer.

It doesn't have to be—a whole box—please—just a carrot—or something—anything.

Right, that's it.

The older warden grabs his arm and pulls him back onto his feet. Atlas spies the handcuffs in the officer's other hand. Panicked, he yanks himself free and scampers away. The warden doesn't follow him.

And don't show your face around here again, he shouts.

Atlas barely has the energy to catch up with the elderly man struggling to carry his rations.

Would you like me—to help you—with that?

Atlas makes a grab for the food.

Get the hell off!

The old man pulls the box out of reach but loses his grip and drops it. The contents spill onto the ground and Atlas takes his chance. He reaches for the rice but the man beats him to it. Then, seeing an apple rolling towards him, he picks that up instead and makes to run away. But it isn't running. It's a limping, scurrying, lolloping movement in which his arms are more animated than his legs. But he has his apple. He has his apple, an actual apple, and he is going to eat it. Excited anticipation rises through him and he can already feel the fresh, crunchy fruit slipping down his throat. People are shouting after him. He is suddenly sure someone will catch up with him any second now so he slows his pace and brings the precious apple to his salivating mouth, its smooth skin on his lips, its delicious sweetness fills his nostrils, and just as his teeth begin to break its hard, cool flesh, his left foot trips over his right and he is flying for a moment, and then plummeting in slow motion. As his body plunges, he lifts his face to watch the apple rise into the air, up, up, up and out of sight.

· · ·

It's nigh on impossible to climb onto the lap of Nathaniel Castleport nowadays. And he's not always convinced the endeavour is worth the cost in calories. However, sometimes, if he lies up here long enough and allows his eyes to relax so the statues and buildings around him fall out of focus, he can just about reconstruct an obscure sensation he finds beneficial in these times of scarcity. And although the experience is never perfect, he is almost, almost comfortable in his mind. The clouds bounce with colour, and the air is thick and easy to breathe. The world is weightless and mild. And there, was that it? Did he see it? Yes, he probably did, a single glint of joy passing by like a shooting star.

This, he thinks, might be happiness. Almost. Very nearly. Not quite, because this isn't the real thing. This version has been refurbished and reformed from fading fragments. He should've done more to absorb and preserve the sensation when he had the chance, in those rare moments way back then. It hadn't seemed necessary. Because happiness had insisted she would return. Just enjoy me, she'd said. Drink in this moment and forget about the future because I'll be here for you, no matter what. If only he'd taken a sample for reference, a test tube to uncork later when happiness did what she always does and abandoned him.

But up here, he can find her echo. He can unfold it and smooth it out on the legs of this iron monster and do his best to relive a slither of the elation he once knew. And if he does it well enough, if he can tune out the ache in his belly and the cold air that scrapes at the stretched skin of his torso, then he will crawl deep, deep, deep into the memory, out of Moss's reach, far away from the shadows and columns of darkness, back underground to when everyone wanted to be a part of an idea that traversed the corridors on saddled whispers and promised the kind of immortality won only from being in close proximity to something so wonderful.

· · ·

If Angela never comes back to him, that's okay.

If he expires here tonight, that's okay.

If they never find his bones, that's okay.

If nobody ever hears about who he was or what he did, that's okay.

ARRINA

It tickled her, the sight of Dr Brown exerting himself, all grunts
and twisted elbows. She wondered if this was how he looked
while bent over her. Even if she kept her eyes open during sex,
her vantage point wouldn't allow her to see him in this position.
It was more the thought of how he'd look to someone observing
them she found amusing. The light from the neighbouring
houses revealed the large patches of sweat mooning down his
back and underarms, the reddening of his face and neck, the
painful angles of his joints. She could have offered to take a turn
digging but witnessing him drip into the expanding trench like
this was the most fun she'd had in weeks.

It had been almost midnight when he tapped his fingernails on
the window of her accommodation, his urgent face beckoning
her outside. He'd whispered too softly at first and looked irritated at having to repeat himself three times before she understood he wanted her to distract the security guard at the gate.

Bernie was struggling with a game of Patience. He swiped
the table with frustration as Arrina entered the hut. She ignored
the cards on the floor while apologising for the late visit,

assuring him she wouldn't stay long. Work was busy, she said as she moved to the middle of the room to keep his eyes away from the window. With so much to think about, she found it difficult to relax. He could relate, he replied. His grandson's illness kept him awake. Arrina nodded and asked after the boy. She turned down his offer of a mug of tea, wished him good night, and stepped back out into the darkness, intending to return to her bed. A movement to her right drew her attention to the gate. Dr Brown beckoned her with a quick wave from the other side. Without questioning, she crouched, ducked under the barrier, and jogged towards him, a little startled at how easy it was to leave.

He stopped digging and cursed under his breath.

It's here—somewhere—buried the damn thing myself.

He rested his arms and then his chin on the handle grip of the upright spade.

Should've marked it—with something—for fuck's sake.

Then he straightened up and surveyed the lawn.

Unless those—fuckers—have stolen it.

Other than him telling Arrina where they were going, the walk to his house was in silence. When they arrived an hour later, Dr Brown retrieved a rusting shovel from behind the old garden lab, circled the rectangle of grass between it and the house, and then, having decided on a spot, started digging.

This won't—shouldn't take long. You—keep watch.

He struck plastic while working on the third trench. By then, the mud had absorbed his initial eagerness. He groaned as he lugged three cool boxes from the soil onto the grass. Inside were several blue aluminium canisters. Without pausing, he removed a ball of screwed-up carrier bags from his jacket pocket, and within a few minutes the pair were walking back towards the compound, each carrying two heavy bags of containers.

Don't—don't let them clunk—against your legs—like that.

What even are these?
This—this is the agent.

They asked him about it once, the agent, back at the Facility. They knew he kept it in the safe and that it contained a chemical that attracted the Particle, but they craved the specifics. Even so, while they believed he would be happy enough to answer, the amount of time the question had remained unasked for made it awkward. It was as if by missing the undefined window of opportunity the required words had become too unwieldy on the lips.

Perhaps Ahmed longed for the details more than the others. He waited until Dr Brown was in the lab and the safe door was slightly open. This allowed him to ask about the agent as if in passing, as if it had only just occurred to him to do so. Casualness seemed important. It might, he may have thought, ease the question of him. And possibly it did, as he managed to compose the enquiry perfectly well. However, his delivery was so quiet that three of his colleagues felt compelled to repeat the words on his behalf to help them reach their intended ears. With the excitement and enthusiasm of a new declaration of love, the researchers stumbled and tripped over each other utterances, pulverising Ahmed's careful syntax in the mayhem.

What is, can you tell us, what, the, makes up the agent, please, the ingredients, agent made from, formulation, please?

Arrina hadn't joined the verbal stampede but it was she who the doctor smiled at once he'd untangled exactly what he was being asked.

All in good time, he said. Which was a time that had still not arrived before he disappeared and they discovered the ransacked lab and the empty safe.

• • •

His head twitched like a sparrow as they negotiated the journey back. Every passing taxi, every late-night pedestrian, every unexpected noise caused him to tense up and search for potential escape routes. Meanwhile, Arrina scanned the streets for payphones, logging their locations for a possible unauthorised jaunt from the compound in the future. By the time they'd snuck past the guard's shed again and climbed the stairs to Dr Brown's quarters, Arrina's shoulders were on fire. She watched him get on his hands and knees and push the canisters under his bed. He removed his muddied clothes, put them into one of the bags, and threw that under too.

Only you—and I—know about this. Do you—understand?

Is that safe, keeping them under there?

Nobody knows they're—here—which is—which is the point.

No, I meant safe, as in. Never mind.

He was sitting on the edge of the bed in his underpants, his extremities brown with soil and sweat.

Maybe—we—could—

I'm going to get some sleep.

————

By Extraction Day eve, Arrina was struggling to stay awake. Nothing had run to schedule and too much work had been crammed into too little time. It was late and she was so tired that she walked straight past her own quarters and into Dr Brown's.

He was lying naked, face down on his bed.

Arrina made to go, and hesitated. She had watched him become increasingly agitated throughout the day, losing his temper with the technicians as they carried out rushed, last-minute adjustments. She suggested he go to bed and leave them to finish off, that they could manage without him. It was one in the morning. He needed his sleep. He'd looked at her with utter contempt. It only lasted for a second but it took her by surprise. Then he nodded and disappeared. She'd imagined him pacing the length of his box, worrying holes in the carpet for the rest of the night. But here he was, already asleep. She closed the door and lay next to him.

He stirred, turned, and smiled at the sight of her. They embraced and he asked how the preparations had gone. She said everything was fine and he could forget about it for tonight.

You should go back to sleep.

He turned over and looked at the ceiling, putting a hand on her thigh. The moonlight skimmed the surface of his eyes.

We're—almost there.

Arrina waited for his eyelid to close again. When they didn't, she asked what he would do when all this was over.

Dr Brown yawned.

I can't be sure it'll ever—be over. I—think this is life's work. My—life's work.

Their tiredness creaked the air between them.

I'll stay—for a while—look after things—monitor it all—take care of the Particle—until it can be neutralised or whatever—stored safely—maybe.

There was a moment of silence before Atlas returned the question.

I'll travel.

—where?

Everywhere I can. I'll just keep going until I stop. I have the money now. Farfalla is paying me well.

I thought—I—

Atlas's hand left her leg and his face pulled back.

—I'm not sure what I thought. So you'll set off—with your money and—and—we'll never see you again? Arrina—the nomad.

Yes. Nomad, as in, not mad.

Later, Arrina woke facing the edge of the bed, the duvet wrapped around her twice. She watched Atlas walk through the darkness towards the sink. But then he stopped before reaching it. He turned to the window where the gasholder would be cutting its silhouette into the stars.

What are you doing?

She waited for his response and was about to repeat her question when he replied:

To be honest—I don't know.

ALFONSO

Security Operative (Night Shift). That's what the job advertisement said. But Alfonso doesn't add to the overall safety of the place. Not as far as he can tell. If he were to rename his position he'd say he was a List Checking, Phone Call Making, Push Button Operator (Graveyard Shift).

His job is to check the names of visitors against those on a clipboard, phone the person they're here to see, and then press a button that opens the gates. So far, he has performed these duties twice. He has been in the role for almost three weeks. But this is the middle of the night, he tells himself. Of course things are slow. The man who used to do nights now does days. Alfonso sees him at the handovers between shifts. His name is Bernie. There's been nothing to hand over yet, just a minute or two of chatter before whoever is heading home heads home.

The hut is a portable cabin with a single sliding window. A small red sign with white writing instructs visitors to REPORT HERE. Inside, a tall stool and lectern are positioned next to the window. Alfonso sits on the former, and the telephone and clipboard on the latter. The button is fixed to a metal box the size of a fist, which, in turn, is mounted on the wall just a little out of his reach. The only other furniture is a two-seater sofa in black pleather, a coffee table covered in old newspapers, and a decrepit office chair on wheels that moves of its own accord.

An internal door leads to a bathroom. There is a toilet, which Alfonso cleans daily, a sink with a wall-mounted soap dispenser that is always precariously close to empty, and a stained bath with a dripping showerhead above it. The stain looks like a puddle of piss. He wants to mend the shower head but he needs his toolbox. Every time he goes in to relieve himself, he curses for forgetting to bring it from home again. His memory used to be excellent.

The uniform is similar to the one he wore as a traffic warden. Cheaper and thinner, though. But it fits him better. Jen and he laughed when he first put it on. She worries about him returning to work so soon after the incident. She thinks he should take his sick pay from the council and wait a while longer. But she also hugged him and said she'd support whatever decision he made. You know I love a man in uniform, all flirty eyes and pouted lips to make him laugh.

She and Mil have spoiled him since he left the hospital. He was tempted to stay put. If it hadn't been for the itch inside his head he might have let them nurse him into old age, allowed their love to smother him to a quiet, comfortable death. They agreed he'd return to work but not to the Castleport City Council Traffic Department. Neither of them liked the idea of him walking the streets. Not for a while at least. He just needed something to keep him busy, to occupy his brain and hands. So this isn't exactly the ideal job, far too much time spent doing nothing. He is little more than meat in a box. But the pay is okay and for now it'll help. He'll look for better opportunities once his confidence returns.

A young woman from the compound sometimes pops by on an evening, filling an hour or so. He doesn't know her name yet and it's too late to ask now. There are four female names on the staff list, so she's one of those. He won't be guessing which though. It might offend her and he'd hate that. She's a little unusual, which he appreciates. When she comes, she parks herself on the sofa and they chat. It's easy enough to talk to her but he prefers to listen. Her voice is unlike any he's heard before and he could listen to her go on about the weather all night if that was something she was inclined to do. But there are also long silences that are oddly comfortable. These quiet moments allow him to look inward in a way he doesn't when alone. When a stranger appears happy to sit there while you wade around your thoughts, it's as if they have given you permission. That's what it's like. And although she has never said so, he knows she is right there if he needs her. At home, he tries hard not to think about the incident. But when this young woman is with him, he can slip into memories and confront his actions in a calm and steady manner that never seems to unsettle him. He even talks to her about it a bit, and her questions don't upset him. What's odd is that she didn't know about it before he told her. She's probably the type who never watches the news, and he can't blame her for that. She asks about the feelings he experienced rather than about the occurrence itself. Whenever he speaks about it, he finds new ways to explain how he felt and wonders if his memory of the day is changing or if there are infinite ways to describe it.

PART VIII

ATLAS

If Atlas Brown could feast on his demons, he'd be a beast of a
man. As it is, going to bed hungry is its own special kind of
agony, worse even than going to bed knowing one is to blame
for the collapse of society. On the upside, the growing emptiness
in his stomach dwarfs the turbulent glut in his head. It tramples
troubled thoughts to death without trying. It's the behemoth of
all troubles. And it tires him, this monster. Hunger is exhausting
and he will sleep the sleep of the almost dead, away from the all-
consuming ache. First, however, before he enters that blissful
relief, he consults Reflected Atlas, who commiserates with gusto.

Yes, the man who tried to save the world is starving.

I—don't deserve this.

Reflected Atlas shakes his head.

No. You don't. There should be daily deliveries of fresh food
to your door, a procession of worshipers carrying offerings to
their saviour. You should be gorging on the love of the people.

They don't—love me. They don't know I'm here. Or that I—
exist.

Oh, but imagine if they did.

And in the beat of a wing on a dying moth's back, Atlas

enters a large, traditional lecture theatre filled with hundreds of undergraduates.

It's Dr Atlas Fucking Brown, he hears a student exclaim under the booming applause. He strides to the lectern. Atlas can tell a crowd like this anything he wants. He has their respect. Their awe. All he has to do is open his hand and let them feed from his palm. He looks up at the theatre's ceiling, sighing through his nostrils. No niceties today. Just straight in. Hammed up, though, because he is who he is.

Can everyone who has ever experienced fear stand up? says Atlas. I'm serious. Stand up.

Everybody stands.

Thank you. I'd like you to remain standing for a moment. Now, if the fear you're thinking of was in connection to money, for example, I don't know, you thought you were about to lose some or didn't have enough to pay your rent, please sit down.

The students look about them. After a few seconds, over half the audience has sat down again. Ripples of chatter and laughter.

Okay. Those of you who were fearful of losing someone, a friend or a family member, maybe they were gravely ill or had been in an accident, sit down, please.

Forty or so people still standing.

This is going well, he thinks to himself.

Anyone who was *not* afraid for their own life, please take a seat.

Nine remain.

Finally, if you feared for your life but only for just a second or so. For instance, you stepped out in front of a bus and jumped out of the way or something like that. Then you know what to do.

Four remain on their feet. Two males, next to one another at the left of the theatre, and two females, one at the back, the other near the front.

Thank you for your honesty. Please, sit. So, this experiment suggests that around three percent of you have feared for your lives and a little over one percent have done so for longer than a split second. I suggest that the other ninety-seven percent are liars or have no idea what it is to be fearful.

It's like throwing a turd into the crowd. Discontent flounces through its ranks. Atlas can see brows furrowing, heads shaking, backsides shifting in seats. He is always delighted by how little it takes. He continues.

Genuine fear triggers a fight-or-flight response in the brain. Can any of you really claim to have experienced this reaction when your student loan didn't arrive on time? When you discover your mother is knocking on death's door, do you have the burning desire to flee for your life? Or wrestle the doctors? What most of you think of as fear is nothing more than anxiety. Or anger perhaps.

Fear, though, fear is what pumps through your veins when some savage in a bar lets you know he's going to push a broken bottle into your face. It's when your car breaks down on the rail crossing just as the train comes around the bend. When you wake up to find your house on fire.

A man in a baseball cap and black t-shirt that declares *No Fear* shouts out that it's just semantics.

Just semantics? Atlas asks. Just meaning? Nothing more than the thing that separates us from the apes? That's fine. But while you dream about swinging through the trees with your contemporaries, the rest of us are going to talk about fear.

Most of the undergraduates are laughing with him. A couple are even clapping. Of course they are. This is the easiest crowd he's had for a while.

Now where was I? Ah, yes, fear is a word that is dropped into the narrative as liberally as a chef seasons a chicken carcass. Politicians fear recessions. Doctors fear the rise in child obesity. Middle-aged men fear losing their hair. Imaginary students fear imaginary speaker who humiliates imaginary heckler in imaginary lecture.

The laughter is overenthusiastic this time. Atlas finds it a little uncomfortable. As he makes a mental note to steer clear of any more humour, a woman from the one percent raises her arm.

Dr Brown, you wrestle with these make-believe scenarios—the seminars, interviews, articles, etcetera—that can never happen. You do it again and again, and every time you feel worse for it. Why punish yourself like this?

Why? Because what else do I have? This is the only glory I'll ever get. Imaginary renown, phantasmic acclaim. Figmental fame. It's this or nothing.

If you don't mind me saying, this *is* nothing.

How can it be nothing when it fills me with such pride to stand here before you all?

You look annoyed.

Never mind how I look. I would like to ask you a question. What happened to you that made you fear for your life?

I'd rather not say.

The woman sits back down.

Well, as I'm imagining you, I suppose it could be anything I want it to be. So, you were holidaying in South America somewhere, and you were a victim of a carjacking. Your companion, let's make them a he and say that he was your fiancé. So this fiancé of yours resisted the robbery and was shot in the head before your eyes. And then the gun was pointed at your face.

If you say so.

Good, because this helps me get to the point I want to make.

You're welcome.

Thank you.

During this exchange, the structure of the lecture altered and now Atlas is standing on a stage with the audience below. There is a sofa at his side. He sits. The young woman from the lecture theatre is across from him on another couch positioned at a right angle to his. Between them is a low wooden table with two microphones on stands, a pitcher of water, and five glasses. The crowd is out there in front of him. The lights have been dimmed but he can see their faces well enough. The idea of a live Q&A podcast has never occurred to him before. He likes it. It's relaxed, kind of natural. It suits a man like him.

Are we expecting guests?

Yes. But we're keen to hear from you first.

Who else is joining us?

You don't know them, a wealthy North American investor who claims he owns the intellectual property rights for the Hate Extractor, an Eastern European crime lord who says you owe him a lot of money, and the artist, Bute Blue, who is promoting her new exhibition. It's called *Scar*. I was supposed to see it before the interview but didn't have time. I think it's about domestic abuse. But that's for later. You were saying?

Oh yes. A gun aimed at your head. Well, what I was trying to say is that most of us never experience fear like that. And by 'most of us', I mean the majority of people in here tonight, the white, middle-class males. For us, it's rare, especially here in the molly-coddled West.

Atlas pauses. They come naturally now, these rhetorical intermissions. He glances at the audience, which seems to have multiplied since he last looked. It reminds him of a photograph taken from the main stage at Glastonbury, a field of tiny heads. He's surprised to see the interviewer among them, right at the front, sitting on the shoulders of the *No Fear* guy.

Arrina now occupies the sofa opposite him. She nods her head.

Please, go on.

My pleasure. Even though actual fear is rare, it arrives in our consciousness fully formed. It's as if every one of us is walking around with a preassembled, fuelled-up V8 engine in our heads, revving away in the background in case we need it.

So, you're saying that fear is always in us.

I am indeed. But if you've encountered fear, the real deal, come face to face with it and the way it rushes you with such ferocity, screaming in your face like a starving tiger, burning your sanity to a crisp in an instant, you'll appreciate that, because of its sheer enormity, it's nigh on impossible to imagine that such a beast is always there, waiting in the darkness for its cue. How can a thing like that, something so large and vicious, be lurking in your brain without you knowing about it?

Atlas taps the side of his head with a finger.

But it's there, in your amygdala, two small almond-shaped clusters of nuclei in your temporal lobes. It lies dormant for years, watching the images and sounds flow in through your senses and onto the cognitive factory floor, observing them as they're moulded into the meanings that form your grasp on the world, your take on reality. It waits for the glitches, those tiny changes, microscopic malfunctions that stop the cogs from turning for the tiniest conceivable slivers of time. It's searching for those minute irregularities, the creak in the hallway or the unexpected shape in the shadows that cause you to pause and ask yourself, what's that? And in that moment between you noticing the unusual stimulus and rational thought stepping in with an explanation, fear rushes at you like a runaway train. But mostly, it isn't quick enough. You feel its approach but then you remember you didn't close the kitchen door and the cat must have got out, that you left the central heating on and it's just the radiators groaning.

Where are you going with this?

You'll find out if you try applying a little patience.

Maybe you should've suggested that to our audience.

Atlas looks out. The field of heads has disappeared, leaving behind only muddy grass. Not a soul in sight. This won't do, and so he conjures a parliament of owls. Feathered wisdom on the branches of old trees. Arrina, the sofas, and the stage have gone too. It's just him sitting cross-legged on rocky ground, avian eyes shining yellow in the fading light.

I was about to say that sometimes fear *is* quick enough, or rather, reason is too slow. Or, reason doesn't turn up at all because it turns out that the shape in the shadows is actually a horde of salivating wolves or a gang of machete-swinging militiamen, and you're cornered. And it's you and your fear versus your imminent demise.

One of the owls, the one wearing the mortarboard and monocle, swivels its head around three hundred and sixty degrees and then asks through various twits and hoots if Atlas thinks he might get to his point any time soon.

Yes, I will. Right now, in fact. Why is everyone in such a hurry today? My point is that during these prolonged exposures to fear we produce large enough quantities of alarm pheromone to attract the hate parasite, the Particle. This is what I'm trying to tell you.

The owls' eyes widen, illuminating the clearing beneath the trees in yellow light. The chief bird's monocle falls and dangles below its branch.

I know. It's quite something, isn't it? But even better than that is what the Particle does to the human mind. Admittedly, the research hasn't been peer-reviewed yet. I've been unable to go through the usual scientific channels to test my work but the evidence is overwhelming.

The light fades to less than its original luminosity.

Don't narrow your eyes at me. I was in a difficult situation. You don't understand the pressure I was un

There's a rumble.

Atlas feels tremors in the centre of his being. It echoes in his chest and rattles his jaw. But the ground beneath him is also vibrating. It's an internal quake so powerful that it shakes the rocks, so powerful that it shakes the trees, so powerful that it shakes the sky. So powerful that the whole universe shudders. The owls open their enormous wings and lift from their branches.

Hey, why are you leaving? I'm not

finished

with

you

And he's back in his metal box, curled on his bed, his legs pulled up tight against the pain of his bellowing stomach.

Let's play What-If.

I don't—do—I don't do what-ifs—can't

Reflected Atlas chuckles.

That's actually hilarious.

If Atlas knows anything it's that nothing is funny. Certainly not what he or his reflection has just said. Not that he is curled up in a ball on his bed. Nor this slow fall into oblivion. But then, he knows nothing at all. He would not be in this predicament if he had even the slightest clue about anything. A three-year-old wouldn't have ended up like this. His stupidity is starving him to death. He deserves it, he thinks. This is evolution doing what it does, abandoning the weak.

Come on, Atlas, you love a game of What-If.

—no.

I'm not taking no for an answer. So what if, what if… ah, I've got it; what if the extraction, the actual event, had been everything you'd dreamed of, Atlas. Imagine that.

Not—now.

But imagine it.

Please—shut up, this isn't—isn't the time.

Atlas wonders if hanging something over the mirror would mute it.

Your face on screens everywhere. A major broadcasting event. Streamed to an audience of billions. Ah, it would have been fantastic.

He'd need to find the strength from somewhere though, to stand up, locate a shirt or a towel, and walk all the way over to the other side of the box to drape it over the glass.

The biggest of its kind ever. An extraordinary moment. Historical. Imagine it. Images of you and your machine beamed all over the world.

He could use the sheet he's lying on. That might save a bit of energy.

On every television, every tablet and phone, at every cinema, watched by every living person in real time. It would be like one of those 'where were you when Princess Diana died' moments.

Atlas reaches out to the edge of the mattress and grips the bedsheet in his fist. His fingers and wrist and forearm protest.

A big introduction by some insanely famous person, like a movie star or singer. George Clooney, maybe. Rihanna or Taylor Swift. Oh, oh, I know, Barack Obama. He'd be all over this. Or, what's her name?

He would shout at the mirror again, tell it to shut the hell up, but he needs to concentrate on the sheet. He tugs with both hands this time but it doesn't give. It's difficult to keep his fingers wrapped in the fabric.

That one who married that other one, you know, who adopts all the children. What is that woman's name? Anyway, someone like her.

He tries again, harder, clenching the sheet as tightly as he can. And he yanks, and blades smash through his knuckles, elbow, shoulder, neck, back, skin, eyeballs, frontal sinus, frontal lobe, cerebral cortex where it splits in two, sending pain charges into both hippocampi and then the amygdalae, only to regroup and plough deep into the neocortex so that, like after a volcanic eruption on a far-off island, a tidal wave of memory begins its journey to Atlas's consciousness where, any second now, he'll be overwhelmed by recollections in which he'd hoped never to swim again.

We could put them at a fancy lectern, like at the Oscars. Or, or, how about we make it a bit more free-flowing, Eurovision-style, the Extractor all lit up behind them. They'd interview you, of course. And there'd be dancers, which is a little old-fashioned but what the hell, and music as well, some big shot rapper or someone, but then, thinking about it, better to treat extraction as if it's a space launch, set it far back, especially now that we know how dangerous it —————— and his reflection's voice is fading into the background again, this time under the excited chatter that bounces off the hangar walls. It is Extraction Day and Atlas is standing by the machine on the new platform. The group below him is larger than expected. Bunting hangs from the ceiling, and bunches of balloons quiver against sloping walls and railings, all of it at Farfalla's request. The American has invited three dozen or so of his colleagues and associates. Below Altas, Angela chats with whoever that is next to her. And there's Oblonsky and his entourage keeping themselves separate from other guests. Others too, possibly family members of compound technicians, here to find out what their husbands, wives and partners have been doing for all these months. On Atlas's reckoning, he is looking at around a hundred people, all staring back at him.

Farfalla is at his side, his features foxtrotting across his face.

It's okay, he says out of the corner of his mouth. Everyone's vetted and NDA'd up to the eyeballs. If anyone so much as thinks about this again after today we'll be onto them like a pack of wolves. We're watertight.

Atlas is finding it easier to be cordial, partly because this is a deep memory and his emotions, speech, and even his hair and clothes have been smoothed and graded to improve the aesthetic experience of his mind's eye, but also because he has amended his assessment of the American several times since the trial extraction. It has moved by degrees from the sinister conman who'd planned to sell the Particle from day one to a guileless but likeable capitalist incapable of passing up an opportunity. But now that Atlas has decided the only way he can proceed is to pretend there is no sale, Farfalla's initial persona of the big-hearted philanthropist has made a welcome return. The mediation cd says to focus on the stories we tell ourselves. And Milo Farfalla and Atlas Brown are good men doing a good thing.

The compound technicians understand the running order. They've had it drilled into them a hundred times. The practice sessions were akin to rehearsals for a complex piece of theatre. There are actions to perform and lines to recite. There should be no need to deviate from the main script, but every actor knows what to do should things veer from the plot. A flowchart of possibilities covers all conceivable variations. If A happens, then inform B and action C, if D happens, and so on and so forth.

From the platform, Atlas can see everyone is in place. Other than the three hazmat-clad technicians by the gasholder, the rest wear their new white lab coats, yellow hardhats and large safety goggles. Someone raised the question of uniforms during rehearsals. Atlas wasn't keen. They look like walking clichés. However, now that he sees how many people are here in the hangar, he's happy he can pinpoint those he is relying on without difficulty.

He taps the microphone. Hello everyone.

All eyes on him. This is okay. He feels relaxed. But then, speaking to this crowd is a peripheral activity. It doesn't matter what they think. Today is all about the Extractor doing what it's supposed to do. No need to persuade anyone about anything. He'd considered starting with something about this being their day, for them to remember forever, but really, it is his. His day. So he will not try to inspire or impress them. If they remember it, then great.

To those of you who don't work here, thank you for coming. To the rest of you, I think you already know you have my eternal gratitude for your immense efforts during the last months. In just a moment, we'll start the Extractor behind me. And then, when you wake up tomorrow, the world will be a different place.

The crowd follows Farfalla's cue to clap.

I'm sure you've all got a rough idea of what'll happen in the meantime. But so there's no confusion…

Atlas gives an abridged account of the discovery of the Particle and the invention of the machine and sketches a picture of a world without hate. This last part of the speech is directed at Oblonsky. Of everybody there, Atlas wants that man to understand what they will achieve today. His words may touch something in the man's soul, stir his sense of decency, and influence the Particle's future if he does manage to get his hands on it. It pains him to be so idealistic in public like this, but he has to try.

The button was Farfalla's idea. He wanted drama. The hard hats and lab coats were a start but not enough. He demanded something more, a moment in the proceedings that would awe the audience. It is the most important button in human history, according to Farfalla. A metal disc, frisbee-sized, spray-painted red, mounted on a few short springs and attached to the machine's front panel. The script had to be amended to accommodate it, so now Arrina is to activate the extraction on the tablet when she sees Atlas push the button. The button that does nothing.

The crowd is silent as he takes the rehearsed steps towards the Hate Extractor. Pistons pump adrenaline into his veins. He finds it difficult to believe he's reached this day. He contemplates the button, his back to the compound. He remembers the months inside his garden lab, the agony and the joy of searching for something he had only the faintest inkling might exist. He remembers his carelessness. He remembers the violence he unleashed on his wife and the scar he left on her. He remembers how close he came to destroying his career. He remembers his gratitude for being permitted to return to the Facility. He remembers Moss's ultimatum. He remembers absconding. He remembers the lies in the newspapers. He remembers his forsaken brother, left to deal with the fallout of his disappearance. He remembers the murdered. He remembers the maimed. The displaced. The orphaned. The tortured. He remembers the Particle. He reaches out and presses the button with the flat of his palm.

The familiar hum is barely audible at first. Within thirty seconds, it has built up into a deep, booming pulse that squeezes Atlas's bones. He turns to Arrina, who stands away from the audience, near the platform, monitoring the system on her tablet. She looks up at Atlas and nods. Noticing this, Farfalla rushes to the microphone to announce extraction has begun.

The caterers pour into the hangar as the musicians take their places. The two men stand alone on the platform.

Farfalla leans into Atlas. Delight whirls over his face.

Well done. You did good.

He kneels at the platform's edge and takes two champagne flutes from a waiter below. He hands one to Atlas and turns to the crowd, who raise their glasses to him.

Here's to a better future. To a future we want!

Atlas climbs down from the platform and checks the monitors along the pipeline and by the gasholder. The readouts match. All is well. Then, when he is sure the team is satisfied with the initial progress, he feels his tension ease a little. The music from the brass band masks the sound of the giant drum as it judders slowly upwards, and Atlas finds himself enjoying conversations with guests and the few technicians who aren't required during extraction. While he's speaking, he searches the crowd for Arrina. He'd like to share some of this moment with her. Behind him, Farfalla is singing his praises. Atlas is a genius, saving the world, going down in history as the man who set humanity in a new direction. Occasionally, the American beckons him into a small gathering, puts his arm around his shoulders and squeezes tightly.

Here he is, Doctor Hate!

Oh, but surely we should call him Dr Love, says a guest, beaming at her own wit. Farfalla laughs as if this is the first time he has heard this suggestion today.

An hour or so passes. Atlas is tired. He retreats to the platform to check on the machine.

Arrina is climbing the steps. He braces himself for bad news, a technical problem, a leak, but as she nears he can see she is calm.

How do you feel?

I've never talked as much as this in my life.

Or smiled. Everyone wants a piece of you today.

My face, it hurts. I'm not used to it. I came up here for a rest.

Well, I just wanted to congratulate you.

Thanks. Thank you.

They stand like that, facing one another, for a few seconds too long.

I should probably.

Yes, me too.

She reaches out her hand. He takes it.

Well done, Dr Brown.

As they descend the steps together, Atlas sees that the only people keeping their emotions packed away are the suits huddled around Oblonsky. Stoney faces, sunglasses, and earpieces. He plays with the idea that these men and women are enjoying themselves beneath the stern exteriors. How can they not be? They know as well as everyone else here that, at that precise moment, hundreds of murderous events are already running out of fuel. Genocides, homicides, infanticides, wars, rapes, mutilations, humiliations, and beatings are stopping, never to be repeated. Maybe, like him, they imagine the Particle as thick, toxic smoke, billows of it being wrenched from tank cannons, gun barrels, battlefields and ruined cities, out of the mouths of soldiers, terrorists, police officers, politicians, enormous clouds of hate swarming in the atmosphere, melding and moving at speed towards this tiny corner of England. Soon all the hatred in the world will be here.

Right here.

An unfamiliar sound interrupts his thoughts. The fake button has fallen onto the platform floor. Eye-level with the oscillating disc, he wonders for a moment if he should climb back up the steps and reattach it to the machine.

Moving through the crowd, Atlas detects a change. Not a smell or a temperature or a sound, something else, like air density, like it has thickened or thinned, it's impossible to tell which. Or gravity maybe. Is he feeling heavier than he did a minute ago? Lighter? Whatever's going on, the general mood appears to have altered, and although he knows it is probably only him, his mind playing tricks on him, he is very aware of a creeping menace in the immediate atmosphere. And then there is this other issue. He can't quite pinpoint it either, and this must be his imagination because it seems as if everyone has been replaced with look-a-likes while he was distracted by the falling button, and now they're waiting to see if he'll notice. He catches a sideward glance from a waitress holding out a tray of drinks for two women. They shake their heads and one of them laughs at a comment the server makes. All three turn Atlas's way. Just as he wonders if they are making fun of him, his attention is drawn to a movement above them. It's almost visible against the dark hangar roof. A ripple or a quiver.

Like eye floaters, barely tangible cells drifting in all directions, and, unless he's mistaken, more solid than he's used to seeing. Darker, fuller, shifting away quickly as he moves his gaze from one location to another.

Like fireflies in negative, grey trails skating across the unlit metal, fading to nothing as soon as he tries to focus on them. There, but not.

Like echoes of a dream. Dust from a different time.

In the muffled acoustics, a tune ends. A champagne flute smashes on the concrete floor. A woman shouts something indecipherable. In the corner of Atlas's vision, every head in the hangar turns towards her, her face as tight as a fist as she bellows into the back of one of Oblonsky's men.

Look what you've fucking done, you fucking ape.

As the man turns to her, her hands chop the air in front of his sunglasses. But Atlas is transfixed on the fine erratic scores overhead. A swarm of pencil lines moving quickly together, twitching like small birds. Changing direction, advancing and retreating, down and to the side. Zooming, zagging, halting. Edging forwards, diving, pulling back. And again. Purposeful and sharp, probing. Then parting and disappearing.

Apologise to me, you piece of shit!

Now moving together but independent of one another, the occasional stroke peeling off, exploring, bouncing off invisible molecules. It's as if they're scouting for something. Searching for hidden dangers, opportunities to feed, before returning to the delicate flock.

Atlas directs his focus at the machine. The air above it is alive, thick with movement, blurring trails pour into the funnel.

Atlas?

A hand on his shoulder, Farfalla's, brings him back. As Atlas turns to him, he sees Oblonsky's man push his palm into the woman's face. She falls backwards, knocking drinks out of the hands of those around her. Another man punches the sunglasses off Oblonsky's man, and guns appear from under the jackets of the entourage.

The trails are swarming over the incident, thicker there than anywhere else in the crowd. Atlas looks again at the Extractor and sees that most of the streaks are being pulled into the funnel, but not all of them. The funnel isn't wide enough to take them all; it can't catch them all as they come torrenting down through the hole in the roof. And now it dawns on him. He is flooding the hangar with Particle.

He screams.

We need to turn off the machine.

He grabs Farfalla by the arm. He drags him up the steps to the platform and pushes him towards the microphone stand.

Tell them to get out of here, run, tell them.

He's still screaming. He runs towards the machine. Slams his body against it. He's kicking at the power cables as he remembers he needs the tablet to turn it off. And now he is at the front of the platform searching for Arrina in a crowd, a crowd that has turned on itself, a froth of violence. He's howling, Arrina, it's here, Arrina, it's here.

Reflected Atlas is calling his name. He is saying that playing what-ifs wasn't a great idea after all. They should probably do something else. But Atlas can't climb out of the memory because the seconds contained within it have opened up like hours to accommodate every single vicious detail and now its sides are too deep, too steep. The shrieking compound technician in his flailing white coat who jumps onto Oblonsky's back, his fingers boring into the Estonian's eye sockets and mouth, tearing through his scream, ripping cheek flesh from the skull, and bringing his large frame crashing to the ground; the sobbing security guard who's body convulses as he lifts his firearm and shoots into the roof of the hangar and then lowers it and takes aim at the crowd; the bewilderment on a guest's face as it is punched three, four, five times in rapid succession by an assailant she can barely see; the saxophonist swinging his instrument like an olympic hammer thrower before driving it into the side of the bandleader's head; the cracked yellow hardhat that coin-rolls over a blood-splattered floor until it comes to a stop next to a dropped handgun; a lab coat wrestling with a black suit; another shot, and another, bodies deflating and crumpling; the walking wounded rounding on each other with broken table legs and crockery; one of Oblonsky's people holding the barrel of a gun between his teeth, pulling the trigger, and sending a pink mist into the madness behind him; an injured waiter rushing into guests wielding a champagne bottle by its neck; a second kneeling on the back of a grounded guest, fists full of hair, smashing the red mess into the concrete; scarlet footprints scraped over grey flooring, around lifeless bloodied bundles, and under the quivering last breaths of the dying who drag themselves towards a final stabbing, shooting, smothering; and the Particle swarming, in through the eyes and out through the mouths, in through the gashes, out through the slashes, a frenzy of hornets tightening around triggers, throwing their weight behind wielded blunt objects; all of this while Atlas is pulled and dragged and heaved out of the hangar by a masked Farfalla.

ALFONSO

Alfonso is running.

He is surprised to find he can still move at speed.

But then, today was weird from the off. All day he's been feeling uncertain about his place in the macrocosmic structure. Not in a good or bad way, he has just been a little out of kilter. He noticed it at the start of his shift. The tone seemed off. There's a ley line that passes through the outskirts of Castleport. Alfonso doesn't understand much about these things or where this one is precisely and has wanted to read up on them for a while, but he knows they are supposed to contain great energy. So, the strange atmosphere might have something to do with that. It's as if the air is magnetised, and just as certain aromas can send you reeling back to a particular time, he suspected the cosmos was trying to drag him off somewhere else. Whatever it was, the magnetism is stronger now, and here he is, being dragged away on legs that haven't moved this fast in years.

Bernie hanging around for a few minutes longer than usual can't have helped. It doesn't take much to tilt a day. Alfonso had agreed to swap shifts because Bernie's grandson had an important hospital appointment. He didn't go into detail. The man was only being nice by showing interest in him after clocking off. He asked about Alfonso, what he used to do, his family, and what his daughter plans to study at university. He enjoyed the chat. Seeing Bernie so often and neither of them going to the trouble of getting to know the other had made things a little uncomfortable, so he appreciated the effort. He is all for taking the edge off awkward situations. So, he'd thought, that might've been all it was, a minor change in the dynamics causing this odd atmosphere.

He didn't spot the new clipboard on the desk until after Bernie left. There was a long list of people with clearance to enter the compound that day. He did wonder if this, the event or whatever was obviously happening today, wasn't the real reason Bernie had wanted to trade shifts. Nothing to do with his grandson at all. If he had known about the event, he might have invented an excuse to get out of it. For a moment, Alfonso felt sorry for his colleague and then ashamed for jumping to the conclusion. Either way, the gate had so much use today that it began to squeak.

It isn't dignified, this sprint-cum-limp he's doing. His arms are down by his sides and his legs pull him along the road surface like a hermit crab. Alfonso and athleticism have never been friends. 'Look at Alfonso go' is a sentence rarely uttered. And then there are the injuries, fresh from the incident. His pink scars hide pains and aches that will take a long time to fade. Some may never leave. No wonder his running style is awkward. But today he doesn't care. Nor does he care he is breaking the terms of his employment by leaving his hut and approaching a restricted area.

From the hut, the compound is nothing to look at. A wall of rusty shipping containers, from behind which poke the tops of four floodlights. Beyond these, the latticed structure of the old gasholder scratches at the sky like claws. As Alfonso gets closer, perspective pushes the rusting barrier higher and the lights and iron struts sink until they are out of sight.

He has only vague ideas about what goes on behind the wall.

He likes to think it's a new development, like a sustainability project of some sort, the type he hears about on the radio news. Maybe a bio-dome, if that's what they're called, or one of those plants where they turn discarded food into energy. Something eco-friendly would be nice. Especially here, in this part of town. It used to be so busy with hundreds of little factories and businesses. All gone now, though. Relocated or shut down to make way for some council initiative that never happened, cancelled before it began. Yet another enormous waste of money. The place really needs sorting out. If this is the start of a green revolution, the kind the politicians talk about, right here in Castleport, that would be exciting. When he asked the girl, she shrugged. She explained it was confidential. No big deal, it was Jen who wanted to know, anyway. She quizzed him again over breakfast a week or two ago. It must be important, she replied when he told her what the girl had said. Jen's the one speculating about it being environmental. She's always doing that, taking wild guesses with no evidence to back them up.

The noises coming from the compound were responsible for luring him out of the hut and getting him running. There'd been music earlier. He had left the door open so it would waft in and keep him company. A couple of tunes he recognised, though he wasn't able to name them. He'd hummed along. There was some kind of announcement too, but the amplified words didn't reach his ears intact. He couldn't say how long it was until the other sounds began. His mind was on the air, thinking that it was heavy. Pre-thunderstorm heavy but sort of thicker. He was wondering if it was stress. Not his, theirs, like a tension emanating from the other side of the containers. He's perceptive that way. He picks up on other people's anxiety, which is one reason he was great at his old traffic warden job. Or terrible at it, in Mr Alexander's view. He has enhanced powers of empathy. That's what Jen says. And whatever's been happening in there today, it's irregular. The other noises might have been shouting. The music had stopped. And as he listened, he realised he was right about the cosmos, it did want to take him to somewhere very familiar. His first thought was to shut the door and sit crossed-legged on the sofa, close his eyes, and visit his good place so he could be in the golden, rippling meadow to watch the blossom trees sprinkle small pink petals and let the sun soften his bones. But he was already outside, running towards the forbidden compound.

The sounds are clear now. Screams and roars and a loud popping sound, over and over.

He is close. His fists are clenched, his jaw is viced.

Two men in masks, one wearing a lab coat and the other a suit, sprint out from behind the container wall and head straight at Alfonso. They yell at him. But he doesn't try to hear them and ducks his shoulder to dodge their grasping hands as they pass. Alfonso rounds the corner and sees the inside of the compound for the first time, and his old legs cannonball him towards the mayhem.

PART IX

ANGELA

The service station consists of two sections, a single building on each side of the barren motorway. One is an empty, three-storey, flat-roofed Travelodge, and the other is a collection of derelict fast-food concessions huddled around a large atrium where people once ate at tables that are no longer there. The buildings are connected by an enclosed footbridge through which weary drivers once traipsed in search of inferior coffee or an inadequate night's sleep, depending on their direction of travel.

When Angela drove into the complex for the first time, she was surprised by a collection of camper vans, transits, and a few small motor homes parked in an approximate circle near the wooded area of the car park, away from the property. Five men emerged from the cluster on hearing her engine. Big coats and boots, rough, empty faces. Children peeked out at the uninvited visitor through the gaps between the vehicles before being pulled back into the safety of the encampment.

Angela climbed out of her van. Then, as now, she wore a black tracksuit with three golden lines running up the sides of her legs and arms, matching training shoes, a black beanie, and a small black rucksack. She walked to the passenger door, opened the glove compartment, and removed her handgun. She didn't point it at the men, only showed it to them in her open palm. They nodded and turned back to their encampment. She put the gun in her bag and got to work. That was four days ago.

It's a methodical search. Angela has picked her way past fallen ceiling tiles and collapsed partitions, over toppled displays and through ransacked kitchens, and opened all the cupboards, cabinets, and doors she can find. During her previous visits, she searched the restaurant building and most of the hotel, moving through each section systematically, exploring every shape and crevice in the walls and floors. When she returned home from her third visit, Dan asked her not to go back. They came close to arguing. He said it was too dangerous, that the more often she went there, the more likely something terrible would happen, that he and the children needed her here with them. They do, she knows that. She told him she would try one more time. If she couldn't locate what she was looking for, then maybe it wasn't there to be found anymore, or she had made a mistake.

Angela enters Room 116 of the Travelodge. It's smaller than the others, squashed between a corner of the building and the main hotel entrance. She has her routine down now: she stands in the centre of the bedroom and looks hard for a few minutes, searching for anything unusual; inspects the small, doorless wardrobe and runs her hands along its inside, checking for any irregularities in texture and form; pulls out the drawers from the chest; takes down the abstract framed print from above the headboard; strikes the walls with the heel of her hand while assessing consistency and listening for hollows; conducts a visual examination of the carpet for unevenness or breaks in the pattern; manoeuvres the bed to reveal the floor beneath it, scanning as she goes.

Rather than the usual shower-over-bathtub setup, this room has a corner cubicle. Inside it, at the bottom of a tiled wall, Angela sees a panel, about a metre-squared, also covered in tiles. Not so invisible, but not so inconspicuous either. She takes a hammer from her rucksack and taps the panel's top edge until she is satisfied this could be what she is looking for. Then she batters the corners with all her might. Ceramic splinters explode against her face and safety goggles and the square starts to come away. Soon she is prising it out with the hammer's claw. And there, behind it, deep stairs descend into a dark concrete cavity.

She slumps onto the floor of the cubicle.

At bloody last, she sighs, wiping sweat from her forehead with the arm of her tracksuit.

While she rests, she imagines the kind of person who might have used this shower. In her mind's eye, a forty-something sales rep, his face in the hot jet, lets the day's labour wash from his body. The drumming of the water against his skull drowns out the sounds of the panel being unlocked from the other side. Nor does he hear the young woman clearing her throat. He reaches for the shampoo dispenser, opens his eyes, and sees the large dark hole where, only a moment ago, there'd been a white wall. It takes a second to notice four apologetic faces peering at him.

Angela returns to her van. She removes her small rucksack and exchanges it for a much larger, heavier one, also black. On her back, it feels like she's lost an inch in height. Next, she puts on an LED head torch, stuffs three packs of triple-A batteries into her pockets, and eases out her folded Brompton bicycle. Then, after reminding the watching travellers or refugees or whoever they are that she is armed, she returns to the building and the stairs that will lead her down into the abandoned Facility.

The steps are too long to stride down one at a time. The descent is slow and painful under the weight of the rucksack and the bike. She wishes her legs were longer and her knees younger. Her torch casts shadows that change the shape of the stairwell, stretching and shortening, swelling and shrinking the narrow space ahead. It takes twenty minutes before she reaches the bottom.

A single door. Through it, there's an office containing three desks and five chairs. Angela puts down the bike, removes her bag, and sits with her legs up. She casts her circle of light over the room. Empty shelves, monitors without computers, scattered papers around a photocopier, an open filing cabinet. On the back of the door she has just passed through, a red sign reads

EMERGENCY EXIT

She has a map of this Facility sector, pilfered long ago. She doesn't remember her reasons for taking it. Maybe it was the thrill of breaking the law. A compulsion. Or she'd had a bad day, had had enough of the relentless misogyny and wanted to take some quiet revenge. Perhaps she knew somehow that she would need it, that in the future the place would be little more than a dark, deserted labyrinth, and she would be back underground needing to navigate from Point A to Point B. Whatever the reason, she has it. And right now, it's her most valuable possession.

Point A is the emergency exit she entered through. Point B, circled in red ink, is another. It should take her about two hours. That accounts for taking just one wrong turn, provided she realises her mistake before it becomes problematic.

This is a last resort. Angela knows she will face troublesome questions when she arrives at her destination. If there was another way to reach Atlas and avoid explaining herself, she would have taken it. Every other route is blocked. If she'd tried harder or searched for longer she might have found an alternative but fuel is so scarce these days and all that driving was attracting attention. She was even stopped at a blockade and held for two hours in the back of a small lorry while her warden captors worked out whether the knitting needle they discovered in her car was a dangerous weapon. She was scared in there, alone, convinced they were going to do something terrible to her.

It was a dark moment, but she will tell him about it to make sure he understands how difficult it's been to get to him. She'll make a joke of it, about how she could have held these so-called tough guys hostage with her knitting needle. And if life were perfect, he'd laugh, delighted to have her there safe and sound, to have the food and water she's brought. He'd apologise for the state of the place and later they'd play a game of chess and drink a glass of this homemade wine she is lugging through the Facility corridors. No interrogations, no explanations. As if nothing happened, as if she has never been away.

This all depends on him still being in the land of the living. Which he is. Of course he is. That is not a train of thought she wants to follow. Finding his skeletal body on a bloodied mattress or hanging by the neck from the gasholder, these are the kinds of scenarios that keep her awake. He is unlikely to have prospered while she's been absent. She knows that much. Atlas may be clever, but he's not resourceful. It'll have been a struggle. It's possible that he's been trapping rats or pigeons and cooking them over some barbecue contraption fashioned from bricks and coat hangers. She can picture him gnawing on their bony carcasses while cursing her for the indignity of it all. But he will be alive. And he'll be curious, like he always is. And she won't get away with saying nothing, dismissing her method of arrival as some trivial detail. The only choice she'll have is to explain everything, the service station, men and mobile homes, a bike, a torch on her head, how strange it was to be underground after so long. He'll hear her story, but parts of it will seem to fold over others as if the structures that should hold it together are dissolving. Her sentences won't make sense, or they'll make the wrong sense. As he looks out into the compound, he'll see the corner of the brick shed peeking out from behind the gasholder. And he might say, That shed over there? That's a Facility emergency exit? And you've just come through it? I don't... And that'll be it. In those seconds he will watch her features change from known to unknown, her breezy ways replaced by a weightiness, her eyes wet, her mouth loose. She'll be staring back at him, watching his world shrink, entire cities and towns and oceans and rivers and forests and deserts and mountains being rolled up like an infant's play mat. Until there is nothing left but the two of them.

His mouth will open, but no sound will come out. Instead, his eyes, those small dark holes behind the smeared, scratched glasses, will reach out and implore her to explain. And that'll be all the permission she needs to let go of the secret she has been holding back for years, ever since she met him in that remote house on the Scottish island of Barra Head when he was the ungrateful hideaway and she was the focus of his frustration. And she could, if she wishes, allow the truth to burst forth as if from a cracked dam, relinquishing her command of the situation and leaving the conclusion to the churning chaos of emotion. But she doesn't have to. There are choices. She has already chosen between letting a man starve to death or bringing him food. As she has taken the second option, she can now choose between confessing through a bubbling, sobbing mess or via a controlled, well-planned strategy.

Implementing the strategy requires her to be clinical and detached. She will not cry. She won't apologise. This upcoming episode is a game in which the victor is the person who remains composed throughout. She must be assertive and, to a certain extent, ruthless.

Angela moves through her plan as she pedals, starting with the setting. He should be in the kitchen before she begins. She wants him in front of a bowl of soup, something nourishing to soften his bones and ignite his endorphins. When she thinks he's ready, she'll begin with Dr Nichols. Atlas will remember Nichols, she's sure. She was the Facility scientist responsible for the Arachnophyr, the spider-like microrobots designed to infest positions behind enemy lines before detonating. However, the most memorable thing about Nichols is that she disappeared before the project was completed. The official line was illness, and those acquainted with her knew that before she vanished she'd been under considerable stress. But the reality is that her sudden absence had nothing to do with health.

Evidence suggests that designing creative ways to kill people can do unpredictable things to a scientist's mind, and Nichols wasn't the first researcher who'd run away. Although it was rare, it was a problem for the Facility. Scientists discovering moral compasses and absconding mid-project disrupted its time-critical workflows and impacted its margins. It knew from experience that dragging staff back underground to complete their work usually ended badly. So it developed contingency playbooks. Like set pieces, these strategies could be implemented when needed. The idea was that if someone was going to go rogue, it would be better if they did it in a way the Facility could control.

She has to make accommodations for his questions. Angela can't expect him to sit through an entire monologue without interrupting. For a start, he's bound to ask how she knows about Nichols. And she will promise an answer soon enough. Please, don't rush me.

For Nichols, the Facility faked a group of eco-terrorists that wanted to attack oil refineries and such likes because, well, you know, saving humanity appeals to certain personality types. She'll say sorry for the bad joke if he notices it. They made contact with Nichols, took her to a property on Barra Head, and helped her finish her project. Yes, the same island where Angela had put Atlas into hiding, but he won't make the connection. When the work was done, the Facility's people swooped in and reclaimed possession. But, strictly speaking, it had never been lost.

By now, he will have finished his soup and she'll offer him more. Regular moments of calm ordinariness like this will be necessary. While refilling his bowl, she'll ask about his sleep, if he's been getting enough, and he'll reply that sleep is all he does. That and thinking too much.

What about? The usual?

Everything, he'll say, all of it, people, food, imminent death, things he could have done differently, yes, the usual.

Punishing yourself?

If I don't do it, then who is going to?

Steam will rise from the bowl and fill his nostrils while Angela busies herself at the sink, letting the quiet thicken between them. His spoon will be hovering above the soup. He won't have eaten much of the second helping. I should finish my story, she'll say as she sits down again. And he'll nod slowly. You asked me how I knew about Dr Nichols.

Now it'll be time to tell him she worked for the Facility. In security. That she joined straight from university. Atlas will frown and ask how long she was there for, expecting her to reply that it was only for a couple of years and that she left for the private sector, wanted better prospects and pay, and eventually landed a role at Farfalla's company. Well, this is the thing, she will say as if she is doing little more than passing him the salt, I was made redundant when it closed down after extraction. There will be nothing from him for a few seconds, followed by words that do not string together. Buts and Not Possibles and I Don't Understands, his voice weaker than when she arrived, his face crumpling. However, his frustration will find a way through the debris of confusion, so Angela will press on before it can reach her. She'll inform him it was her job to observe the flight risks, watching for erratic behaviour, especially from people working on national security projects. She flagged Atlas as a potential threat because of how he was dealing with Moss's new directive.

If he accuses her of spying on him, of lying to him, she will rebuff with an unimaginative I was doing my job, like you did yours. Back then, he was just another possible absconder with valuable knowledge. She wouldn't have picked him out for special attention if he hadn't withheld the agent's formulation.

Not disclosing it made him a person of interest. Then, as predicted, he did a 'Nichols'.

You flew the coop, she'll say. We were right.

Even though Atlas tends not to follow standard behaviour patterns, it's helpful to think she can predict his reactions. For instance, there'll be his reluctance to believe her. He will hope that at any moment she'll shout, fooled you, and they'll drop to the floor in fits of giggles. Clenched eyes and aching jaws. But when he asks her if there was a playbook for him and she swivels her hand on her wrist, drawing a coil in the air, and says, this is it, or this *was* it, he'll realise how foolish he is being, and despair will begin to replace his optimism.

She'll tell him about the compound in the early days and how the land was already earmarked for the new directive. Located right on top of the Facility, with a gasholder for storage, decent access, and no nearby residential areas, it was perfect. Even before Moss had spoken to Atlas about the project's change of direction, money had been set aside to develop the site. And when they launched the playbook, it made sense to stage it there. The only substantial alteration to Moss's plan was that instead of developing localised extraction, which he'd wanted Atlas to work on, he had to settle for complete extraction. That was how they were able to give the scientist the impression that he was in charge and ensure his full cooperation. Afterwards, Moss would assign a team to find ways to use the trapped Particle to carry out the original initiative.

She has to keep the rhythm up. If she's to hold the power throughout this exchange, Atlas can't be allowed to start joining dots all by himself. She must move to the next revelation before he recovers from the last, then do it again and again in a continual bombardment of truths to maintain his disorientation.

It's Milo Farfalla's turn. He was a character performed by a man called Alan Mills. From Belfast. The playbook required someone who could make things happen without raising suspicion, and a wealthy investor was perfect. He had a full digital life, online presence, social media, everything needed to construct a believable persona. Or real enough for people who aren't experts in such matters. Atlas will process this new information quickly and will want to know who else was fake. She will be ready to list them before he can ask. But first, she'll assure him that Arrina and K knew nothing about the scheme. These details will ideally send his mind on a different trajectory for a short time, keeping him off-balance and her out in front. Then she'll run through the false names of the compound technicians: Terry, Mike, Susan, Phil, and so on, all of them Facility employees. As he is trying to remember their faces, she will hit him with a catalogue of other deceptions: putting him into hiding, the newspaper stories, the raid on his house, interrogating his old team and having them followed, and she'll go on, saving Ralph, the man who played Oblonsky, until the end.

He worked with her in security. He was quite a nice guy in real life, she'll say. We made his character foreign so he wouldn't have to speak. His acting was terrible, but he looked the part. For a reason that was never explained to me, we had to get hold of a sample after the test run. That's why Ralph was there. A team had been set up at the Facility especially. But after the accident, we decided to wait until after full extraction. Someone in health and safety likely got wind of it.

The accident. The Particle spillage in the middle of Castleport that led to all those deaths and life-changing injuries, that is something she is unsure about. Atlas may know about it already. Angela and everyone else at the compound had been ordered to keep it quiet, but secrets leak. It's a judgment she will make when she has to. If he knows, he will accept her statement. If he doesn't, well, she'll have to remind him of the vehicle that took the Particle sample and explain how it crashed a few miles away in the town centre, even though it should never have been there in the first place because driving a cargo like that through a densely populated area broke every health and safety rule in the book. About how many members of the public were around as the tanker leaked its load. How horrible it was. The numbers of injured and dead. Perhaps his head will be in his hands as he listens. Cold soup between his elbows. And the last scrap of hope will cough up its lungs, bend over, and die. And Angela will still be in control.

Outside on the steps for the final reveal, she thinks. Atlas will follow and sit next to her. After staring at the gasholder for a while, he will say something about it all being a lot to take in. He might commend her on doing an excellent job of hiding it all from him, that he had no idea. Or he'll become self-reflective with a few words about how it changes the way he sees this whole thing, how he sees himself. That he's such a fool. She will try to explain that none of it matters anymore.

Look, she'll say, pointing to the giant drum. You won, Moss lost.

And when he asks about how the Facility planned on taking control of the Particle after extraction, she'll begin the last chapter, the part of the story that angers her more than any other. At least the Castleport accident was just that, an accident. What happened at the compound was utterly preventable. A horror show created by Moss's paranoia. Or stupidity. More likely both. The original plan had been simple. The only people present should have been staff, including her, Atlas, Arrina, and Farfalla, along with the Facility security officers pretending to be Oblonsky's soldiers, who'd been there since the Particle sample had been removed. As soon as extraction was completed, the latter were to arrest Atlas, seize the agent, and secure the gasholder.

That was it. But Moss suspected Atlas knew what they were up to and would somehow thwart the takeover. Angela tried to talk him down, but he wouldn't listen. He wanted extra bodies inside, ready to pounce no matter what Atlas had up his sleeve. So she arranged for Ralph, or Oblonsky, and his fake bodyguards to be there too. That seemed like a feasible thing to do and unlikely to raise Atlas's suspicions. Then, two days before the event, Moss insisted she doubled the numbers. She had no choice but to brief additional officers to pose as Farfalla's guests and technicians' family members. But while this stretched the boundaries of credibility, it wasn't over yet. Hours after she'd made these arrangements, Moss demanded more officers, more technical staff, and some military for good measure. Angela was at the end of her tether. She argued against it, but it was pointless. The result was a ridiculous party full of Facility staff pretending to be guests, musicians, and caterers, many of whom were armed. And eight marines crammed into the brick shed behind the emergency exit. It was a disaster waiting to happen. So when the hangar flooded with Particle, instead of just a few people to evacuate, the place was so crowded it would have been impossible to act fast enough to save lives even if there'd been a warning.

Alan, who played Farfalla, gave a statement about what happened up until he pulled Atlas out of the hangar. The rest is sketchy. It appears that when the soldiers heard the shots, some of them scrambled through the emergency exit and got caught up in everything that was happening. However, the medics in the cleanup operation found evidence that most of the marines opened fire on each other before leaving the shed.

Moss was never held responsible, she should let Atlas know that. When the Facility closed, he was transferred to a role in Intelligence. She'll not make the obvious joke because she won't want to dilute whichever emotion is chewing Atlas up at that moment. Whether it's anger or depression or something in between, it will be out of control and unfocused, with some of it directed at Moss, some at the Facility, or the government possibly. Some at Alan. Some at himself, that's for sure. And some, but not a lot, at her. She is on his side, that should be his conclusion. When he finds out she never used an alias, that the whole thing was just a job to her, and now she's here with food and the truth, how could he not forgive her? At that point, if he seems pliable enough, and if it is safe to do so, she will call his bluff and offer herself up as a target for whatever it is he is feeling. And he'll say no, he doesn't think he can do that.

Later, they'll drink the wine. Atlas might talk about how he's been coping since her last visit and make her laugh at some of his stories. Later still, she will say she's tired and ask if she can stay the night. Atlas will offer his bed and she'll adorn her blankest face and tell him she'd rather sleep inside the gasholder and they'll laugh again. She'll take one of the lower floor cots and fall asleep in minutes. Perhaps even later, emboldened by the alcohol, he'll look in on her. There will be a slight grin on her closed eyes. It'll seem she is having the best of dreams, which will please him, and he'll remember that an hour or so ago she said to him, I like you, Atlas, you daft old bastard. He'll think, I like you too, because how else should he be towards someone who does this kind of thing for him, this saving of his life? This nourishing of his body and soul? And any residual feelings of betrayal will evaporate.

The Facility passageways seem longer and narrower than they used to be. These once strip-lit corridors are tunnels now. Her speed reveals gentle slopes and curves she never noticed on foot. She could be cycling through the lava tubes of an ancient volcano.

And maybe these imaginary tubes are freshly carved by a recent eruption because she feels warm and unexpectedly safe down here. The moment takes her back. She is lying on the upper bunk in a tiny bedroom she once shared with her sister in her parents' Tyneside flat. Before Katie moved out, this room had been a dazzling hellhole of pink, floodlit by a naked, high-voltage lightbulb and further illuminated by the infeasibly white teeth of several George Michaels and Andrew Ridgeleys beaming down from every wall. Angela's tastes were so deviant in Katie's mind that not a single artefact of her own was permitted to be on show. The post-Katie era was better. Angela painted the walls black, draped dyed charity shop lace over the small window, took charge of the precious Sanyo GXT stereo, and replaced the posters with real artists. The Mission, Siouxsie Sioux, The Cure; Robert Smith's smeared lips supplanted the inane pearly grins of the Wham! boys. And all of it softly lit by her mother's stash of blackout candles.

It was a moment of dark perfection. Of crimped, overly-sprayed, jet-black hair. Of thick ivory foundation, heavy eye makeup, and black clothing. Of Fields of Nephilim, Bauhaus, Sisters of Mercy groaning the soundtrack to two unsmiling, sunlight-dodging, depression-faking years. Of revelling in her classmates' snubs, her teachers' disapproval, and her parents' bewilderment. And of retreating to her crypt and her candles and her music. This room followed her everywhere back then. Whether or not she was inside it, it contained her. Its spirit shielded and cradled her and made her feel, well, the only word she could ever find was cosy. She hated the word, but nothing else came close. A cosy goth. It was all wrong. But this sense returns to her here, all these decades later, deep underground, and she still has no other word. She suits it better now, even as she cycles through forsaken burrows, glides past caves that used to be laboratories, and slices through caverns that were once canteens and conference rooms and halls. She pedals on, her grin as wide as her handlebars.

. . .

One battery change and a minor collision later, she arrives at the foot of the ladders that will take her directly to Point B and the second emergency exit. She dismounts, fights the urge to lock up her bike, and starts climbing.

The aluminium ladder is attached to the inside of a concrete cylinder, like a chimney. However, instead of the walls being caked in soot, Angela's face is only inches away from streaks of dried blood. There is a faint metallic scent. She tells herself it is paint and thinks again of her teenage bedroom, splashes of black emulsion on the carpet, skirting boards, window sills, and the acrid aroma that signalled the beginning of that new life. But as she heaves her bag further up the ladder, the patterns merge until there is more blood than concrete. The stench thickens, the metal giving way to rotting fish, old piss and vomit. She tries breathing through her mouth, but the taste is worse than the smell. She feels it lining her throat, seeping into her pores, coating the membrane of her eyeballs.

At the top of the shaft, Angela clambers out of the hole and onto the rough floor. The effluvium up here is physical, air so thick it leadens her movement as she reaches out to lean on the wall. Brick encloses her on four sides. Twelve by eight foot, sloping towards the ground at one end, a metal door at the other bearing an identical Facility emergency exit sign to the one that led to the Travelodge. She craves the cold, clean atmosphere beyond. To breathe it in deep and fast. For it to cleanse her mouth, nostrils, and lungs. In three slow steps, she has the panic bar in her hands. She pushes. The door does not open. She tries again. Then again. She shoulder barges it while holding the bar down. It's as if she is throwing herself against rock. There isn't the slightest give. This time she growls into the darkness, runs at the exit, and slams her entire weight against it. Pain bites through her right arm and hip. She is on the floor, and the way out remains shut.

Angela catches her dismay. She needs to be rational. It's okay, she says. No need to overreact. Back on her feet, she shines her head torch on the rusting surface, at the bar, at the lock mechanism. There has to be a logical explanation for this. But despite the calming tone of her inner voice, she loses patience. She turns away and fails to notice the welding that undulates like a fluted pastry crust along the top, bottom, and both sides of the door. She fumbles in her bag, searching for something, anything she can use, and curses herself for leaving the tools in the car. Dead blood in the air stings her eyes and throat. Gripping two food cans, she bang, bang, bangs at the metal slab and shouts his name. Atlas, help me. Atlas, let me out.

ATLAS

The bang, bang, banging begins in the far reaches of his comprehension, where the forest of confusion grows thicker by the day, by the hour, dropping its seeds, putting down new roots. And this noise, this metallic din that clanks and clangs its way towards his consciousness, is careful to avoid clearings and glades lest it should be spotted early. It rattles through thickets, crashes through undergrowth, hidden from Atlas's grasp.

He is oblivious. He stands before his mirror, preoccupied by the marks on its dusty surface. These alterations, made with a wet finger, are of a broad, open grin and enormous eyes. Through the evening gloom he recognises the comical aesthetic of these additions. When he aligns his face so that the fat, toothy smile is over his thin lips, and the big, delighted eyes with their spiky upper lashes are superimposed on the dry, greying holes under his glasses, his mood lifts like a hot-air balloon, its basket filled with puppies and kittens and giggling children, rising to the apex of a rainbow. It feels like the first spring sun, a rush of new love, bread in the oven, a warm blanket over cold bones. Then, if he moves a little to the left or right, the effect is lost, and his spirits plummet into darkness. He tries this repeatedly. Left to right, left to right, up and down goes his emotional barometer.

Joy and despair, just millimetres apart, relay switching. Into the image and out again, a rhythm appears. Happy to sad, cheery to blue, gleeful to glum, good day to bad day, in and out, in and out, each shift drenched with translucent memories.

And in, to all the restaurants he's ever eaten at, a thousand waiters placing a thousand meals in front of him, the carbonaras, the curries, the crispy ducks, the shakshuka with extra chorizo, the stacked, oozing burgers, the chips and fries and wedges, the sourdough pizzas, the full English breakfasts with fried, poached, scrambled eggs, melt-in-your-mouth pork belly.

And out to where two ghostly figures in respirators sprint silently across the compound tarmac. The suited phantom tows its lab-coated companion by the arm, hurrying around the end of the shipping container wall and past a security guard who hobbles at speed in the wrong direction. And they're running, running, out through the gate, over empty roads, beyond the mounds of rubble, demolished factories, deserted warehouses, running and running until they collapse on a grass verge. Atlas feels the thumping of their hearts in his own chest. The man in the suit pulls off his respirator. Farfalla's eyes pour into his phone, thumbs drumming the screen. The other is shaking his head, pointing back to where the distant gasholder is jolting up its iron cage, and a voice, his own voice, muffled under the mask, the machine, it says, he says, the machine, his words cut off by the sound of gunshots. He is trembling and stuttering and wondering aloud about damage to the extractor and if they should go back, they really ought to get back right now. And then more gunfire that buzzes like an untuned television until, eventually, it splutters to a stop. Farfalla's face is pulsating.

Nobody is going back in there, he says.

And in, to the bite of crispy roast potatoes, of garlic naan, of Cumbrian sausages, of buttered toast, of puff pastry, of fried rice, fried noodles, fried egg sandwiches, of burnt marshmallows, of melted cheese, of hot paneer, of medium rare fillet.

And out again, to drinking weak coffee in a sterile welfare

van while hazmated people turn off the machine, scan for leaks, search for survivors, clear the casualties and clean the grounds. The clear and clean, that's what the American calls it, like it's a brand. We'll see what they find in the Clear & Clean™; Clear & Clean™ is going well; we won't know that until after Clear & Clean™. The bodies, most aren't bodies anymore. He's told that those they can identify and move in one piece are taken to their homes where doors are smashed, contents ransacked, and valuables removed so their fatal injuries will be understood and processed by grieving families. A burglary gone awry is easier to comprehend than the truth. All other remains are disposed of responsibly and with respect. He doesn't dare ask which grouping Arrina belongs to.

And in, to the texture of hot chocolate, of double cream, of cold milk, of stout, of orange juice with bits, of latte, of baked Camembert, of lemon sorbet, of vanilla ice cream.

And out, to not having these things, to never having these things again, to not trusting his memory of what these things were, how they were.

And in, to his metal box, inside the compound steam-cleaned of its deadly past, the two of them in their usual places, whiskies in hand, like before, watching the ticker tape slide along the bottom of the muted tv. Tanks retreating from the Crimean Peninsula. Images of crowds, cheering, fists clenching blue and yellow flags, sky and wheat. A correspondent on Constitution Square gestures towards the Verkhovna Rada behind him. It's working, either he or Farfalla says to the other. Look at what's happening. We did the good thing we said we would.

And out again, to the words I wish the others could have seen this, a phrase that echoes like valley church bells, I wish the others could have seen this. The following minutes mutate into the kind of time that grown men don't know how to handle. Quietness falls where only days before it seemed the noise would never cease. Farfalla's features are slow as he utters another sentence, one that would make a fitting end to this story:

I didn't think it would cost so much. But instead of credits rolling over a melancholy orchestral piece, his phone rings. Uh-huh. Uh-huh. He stands. His face is motionless for once. Then Atlas's partner through all of this, his enabler, his catalyst, his cash cow, his sounding board, and the nearest thing he has to a friend, is nodding and opening the door. Heavy footsteps strike the aluminium steps. By the close of that day the new security detail is gone. Then the skeleton technical staff vanishes and the workstations are empty. The food deliveries stop. He locks himself in his accommodation. Is this it, then? He hides under his bedcovers, squeezes his eyes shut and tries to evaporate.

And in, to when he held to his chest a dream of what this compound could become. There he is, basking in the kind of optimism that can only be found in the manifesting of a whole-some future. He is projecting certainty into the universe, confi-dent that it will respond with a network of air monitors that sift the atmospheres of every conurbation around the world, capturing and pinging data granules via satellites and deep-sea cables to a bank of screens where his handpicked specialists assess and analyse real-time intelligence to answer a single ques-tion: is the Particle still out there?

And out again, to the reality of nothing. To no global network, no team, and no concerted effort. Only a sad little man scraping around the internet for secondhand reports of riots, new conflicts, for evidence. The lonely Particle Hunter lying in wait for war to break out.

And in again, to Angela and the smile that fills his chest with a kaleidoscopic joy the first time he sees her after extraction, reporting for duty, she says, bright and breezy, brandishing supplies. The woman he once found so easy to despise is sing-songing her apologies. I should be dead, she says, I was in a toilet cubicle when the gunshots started, she says, it was terrify-ing, she says, until something else took over. Similar to rage but deeper, fevered, wild. Hit her head against the cistern, she says, came to in a hospital bed. And she laughs at herself and it sounds like music. And this melodious being keeps coming to him. Every week, his feeder, pharmacist, advisor, therapist, nurse, and anchor to reality, she brings a lightness with her that sustains him as much as the food and drink.

And out again, to when her visits stop. His lifeline stops. The point of it all stops. Everything stops. And everything stops.

And in, to a flickering compilation of Arrina Heal. Her face up close. Her in the distance through dusty Venetian blinds. Sitting next to him in the truck. On his sofa, drinking his wine. Her silhouette in the darkness, her weight on his thighs. Her spine curved against his chest. Her sarcasm, her scepticism, her visits, her warmth, her near-imperceptible touch, her tight, focused face as she powered up the machine. Her.

And out again, to her absence.

And in, walking to clear his mind, walking for the exercise, walking for the sake of it. The Great Peace is still young and such things seem so normal. Most shops are shut. Lights off, doors barred, like the monotone Sundays of his youth, those hours that lasted for days. But here, to his left, a pinprick of colour, a store display that pulls him towards it. Toys sparse behind blocks of bright vinyl. Down one aisle someone is kneeling, attending to a shelf. Slim, blonde hair tied up, shaved at the sides, just as her's was. And when the woman turns he sees her. Actually her. His chest heaves. He pushes his hands against the window and launches towards the store's entrance. Arrina, he is thinking. Arrina, Arrina! He shakes the locked door by its handles, bangs it with an open palm, clattering the frame. He shouts for her. Peers into the interior. Nothing. He returns to the window worried he'll miss her at the door if he isn't quick. But she's not in the aisle, so he rushes back. An almighty high, these seconds in which she has come back to him, when she hasn't perished after all, and life really is a thing of beauty.

And out again, to the realisation that this person on the other side of the door is not her. Similar height, similar build, similar hair, but different. A different woman. Fuck off or I'm calling the wardens, she shouts through the glass. He raises his hands and backs away. Sorry—sorry—I am.

In and out he goes, Metronome Man, rocking slowly on the balls of his feet, a human pendulum, his movement accompanied by an internal beat that keeps his rhythm. He can hear it, distant and close, inside and out, like the sound of his heart palpitating through his open mouth as he lies in bed. But this is an interesting noise, this pulse. Different with its hard edges and sharp corners, not at all fleshy. More metal than muscle, more clinking than ticking. A tin heart, is that what this is? Is he powered by a rusty bucket that rattles as he sways, fallen rivets and bolts rolling and clanging against its flaking hull? Is this what he is now? And so he stops his oscillating. Brings himself to stillness. The finger-drawn features pause over his face, and he listens.

And here it comes, the clatter and clunk, the clangour and clash, bang-galloping out from the forest and into the diminishing clarity of Atlas's mind. This noise. This noise is not inside him, he realises. It is coming from out there.

Reflected Atlas bursts into life.

What's that?

Shit—be—quiet.

Is it footsteps on gravel, on the aluminium stairs? Is it, is it wardens?

He doesn't remember finding the empty whisky bottle as he ran or jumped or, more likely, scuttled behind the sofa. But he's armed now. And while he may not have the strength to swing it, his grip on the smooth, hard neck is all the reassurance he can hope for.

The noise is real and there is no way out. At any moment the door will explode and he'll be face to face with his fate. Atlas's mind limps off in search of silver linings. If it is wardens, they might have something to eat. I will tell them everything and they'll feed me. I'll hand over the gasholder and more power than they can ever imagine and they'll take me to wherever they live and feed me and feed me and feed me. I'll help them design ways to use the Particle, and they'll, and they'll

Why don't they just come in and get it over with? interrupts Reflected Atlas.

Atlas shushes the mirror but has to admit it has a point. Why don't they? There are only so many steps a warden hellbent on Atlas's downfall can take across the compound and up the stairs. But the noise is still hammering and pounding without getting closer. If it is footsteps he hears, then it has to be a standing march, metal-soled boots striking gravel, Alexander's army trying to intimidate him. To scare him out of hiding. Or. Or. There is something familiar about this terrible racket. His hungry mind clambers through the data until he's in front of a slideshow, young expectant faces before him, a robot dog galloping on the screen behind, its paws beating the rocky terrain like a pneumatic hammer. That's it. That's what it could be out there. A defective QiNT. It is. Has to be. The damn fools have got hold of a Sniffer. Of course! Messing with hardware they don't have the first clue about operating and software they can't understand, letting the machine loose and hoping for the best. And now it's in the compound, with its malfunctioning head caught in an empty crate by the hangar, smashing its ridiculous claws into the ground as it tries to free itself. Someone in a control room somewhere is shouting, I've lost the bot, system error, it isn't responding, electrical overload, camera down, come in Sniffer, Sniffer come in.

Atlas wonders about the battery life of a thing like that. It can't be much. It'll have been running for a few hours already, more than likely. When it fizzles out they'll send a search party to retrieve it.

Yes, but we don't want that though, do we? says Reflected Atlas.

No—we don't—.

You should go out there. Set it free so it can run out of power somewhere else.

I am—not—going—out there. Atlas is crawling out from behind the sofa.

You don't have a choice, though, do you? If you do nothing, then they'll find us.

Maybe—maybe they will. Maybe that's not—not such a bad —such a bad outcome.

Maybe it's awful, a terrible outcome because we don't have a clue about what'll happen, what they'll do to us, or how they'll, well, you know, deal with all the hate out there.

I—refer you to—to my previous reply. Atlas's words are faint and strained as he drags himself towards the window.

Which statement is that Atlas? Because you're not making sense. Oh, I see.

—what?

I see what's happening.

And what—would that be? He stops and rests, allowing his face to press into a discarded once-white shirt. He is no longer convinced he is speaking aloud and that his reflection isn't reading his mind.

You've given up.

Oh, fuck—off. I haven't eaten for—I don't—just leave me— alone—please.

Hang on. I've had an idea, Reflected Atlas says.

Spare—me.

What if the robot has supplies? What if it's been sent here to save you? What if she sent it? Angela. What if Angela sent it?

Atlas's eyes crack open. It is a fascinating idea. In the realms of possibilities, it doesn't seem too outlandish. She might have done. Saddlebags over the robot's back bursting at the seams with bread and soup and cheese and carrots and chocolate and ham slices and rice and tubs of vanilla yoghurt and he is on his feet and baked beans and marmalade and noodles and bagels and he opens the door and honey and coffee and peanuts and potatoes and grapefruit and butter and gravy and pistachios and tomatoes and roast chicken and steps outside into the darkness and onto the aluminium platform. Only, now he's out here, it's clear that the noise isn't coming from the hangar. It's coming from the direction of the gasholder. And there's another sound. A sound within the sound. A voice. Or voices. Quiet but urgent. Like whispered screams. It calls him by his name, pleads with him to help it. Atlas, let me out.

He eases his tired body towards the stairs, and when he puts his left foot down on the first step, the sound reaches a crescendo of metallic clatters accompanied by a faint wail. Atlas pauses. Now there is nothing but the whistle of a light wind cutting through the compound. Something is wrong. This is a trick. He is being lured out here and he must be cautious. He glances at his box behind him. That's where he should go. If he were sensible. If he cared about his wellbeing, he'd limp his way back to bed and forget that any of this ever happened. But that's not going to happen. He puffs out his chest. Dr Atlas Brown will not be bullied by his own prisoner.

The shadow silhouette of the gasholder, a giant demon's head, its horns piercing the late evening clouds, scowls at Atlas as he descends. He can feel its glare, willing him to make a mistake, to trip or slip and smash his skull open on the gravel, to lose his mind to fear and release its innards. He senses hate's infinite patience. It knows its time will come again, that this is a temporary respite before a reckoning. A dormant tumour, all the hate in the world, right here in England, waiting for its moment.

He spreads his arms wide against the colossal container and presses an ear against it. He is sure he hears it move through eight inches of metal, silicon, and resin. A hurricane of wrath. Yes, he can definitely hear it swirling in there. The Particle, a single entity in many parts, the swarm, the legion, seething, raging inside a giant drum. Outraged, thrashing at its prison walls, incandescent, boiling with fury, shrieking threats and retribution, gnashing and barking, a writhing, salivating devil.

Atlas closes his eyes.

He strokes the gasholder with his fingers and whispers shhh
—shhh.

It whispers back, moaning under crushed breath, like furtive
sex, flooding the air with hushed affirmations—smouldering
through cracking incisors————————we are————————
we are————————the fists, they tell him————————don't
forget————————we are the teeth————————never
forget————————we are ————————we are
————————we are the————————elbows————————
we are the nails————————we are the boots————————
true to our roots————————we are the sticks————————
we are the drones————————we are the broken bottles
————————we are the crowbars————————smashed
limbs and face scars————————we are the chair legs
————————we are the truncheons————————we are the
nightsticks————————we are the noo—oo—oose
————————we're on the loo—oo—oose————————

we are the razor wire————————we are the kniVes and
shanks————————the hackers and choppers and rippers
————————we are the————————we are the swords and
————————the Molotov cocktails————————we are the
machetes and————————the suicide vests————————we
are————————we are————————we are the axes
————————we are the hammers————————we are
————————we are————————we are the shillelagh and
hanbōs and————————the sickles and arrows and ice picks
and whips————————and the in through the nostrils
————————and out through the blades,————————out
through the scythes————————out through the hooks
————————and out through the bows and the spears
————————and the batons and stakes————————we are
the matchsticks, the gasoline————————the flamethrowers
————————we are ————————we are————————we
are the scratching, the stabbing, the gouging ————————the
skinning, the melting, the burning, the burrowwwwing

——————————the slicing, flaying, exploding——————————dis-
mem-ber-ing——————————de capitating——————————we are
the tanks, let's ride——————————puncture, tear, rip, pop, burst,
crush, maim——————————la cer ate——————————we are the
pool cues——————————we are the bayonets——————————we
are the daggers——————————we are the triggers
——————————in through——————————eyeballs and out
through crosshairs——————————we are the levers
——————————bombs away——————————we are
——————————we are——————————we are the sulphur
mustards——————————we are the bio bio biological agents
——————————the nerve agents——————————the rip-the-
brain-apart agents——————————the you-can't-hyd-rogen
cyanide——————————hung drawn and quartered
——————————we are the flails——————————we are the
gallows——————————we are the guillotines——————————we
are the falXes——————————we are the deathly, deathly death
stars——————————we are the knuckledusters——————————
we are the firebombs——————————the car bombs
——————————in through one hole and out through another
——————————we are the napalm bombs——————————incen-
diary bombs——————————homemade nail bombs
——————————the laser guided bombs——————————bunker
busters——————————cruise missiles——————————landmine
after landmine after landmine——————————we are the
——————————we are the hates——————————we are the hates
——————————we——————————are——————————we
——————————are——————————

we are the hates——————————

ACKNOWLEDGMENTS

The biggest thank you goes to the talented, insightful, incredible Carolyn Thompson for years of encouragement and support, soundboarding services, editing expertise, and for your sensitive handling of my fragile ego throughout.

Also, thank you to Reuben and Martha Hughes, Sweta Pathak, Sophie Honegger, and my brothers Stephen and Andy for your early reading, feedback, and invaluable design advice and help. And to Lesley Sharp for your last-minute intervention.

Also to Keith Glover, without whom Genghis Khan might have been king.

And thank you to everyone else who has tolerated my droning on and on about this book since the days when it was nothing more than a vague idea.

Finally, several printed and online texts helped me write this novel, especially *Ethnolinguistics and Cultural Concepts: Truth, Love, Hate & War* by James W. Underhill.

ALSO BY SEF HUGHES

Salt Water (and other short stories)

Dark, heartbreaking, funny, twisted, bleak, and hopeful in unequal measure: eleven short stories that take you to the curious extremities of human relationships. Available via sefhughes.com.

Praise for Salt Water:

"Like the literary fiction equivalent of a deep-tissue massage for someone who had no idea how tense they were."

"The unspoken despair in Tap Tap and Noel Hardy is so painfully delicious."

"I found myself gripped and intrigued, tickled by the metaphors, and deeply touched by the characters."

The Overflow Pipe

Suicidal seagulls, parasitic palm trees, parallel universes hiding inside buckets... visit sefhughes.substack.com to subscribe to Sef Hughes's free fiction newsletter for regular short stories, flash fiction, and updates.